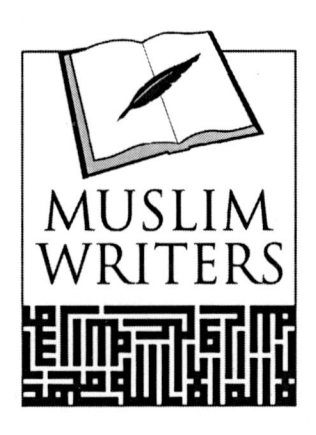

MUSLIM
WRITERS

Also by Jamilah Kolocotronis

Echoes Series:
Echoes (Book 1)
Rebounding (Book 2)
Turbulence (Book 3)

Innocent People
Islamic Jihad

Ripples

Book Four of the *Echoes* Series

by

Jamilah Kolocotronis

Muslim Writers Publishing
Tempe, Arizona

Ripples © 2008 by Jamilah Kolocotronis
All Rights Reserved.

No part of this book may be reproduced or transmitted in any form or by any means, graphic, electronic or mechanical, including photocopying, recording, typing, or by any information storage retrieval system, without the permission of the publisher.

This work is a work of fiction. Names, characters, places, and incidents are the product of the author's imagination or are used fictitiously and are not to be construed as real. Any resemblance to actual events, organizations, locales, or persons, living or dead, is entirely coincidental.

Published by Muslim Writers Publishing
P.O. Box 27362
Tempe, Arizona 85285
USA

www.MuslimWritersPublishing.com

Library of Congress Catalog Control Number: 2007943049
ISBN 978-0-9793577-6-3

Book cover graphic courtesy of www.dreamstime.com
Book design by Leila Joiner
Editing by Amel S. Abdullah

Printed in the United States of America

Ripples

Dedication

To my very understanding parents
Who tolerated my youthful explorations
And gave me room to find my own way

Acknowledgements

I would first like to acknowledge the continuous support I receive from my husband and children. I know it isn't always easy to live with an author.

Specifically, I want to recognize the contributions of two of my sons, Adam and Musa, to this novel. When I first told Adam my idea for the novel, he gave me invaluable feedback which ultimately determined the direction of the story. Musa, an aspiring writer, often serves as a sounding board for plots and plot twists.

I want to thank Empish Thomas for her professional advice about living with disabilities. It would have been very difficult for me to write Kyle's story without Ms. Thomas's contributions.

I also want to thank S. E. Jihad Levine. In addition to her continuous encouragement and support, she helped me refine the section about Kyle's program, "Kids Who Care."

I appreciate the efforts of Amel Abdullah, my editor, who caught my errors, patiently worked with me, and made sure the story flowed smoothly. And, as always, I have deep appreciation for my publisher, Linda Delgado, and her determined professionalism.

Table of Contents

Prologue 13

Me 15

My Family 21

My Life 39

My Turn 47

Friends and Brothers 67

Jagged Edges 107

Tough Choices 147

Negotiating the Curves 173

Meeting the Challenge 197

Taking Chances 213

Ramadan 257

Eid 269

Positives and Negatives 277

Dreams and Nightmares 285

Dreams and Nightmares Continue 311

What Happened to Isaiah 335

Separate Paths: Isaiah's Redemption 347

Separate Paths: Kyle's Recognition 363

Separate Paths: Jennifer's New Reality 377

All Grown Up 399

Epilogue 411

Prologue

As a little boy, Isaiah was enthralled as he watched his father perform every Sunday. The same man who had patiently taught him to ride a bike stood before the congregation, his voice booming, as he called the sinners to salvation. Isaiah looked up at his father in awe then, as he stood there larger than life, and swore that, one day, he would be like him.

Something changed, though, when Isaiah was thirteen or fourteen or fifteen. One day, he looked at his father and nearly laughed, right there during the church service. The old man stood in his suit and tie, his voice still booming, and spoke of the terrible tribulations of Hell and damnation. It was theater, poorly scripted, and painfully tedious.

Me

*There are ten men in me,
and I do not know or understand one of them.*

—Carl Sandburg

Isaiah

Every morning, I wake up grinding my teeth. And I listen. First, he uses the bathroom. Then he comes for me. "Isaiah. Don't be lazy." If I don't open my eyes within sixty seconds, he pulls me onto the floor. "Wake up," he says firmly. "The Lord does not love the slothful." I've become a light sleeper.

～

After dinner, I clean up the kitchen and head upstairs to study. I need to keep up my grades.

I'm reviewing for a history test when he walks in and tears the book away from me.

"Why do you waste your time on this nonsense?"

"It's history, Dad. We need to know it so we can avoid the mistakes of the past."

"Everything you need to know is in the Bible."

"I've memorized my verses for the day. The Book of Colossians, verses five through eight."

"Recite them."

I close my eyes and concentrate, knowing what will happen if I miss a single word. "Mortify therefore your members which are upon the earth; fornication, uncleanness, inordinate affection, evil concupiscence, and covetousness, which is idolatry. For which things' sake the wrath of God cometh on the children of disobedience: In the which ye also walked some time, when ye lived in them. But now ye also put off all these; anger, wrath, malice, blasphemy, filthy communication out of your mouth." I did it. I was afraid I would forget how to say concupiscence.

Dad shakes his head. "I've told you not to close your eyes."

"It helps me remember."

"You must memorize the Scripture with your heart, not only your tongue. One day, you will recite the Word of God before the multitudes. You must be confident when you stand at the pulpit. The Lord does not love weakness in His Servants."

I lower my eyes. "Yes, sir."

"Your voice will reach millions. You will travel the earth, spreading the message of Christ's redemption."

I want to study the remnants of ancient civilizations, not spread the Word of God. I remain quiet. He wouldn't understand.

"You will memorize the next four verses for tomorrow. There will be no more history tonight. Open your Bible."

I pick up the Bible and stare at the page. I'm tired of memorizing.

Dad moves on to test Jacob and Benjamin. Jacob has only one verse. Benjamin, who's younger, has two. He makes a mistake. Dad punishes him on the spot.

When he's done with Benjamin, he comes back to me. "Forget about history." He grabs my textbook and takes it with him.

I hear his footsteps on the stairs and jump up to get my notes from my backpack.

My brother Jacob looks over. "You heard what Dad said. No more history. Open the Bible, or I'll tell. You, too, Benjamin."

I place the notes on my bed and reach for the Bible. Jacob will tell. He smirks while playing a video game he sneaked into the house. He should be reading the Bible, too, but he knows we can never tell on him.

∼

I wake up early and study for my history test under the covers. I think Dad is still asleep, but I can't take any chances.

He's trying to mold me into the next great evangelist. It's been his dream, he says, since the day I was born. He won't listen to my dreams. They don't matter.

Ripples

Kyle

Every morning, I take stock of who I am. Kyle Adams. Son and brother. Former offensive lineman. Former fiancé. Former father-to-be. Paraplegic. I look at the foot of my bed. My chair awaits.

∼

Mom knocks. "Kyle, you need to get up. I don't want to be late for work."

Every morning, she drives me to Hope Center. She's the director of the health clinic. I work there, too. I stuff envelopes.

I drag myself out of bed and into my chair. It takes me an hour to complete my morning routine. By the time I wheel into the kitchen for breakfast, I'm ready to go back to bed.

"Grab a bagel, and eat in the car," says Mom. "I have a meeting this morning."

"I'll skip breakfast."

"No, you need to eat. I'll make your bagel. Get in the car."

And so begins another exciting day.

∼

Some mornings, I'm so frustrated that I yell at everyone in the house because my bagel broke apart in my hand. Other mornings, I'm so angry I feel like throwing the damn chair out the window. And there are mornings when hopelessness washes over me, and I want to stay in bed and never get up.

I'm always lonely. Every morning, and especially every night. My beautiful Amy and the child she was carrying—our child—are dead. Why couldn't I have died with them?

Jennifer

Every morning, I wake up smiling, with my handsome husband beside me and our beautiful baby still asleep in his crib. I used to dream about having Nuruddin's baby. I knew it would be wonderful.

Nuruddin is such a sweet husband. When I was pregnant, he came to all of my doctor's appointments. He massaged my feet. He even went out some nights to buy chocolate almond fudge ice cream. When the pains started, he rushed me to the hospital and reminded me how to breathe.

He says I cursed him out during labor, but I think he's exaggerating. It did hurt—I remember that—but, as I gaze at my sleeping baby boy, I know it was all worth it. His tiny hands are curled under his chin. He smiles a little. He must be dreaming. I'm tempted to wake him. My arms yearn to hold him. I softly brush through his black hair with my fingers and kiss his little forehead. He stirs and whimpers. He'll be awake soon.

Our son. He is the most beautiful baby who has ever been born.

My Family

Family love is messy, clinging, and of an annoying and repetitive pattern, like bad wallpaper.

—Friedrich Wilhelm Nietzsche

Isaiah: Part One

Tension has been building between my father and me since the day I was born. He has scolded and corrected me every day of my life. I don't know why.

This last year has been the worst. On the day I told him I was going to Loyola University instead of Redemption Bible College, where he teaches, he lectured me for two hours before punishing me. For a full week, he did everything he could to break me—confining me to my room, confiscating my books, forcing me to read the Bible from sunrise to sunset. I wouldn't give in.

Now, he barely talks to me, except to bark orders day and night and demand I memorize my verses. These last few days have been especially rough. I aced my history test on Tuesday, but, that night, I stumbled over two of my Bible verses. He punished me immediately. I will never be too old for his wrath.

Last night, I messed up again. This morning, he ordered me to skip my classes and memorize the Book of Colossians. All ninety-five verses. I couldn't stand up to him. I stayed in my room all day and forced my brain to absorb the words. All one thousand five hundred and eighty-two of them.

∽

At 4:55 PM, I stop studying and listen. He walks in the front door at five, right on schedule. Three minutes later, he's standing in my doorway.

"Did you learn your verses as I instructed?"

"Yes, sir."

"Recite them to me."

I want to close my eyes—I've never had to learn this much in one day—but I know he'll punish me. I look straight ahead, focusing on the doorknob, and begin.

After ten verses, he stops me, picks up the Bible, and nods. "Go on."

I continue to recite, focusing on the doorknob and the syllables I must say perfectly. Twice more, he stops me and checks.

One more verse. "The salutation by the hand of me Paul. Remember my bonds. Grace be with you. Amen."

"That was good, Isaiah. You are on the right path to serve our Lord."

He almost never compliments or encourages me. I dare to smile.

"Keep studying," he says. "Tomorrow, I want to hear verses one through ten of First Thessalonians."

I have a short report to write for my economics class tomorrow. I won't sleep tonight.

He stands in the doorway. "You are gifted. Don't waste your God-given talents on frivolities."

When he's gone, I fall onto my bed, relieved.

"Don't forget," says Jacob. "You have ten verses to memorize."

Was Abel as annoying as my brother?

Ripples

Isaiah: Part Two

For the last week, he's given me ten verses every night. I'm not getting much sleep, but I'm able to pull it off. I hope he eases up soon. I can't keep this going much longer.

He tested me as soon as he came home. I aced my verses. He nodded, without comment, and went on to Jacob and Benjamin.

It's a Friday night. I'm caught up with all my schoolwork. It's time to relax. I grab a book.

I hear his footsteps in the hall. I should put the book away before he catches me, but I want to finish this chapter.

He pushes the door open. He never knocks. I know it's his house—he reminds me of that nearly every day—but I wish he wouldn't barge in all the time.

"It's time for dinner, boys. Wash your hands. I expect you downstairs in two minutes. Do you hear me, Isaiah? Don't dawdle. Benjamin, wash your hands thoroughly. I don't want to see dirt under your nails."

I obediently close the book and head for the bathroom. He stops me.

"What are you reading?"

The book is lying on my bed. I should have hidden it.

"What is that?" my father demands. He walks over and grabs the book. "Why would you bring this filth into my house?"

Before I can reply, he whips out his belt and hits me across the chest without waiting for me to take my usual position. My breath catches in my throat. I bend over and wait for the next blow. The belt whips across my spine. I know better than to flinch. I hold my breath and count the lashes. One. Two. Three.

Anger flashes in my brain. The belt comes down a fourth time, landing between my shoulder blades, and I can't bear it one more second.

I've often dreamed of fighting back, but I was afraid of the consequences. Suddenly, I don't care. I spin around and snatch the belt from my father before he can complete his fifth blow.

He gasps. I raise my hand.

"Stop hitting me!" I scream.

"Give that to me, Isaiah." His voice is calm, as usual. "You must receive your punishment." He comes closer and tries to grab the belt from me.

I jump away. His hand hits the closet door. He pauses a moment, grimacing, before pursuing me. I raise the belt, striking the air so he can't get too close. He reaches again and misses. I rain down blows on his shoulders and chest. He backs off a little.

Jacob looks up from his game and watches. He's used to seeing me get beaten, but he's never seen me fight back. He stares with disinterested curiosity.

I glance at my brother. My father lunges at me. We struggle for control, falling to the floor. I quickly overpower him, rolling on top and pinning him against the carpet.

"No, Isaiah," he pleads. How many times have I begged him to stop?

I bring the belt down on him, striking his chest, shoulders, and face. He cries out. His pain fuels my anger. Fury seizes me. I toss the belt aside, pounding him with my fists.

He struggles, trying to break loose. I grab his shoulders and hold him down. I move my hands to his neck and apply pressure. I imagine squeezing the life out of him, stopping the beatings forever.

"What is going on?" Mom shrieks in the doorway.

I quickly stand, ashamed for her to see me this way. My father gasps and coughs. Mom runs to him and helps him rise slowly to his feet.

He wheezes. Mom stands beside him, wringing her hands. I wait, suspended, while he recovers.

"Get out of my house," he whispers. "I never want to see you again." He grabs the book and storms down the steps.

Mom stops him. "He's our son," she says softly.

"Isaiah is dead." He pushes her to the side. Halfway down, he pauses. "Start packing, Melinda. Call your sister. Tell her we'll be there in time for the Sunday service."

"No, Chris. I don't want to leave." She cries. He walks away.

When the front door slams, I spring into action. How much time do I have? Maybe an hour, if I'm lucky. I pull my suitcase from the closet and throw in my clothes. I stuff all the books I can fit into my

Ripples

backpack. I go to Jacob's desk and grab the laptop computer.

"That's not yours!" he yells.

"It is now."

Mom is sobbing in the doorway. "No, Isaiah, you can't leave."

Ruth stands next to her, silent.

Benjamin grabs my arm. "Don't go, Isaiah." He cries hard, wiping away the snot with his sleeve. Mom doesn't correct him.

Martha clings to my mother's skirt. I reach down to touch her face. "I'll see you later, kid."

"No!" Mom screams.

"I can't stay." I shut my suitcase, grab my backpack, and tuck the laptop under my arm. Mom grabs my sleeve. I jerk away.

I throw my things into the car and glance once more at my home. My mother cries in the doorway.

Ruth stands at an upstairs window and slowly waves.

Kyle

Last week, we returned from our vacation out West. I wish we could have stayed. They all said they were happy to be home, but there's nothing for me in Chicago anymore.

On the day we returned, Isaiah was waiting on our front porch. He looked upset, but he wouldn't tell me why. I need to find out what's going on. I won't call when Uncle Chris is home, though. He never did like me.

I'm not sure Uncle Chris likes Isaiah that much, either. Isaiah doesn't say much, but it's easy to see he doesn't get along with his father. He could probably use a friend.

~

I never imagined my life would be this boring. Mom and Dad are relaxing on the couch, watching some old movie. Matt is in his room. And I'm doing my homework at the kitchen table. On a Friday night. That's how it's been since the accident.

I'm in the middle of writing an essay on the causes of the Civil War when I hear the screeching of brakes and, a moment later, pounding at the front door.

"Can you get that, Kyle?" Dad calls. He and Mom look real comfortable. I head for the door. It's not like I have anything better to do.

I turn on the porch light. It's Uncle Chris.

Dad looks over. "Hi, Chris. Come on in."

My uncle's face is red. He stomps into the living room, holding a copy of the Qur'an.

"I found Isaiah reading this!" he shouts. "What are you doing to my son?"

Dad turns off the movie. "I'm not doing anything. What are you talking about?"

"I don't understand you Muslims. You're not content to destroy your own souls. You want to spread your cancer. But why did you have to go after my son?" He's nearly crying. I've never seen Uncle Chris like this.

Dad stands. "When I converted, Isaiah wanted to know about my journey. He asked about Islam. I told him he would have to find out on his own."

"When did he ask you? When have you been talking to him?"

"He comes over about once a week."

"Without my permission."

"For God's sake, Chris, I'm his uncle. He's eighteen years old. Do you still hold his hand when he crosses the street?" Dad smirks. "You've got to loosen up on your kids."

"Like you did?" Uncle Chris points at me. "So my son can end up like that?" I know he doesn't like me. He still blames me for that time I rode my bike through their flowers.

"Leave Kyle out of this."

"You let your son ruin his life. Now you're going after my son, too."

Dad's voice gets louder. "I told you, leave my kid out of this."

Uncle Chris hurls the Qur'an to the floor. "I can't believe he brought this filth into my home."

Dad rubs the back of his neck. The first sign he's about to blow. He walks over to my uncle and quietly says, "I think you'd better leave."

"You're throwing your own brother out of your house? Is that what your Islam teaches?"

"No, but I think you'd better leave before we both regret it."

"And if I don't?" Uncle Chris shouts in Dad's face.

"Back off, Chris." Dad pushes him, just a little.

Uncle Chris pushes back. "Why did you go after my son?"

"I didn't do anything to Isaiah."

"Didn't you tell him to read this garbage?"

"I'm warning you, Chris."

The punch comes from nowhere.

Dad hits back.

Dad and Uncle Chris never fight. Dad says they used to wrestle a little when they were kids, but I'm sure it was nothing like this.

Uncle Chris's first punch gets Dad in the eye. Dad punches my uncle's shoulder. Uncle Chris comes back, going for Dad's jaw. Dad blocks the punch and pushes my uncle away. Uncle Chris slams Dad into the wall. He slumps to the floor. I hope he's okay. I should help him, but I don't want Uncle Chris hauling off at me.

Dad sits on the floor, trying to catch his breath. "Look," he gasps, "I don't want to fight. Leave now, and we can forget this ever happened."

Uncle Chris kicks the Qur'an. "You couldn't leave Isaiah alone. He was a good boy. He wanted to travel the world, spreading the Gospel and leading people to the love of Christ, but you wouldn't leave him alone. It doesn't matter now. He's dead."

"What?" What?

"He's dead to me. I'm leaving Chicago so I can save the children I still have before Satan gets his claws into them."

Dad stands up slowly. "Settle down, Chris. Let's talk this out. Don't run away. I'm your brother."

"Go to Hell." My uncle turns and walks out. I always knew he could curse if he really wanted to.

Dad slips on his shoes and runs after him. "Chris. Come back."

The tires screech as my uncle roars down the street. Dad stays out there for a long time. When he walks in, his eyes are red. He picks up the Qur'an and kisses it. Mom hugs him.

Six months ago, Dad thought I was a loser, but, tonight, he stood up for me. I go over. He breaks away from Mom and puts his arms around me.

~

Isaiah comes maybe thirty minutes later. Dad has been pacing, waiting for him.

He walks in carrying a suitcase, a book bag, and the laptop Jacob always hogs. "Can I stay with you for a while, Uncle Brad?"

"What happened?"

"When he came into my room and found me reading the Qur'an, he went berserk. I packed while he was gone. Mom is crying, but I can't stay." He points to Dad's left eye. "My father did that to you, didn't he?"

Dad's eye started swelling soon after Uncle Chris stormed out. Mom put an ice pack on it. "We haven't fought in over thirty years."

"Can I stay here?"

"What about your family?"

Ripples

"Dad's been bugging me constantly—either I quit Loyola and go to the Bible college, or I'm dead to him. What happened tonight put the nail in the coffin. I'm dead." He stares at the floor.

Dad hugs him. "You can stay here as long as you want."

"I think they're moving to Arkansas. Mom's sister, my Aunt Debbie, says their church down there needs a minister. My father keeps saying he has to get away from all this godlessness."

"We were always so close. Everything has changed."

"I know. Anyway, I'm dead now, so I can do what I want. And I want to become a Muslim."

What are you saying, Isaiah? Are you insane?

"I understand how you feel," says Dad. "You're upset, and you want to change your life. But you need to slow down. You're not ready yet for that commitment."

"You're just saying that because you're afraid of my father."

"That's not true. But, if you convert, you will lose him, possibly forever."

"I don't need him. And he has four other children to dominate. He expects Ruth to marry one of his students. Jacob, Benjamin, and Martha won't be allowed to leave the house, not after what I've done."

"Did you tell him you want to become a Muslim?"

"No. I was studying Islam, that's all. But, after the way he acted tonight, if that's how it is to be a Christian, I'm done with Christianity."

Dad pats Isaiah's back. He doesn't see Isaiah grimace. I wonder what's wrong. "Take it easy. You're upset. A few weeks, a few months from now, you may feel very differently."

"We'll see. Can I have my Qur'an? I want to keep reading."

Dad hands it to him. "Take it slow."

Isaiah rolls his eyes. Dad doesn't notice.

"Let's get you settled in," I say. "Do you want to stay with me or with Matt?"

"Matt has the bunk beds. You can stay in there," says Mom.

She's right. My room is a little bigger, but the wheelchair takes up space.

"Can I eat first?" says Isaiah. "I'm starved."

"You didn't have dinner?" says Mom.

31

"No. My father threw me out before I had a chance to eat."

Dad frowns. "That doesn't sound like Chris."

"You would be surprised."

There's something he's not telling us. I can always tell when Isaiah's lying because his ears turn red, but I never rat on him.

"Let's go to the kitchen and heat up the leftovers," I say. Maybe he'll tell me when my parents are out of earshot. I fill a plate, too, and eat with him. "What really happened tonight?"

"Like I said, Dad got mad because I was reading the Qur'an."

"What else?"

He touches his left ear and looks down at his plate. "I don't want to talk about it."

He's shutting down. Classic Isaiah. I change subjects. "You really want to become a Muslim? You must be crazy."

He smiles a little. "Haven't I always been crazy? What about you? Aren't you curious about Islam?"

I pat my paralyzed legs and grin. "My wild days are over."

Ripples

Brad: Losing My Brother

I've been lying here in the dark for hours. I never imagined. Not Chris and me.

He threw the Qur'an on the floor. I should have picked it up immediately, but I was shaken. All I wanted at that moment was to end the fight and pretend it never happened.

I knew Isaiah would come. He had nowhere else to go. I don't know why it took him so long to get to our house. Maybe he needed to cool off.

Chris and I have been best friends for nearly fifty years. I won't lose my brother.

∼

I call Chris in the morning. Melinda answers.

"I need to talk with my brother."

"He's at the college clearing out his office." There's a hard edge to her voice.

"You can't let him do this, Melinda. Running away isn't the answer."

"Is Isaiah there?"

"Don't worry. We'll take care of him until this all gets straightened out."

"Is he a Muslim?"

"No. You know Isaiah. He's always been a curious kid. Can you ask Chris to call me?"

"I'll give him the message," she says. Then she hangs up. I've never heard Melinda so tense.

I need to put in a few hours of work on the mass transit system we're developing. On the way to my office, I call Chris's cell. It's out of service.

In the afternoon, I drive over to their house. A moving van is parked in the driveway. Jacob is walking out with a box.

"What's happening? Where are you going?"

He looks down. "Dad told me not to talk to you."

"Where is your father?"

"He's in the house."

I knock. No answer. I ring the bell. I pound. "Open the damn door, Chris. We need to talk."

"He won't come out," says Jacob. "You need to go home."

"But he's my brother."

"I used to have a brother. Isaiah is dead now." His face is expressionless. What is Chris doing to his children? I want to grab Jacob by the shoulders and shake him.

I rub my neck instead. "I have to talk to Chris."

"I shouldn't be talking to you. My father won't like it." He comes closer and whispers, "Tell Matt I'll miss him." He heads for the house. "You'd better go now."

I walk back to my car and wait for my brother to come out. After ninety minutes, I give up and drive away.

I go to the house again in the morning.

The moving van is gone. I peer through the naked windows. The rooms are empty. I'm still standing, staring, when a plump middle-aged woman drives up and posts a "For Sale" sign in the yard.

"Are you interested in this house? I would be happy to show it to you."

"No, thank you."

~

Isaiah has lived with us for a week now. He is already becoming one of the family.

On Saturday afternoon, while Beth is out running her errands, Isaiah walks out of the bathroom with only a towel around his waist. I stare at his shoulders and back. He is covered with scars, cuts, and bruises.

"How did you get those marks?"

He looks down. "You weren't supposed to see them."

"What happened, Isaiah?"

"I can't tell you."

"You can trust me. I want to help."

He sighs deeply. "Okay, you know how angry Dad was. When he saw me reading the Qur'an, he hit me with his belt, like he usually does. I got mad, too, this time, and fought back. That's why I had to leave."

Ripples

"Usually? This time? He's done this before?"

"Sure. I'm always getting into trouble."

"You could have come to me. I could have made him stop."

"No you couldn't. It's in the Bible. 'Withhold not correction from the child: for if thou beatest him with the rod, he shall not die. Thou shalt beat him with the rod, and shalt deliver his soul from Hell.' The Book of Proverbs, chapter twenty-three, verses thirteen and fourteen. I deserved it."

"No, Isaiah, you never deserved that."

"I was bad."

"No kid deserves to be beaten. I know what I'm talking about. And I read the entire Bible. I saw those two verses, but others speak of love and mercy. While you're reading the Qur'an, you should also be reading the Bible, if you really want to know."

He nods. "I'll do that. Thanks."

I wish I had helped him sooner—when he was a little boy being beaten by his father.

He is never going back to them.

Jennifer

Before I married Nuruddin, I was easily bored, but I've spent the last year concentrating on my little family, and I have never been happier.

My days are full of my baby. I keep a record of all of his firsts, writing daily in a journal about his progress. When the baby is asleep, I cuddle with Nuruddin. Between my beautiful son and my wonderful husband, I really don't have time to think about anything else.

When Aunt Beth calls, I've just put Ahmed down for a nap.

"How are you, Jennifer?" she says. "And how is that sweet baby?"

"He's wonderful."

"We're having a barbecue tomorrow, and I was hoping you could come. I can't wait to see Ahmed again."

"Won't it be too cold?"

"They say it will be in the seventies. You know how strange the weather is. Can you make it?"

"If it's that warm, it should be safe to take the baby out. What would you like me to bring?"

"You don't have to bring anything. I just want to see that baby of yours. Your mother must love playing with her grandchildren."

Kyle will probably never have children. Poor Aunt Beth. "Yes, she does. I guess we'll see you tomorrow then."

After we say our goodbyes, I tiptoe into the bedroom and gaze at my son. I am the luckiest woman in the world.

∼

My little brother, Luqman, is playing with the hose. The minute I walk into the yard, he takes a shot at me.

"Stop that!" I scream, shielding my baby.

"Luqman," Aisha calls, "Put down that hose right now."

"Why?" He shouts back.

"Luqman." She gives him that look of hers. He drops the hose and runs off to play with the other kids.

I look around. "Where is everybody?"

"We're all here," says Aisha.

Ripples

"What about Aunt Melinda and Uncle Chris? Are they in the house?"

"Didn't you hear? They moved to Arkansas."

"Arkansas?"

"Melinda's sister lives down there. They wanted to be close to her."

How could I not know that my aunt and uncle moved to a different state? I nod. "I hope they like it there." I wonder how Isaiah is handling Arkansas. He's probably bored out of his mind.

Water splashes my back. I spin around. "Luqman, I told you to stop that."

Kyle is holding a squirt gun. "Gotcha." He grins.

"Aren't you too old for that?"

"You're the old one around here, Jen. Did you know they have creams to get rid of the wrinkles?"

I touch my face. He wheels away, laughing. "Gotcha again."

Why do I even bother?

Isaiah walks up and sets a bowl of chips on the table. "Don't eat the whole thing, Jen. Save some for the rest of us."

I'm too stunned to shoot him a comeback. "Aisha said you moved to Arkansas."

"They did."

"What are you doing here?"

"They told me to stay and keep an eye on you," he says with a straight face, walking away.

All right. I'm too old to play games with my goofy cousins anyway.

Later, while we're eating, Aunt Beth tells me what happened. "I never thought I'd see Brad and Chris fighting like that."

My quiet Uncle Chris kicked Isaiah out, punched Uncle Brad, and left Chicago. And I knew nothing about it. I guess there is a world outside of Nuruddin and Ahmed.

My Life

Life is like an onion: You peel it off one layer at a time, and sometimes you weep.

—Carl Sandburg

Isaiah

I keep dreaming about that night. Sometimes, nothing happens. I go to the bathroom to wash my hands, and we sit down to eat dinner. Other times, Mom doesn't come, and I'm staring at my father's lifeless body. Last night, I dreamed I was speeding down the highway with the police close behind. No matter how far I drove, or how fast, their sirens wailed. I couldn't escape.

I would not have fought him if he had just stopped beating me. He's hit me ever since I can remember. When I was little, I got in trouble for climbing on the furniture, talking too loud, fighting with Jacob, or forgetting to wipe my muddy feet. Sometimes, I didn't say please and thank you. Sometimes, I broke my toys or ripped the knees out of my pants. The last few years, he's hit me for getting B's on my report card, sleeping past 8:00 AM on Saturday, and talking to girls at church. Whatever I did, I always knew the belt would come next.

Mom never hit me—I can't imagine Mom hitting anyone—but, when Dad came home, she would tell him about the trouble I had caused. Out came the belt.

Dad never hit Jacob. Never. When Jacob and I fought, I started it. When our room was a mess, it was my fault. When we were playing ball in the kitchen and some of Mom's dishes got broken, I got blamed. Jacob never did anything wrong.

And not even Jacob is as perfect as Ruth. Everyone calls her an angel. I like Ruth. She never protected me, but, sometimes, when I was little, she held me afterward. A few times, she helped me cover my tracks. Like the time I spilled grape juice all over the living room carpet. Mom and Dad were out visiting sick people. Ruth grabbed the rags and started scrubbing. It took a while, but we got the stain out before they came home.

Martha will never be hit. She's only five, and she doesn't get into much trouble yet. Besides, Dad likes the girls better.

Benjamin has been getting hit since he was little, and it's worse now that he's showing signs of puberty. I'm gone, and he's Dad's only target. I wish I could help him.

~

I like living at Uncle Brad's house. He and Aunt Beth have only a few basic rules, like cleaning up after myself and letting them know where I am when I go out. There's a midnight curfew, but I'm never out that late. Between my classes and my job at the pizza place, I don't have time for a social life.

They are so much different than Mom and Dad. No Bible readings. No memorization. No dragging me to church on Sundays. Aunt Beth goes sometimes, but she doesn't make a big deal out of it. Uncle Brad goes to the mosque every Friday. Last week, I went with him. He gave me a chair, and I watched them pray. I'd read about the Islamic prayer service, but I hadn't realized how different it is. No pews, no hymnals, no choir.

They also ask me about my studies. My father just lectured me about the Bible, but Uncle Brad and Aunt Beth are interested in the history I'm learning. Last night during dinner, we discussed the problems in the Middle East. Kyle and Matt joined in. It was exhilarating.

I miss Mom, Ruth, and Martha, and I worry about Benjamin, but I don't want to go back to them. I never realized life could be this easy.

Ripples

Kyle

Isaiah has lived with us for a month now. That's wrong, what Uncle Chris did to him, but it's good having Isaiah around. We hang out together in my room every night after studying. He goes into the kitchen to get the ice cream and chips, and we sit around, talking and eating, until midnight or later. Nothing important. Just stuff.

Except for being thrown out by his father, he has a pretty good life. When he finished high school, he got a car from Gramma's estate. I'm still waiting on my car. Plus he has a part-time job and a scholarship to Loyola while I'm performing meaningless tasks and stuck in a community college. He's where I would be if I hadn't messed up.

And I'll never get there. I should be married to Amy, playing with our son, and attending a top-rate college on a football scholarship, but that life is gone. I don't know where to go from here.

There are days when I don't want to get out of bed. I'd rather keep dreaming about football, Amy, and our baby.

I want to be angry, but there's no one to blame, except myself.

～

My life isn't totally bleak. I'm taking three classes over at the community college—algebra, history, and English. I breeze through the algebra and English. Isaiah helps me study for my history tests. It's gonna take a while, but one of these days, I'll graduate.

And I have my job. When Uncle Joshua first brought me to Hope Center, he put me to work stuffing envelopes. It was busywork to keep me from thinking about how much I had screwed up. A month ago, they finally put me on payroll, but I still don't do much more than stuff envelopes. I think they gave me this job out of pity. Do your duty. Hire a crip.

I have some ideas, though, and, if they pan out, I'll be on my way. I need to be more than just the local crip.

Life isn't hopeless, but I lost so much. And it's gone forever.

Jennifer

We had another nice day today, so I took Ahmed for a walk. I'm glad Nuruddin insisted on living in this neighborhood. I picked up a few groceries and even did a little window shopping. I wanted to browse in a bookstore, but Ahmed started fussing the second I walked in. An old woman frowned. I quickly left.

He's been crying for the last two blocks. I know he's hungry, but I can't exactly stop in the middle of the street and open my blouse. I push the stroller into the apartment. "Hold on. Mommy needs to put these bags in the kitchen. I'll be right back. It's okay, honey."

I drop the groceries on the kitchen floor and run back to my baby. He's screaming now. My milk drips steadily. It's a good thing I had those grocery bags to hide behind.

I scoop him up and carry him to the couch. "My poor baby. It's okay, Ahmed. Here you go." He stops screaming.

I lean back into the couch and concentrate on my baby. I love him as much as the day he was born. More, even. His sweet smell, his soft skin, his little curled-up fists. I close my eyes and enjoy the moment.

Nuruddin kisses me on the cheek. "Hi, Jenny. How was your day?"

I open my eyes. "When did you get home?"

"A few minutes ago."

"Why didn't you say anything?"

"I had to put the groceries away. The ice cream was melting all over the floor."

"Oh, I guess I fell asleep."

Nuruddin runs his hand through the hair of our sleeping baby. "Don't you ever put him down?"

"I fell asleep. I'm sorry."

"Don't get upset. That's not what I meant. But I think you're spoiling him." He laughs. "If you carry him all the time, how will he learn to walk?"

I softly kiss my son's head. "I'm in no hurry for him to grow up. He is my most precious baby. I love him so much."

"More than you love me?"

"Of course not." Something occurs to me. "How in the world did your mother manage to love and care for eight children?"

Ripples

"You'll have to find out."
"Not me. One is enough, or maybe two."
"I thought we would have nine."
"Are you crazy?"
"I'm crazy about you." He comes closer for a long kiss.
A sweet baby boy. A handsome husband. My life is nearly perfect.

My Turn

The pessimist sees difficulty in every opportunity.
The optimist sees the opportunity in every difficulty.

—Winston Churchill

Isaiah: Part One

I've lived with Uncle Brad for almost three months. Every morning, I hear Matt get up early, while it's still dark. I wonder why.

This morning, I follow him out of the room. He's praying with Uncle Brad. I watch for a moment before sneaking back.

When he comes back, I ask. "Are you a Muslim?"

He grins. "Not yet, but Dad's going to let me fast this Ramadan. I can't wait." He goes on and on. I go back to bed.

I've read the Qur'an three times now. I read the Bible, too, because Uncle Brad insisted. I've memorized most of it. Twice.

Sometimes, the songs I sang in church run through my brain. I feel like beating my head against the wall. Instead, I listen to one of Uncle Brad's Qur'an CDs. I don't understand many words yet, just a few I hear my uncles say often. I like the way they sound.

Every day, I tell Uncle Brad I want to be a Muslim. He always says I'm not ready. I don't know what more he expects from me.

∼

I just received an email from Ruth. She got married last week to some guy named Andrew Stone. I know him. He was one of my father's students. He always hung around our house, trying to make a good impression on my esteemed father, the Reverend Christopher Adams—quoting the Bible and discussing the parables ad nauseam. Dad kept telling me I should be more like Andrew. That jerk had better take good care of my sister, or I will hunt him down.

Ruth says they plan to travel to Indonesia in a few days to do missionary work. "Spreading God's Word," she calls it. She knows how I feel about that. I write back and tell her to have a safe trip. I never thought it was right to barge into someone else's country—food in one hand and Bible in the other—and try to convert people who haven't asked to be converted.

I wish I could see Ruth before she leaves. If I jump in my car and drive straight through, I could be there in time, but I have a test tomorrow. And I don't even want to be in the same state as my father.

Jamilah Kolocotronis

Isaiah: Part Two

I'm working on a term paper when Matt runs into the room and leaps onto his bed. "Yes!"

I ignore him and keep on typing. But he does this little victory dance, and I can't concentrate. "Why are you so happy?" *And can you keep it to yourself?*

"I'm going to become a Muslim."

I look up from the computer. "Oh, yeah?"

"Dad says he'll take me to the mosque on Friday and let me declare the *shahadah* in front of everyone. I don't think my mom really likes it, but she'll let me do it. I can't wait to be a real Muslim."

He keeps yammering. I save my work and start planning my strategy.

Five minutes later, Matt is still talking. I walk out, looking for Uncle Brad. He's in the kitchen, fixing supper.

"Matt just told me he's converting."

Uncle Brad turns around, smiling. "Isn't that great? I think he's ready."

"Can you take me, too? I want to be a Muslim, too." Okay, I sound like a ten-year-old, but this means a lot to me.

He sighs. "I don't think you're ready, Isaiah."

"What do you mean, I'm not ready? I read the Bible, Genesis to Revelations. I'm reading the Qur'an for the fourth time. What more do you need?"

"Why do you want to be a Muslim?"

"I want to start a new life." *Far away from everything my father stands for.*

He shakes his head. "You're not ready. Keep reading."

"What makes you such an expert?"

"I have some experience under my belt. Listen to me, Isaiah. If you wait until you've grasped both the knowledge and the spirit of Islam, your conversion will be much smoother. You must have the right intention."

"I intend to become a Muslim. Isn't that enough?"

"No. Keep reading and praying. It will come to you, and, when it does, you will know exactly what I'm talking about."

Ripples

"Forget you!" I storm out of the house and climb into my car. I hit the expressway and drive for over an hour before I'm calm enough to go back.

When I walk in, Uncle Brad is cleaning up from dinner. He glances at me. "Are you hungry?"

That's it? I know he won't beat me, but I can't believe I'll get off without even a lecture.

"What do you have?"

"Sloppy Joes. Sit down, and I'll fix you a plate."

I eat while he loads the dishwasher. "It's too bad you couldn't eat with the family," he says. "We missed having you here."

"I needed to cool off."

"Where did you go?"

"Nowhere. I just drove."

He calmly wipes the stove and counters. How could he be my father's brother?

I finish eating and wash my plate before heading for my room.

"Wait," says Uncle Brad. "I don't want you leaving the house again without telling me where you're going."

Here it comes. "Why?"

"It's a house rule. And I care about you."

"You never cared where Kyle went."

"That was in the old days. We have new rules now. I expect you to follow them."

"What if I don't?"

He frowns. "Stop acting like a child. You know I won't hit you, and I probably won't even yell, but you're old enough to take responsibility for your actions. I expect you to do so." He turns off the kitchen light. "I'll see you in the morning."

That's it. No argument. No power struggle. No sermon. Tomorrow, I'll tell him I've decided to convert. Hopefully, he'll support me.

I go back to the room and try to study, but Matt won't settle down. I keep reading the same sentence.

"I can't wait," Matt says. "Dad promised he'll buy me new clothes, like the ones Uncle Joshua wears."

I look up. "Why do you want to dress like that?" Baggy pants and a long shirt. It looks messy.

"It's different. Wait until the kids at school see my new clothes."

They'll probably beat him up. I've completely lost my concentration. I close my book and walk out, slamming the door.

Kyle is studying, too.

"Does your little brother ever shut up?"

"Not unless I hit him."

"I can't study."

"So you came in here to make sure I flunk my algebra test?"

Nobody wants me. "Sorry." I walk to the door.

Kyle grins. "I know this stuff. Go get the ice cream."

~

I corner Uncle Brad during breakfast. "I want to go the mosque with you and make shahadah today."

"Let's talk about this, Isaiah. What do you believe?"

"I believe in God."

"Good. What else? What about Jesus? Do you believe in the Trinity?"

"I know what the Qur'an says. Jesus was a prophet. There is no Trinity. It's just the One God, that's all."

"Is that what you believe?"

Is that what I believe? My father says anyone who doesn't embrace Jesus Christ as his personal Lord and Savior will suffer everlasting punishment. I don't want to think about all those hours I spent listening to his talk of hellfire and damnation.

So is Jesus a prophet, like they say? I don't know. I still haven't thought it all the way through.

"Sure. If it's in the Qur'an, it must be true, right?"

"Do you believe what's in the Bible?"

"Some of it."

"Which parts?"

"What's with all the questions? I told you I want to be a Muslim. Isn't that good enough?"

"Not for me."

"Forget you." I learned to say that instead of cursing. It saved me from the worst of the beatings. I trudge into my bedroom, slam the door, and throw myself on the bed.

Ripples

Uncle Brad refuses to help me take the shahadah, or even take me to the mosque with him tomorrow. I don't know what's wrong with him.

∼

In the afternoon, I skip my economics class and go to a small mosque I pass every day on my way to school. I walk in and tell someone I want to become a Muslim. He asks me a few questions. Do I know what Islam is? Have I read the Qur'an? Do I know about Prophet Muhammad? I answer perfectly. He listens as I take the shahadah.

I'm a Muslim now, and there is nothing anyone can do about it. I dare them to try.

∼

I haven't heard from my parents for three months. I'm dead, my father said. Up until two days ago, I wasn't sure he really meant it.

Ruth had been emailing me from Indonesia. She likes it there, even though they have to sleep inside mosquito nets, and it's always hot. The people are friendly, she said, and anxious to hear the Word of God. I didn't comment.

She told me that the family is doing well. My father enjoys having his own little church down in Arkansas. Mom home schools the kids. I'm sure both my parents watch them closely to make sure they don't turn out like me.

In her last email, Ruth sent me their phone number. I called right away. It was Tuesday afternoon, and my father shouldn't have been home, but he was. He answered.

"Hello?"

I froze for a second before clearing my throat and saying forcefully, "I need to talk to Mom."

"Isaiah," he whispered.

"Can you get Mom, please? I miss her."

There was silence for a minute or two. "Dad? Are you there? Where's Mom?"

He hung up.

Yesterday, I tried again. The number was no longer in service. I emailed Ruth right away, but she hasn't responded.

I'm glad I made shahadah. Now I won't have to belong to the same religion as that hypocrite.

I begged Uncle Brad. I wanted him to be the one to convert me, but he wouldn't. I won't ask him for anything else.

Isaiah: Part Three

I am a Muslim.

When I walked into the mosque this afternoon, it was nearly empty. I wanted to be there for the Friday prayer, but I got stuck in traffic. I found one man sitting alone, reciting the Qur'an. I walked up slowly behind him. He kept reciting. I waited. I wasn't going to leave the mosque without converting.

Fifteen minutes later, he turned to me. "What do you want?"

He was intimidating with his long black beard and strong voice. His face showed no expression. I nearly walked away, but visions of my father flashed before my eyes. I gulped and said, "I want to be a Muslim. Will you convert me?"

"Conversion comes from your heart," he said. "I can help you. Why do you want to be a Muslim?"

I knew what he wanted to hear. "I believe in Allah, and I want to worship Him."

"Have you read the Qur'an?"

"Yes. Four times. It's beautiful."

"Do you believe in the prophethood of Muhammad, peace and blessings be upon him?"

"Of course I do. He was sent by Allah to guide us."

"Good. Repeat after me."

I said the words perfectly. He offered his hand. "*Assalaamu alaikum*, my young brother." He had a strong grip.

"Thank you," I said quietly.

"There are many things you must learn. We will start with the prayer."

∼

By the time other men started trickling in for the afternoon prayer, I could stand confidently with them. A warm feeling spread through my chest. I was a Muslim. I belonged there.

After the prayer, my teacher said, "You must be hungry. Come with me."

We walked to his apartment on the second floor of an old brick building. I looked around. The room was bare except for three green cushions propped up against the wall. No table. No couch. He asked me to come into the small kitchen with him. We talked while he cooked. I was in awe of his knowledge and paid no attention to the food.

When he was finished, he brought two pots to the middle of the room and gestured to a sheet in the corner. "Spread that out." He put the food on the cloth and asked me to sit with him on the floor. "Get the plates."

"Would you like me to get the utensils, too?" I asked.

"We will eat with our hands."

I stared at the pots. What had he prepared?

"I usually eat rice and lentils," he said. "We don't need fancy foods to sustain ourselves."

So we ate without meat or salad. No table or forks. I wondered why Uncle Brad and Uncle Joshua don't eat that way.

∼

We've talked for hours. It's stimulating, but I'm tired. "I'd better go home. It's late."

"Come tomorrow," he says. "You have much more to learn."

We shake hands. "I'll see you tomorrow."

He nods. "*Insha Allah.*"

I drive back in the dark after making another prayer with him. I feel different.

When I walk into the house, most of the lights are off. They're watching a movie. Uncle Brad looks over but doesn't say anything. I head for my room and open the Qur'an.

Twenty minutes later, there's a soft knock. I'm concentrating. Uncle Brad opens the door.

"Isaiah."

I'm studying a verse about Jesus. What exactly does it mean?

"Isaiah." He raises his voice.

I look up. "What is it?"

"I need to know where you were this evening. Why were you late?"

Ripples

"I had a study session at the library." I turn back to my reading.

"You had a study session on a Friday night?"

"You know how tough Loyola is." Would you just leave me alone?

"You should have called to let us know you'd be late."

"I forgot." Can't you see I don't want to talk?

"Don't let it happen again." He walks away.

I turn back to the verse. "That they said (in boast), 'We killed Christ Jesus the son of Mary, the Messenger of Allah'—but they killed him not, nor crucified him. But so it was made to appear to them." I have read this passage at least ten times, and I can't quite get my mind around it. It's revolutionary. I wonder if my father knows Muslims believe this.

What are they doing right now? Do they know how much I changed today? Do they care?

∼

When Matt gets up for the morning prayer, I wait a few minutes and go to the bathroom for my ablutions. I stand behind Uncle Brad and Matt, raising my hands. "*Allahu akbar.*"

At the end of the prayer, Uncle Brad stares at me. I offer my hand. "*Assalaamu alaikum.*"

"What's going on?"

"I went to Masjid Darul Islaam yesterday and made shahadah. You can't stop me."

He rubs the back of his neck. "I never wanted to stop you. I only want to be certain you're becoming a Muslim for the right reasons."

"I'm smart enough to know what's right. Anyway, it's done."

"In that case," he extends his hand, "*Walaikum assalaam.* Remember, if you need help, you can come to me."

"I met someone at the *masjid* who will teach me. His name is Faruq. I ate dinner with him, and I'm going back later today."

"Okay. Well, congratulations."

"Don't pretend. I know you don't approve, but I don't care anymore."

He doesn't respond. I go back to my room.

Jamilah Kolocotronis

Kyle: Part One

Every morning, I roll into Hope Center, hoping they'll give me serious work for a change. Two weeks ago, I emailed some of my ideas to Bob Warren, the director. No response. I'm still answering phones and stuffing envelopes. Some people think that's all a crip is good for.

Most people don't like that word—including a lot of the crips I know. One of the counselors in rehab lectured me for twenty minutes about it. "You must develop your self-esteem," he said. "Use of labels will only impede your progress. You and I are people with special needs. That's how we must think of ourselves." Like his way of saying it was more positive. Someday, I'll invent a word to capture the essence of the wheelchair-bound lifestyle.

So, I have a nowhere job where people see a wheelchair instead of me. I'm acing my college courses, but it will take me years to graduate. I'm frustrated. I'm bored.

And I'm so lonely it hurts. Our baby would be crawling now. Maybe walking. I know our child was beautiful. He would have excelled at everything he tried. Top student, ace quarterback, model citizen. He would have turned pro before he was twenty. He could have had a wonderful life, but he never had a chance.

Sometimes, if a person loses someone he loves, people say, "You can try again. You can fall in love again. You can have another child." They don't even try to pull that crap with me. They know I had only one chance. Now it's gone.

Ripples

Kyle: Part Two

What is wrong with this family? My little brother is practically wetting his pants because Dad took him to the mosque and let him dress up like a terrorist, and Isaiah acts like he's waging a major rebellion. "Uncle Brad thinks I'm not ready, but I'll show him," he says. I don't know why he makes such a big deal out of everything.

I'm just trying to survive without punching someone. I get out of bed, which is a feat in itself. I sit at my desk for eight hours and perform meaningless tasks. Some nights, I come home and watch TV until I can't keep my eyes open. Canned laughter intrudes on my dreams.

∽

It's another Friday afternoon, and I'm stuffing envelopes. One after the other. I can barely stay awake. I roll to the break room for another cup of coffee.

Bob Warren walks up to me in the hallway. "How are you today, Kyle?"

He's barely talked to me since I started here. I'm surprised he knows my name. "I'm okay."

"Let's go back to your office. There's something I want to discuss with you."

I'm being laid off. I knew it would happen. Why should they pay me when they can find volunteers to stuff their envelopes? I take my coffee back to the office and sit behind my desk. I wonder how long they'll let me stay.

Warren keeps standing. "You look bored. I read your email, and I think you can handle something a little more challenging. What do you think?"

"Sure." Anything would be more challenging than this.

"You know the center depends on the help of volunteers. We need someone to recruit additional volunteers and coordinate and oversee the work of all those who come to help. Are you up for the job?"

I'm not being let go? Yes! "Sure."

"Good. I'll email you the list of our current volunteers along with areas where we need more help. If you do a good job, next month I'll ask the board to give you a slight raise."

A little extra cash is always nice. "I'll get right to work on it."

We shake hands, and he leaves. He's giving me this chance to show what I can do. I can't blow it. In fact, I'll be the best damn volunteer coordinator the world has ever seen.

∼

During dinner, Dad rubs his neck. "I wonder where Isaiah is."

I know where Isaiah went. He swore me to secrecy. For a smart guy, my cousin can act awfully immature. I keep my mouth shut. Secrecy is something I respect.

All during the meal, Matt keeps babbling about becoming a Muslim. Mom presses her lips together, which is what she does when she's upset. My stupid brother doesn't notice.

Dad does. He interrupts Matt. "How was work today, Kyle? Did anything interesting happen?"

He asks me that all the time. I finally have something to tell him.

∼

I've been on the new job for almost a week. Every day I have one or two volunteers come in to stuff envelopes and answer the phones. Most are teenagers who need community service hours to graduate.

Recruitment is the hardest part. We need people to teach ESL and GED classes and give workshops on health care issues. We also need translators in our clinic and volunteers to coach our basketball, football, and soccer teams. I've sent notices to area churches asking for help. So far, only a few responses have trickled in.

Mom stayed home today with a bad cold. I'm sure she caught it at the clinic. She could stay in her office, but she likes to greet the patients. I wonder why she wants to spend her days around sick people.

When Dad picks me up at six, he asks, "How was work? Anything interesting?"

"Signing up volunteers is harder than I expected. What about you? Did Hendricks give you any trouble today?"

"The usual. I have four more months. I don't think I could last a day longer."

Ripples

"You really plan to open up your own garage?"

"When I was in high school, being a mechanic was my dream job. Everyone said I should get into engineering instead because there was more prestige and more money. So I did."

"Sounds like a dream deferred."

"Something like that. What are your dreams, Kyle?"

"I don't have any." I used to.

He pulls onto our street. There she is, parked at the curb in front of our house. My dream. Matt is standing next to her, keeping guard.

"She's here!" I open the door while the car is still moving.

"Hold on." Dad laughs. "Let me park first."

The second he stops, I pull my chair out, swing in, and go over to inspect her. She's beautiful.

Dad peers through her window. "This is a good model. She should last you a long time."

I pull on the door handle. It's locked. Matt runs into the house to get the code.

"They brought the car a few minutes after I got home," he yells, running back out. "It's nice, Kyle."

Real nice. And she's all mine. I swing in and check out the interior.

Isaiah saunters over. "Nice wheels. Do you want to race?"

My father clears his throat and shakes his head.

"Don't worry, Dad. I'm not that stupid."

Mom comes out and looks her over. "Congratulations, Kyle." She hugs me. That's Mom.

Dad was supposed to cook dinner tonight, but he forgot all about it. Mom orders pizza. She makes me come in to eat with them. After dinner, Dad, Isaiah, Matt, and I go back outside.

"I looked through the instruction manual, and I've figured out how these hand controls work. Do you want to take her for a spin?"

Dad is always using those old clichés. Sometimes, I don't know what the hell he's talking about, but I understood that one. "Let's go."

I climb behind the wheel, pull in my chair, store it in the overhead compartment, and start the ignition. Smooth.

I'm glad we live on a quiet street. I jerk, trying to figure out how to stop and start. I haven't driven in nearly two years, and these hand controls will take some practice.

"Take it easy, Kyle. Keep her steady. You know how to operate a stick shift. This isn't much different."

After an hour, I think I have it. I pull into the driveway and shut her off. "I can't wait to drive her to work tomorrow."

"You have to wait. Chicago traffic can be rough. You need to master these hand controls before you get out on the expressway. And you don't have a license or insurance yet. Why don't you study the manual?"

I want to argue, but he's right.

I can't wait to take her out again.

Ripples

Jennifer: Part One

I just put Ahmed down for a nap. I should have time to take a shower and start dinner before he wakes up crying.

I'm about to turn on the water when someone knocks. I don't answer. It can't be too important.

"Jennifer. Open the door."

It's Mom. I throw on my robe and let her in.

"You're not busy, are you?"

"Ahmed's finally asleep," I whisper. "I have a little time to myself."

"Don't let me interrupt. I'll wait."

"You don't mind?"

"I remember how it is to have a little one. Don't worry. I'll just make myself at home."

I laugh to myself. Mom always makes herself at home, no matter where she is.

She goes in to peek at Ahmed. I climb into the shower and revel in the hot water massaging my back.

When I walk out, refreshed, Mom is holding my screaming baby. "I can't get him to stop. He must be hungry."

"I'm sure he is," I sigh. He's always hungry. I need to start him on cereal.

While I nurse the baby, Mom tells me why she came. She always has a reason.

"I'm worried about you, Jenny. I know you enjoy playing house, but you were meant to do more. Before you married Nuruddin, you promised you would continue your education. You've been out of school for months now."

"I wanted to take this semester off to be with the baby. If I return in the fall, is that soon enough?"

"What if you get pregnant again? It could take you years to finish."

"I'll go back in August, no matter what. If I do get pregnant, I'll have to work around it." I sure hope that doesn't happen. Nuruddin doesn't believe in birth control.

"Where are you going to find a sitter?"

"I don't know. I guess I'll advertise. I haven't thought about it yet."

"You didn't ask me."

"You have your work."

"I can cut back. My paintings are selling, and I don't have to take on so much extra work. If I arrange to keep my mornings free, would you leave my precious grandson with me?"

"Of course I would, Mom. That would be great."

"Good. I'm glad that's settled." She walks to the door. "You're going back in August, and I'm going to spend more time with my little Ahmed."

I have to admit, there are times when I think I shouldn't go back to school until my baby is older. Maybe when he starts kindergarten. But I promised Mom. She will never forget.

I gaze at my nursing baby. I can't imagine leaving him with anyone. Not even Mom.

~

I made curry for dinner. With help from Safa, Dad, and a few of our friends, I'm learning to cook the foods Nuruddin likes.

"This is good," he says. "You're a quick learner."

"Is it as good as your mother's?"

He smiles. "Sorry, Jenny. I don't think anyone cooks as well as Mama."

Why does he always have to be so honest? I frown. He doesn't notice.

"That reminds me," he continues. "Mama and Baba will be coming soon. They're still trying to get their visas. Your father is paying for their trip."

"They're coming?"

"Yes. I can't wait."

I guess he can't, but what about me? No matter how well I cook, I will never measure up to their standards. I'm not a Muslim. I don't cover my head. I don't speak much Urdu. I'm just this silly blonde girl who fell in love with their son. Not at all what they imagined for him, I'm sure.

Ripples

Maybe they won't get their visas. It's hard for people to get into the States, especially from Pakistan. And they're really conservative. His father has a full beard and always wears tunics. His mother doesn't just cover her head, she covers her face, too. I've never even seen a picture of them because they think photos are forbidden in Islam. They could easily pass for terrorists.

Nuruddin wants so much to see them, but I'm not ready to meet his parents. I don't know if I'll ever be.

Jennifer: Part Two

Nuruddin will graduate soon. I can't wait. I hope he'll be able to relax once all his studies are out of the way.

My brother Jeremy is graduating, too. He just called to tell me he was accepted. He'll be going to law school at the University of Chicago. I'm very proud of him.

∼

Ahmed crawled all the way across the room today. I clapped. He reached for me and laughed. I love him so much. I can't believe he loves me, too.

Before I met Nuruddin, I planned to attend an Ivy League school and find a job in New York writing for a major magazine. When Nuruddin got off that plane, and I looked into his beautiful dark eyes, I decided to graduate from a top Chicago university and break into the local literary scene. After we were married, I wanted to finish my degree and find a nice job somewhere. When I became a mother, I started living only for the sweetness of my baby.

But he won't be a baby forever. I need to reclaim my life. Before Ahmed was born, I couldn't understand how a woman could waste her life raising children. I have to be careful not to fall into that trap.

Nuruddin and Jeremy are building their careers. Raheema will graduate in August, and she already has a job with the Great Lakes Commission. While they're all making important contributions to society, will I be just a mother?

I may never write for a major New York City magazine, but I should start thinking about my career again. It has been months since I've written as much as a sentence. While Ahmed takes his afternoon nap, I sit in front of the computer and stare at the empty screen. What do I want to say?

Friends and Brothers

*Be careful what you set your heart upon—
for it will surely be yours.*

—James Baldwin

Isaiah: Part One

I spend most of my time with Faruq. He's knowledgeable about Islam, and he takes his faith seriously. I'm honored to learn from him.

During the day, Faruq works as a butcher in a Muslim meat shop. He often spends his nights praying at the masjid or reading the Qur'an in his apartment. He fasts at least two days every week, sometimes more. He doesn't have furniture, a car, or a phone. He says he wants to live his life in imitation of the Prophet, peace and blessings be upon him.

On Thursday, he hands me a bag.

"What's this?"

"You're learning to follow in the footsteps of the Prophet. You need to dress like him."

I carefully examine each gift. He's given me two white robes, two *kufis* to wear on my head, a pair of leather socks, and a stick called a *miswak* for cleaning my teeth.

"Put away your Western clothes," he says. "Give them to charity. From now on, you will dress only as the Prophet dressed."

When I get home, I gather most of my clothes and put them in a box.

∼

In the morning, Uncle Brad gives me the once-over. "You look nice."

"Why don't you dress like this? Are you a true Muslim?"

He raises his eyebrows. "I have a robe I sometimes wear, but Islam allows for many different styles of dress, within limits. My clothing is loose, and it covers me properly. That's good enough."

I walk away, shaking my head. "You're wrong." I'd like to teach him more, passing on my lessons from Faruq, but I don't think he'd listen.

On my way to school, I drop off my clothes at a thrift store. They will keep someone warm, and I will receive more reward for helping needy non-Muslims.

∼

I spend the weekend at Faruq's apartment. He patiently teaches me how to read the Qur'an in Arabic. We study all day Saturday, stopping only to go to the masjid together to pray. I sleep a few hours Saturday night before Faruq wakes me for the late night prayers. I doze a little afterward and wake to hear him quietly weeping as he reads the Qur'an. He's told me the Qur'an often moves him to tears.

A minute later, Faruq stands and calls out, "*As salatu khairun min an naum.*" Prayer is better than sleep. I go with him to the masjid in the early dawn. After listening to a lecture, we return to the apartment, eating bread and honey for breakfast. He continues to teach me the Qur'an until lunch time when I help him prepare the rice and lentils. After the midday prayer, we each take a short nap.

I wake up and glance at my watch. Faruq is reading the Qur'an. I wait until he pauses. "I need to leave."

"Stay until the next prayer."

"I have a test tomorrow and a paper due on Wednesday. I'd better get to work."

"What are you being tested on?"

"European capitalism."

"And your paper?"

"The effects of the African slave trade on early eighteenth-century presidential politics."

He frowns. "Why do you bother with these forbidden topics? If you continue to pursue useless knowledge, you will lose all blessing." He glares at me. "Everything you will ever need to know is contained within two sources, and two sources only. The Qur'an and the *Sunnah*."

He must be right—he knows everything about Islam—but I'm uncomfortable. I worked hard to earn my scholarship. And I enjoy my classes. I feel a weight in my chest, and the room suddenly feels too small. "I'll think about it."

"Think hard, Brother. Pray hard. Be very careful, lest you are led astray by the *Shaytan*."

He doesn't know what he's asking. I've worked too hard to throw it all away. I nod. "I'll see you later."

"Insha Allah. Assalaamu alaikum, my young brother."

"Walaikum assalaam." I rush to my car. I need to get started on that paper.

Ripples

∽

I dash across campus to my first class. I love being here. There's an excitement I can't find anywhere else.

When I'm at the university, I feel free. I have always loved learning, so I don't really mind the tests and papers. Between classes, I sit in the library and study, or, if I'm caught up with my work, I relax at the CFSU—Loyola's student union. There, I'm free to drink soda, indulge in junk food, or even play pool. All those things were forbidden by my father.

After Faruq's warning, I start noticing other things about college life. The guys who curse and joke. The girls who wear their clothes short and tight. I noticed the girls before, of course. Dad always told me it was sinful to look at them.

That's what Faruq says, too. But Faruq is nothing like Dad. He doesn't yell or abuse me. He cares about me for who I am.

I pay closer attention to the professors, too. My medieval history prof cites scholars who believe societies were tied down by their religious beliefs. Only through enlightenment, after breaking free of their religious bonds, were they able to achieve their full potential. I used to find his lectures interesting. Now I look for Satan in every word.

But, no matter what Faruq says, I can't give up on my studies. I avoid him all week, making my prayers either on campus or at Uncle Brad's house. I respect Faruq, but I can't obey him. Not on this point.

∽

On Friday, I pray at a mosque near the campus with about thirty other students. I don't know anybody. I spend most of my time in the library.

Dr. Fauzan gives a sermon about the importance of education. The first word revealed in the Qur'an was "Read." The Prophet, he says, told us to seek knowledge from birth to death. Dr. Fauzan talks about useless knowledge, but he means things like celebrity gossip. Our studies here at the university, he tells us, will prepare us to lead the Muslim community. Through knowledge, we will all be strong.

I walk away from the service wondering who is right. Dr. Fauzan or Faruq? Dr. Fauzan is highly educated and seems to be a good Muslim. Faruq has dedicated his entire life to imitating the Prophet. Who should I listen to?

I'm deep in thought, staring at the sidewalk, when I bump into someone going the other way. Books and papers scatter. "I'm sorry." I pick up the books and hand them to the girl standing in front of me. She's very pretty.

"Thanks." She smiles and offers her hand. "My name's Becky. What's yours?"

"I, um, I'm Isaiah." Faruq keeps telling me to take a Muslim name, but I haven't found one that suits me yet. "I, uh, I can't shake your hand. I'm a Muslim."

"I'm sorry, Isaiah. I didn't mean to offend you."

I study the cracks in the sidewalk. "It's, um, it's no problem. Don't worry about it. You didn't know."

"I should have known," she laughs. "Not many guys dress like that. What country are you from? Your English is very good."

"I, um, I'm American. I converted to Islam, not too long ago." Two weeks now.

"That sounds interesting. Why did you convert? Let's sit in the student center, and you can tell me about it."

"I, um, I'd better not. I have a class this afternoon."

"What time does it start?"

"At, um, in about an hour."

"You have time. Let's go." She grabs my hand. I jerk away.

"Oh," she giggles, "I forgot. Come on."

I shouldn't go. I need to be careful. Her clothes aren't tight—just jeans and a Chicago White Sox t-shirt—but, still, she's a girl.

Faruq says we need to tell others about Islam. She wants to know. She's a girl, and my father always told me to stay away from girls, but my father can go to Hell. I smile at the thought.

"What is it?" says Becky. "What's so funny?"

"Oh, uh, nothing. Are you coming?"

Ripples

Isaiah: Part Two

Ramadan starts on Tuesday. Uncle Brad fixes an early morning meal. Aunt Beth sits with us.

"Make sure you eat enough, Matt. If you feel sick, you can stop fasting."

Matt grins. "I'll be okay."

I wish my mom were here to fuss over me.

∼

Becky walks up to me in the CFSU. "Hey, Isaiah, how are you? I didn't see you around yesterday."

She was looking for me? "I'm okay."

"You don't look okay. What's wrong?"

I yawn. "Nothing. I'm tired. We woke up early this morning to start fasting."

"You did? How early? Why are you fasting?"

I tell her about Ramadan. She sounds interested. We're still talking when I realize I'm five minutes late for my economics class.

"I'll see you later," she calls as I rush off.

I'm looking forward to it.

∼

I'm nearly through my first day. Fasting isn't too hard.

But Kyle's eating pizza. "Hey, Isaiah, you want some?" he calls out, laughing. My stomach growls. I ignore him and head for my room to take a nap.

At sunset, Matt wakes me with the call to prayer. I stagger to the kitchen. The three of us break fast together as the sun falls into the west.

"Don't eat too fast," says Aunt Beth. "You'll get a stomachache." She acts like she's talking to both of us, but I know she means Matt.

"Don't eat too much," says Kyle. "Leave some for me."

Aunt Beth gives him a look. "There's plenty for everyone. Be nice. We need to respect their fast."

Kyle grins and winks at me. Nothing slows him down—not even a wheelchair.

～

Jesus fasted in the desert. I always wondered about his experience. My father said fasting was unnecessary for regular people. "We're saved by the grace of God through our Lord, Jesus Christ."

If he was in a good mood, I'd mention St. Paul, who said faith without works is dead. My father would reply that we do good works as an expression of our faith. If I pushed it, he'd glare at me. "We must have faith," he said. "Belief in our Savior is the foundation of our lives. 'For by grace are ye saved through faith; and that not of yourselves: it is the gift of God: Not of works, lest any man should boast.' Ephesians, chapter two, verses eight and nine. Our job is not to question, but simply to seek salvation through our Lord, Jesus Christ."

His words keep coming back to me. I put on my headphones and listen to the Qur'an, trying to drown out his voice.

～

On Friday, I go back to Faruq's masjid. We talk a little after the prayer.

"Are you still wasting your time on useless knowledge?" he asks.

"I can't quit school. Not yet. I have to finish the semester." And earn my degree.

Faruq has already warned me about girls. I see Becky two or three times a week, and we talk about our classes. Sometimes she asks me about Islam. She is a girl, but she's my friend. The only friend I have, besides Kyle. Jenny, too, but, these days, she's too busy playing house.

～

Ramadan is over. As I break my fast on the last day, I make a pledge to fast at least once a week. I want to be close to Allah, like Faruq.

Uncle Brad takes Matt and me to the Eid prayer on Thursday to celebrate the end of Ramadan. It's great. I'm a part of something here.

Ripples

My father always said Islam is from Satan, but how can billions of people be wrong?

Aunt Beth takes off from work so she can celebrate with us. We go to a restaurant called The Grand Caravan. I've never eaten Arabic food before. It's delicious.

∼

On Friday morning, I meet Becky at the CFSU.

"Hi, Isaiah. Did you have a nice Eid?"

"Real nice." After lunch, Uncle Brad and Aunt Beth took us shopping. Matt picked out video games. I have a new camera.

"Can you eat now? Let's go have lunch."

We sit together with our burgers and fries. She's my friend. There's nothing wrong with that.

She's majoring in European literature. "I don't know how I ended up at Loyola. A Lutheran from Minnesota," she laughs. "It is a good school, and I have a scholarship. And, if I hadn't come here, I wouldn't have met you." She smiles. I get a warm feeling.

At first, I was so nervous around Becky that I could barely speak. Now, I feel more comfortable around her than almost anyone else. I would like to hold her hand. Twice, I've had dreams about kissing her. That won't happen, because I'm a Muslim, but I guess it's okay to dream.

Finals are coming, and I need to stay on campus to study. I can't quit Loyola. I love learning. I'm getting straight A's. And I want to keep seeing Becky.

∼

On Wednesday, nearly a week after Eid, Becky comes running up, waving a paper. "Did you see this? Do you want to go with me?"

I scan the leaflet. There will be a lecture by a major Catholic scholar about the Counter Reformation. It sounds interesting, but I never knew a girl could get this excited over a history lecture.

"I can't wait." She's nearly breathless. "I've read some of his articles. I've studied the Reformation since I was a little girl. It's a fascinating event. Do you want to come with me? It's tomorrow night."

I can work my prayer times around it. We're not going to a rock concert or anything. It's just a lecture. And it will be a nice break from studying. "Okay, let's go."

~

On Thursday night, I wear a new robe, trim my beard, and splash on a little cologne. A Muslim should always smell good.

"Where are you going?" Uncle Brad asks.

"There's a history lecture on campus."

"Don't be too late."

Kyle grins and whispers, "You smell too good for a lecture."

"Be quiet."

She's waiting for me outside Campion Hall, the freshman dorm. As we walk, she discusses the Reformation and Counter Reformation. She's really studied. I like listening to her voice.

Halfway there, she shivers. It's May, but the night air is cool and she forgot her jacket. I take mine off and put it around her. My hand accidentally brushes her soft shoulder. I feel a chill.

We arrive at the lecture hall fifteen minutes early and talk quietly. Both our arms are on the arm rest. Our elbows touch. I should move away. I don't.

The auditorium darkens. The stage lights go up. She grasps my hand. I let her hold it.

I find the lecture interesting. Becky is mesmerized. She hangs on every word, softly whispering her own responses.

As we leave the hall, she recounts all of the speaker's main points and shares her own interpretation. We go to the CFSU for a snack before I walk her back to her dorm. She's still talking about the lecture. I can't concentrate. She's too close.

We reach her dorm. Suddenly, she stops talking, comes a little closer, and kisses me lightly on the lips.

I put my arms around her. We kiss longer, harder. I feel dizzy. I feel many things.

She pulls away and tries to talk. She clears her throat and tries again. "I'd better go. I have an early class tomorrow."

"You need your sleep," I whisper.

Ripples

"Goodnight." She squeezes my hand.
I watch as she walks away.
She turns. "You'll need your jacket." She reaches for it.
I stop her. "Let me." I caress her soft shoulders.
She kisses me again, and time stops.

∽

My heart is racing, and my hands shake as I drive back to the house. I keep replaying the scene, still feeling her kiss.
I have never kissed a girl before. Dad never let me get close enough. If I tried to talk with a girl at church, I'd get beaten when we came back home. "Stay away from the girls until you're ready to get married," he said.
One day, I felt brave enough to ask, "How will I know when I'm ready?"
"I'll let you know," he said.
I graduated from a Christian boys' school. Ruth wasn't allowed to have her friends over. Except for my sisters, girls were like alien creatures to me.
Until I met Becky. Now the world has opened up.

∽

The house is dark except for one light in the living room. Kyle whispers. "Hey, where have you been?" He turns on another light.
"I told you. I went to a lecture at the university."
He smirks. "You didn't get that grin from any lecture."
Kyle is only six months older than me, but he knows so much more. He had a steady girlfriend from the time he was fourteen. She died, and their baby, too, in the accident. Since then, he hasn't had anyone. "Most girls don't get too excited about a guy in a wheelchair," he often says.
I can't stop grinning.
"Come here, son. Confess your sins to Father Kyle."
I tell him all about Becky. Her spirit. Her softness. Her kisses.
"It's about time. I was getting worried about you, if you know what I mean."

For the next two hours, Kyle fills me in on the facts of life. Not the biology. I learned that in school. The feelings. The things my father refused to teach me.

It's nearly 2:00 AM when I wash up, pray, and go to bed.

I dream of Becky. I'm holding her, kissing her. I never knew I could feel this way.

Suddenly, I'm falling. She reaches for me. I look below me into the raging fire. I gasp and flail.

I call her name. I wake up, breathing hard and holding tight to the mattress.

There is no fire. It was just a nightmare.

The house is quiet and dark. No one heard me.

I take a cold shower before bowing down to Allah, asking Him to save me from the fire.

∼

Uncle Brad shakes my shoulder. "Isaiah, it's time for the morning prayer. Why are you out here?"

I fell asleep on my prayer rug. "I had a nightmare," I mumble, stumbling to the bathroom.

After breakfast, I feel better. It was just a dream. I shouldn't have kissed her, but that won't happen again. I get dressed and hurry to class.

We meet in the CFSU. She smiles. "Did you sleep well?"

I nod, too tired to comment.

"They show foreign films on campus every Friday night. Would you like to go with me?"

A movie. I shouldn't, but there was no fire. It was just a dream. "Sure. I like foreign films."

I go to the prayer near campus. The sermon is about politics. Half of the sermons here are political. I try to pay attention, but my thoughts keep drifting to Becky.

At home, I shower again and get dressed for the movie. I don't feel like wearing a robe. I pick up my red t-shirt and some jeans I forgot in the corner of my closet.

I'm walking out just as they're sitting down to eat. "Where are you going?" says Uncle Brad. "Come have dinner first."

Ripples

"I, uh, I'm going to an event on campus. A foreign film festival. I'll eat something there."

"You smell too good for a movie with subtitles," says Kyle.

Shut up. "I won't be late." I rush out the door before Uncle Brad can interrogate me.

She's waiting for me in front of her dorm. "Good, you're here. The movie starts in ten minutes. We'd better hurry."

I keep my arm away from hers during the film. It's a social commentary on the economic exploitation of the lower classes. Normally, I would enjoy a movie like this, but I'm distracted. She's too close.

Afterward, I take her to a pizza place. On the way there, she reaches for my hand. When I pull away, she looks at me strangely, but doesn't say anything.

She likes mushrooms. "But I can't stand green peppers on my pizza. My brother Denny loves them. Sometimes he puts some on my slice just to annoy me." She talks on and on. I enjoy the sound of her voice.

We walk back to her dorm. "I'd better be going. It's late. My uncle might worry."

"You can stay a little while, can't you? Come up to my room. You can look through my European history books."

"No, I'd better go."

"Just for a few minutes. If it gets too late, you can call your uncle."

A few minutes won't hurt.

We walk into the empty room. "Where is your roommate?"

"Caitlyn went to Indianapolis to see her boyfriend."

I browse her bookshelf. She has quite a collection on the sixteenth century. She has nice posters, too. No kittens or flowers. One is a map of Europe. Some are scenes from Shakespeare. The rest are literary quotes.

I'm scanning a book on Luther when she comes up and puts her arms around me. "I couldn't wait to be alone with you."

I push her away. "No. I shouldn't have kissed you. I'm a Muslim."

"Don't tell me Muslims never kiss. Where do baby Muslims come from?" She whispers in my ear.

"No, Becky, I can't. I need to leave."

"Not yet." She kisses me.

I'm not going anywhere.

79

∼

I wake up with the sun in my eyes. I missed my morning prayer, and last night's prayer, too. I quickly take a shower and pray. I'm about to leave when Becky wakes up.

"Where are you going?"

"I need to go home."

"Come back tonight."

"I shouldn't."

She walks over and kisses me. "I'll see you later."

∼

I carefully open the front door. They're sitting at the table, eating breakfast. Uncle Brad catches me sneaking in.

"Where were you last night?" Here it comes.

"I, uh, I spent the night at Faruq's place."

"I tried to call you."

"I had to turn my phone off during the prayer."

"I told you to let me know where you are."

"I know. I'm sorry. I'll be more careful." I avert his gaze as I rush to my room. I fall into my bed and close my eyes. What have I done?

I keep thinking about last night. It was fantastic. It was wrong.

Kyle comes in. "You weren't with Faruq last night."

"Not so loud. Close the door."

"Where were you?" He's grinning.

"I stayed at the masjid all night."

"Don't lie to me."

"I didn't mean for it to happen. I'm a Muslim. It was sinful. I won't do it again." I run my hands through my hair.

"Hey, slow down. Sinful? I don't know about that."

"You wouldn't know. You don't believe in God."

"I believe in, well, something. Anyway, you need to settle down. What happened is perfectly natural. I'm just surprised it took you this long."

"You don't understand. It was a sin. I'm going to Hell."

"Dude, I know that feeling, but you need to take it easy. Let's say it was a sin. Can't you just repent or something?"

Ripples

"I don't know. This is the biggest sin I've ever committed. I don't know what happened to me. I didn't want to go up to her room, and I didn't want to kiss her, but. . ."

"And you were sober, too, weren't you?"

"Of course. I never drink."

"Hey, I don't know. I mean, as long as you're breaking commandments."

"If my father found out, he would kill me."

"Your father doesn't have to know."

"You won't tell?"

"Me? I have enough secrets of my own. Nothing recent, of course." He pats his chair.

"What should I do?"

"If you like her, keep seeing her. Or you can break up with her. That's up to you. I don't know anything about repentance. You would have to ask someone religious about that."

I think I can figure this out. "Thanks. You've helped."

"Remember, you can always come to Father Kyle."

After he leaves, I consider my options. I have to break up with her. I'll do it tonight. She's expecting me. I'll tell her it was wrong, and we can't see each other again. I'll pray more. I'll fast every day. That should take care of it.

∼

I wear my robe and take my Qur'an with me. "I'm going to see Faruq," I tell Uncle Brad on the way out.

"Don't come back too late. No more overnighters."

"I'll be back soon." How long can it take to break up with someone?

I walk up to her dorm room and knock. I'll be firm. Keep it short and simple. *I'm sorry, Becky, we can't see each other anymore. I think you're nice, and I like being with you, but I'm a Muslim.*

She opens the door and kisses me. "You're finally here."

She pulls me into her room. Incense hangs in the air. Soft music plays in the background. She kisses me again.

I'll break up with her tomorrow.

～

We made it through finals. Becky's roommate left town this morning. Uncle Brad thinks I'm spending the weekend at the masjid. A special retreat. If he gets suspicious, Kyle will cover for me.

Becky has to leave for Minnesota on Monday, and we want to make the most of the time we have left. We won't see each other for ten weeks.

This is against everything I have ever been taught. But I never knew life could be this sweet.

～

She's been gone for a week when the dream returns. I'm holding and kissing her. Suddenly, everything else falls away, and I'm dangling above the fire. I wake up gasping for air.

Ripples

Isaiah: Part Three

I took a second job at a burger place. We text each other every chance we get. I call her almost every day. I'm going to visit her in three weeks. I can't wait.

∼

The nightmare keeps coming. Flames surround me, and I nearly fall in. Each time, I get up and read the Qur'an until the feeling passes.

I don't know which would be worse—falling into the fire or losing Becky.

∼

Everything is set. I took the week off from work. My car is ready for the trip. Becky and her parents are expecting me.

I wait until the night before I leave to tell Uncle Brad, mentioning it as Kyle and I help him clean up the kitchen.

"I'm going out of town next week."

He calmly wipes the counters. "Where are you going?"

"Up to Minnesota. Darul Islaam has a special summer conference for teens."

"That sounds good. Why didn't you tell me earlier?"

"I just found out about it today after the prayer. I think it will help me learn more about Islam."

"Do you have any literature on the conference? Where is it? What exactly will you do there?"

"The usual. Study the Qur'an. Hike in the woods. There's a lake so we can go swimming. I don't have any papers about it. They ran out."

"I wish you had more information. That sounds like a great opportunity for Matt."

Kyle speaks up. "Isaiah, didn't you say everyone has to be at least sixteen?"

"Yes, they do. It's for insurance purposes, I think." Thanks, Kyle.

My uncle sighs. "I wish you had some sort of document for me to look over. It does sound good, but don't you need permission to go on a trip like that?"

"Not anymore. I'm eighteen, remember?"

"That's right."

I think he actually did forget. Everyone thinks I'm still just a curious kid. "I'm really looking forward to this trip."

"I hope you grow stronger in your faith. And don't forget to call. I especially want to hear from you when you arrive to be sure you got there safely."

"Of course."

I did it—with help from Father Kyle.

⁓

I fall asleep easily, but the nightmare returns. The bright flames. The intense heat. The unbearable fear. One night, the fire might consume me. But it can't keep me away from Becky.

⁓

She lives in a small town twenty miles south of Minneapolis, nearly 400 miles from here. It will take me all day to drive there. I pray Fajr, eat a bagel, and head for the door.

"Have a safe trip," says Uncle Brad. "Remember to call me when you arrive."

Aunt Beth hands me a bag full of snacks. "I'm sure you'll want something to munch on along the way."

Matt sulks. "I wish I could go, too. I can't wait until I'm sixteen."

Kyle winks. "Have a good time."

I drive up past Milwaukee without any trouble. I'm on the highway to Madison. Traffic isn't too bad. I'm getting closer to her every minute. This is great.

A red sports car whizzes past me. I speed up. After a few minutes of pushing the pedal, I pass him and zip into the horizon. Victory! I switch into the right lane, cruising along in my black compact.

Ripples

I slip in a Qur'an CD and focus on the words as the miles slip away. I don't see the sports car until he slips by me on the left, honking, with middle finger raised.

He pulls in front of me and speeds away. I press the accelerator and come within twenty feet. But a semi is coming up fast in the left lane. I fall back. The sports car pulls ahead.

He's leading the pack. I pull out behind the semi, ready to usurp him. He's coming up fast on an aging minivan. He swerves into the left lane. Right into the path of the semi.

"Stop!" I yell, knowing he can't hear me. I slam on the brakes and veer sharply into the median. My car nearly flips over. I give it a sharp right to stabilize.

Brakes screech. The semi rolls over the red car. Metal crunches. Then silence.

I climb out of my car and gaze at the wreckage. The red car has been obliterated. The truck is overturned. I smell fuel.

Behind me, brakes squeal as other cars stop. Some crash. The sound echoes.

I'm taking it all in when I see the flames. I run, throwing myself into a ditch a second before the explosion. Screams shatter the air as metal flies.

A minute later, I stand and watch the fire. Shouts and moans emerge from the chaos. I should help, but I'm paralyzed. I stare into the fire.

Highway patrol cars, ambulances, and fire trucks converge on the area. When the fire is out, police and medics clean up the mess. It takes hours. The injured are whisked away, sirens blaring. Other ambulances silently carry the dead. I gaze at the charred wreckage and wait for someone to tell me what to do.

It's nearly dark by the time everything is cleared. An officer comes over. "You can move on now."

I put the car into gear, but I can't move. I see the flames.

The officer waves at me. I slowly pull back onto the highway.

I should turn around and go back to Chicago. What I'm doing is wrong. That could have been me. My body smashed. My ashes scattered on the road. Where would my soul be?

I'll take the next exit and head east. When I'm calm, I'll call Becky. I'll tell her about the accident. She'll be glad I didn't come.

I'm driving slowly in the right lane, muscles tense, when my cell rings. I don't answer.

I hear her voice. "Hi, Baby. Where are you? Is everything okay?"

I miss her. I answer. "I haven't made it to Madison yet. There was an accident and—."

"I just heard. I'm so glad you're safe. You must be tired."

"I can't come, Becky. You wouldn't believe it. The fire. I don't know how many people died. I'm going back to Chicago."

"You're okay, Baby. Don't worry. When you get here, I'll make you forget all about it."

The way she says it sends chills through me, calming the fire. Forget about the exit. I have to see Becky.

My phone rings again. I listen to the message. "Are you okay, Isaiah? Call us."

It's Uncle Brad. I turn off the phone and push the accelerator.

～

I pull up to her house a little after midnight. It's nice—a white two-story frame with green shutters, a double garage, a basketball hoop in the driveway, and flowers growing in all the right spots. It reminds me of the place I used to call home. I ring the bell.

A second later, she pulls me inside. "Isaiah, I was so worried about you." She holds me tight.

I nod, too tired to talk. She leads me to their leather couch and caresses me. "Poor baby. You must be exhausted."

"You have no idea."

She massages my shoulders. "You're so tense."

Her parents are asleep. She takes me upstairs to her room and helps me relax.

～

I struggle to open my eyes. It's nearly noon. I wonder where Becky is.

Ripples

I'm drifting back to sleep when she comes in and kisses me. "Wake up, sleepyhead. My parents can't wait to meet you."

I panic. "Do they know I'm in here?"

"They don't mind."

Interesting parents. "Point me to the bathroom. I'd better get cleaned up first."

I emerge from the shower feeling revived and open the bathroom door. Her father is waiting in the hall. "There you are. We were wondering when you would wake up."

I had hoped to be fully dressed when we met. I grip the towel around my waist and offer my right hand. "Hello, Mr. Wagner. It's nice to meet you."

He takes my hand and grabs me in a hug. I nearly lose the towel. "We've heard a lot of good things about you, Isaiah."

Mrs. Wagner is right behind him. "Isaiah! You're more handsome than your picture. Becky tells us you're smart, too."

I like this family.

~

Becky's parents are the complete opposite of my parents. No rules. No expectations. They say they trust their kids to make the right decisions. I love it here.

We're busy all week. On Monday and Tuesday, we go swimming and boating with Becky's friends. All day Wednesday, we hike. On Thursday, we drive into Minneapolis. On Friday, we swim again.

Becky has two younger brothers. Charlie, who's fourteen, reads. In his room, in the car, every chance he gets. I talk to him about my favorite books. We both like sci-fi. Denny, who's twelve, plays ice hockey. He shows off his trophies—a full case of them. They're both fun to be with. I miss Benjamin.

~

On Saturday, I have to say goodbye.

"I wish you didn't have to go." Becky pulls me close.

"Me, too. But you'll be back in Chicago soon. I'll count the days."

"I'll count the hours."

I don't leave until after lunch. The drive is easy, but when I pass the site of the accident, something comes over me. I pull over onto the shoulder and stare. My chest feels tight.

It's all cleaned up. There are memorials for the four who died here—the semi driver, the guy in the red sports car, and two people who were hit by flying metal. I heard about it on the news.

It could have been me. If I had been driving a little faster. If I hadn't swerved off the road. If I hadn't jumped into the ditch. Then what? Heaven or Hell? I know that answer.

My phone rings. It's her. "Hi, Baby. Are you almost home? I miss you."

"I miss you, too." But I shouldn't be doing this.

∼

I get back to Chicago in the early morning and tiptoe in. I have a few hours to come up with some good excuses.

I haven't prayed since I left. I wash up and bow down. I could have died.

∼

Matt wakes me for the morning prayer. "When did you get here? Why didn't you call?"

I shake my head and stumble to the bathroom. I'm almost too tired to stand up for prayer.

When we're finished, Uncle Brad confronts me. "Where were you? We were worried. You didn't call, and you wouldn't answer your cell."

"Sorry. There was an accident, and it was late when I got there. I forgot." Not really. I turned off my cell while I was with Becky because I didn't want my uncle bothering me.

"I heard about that accident. I could barely sleep, wondering if you were hurt."

"I'm sorry, okay?" Can I go back to bed now?

"I called Darul Islaam. No one knew anything about a retreat. Where were you, Isaiah?"

Ripples

"That doesn't mean anything. The people who knew about it went to Minnesota."

He glares at me. "Stop lying. Where were you?"

I'm too tired to come up with a story. I wish Kyle were here. "I went to see a friend."

"What's his name?"

I look down. "Becky."

My uncle rubs his neck and shakes his head. "Who have you been spending the night with? Faruq or Becky?" he says sharply.

"Who do you think?"

"This is what I was trying to tell you, Isaiah. You're not ready to be a Muslim."

"How do you know what I'm ready for?" I shout.

"Spending the night with a girl? That's not Islam. Do you pray? Do you think about Allah? Or do you only want to be a Muslim when it's convenient?"

"I want to be a Muslim. And I want to be with Becky."

"Then you will have to marry her. Are you ready for that?"

"I can't get married. I barely have enough money to buy my books and keep my car running."

"That is what growing up is all about. You have to make the tough choices and take responsibility for your actions. You've painted yourself into a corner. What are you going to do about it?"

"I don't know. I can't think. Stop badgering me."

"Do you want to be a Muslim? Do you intend to marry this girl? How will you continue your education? How will you support a family? Forget about sneaking around. It's time you started acting like a man."

"What do you want me to do?" I'm crying, which is the last thing I want to do.

"Stop running around. Stay home today, and do some hard thinking about your future."

"I have to go to work."

"Then you will stay home except for work. And, if you are not here when you're supposed to be, I will come and drag you home. Let's get some breakfast, and you can rest. You're probably tired after your trip."

I can barely keep my eyes open. "Yeah. I think I'll skip breakfast."

I struggle back to my room. Matt stares at me. He left right before my confession, but he knows something's up. I don't care. I close my eyes and dream of Becky.

～

I try to get a private moment with Kyle, but, every time Uncle Brad sees us talking, he gives us both something to do. Finally, after lunch, I sneak into Kyle's room.

"You can't stay here," he says, taking off his headphones.

"You're against me now, too?"

"I got hell for covering for you. Why did you go and confess?"

"He had me cornered, and I was tired. I didn't know what else to say."

"If you do the crime, you have to learn how to cover your tracks. Now we're both paying."

"Isaiah." Uncle Brad knocks. "Come on out. I need your help in the garage."

"I told you," says Kyle, putting on his headphones.

"You, too, Kyle. Your mother wants you in the garden."

～

All day, my uncle gives me orders. After dinner, he tells me to stay and help him clean the kitchen.

"Have you decided what to do?" he asks, wiping the kitchen table.

I concentrate on loading the dishwasher.

He grabs my arm. "Isaiah, I asked you a question."

I jerk away. "I don't know!" I shout, turning back to the sink.

"I know this is hard." He starts talking in the same quiet voice my father uses when he's angry.

My shoulders tense. If he lays one hand on me. . .

"You've had a rough life," he continues, "Your father is strict, and he didn't allow you many opportunities to experience life. So, you meet a girl, and you kiss her. Your emotions take over, clouding your judgment. I understand." He puts his hand on my shoulder.

Ripples

I flinch. "It's not just that. Becky isn't just a girl."
"Do you love her?"
"I don't know."
"What do you think you should do?"
"I want to be a Muslim. I want to be with Becky, but I don't want to marry her." Not yet, anyway. "I want to go to school. That's it."
"That sounds like fun, but it won't work. Use your mind, Isaiah."
I shouldn't have told him. "Forget you!" I walk away.
"Come back here, and finish your job," he says firmly.
I sulk. We finish cleaning in silence.

∼

For the last five days, I haven't done anything except go to work and do chores around the house. Becky just called. I loved talking with her, but, when Uncle Brad caught me, he grabbed the phone.
"That's mine!" I yelled.
"I'll take good care of it for you."

∼

On Friday, I tell Uncle Brad I want to go to Darul Islaam.
"Don't stay late. I expect you home for dinner."
I wince as he uses that same quiet voice. "I'll be here."
Fifteen minutes before the prayer starts, I walk in, sit cross-legged on the floor, and remember Allah. Faruq is in the front row, as usual. He turns back once and stares at me. I look away.
The sermon is about hellfire. My father's favorite topic. My stomach knots when I think of him, but I listen anyway. I don't want to get burned.
After the prayer, I stay where I am, remembering Allah, until I hear Faruq. "Assalaamu alaikum." He sits next to me.
"Walaikum assalaam." I avoid his gaze.
"Where have you been?"
I stare at the shaggy green carpet and pick at the fibers. He waits. "I can't leave my school. I want to learn and make something of myself. I want people to finally respect me."

"If you have Allah, you don't need the respect of people."
"I know."
"Why did you come back?"
I keep picking at the carpet. I can't answer.
"What's wrong, Isaiah? What did you do?"
"I committed a major sin." Half of the sermon was about the major sins that lead us into the fire.

He studies me. "Allah said, 'Do not come near fornication.' Do you understand what that means?"

"I understand. It's too late for that."

He puts his hand on my shoulder. "I need to work at the shop this afternoon. Come to my place at five. We must talk."

"I can't. Uncle Brad expects me to be home for dinner."

"Do you serve your uncle, or do you serve Allah? I will see you at five." He walks away.

Do I listen to Faruq or to Uncle Brad? I really need another complication in my life.

On my way back to the house, I remember that verse in the Book of Colossians about evil concupiscence. Sexual desire. My father lectured me about it nearly every day. He made me memorize another verse, too. "Flee fornication. Every sin that a man doeth is without the body; but he that commiteth fornication sinneth against his own body." First Corinthians, chapter six, verse eighteen. He wasn't that strict with Jacob or even Benjamin. Maybe he saw the evil inside of me.

~

Uncle Brad isn't home from work yet. He's busy with that mass transit project and may not get back until seven or eight. Why didn't I stay at the masjid? I should go back. Faruq is expecting me.

My stomach growls. I skipped lunch. I walk into the kitchen and heat up a bowl of leftover beef stew. I'll eat and go back to the masjid.

I wash my dishes and grab my keys. I'm nearly out of the driveway when Uncle Brad pulls up.

He blocks me. "Where do you think you're going?"

"I need to go to the masjid to see Faruq."

"Don't start with me. You're not going anywhere!" he shouts.

Ripples

"Faruq is waiting for me."

"I'm tired of your lies. Get back in the house."

I am sick and tired of being treated like a child. I need to get out of here.

Jamilah Kolocotronis

Isaiah: Part Four

Becky is coming back to Chicago next week. I can't wait to see her again, but what will I say? We have to end this relationship or we have to get married.

On Friday, I go back to Darul Islaam. Faruq glances at me from the front row. After the prayer, he walks over, frowning.

"Why didn't you come?"

"Uncle Brad wouldn't let me."

"You have sinned against your soul. What would happen if you were to die today? You must repent and give up your evil ways."

"I know." I'm trying. Doesn't anybody see that?

"Come tonight. If you don't, you will be a hypocrite, and I will have nothing more to do with you."

I need to convince Uncle Brad.

∼

As it turns out, I didn't have to worry. Uncle Brad and Aunt Beth are going to see a play tonight. They're running late, and my uncle doesn't have time to give last minute instructions. I'm free.

Faruq is waiting for me, his apartment door open.

"Come in," he says. "Close the door. Sit down."

I sit and wait.

"What you did was very serious—one of the worst sins against Allah. There is only one way to be absolved. Allah commanded the punishment of one hundred lashes."

"Are you crazy?" I yell. "I didn't come here to be beaten. I've had enough beatings, and there is no way you or anyone else will ever beat me again. Is that why you told me to come here?"

"What will you say when you stand in front of Allah? I refuse Your punishment?"

"I thought you could help me. Forget you!" I slam the door on my way out.

∼

Ripples

Becky is coming back tonight. I can't eat, and I can barely sit still. I can't wait to see her. I pace. Finally, the doorbell rings.

"Invite her in," says Uncle Brad. "But remember who you are."

I rush to the door. She falls into my arms. It is so good to hold her again.

"I missed you, Baby." She kisses me. "I got your message but I still don't understand what happened to your phone."

"Isaiah." Uncle Brad comes up behind me. "Won't you introduce us?"

I quickly pull away. "Come in and meet my family."

She reaches for my hand. I jerk away. "Do you want me to carry anything?"

"You can carry me. I'm exhausted." She leans on me. Uncle Brad frowns. I pull away.

"I'm glad you had a safe trip," my uncle says.

Aunt Beth hugs her. "It's so nice to meet you. You're just in time for dinner. Let's eat."

It takes a few minutes to introduce everyone and get Becky settled with a cola in her hand. We sit around the kitchen table, eating meatloaf, while Aunt Beth makes small talk—asking about Minnesota and Becky's family. After dessert, she clears the table and disappears. She silently signals Kyle and Matt to disappear with her. Kyle balks, but she gives him a look. He reluctantly wheels away.

Uncle Brad clears his throat. "Becky, I know you and Isaiah have been intimate. Are you aware that this type of relationship is not allowed in Islam?"

"Isaiah hasn't really said anything about it."

Yes, I did. Kind of. At first.

Uncle Brad scowls. "He should have. You two cannot go on this way. I see only two options. Either you stop seeing one another, or you get married."

"Married?" Becky shrieks. She starts to laugh.

I don't know what's so funny.

She laughs so hard that her face turns red. She looks at me. "Where's your sense of humor?" Her laughter dies down. "Are you serious? I'm not ready to get married yet. Are you, Isaiah?"

I might be. "I don't know."

"You must be kidding. We're too young to get married. We still have three years of school left."

"Would you rather break up with me?"

"Why can't things just stay the way they are?"

"It is not permitted in Islam, and I won't allow it," my uncle says firmly.

"Oh," says Becky. "You are serious."

"What should we do about it?" I ask.

"I don't know. I just drove seven hours, and you hit me with this as soon as I get into town. What do you want me to say?"

"I don't know."

"My wife and I will help you move back into your dorm room," says Uncle Brad. "We'd like to get to know you better."

"What about Isaiah?"

"He'll stay here. You two need to talk, but you'd better get some rest first."

Some reunion.

∽

All day, I lie around the house, depressed. I can't see her. I can't talk to her. I can't touch her.

I need her. I have to marry her, but I don't know how we'll manage. I'll have to work more hours. She'll have to work, too. I wonder what her parents will say. They didn't mind me staying in her bedroom. They probably won't care.

The doorbell rings at six. It's her.

I run to the door. Uncle Brad stops me. "I'll get it." He smiles. "Come in, Becky."

Aunt Beth walks out from the kitchen. "Good, you're here."

My aunt made lasagna. Usually, I like her cooking, but my appetite's gone. I watch Becky. She keeps glancing at me.

When we're finished, Uncle Brad says, "Kyle, Matt, go to your rooms." He turns to Becky and me. "You two need to make a decision. What will it be?"

"I want to marry you," I blurt. "Will you marry me, Becky?"

Ripples

"I thought you didn't know what you wanted," she retorts.

"I didn't, but I can't lose you."

"What about my education? How can we afford to live?"

"We'll both stay in school. I'll work harder. We can do it."

"I don't know." She turns to Aunt Beth. "What do you think?"

"It's your life, Becky. Are you willing to spend it with Isaiah?"

She stares at me as if she's seeing me for the first time. I wait. One minute. Two. What's wrong? This isn't rocket science.

"Do you love me?" she says softly.

"Of course I do. I'd do anything for you."

She smiles a little. "I love you, too."

I guess we're getting married.

Jamilah Kolocotronis

Kyle: Part One

I knew Isaiah couldn't keep it up. He's not as good at lying as he thinks he is, but he still didn't have to go and confess.

So, he's marrying her. It must be nice to have someone. My someone is just a picture on my desk and a lot of great memories.

～

My summer hasn't been quite as exciting as Isaiah's. Every day for weeks, I gazed at my car sitting in the driveway. The state made me take a class on hand controls, and I needed insurance. It was more than a month before I could drive her. Nothing comes easy for me these days.

I love climbing into my car, pulling my chair in after me. She's beautiful—bright red exterior with a smooth black interior. Low to the ground and handles like a dream. I pop in some heavy metal and cruise down the expressway, weaving through traffic. When I drive, I'm free.

Until I get to the office. I have air conditioning, but it usually doesn't work. I've sweat all through the summer, wishing I could go home and strip to my boxers.

While I toiled, my volunteers went on vacation. I had to stuff the envelopes. Yeah, it's been a great summer.

～

Before starting my work for the day, I stare at my Amy, caressing her image and missing her.

"Excuse me, are you Mr. Adams?"

She startles me. I put down the picture and look up. She's beautiful. Long brown hair and dark round eyes.

"That depends. Which Mr. Adams do you want?"

"I'm here to volunteer. Does that help?"

"You've come to the right place. I'm Kyle Adams. You can call me Kyle."

"I'm Faiqa Hammadi. What do you want me to do?"

"That's an unusual name. Pretty, but unusual."

Ripples

"I'm a Muslim. My father is from Egypt."

"You're a Muslim? Why don't you wear one of those headscarves?"

"I don't feel like it, okay? Do you have work for me or not?"

"How do you feel about stuffing envelopes?"

"Whatever you need. I'm here to help."

"So you're not one of those high school kids trying to pad your college application?"

"First of all, I'm not a kid—I'm in my second year of pre-med at Northwestern."

"Whatever." I point to the stack of boxes against the wall. "There are the envelopes, and there are the letters. Have fun."

She sits at the table and gets to work. But not before giving me a dirty look.

A few other volunteers trickle in. They are high school kids. One of the guys leans back in his chair and stuffs one envelope every fifteen or twenty minutes. One of the girls goes on and on about some soap opera. Or maybe she's talking about her history class. It's all the same when you're in high school.

While they work, I make and return phone calls, lining up more volunteers. Then I turn to my computer and work on a drug-awareness program for kids. I know, these programs are a dime a dozen, but many don't work. I've been there. I know the secret ingredient. When I finish writing my proposal, I'll find a grant to fund it. They'll have to take me seriously.

Faiqa stays for two hours. Before leaving, she walks over to my desk and looks at Amy's picture. "She's pretty. Is she your wife?"

"No. Almost my wife. She's dead."

"I'm sorry." She pauses, the same awkward silence I've heard so many times. "I'll be back next week. I hope you have more work for me."

"You can count on it."

I glance over at her boxes. She did more in two hours than the high schoolers will accomplish all day.

Kyle: Part Two

Faiqa comes again on Tuesday. I have more envelopes than usual. My high school students didn't show yesterday, and we have a major fundraising dinner coming up.

"How did you get so far behind?" she says, stuffing another envelope.

"I told you. Everyone skipped out on me."

"Why didn't you do it yourself?"

"I can't. I'm the coordinator."

"So you just sit there all day and tell other people what to do?"

"Basically. Are you jealous?"

She laughs. Soft and light. "It does sound like a cushy job."

"Yeah. They even give me my own parking space. It's called handicapped parking."

She snaps her fingers. "You're right. Forget medical school. I need to get a job like this."

She's mocking me. I sigh and turn back to my computer.

After a few minutes, she says, "Maybe not. It takes a special kind of person to work at Hope Center."

I'll take that as an apology. I nod and keep on typing.

Before leaving, she picks up Amy's picture. "How did she die?"

"A car accident. The same one that put me in this chair. Our son died, too."

"That's awful. How old was he?"

"He was seven months away from being born." I swallow hard, yearning for him.

"What was her name?"

"Amy."

"You must miss her."

"Every day."

She bites her lip. "Well, I need to go. I'll be back next Tuesday. Be sure to save some work for me."

"Count on it."

When she's gone, I pick up Amy's picture and think about what should have been.

Ripples

Jennifer: Part One

Ahmed has grown so much over the summer. He took his first step today. I was playing with him on the living room floor when he moved away from the couch and came to me. I called Nuruddin with the news, but he didn't sound excited. He just started a new job, and he's been very tense.

Nuruddin has no problem being away from Ahmed all day, but I don't know how I'll leave my baby when classes start next month. For nearly a year, he's been my entire life. If it weren't for Mom's nagging, I would gladly stay home with him longer.

∼

I'm building block towers with Ahmed when there's a knock. I peer through the peephole. "Michael, you're here!" I scream, flinging the door open.

He hugs me tightly. I haven't seen my oldest brother since last July.

"Look at that uniform. You're so handsome. Did you just get into town?"

"A couple of hours ago. I went to see Mom first."

"How long can you stay?"

"Two weeks. Then it's back to Brownsville for two weeks before they ship me overseas."

"Where?"

"Somewhere in the Middle East. I can't say where. How's my little nephew?" He walks over to Ahmed and sits on the floor. "Can I help you with those blocks? I know a lot about building things."

Ahmed cries and reaches for me. I scoop him up. "He doesn't like strangers. Give him time."

"I'm not a stranger. I'm your uncle. You don't have to be afraid of me."

Ahmed buries his head in my neck.

"Anyway," says Michael, "He's great. You look good, too. Marriage agrees with you."

"What about you? Do you have anyone in mind?"

"Not yet. I can't build a relationship when I'm preparing to leave the country. It will have to wait until I get back."

"Do you want to go overseas?"

He shrugs. "I don't have a choice. In the military, they don't ask for your opinion."

"You've always been the obedient one. This time I wish you would stand up for yourself."

"I'm learning Arabic. I'll be able to hear the call to prayer. It won't be all bad." He glances at his watch. "I need to get going. I haven't seen Dad or Jeremy yet. Mom wants everyone to come to her house tonight for dinner. You and Nuruddin will be there, won't you?"

"I wouldn't miss it. It's so great to see you." I hug him again.

"I'll see you tonight. And you, too, little guy. We're going to be good buddies." He gives me another hug and kisses Ahmed's soft cheek.

I stand in the doorway and watch as he walks away, looking handsome in his uniform. I don't want him to go. He might not come back.

Ripples

Jennifer: Part Two

Dad has invited everyone to his house for a late summer barbecue. Michael leaves on Tuesday.

Uncle Brad and Aunt Beth have a girl with them. She's cute. Isaiah keeps looking at her.

"Hi, Isaiah. Is this your girlfriend?" I tease.

He blushes. Isaiah has a girlfriend?

"This is Becky, Isaiah's fiancée," says Aunt Beth.

"Hi, Becky. It's nice to meet you. I'm Jennifer." I wonder when all this happened.

"Hey, Jen," says Kyle. "Did you cook anything for this shindig?"

"I made the brownies."

"Thanks for the warning."

"You're not going to eat anything, are you? You're carrying enough weight as it is."

"It's all muscle. Oh, and congratulations on the new baby. When is it due?"

"I'm not pregnant."

"Guess you'd better stay away from the brownies then."

He rolls away. I'll get him next time.

∼

After lunch, my dad and the other "old guys," as he calls them, get out on the soccer field. Nuruddin and I sit with my brothers, eating watermelon.

"Are you ready, Michael?" Jeremy asks.

"I have my training. I think I'll be adequately prepared."

"Aren't you nervous?" I ask.

"I'm excited. This is a new opportunity for me, Jenny. I've always dreamed of traveling."

"But why do you want to go to the Middle East?" Nuruddin asks.

"Why not? I'll be in the land of my Muslim brothers and sisters. Sometimes the Army allows service members to go for Hajj. Can you imagine?"

My husband persists. "Going for Hajj is one thing, but you'll be greeting your Muslim brothers and sisters with a gun in your hand."

"I'm a soldier. We carry guns."

"Go somewhere else then. Leave the Muslim lands alone. Hasn't the Army caused enough trouble in the world?"

"I don't have a choice. I must go where the Army sends me."

"You have a choice. You could refuse to fight against your fellow Muslims."

Michael doesn't like to talk politics, but he's polite. "How do you know I'll be fighting them? Hopefully, I can help them. I'm an engineer. I don't destroy. I build."

"If they order you to destroy, you will destroy."

"If they order me to destroy, I will refuse."

"You just said you don't have a choice."

Michael throws his hands in the air. "Help me out, Jeremy. You'll be going into the service soon."

"No, I won't."

"You don't have a choice. You'll be drafted."

"I never registered for the draft."

"You didn't? What are you thinking? You could go to prison for that."

"Maybe. I only know that I could never fight in an unjust war."

"Who's to judge whether a war is just?"

"Think about it, Michael," says Nuruddin. "You will be going into someone else's country, walking into their homes, and threatening them with your weapons. Do you think they will approve of your war?"

"First, I won't go into anyone's home. I'll build bridges. And most people are glad to see American soldiers. We bring relief to the oppressed."

"Is that what you believe? Don't you listen to the news? Soldiers don't bring relief. They kill."

"There have been cases of misconduct." Michael keeps his cool, but I can tell he's tense by the way he grips his fork. "Those were unfortunate. The majority of soldiers are simply doing their duty, and their duty is to help."

"Their duty is to kill," Nuruddin says forcefully. "Have they told you what country you're being sent to? What if it's Pakistan? What if you meet my cousin in the street? Will you shoot him if he opposes you?"

"Don't make it personal."

"It is personal. When you're down there in Brownsville, you're shooting paper targets, but when you go overseas, it will be the real thing."

"I keep telling you, I'm not going there to shoot anyone." Michael stands up and waves a watermelon rind in my husband's face.

"It doesn't matter why you're going. It's an unjust war. How can you give your support to such a cause? Muslims must fight only in the cause of Allah." Nuruddin stands, too.

Michael's face is red. I touch my brother's arm. "I don't like war either, and I hate to think about you heading into danger. Are you sure it's worth it?"

"What do you want me to do, Jenny? I didn't ask to go. I must follow orders."

"Think about it, Michael," says Jeremy. "See if you can find a way."

"Do you want me to break the law, like you?"

"I want you to follow your conscience and do what's right."

"Doing what's right means fulfilling my responsibilities."

"I agree," says Jeremy, "But where are your responsibilities? With the military, or with the Muslim *ummah*? Think about it."

Michael is about to answer when Dad makes the call to prayer. They all line up—Nuruddin, Michael, and Jeremy standing shoulder to shoulder. I watch as they bow down together. After the prayer, they go out on the soccer field. You would never know they'd been arguing.

I don't know if I'll ever become a Muslim, but I like the way the prayer brings people together. I don't want to hear my favorite men fighting.

105

Jagged Edges

Love seems the swiftest, but it is the slowest of all growths. No man or woman really knows what perfect love is until they have been married a quarter of a century.

—Mark Twain

Isaiah: Part One

I'm relieved when classes start again on Monday. I can see Becky and get away from Uncle Brad.

She isn't in the CFSU. Maybe she has class. Or is she waiting for me in the library?

Our table is in a far corner, away from everyone. She's here, reading. I sneak up, kissing her on the cheek.

"You're here!" She's in my arms again. We kiss, long and hard.

There's a tap on my shoulder. I meet the disapproving glare of a librarian. "You need to do that somewhere else," she whispers.

We leave the library, our arms entwined, and go to her dorm room. Forget about classes.

~

I kiss her one last time. "I need to get back. I don't want my uncle to get suspicious."

"I wish you could stay, Baby."

"In five days, we'll be married, and I will never leave you."

She smiles and sighs. "I can't wait. Our lives will be perfect."

~

The wedding is set for Saturday, during Labor Day weekend. It will be very small—just my aunts, uncles, and cousins. And Becky's parents, of course.

Uncle Brad says we must get married Islamically, so, last weekend, he took us to his masjid to talk with the imam. Everything was going well until the imam asked us why we wanted to get married. Becky opened her mouth. "Because we've been sleeping together, and Isaiah's uncle says Muslims can't do that."

Uncle Brad looked away, rubbing his neck. The imam politely stated he couldn't help us. I need to teach Becky to keep her mouth shut.

We went to two more imams. Both turned us away. I asked Faruq. He also refused. Finally, after asking around campus, I found a guy named Uthman who agreed to do it.

Uncle Brad took time off from work today so he could escort us to the courthouse for our marriage license. As we walk back to the car, Becky holds my hand.

Uncle Brad clears his throat. "Not yet."

Will he ever leave us alone? "We're married now."

"Not Islamically."

"You and Aunt Beth never had an Islamic ceremony."

"From what I've been told, it's not necessary because we married long before my conversion. And don't change the subject, Isaiah. This is about Becky and you."

It sounds like a double standard to me.

~

Her parents just called. They're on the expressway. Becky stands at the window, talking to herself.

"Why are you so nervous?" I massage her shoulders.

"I don't know how it will go tonight."

"They like me. What's the problem?"

"They like you as my boyfriend, but Dad isn't happy about us getting married. He says I shouldn't rush into things."

"You love me, don't you?"

"Yes." She kisses me.

I listen for the sound of footsteps. No one's coming, but I pull away. "Not here. It's not safe."

"Are you always going to be so uptight?"

"Wait until tomorrow night." I glance through the open curtain. "They're here."

Becky runs out to hug them. I watch. Her family is very demonstrative. I hope they don't expect me to hug them, too.

"Tell them to come in," Uncle Brad calls from the kitchen.

I walk out. Mr. Wagner hugs me. "How are you, Isaiah?"

You're squeezing me. "I'm okay. Did you have a good trip?"

"It was long," says Mrs. Wagner. "This is further than I expected. Becky, you and Isaiah need to think about moving up to Minnesota."

Ripples

Are you kidding? "We'll think about it," I say.

Aunt Beth comes out to greet them. "Hello. It's so nice to meet you. You have a lovely daughter."

"I know," says Mr. Wagner. "Becky is the light of our life. And Isaiah is a nice young man. I understand he's your nephew?"

"Yes, my husband's brother's son."

"His parents live in Arkansas? When will they arrive? I'm looking forward to meeting them."

My aunt doesn't miss a beat. "Unfortunately, they won't be able to make it. Please come inside and make yourselves comfortable." I didn't know she could be so smooth.

∽

Uncle Brad takes us all to dinner at Tandoori's. Uncle Joshua and Aunt Aisha join us.

"I don't know what to order," says Mr. Wagner. "I can't eat anything spicy."

"You'll like the tandoori chicken," says Uncle Joshua. "I'll ask them to use mild seasonings."

"I'm feeling adventurous," says Mrs. Wagner. "This dish looks good, but I can't pronounce it."

"That's biriyani. I highly recommend it."

When the waiter comes, Uncle Joshua gives him the entire order in Urdu. My in-laws look impressed.

"How did you learn to speak their language?" Mrs. Wagner asks.

Over dinner, Uncle Joshua tells them about his adventures in Pakistan. Everything is going well. I knew there was no reason to be nervous.

I'm finishing my kebabs when Mr. Wagner taps his spoon against his water glass. "I have a few things I need to say. First, thank you for the dinner. It was delicious. Now, I think we'd better get down to business.

"This marriage is very sudden, and I think you're both too young to know what you're getting into. I don't share your uncles' moral views, and I don't see that as solid grounds for entering a marriage. I have never denied Becky anything she wanted, but maybe it's time for me to put my foot down."

111

Becky grabs his arm. "No, Dad, you can't." She stares at him, a tear slowly running down her cheek.

He pats her hand and wipes away the tear. He sighs. "I do like you, Isaiah. I know this is what Becky wants."

"Please, Daddy. I'll never ask for anything else. Just don't stand in our way."

He puts his arm around Becky's shoulders and tries to smile. "If that's what makes you happy, sweetie. I hope you two have a happy and successful life together."

"We will, Daddy. You'll see. Thank you." She kisses him on the cheek.

Becky is smooth. I wish I could control my father that easily. I think it's different for a girl.

After dessert, Mr. Wagner says, "This is a cause for celebration. I know Muslims don't drink, but would you mind if my wife and I shared a bottle of wine with your wife, Brad?"

"I'm a recovering alcoholic," says Uncle Brad. "And they don't serve alcohol here."

"I don't drink either," says Aunt Beth.

"Okay." He smirks. "Becky, you're marrying into a family of fanatics. Are you aware of that?"

She laughs. "Stop being silly, Dad."

I don't think he was joking.

∼

I can't sleep. Should I be doing this? I must love Becky because I can't stand to be away from her, but am I ready to marry her?

I wish Mom were here. She doesn't even know. Imagine what my father would do if he knew. My uncles agreed not to tell him. They've both seen his temper.

I'm marrying the first girl I ever really talked to. Is she the right one for me? When I'm with her, I feel great. But this is forever.

I love being with Becky. I can't wait to get away from Uncle Brad and live on my own. I need to stop worrying. This is my chance to show everyone who I am and what I can do.

Ripples

～

The ceremony will be here at Uncle Brad's house. I can't wait.

At one, everything is ready. I'm dressed. Aunt Beth has finished decorating the living room with white balloons and streamers. The cake sits in the middle of a folding table, surrounded by plates and napkins. Now all we need are the guests and the bride.

Uthman shows up thirty minutes before the ceremony. He asks me to sit with him on the couch.

"Isaiah, are you prepared to take on the responsibilities of marriage?"

"I can handle it." How hard can it be?

He nods. "It won't be all hearts and flowers, you know."

Uncle Brad already gave me this lecture. "I know. There will be bills and things. Don't worry. I can do it."

"Good." He stands. "Marriage takes work. Don't think you can slide by."

What did he mean by that? "Of course. I know that."

Suddenly, I can't sit still.

"Stop pacing, man," says Kyle. "You look like you're waiting for the executioner."

"Are you kidding? I can't wait to be married to her."

"Yeah, I can tell."

When Uncle Joshua walks in with his family, he takes me aside.

"This isn't the best way to start a marriage. Are you sure you're ready to be a husband?"

"Of course."

"I know what's going on, Isaiah. This is one way to solve the problem, though it's not the best way. Do you know what the Islamic teachings are?"

"A hundred lashes."

"And separation from one another. If it were up to me, I would have sent you someplace—even down to Arkansas to stay with your parents—before pushing you into a marriage, but most Muslims in this country encourage their children to marry quickly in these circumstances. I hope this marriage lasts. Be kind to her. On the Day of

Judgment, Allah will ask you how you treated your wife. Remember that."

As if I didn't have enough to worry about. I don't need another way to get into Hell.

~

Becky and her family show up a few minutes before two. She's wearing a simple white dress. I'm wearing a new robe. Her father wears a frown.

"We're ready to begin," says Uthman.

Becky's father accompanies her to the spot where Uthman and I wait. He's scowling.

The service is short and simple. Uthman asks Becky if she wants to marry me, and asks me if I want to marry her. I give her the dowry—some books she's wanted, along with a cheap wedding ring. We sign the contract. Becky insists I promise to visit her family regularly. When we put down the pens, Uthman says we're married. That's it.

There are hugs and kisses. They finally let me touch her again. Aunt Beth serves the refreshments. We eat and talk a little before saying our goodbyes.

Mr. and Mrs. Wagner—they want me to call them Artie and Eileen—have given us the weekend in a fancy hotel. They also bought most of the furniture in our new apartment. Uncle Brad and Uncle Joshua took care of the rest—appliances, towels, all that—and they're paying the rent for the first six months.

We head for the front door, where there are more hugs and kisses.

"Take good care of her," says Artie. I don't like the way he's looking at me.

I avert my eyes. "I will."

Finally, I'm able to drag my wife away from her family. I open the car door, and she slides in. We're really married. I can't believe it.

When I climb behind the wheel, Becky giggles. "Oh, Isaiah, I'm so happy. We're finally married. I love you so much. It will be wonderful. Do you think we should have two children, or three? I was talking with my mother about it last night. She can't wait to be a grandmother—after I graduate, of course." She goes on and on. I grab her hand as I

Ripples

drive down the expressway with her by my side. A warm feeling spreads through me.

At the hotel, a valet parks my car. A bellboy takes our luggage. My wife is still talking. I love listening to her.

We walk into the room, and I kiss her. No more guilt. She holds me tight.

As she sleeps in my arms, I gaze at her. We're married. Everything is perfect.

Jamilah Kolocotronis

Isaiah: Part Two

Marriage is nothing like I expected. I've made it through the first four weeks. I wonder how much longer I can keep this up.

She talks all the time. I mean, all the time—from the second she wakes up to the minute she goes to sleep. Usually, she's still talking when I drift off. Sometimes, she wakes me up and makes me listen until she's ready to sleep.

That's not the worst of it. She used to talk about important things like history and literature, but all she does now is complain. She won't let me spend one minute relaxing on campus without her. She won't let me go to the library alone. She has to know where I am every second of the day.

On top of that, she loves to shop. I wish I'd known that before I married her. At least twice a week, she comes home with more clothes and useless knickknacks. She's already driven us into debt. I thought it would help when she sold her car, but that money is gone. Uncle Brad pays our rent and utilities. Yesterday, I had to ask him for a loan just to put food in the fridge. The boss won't give me more hours, and, anyway, I need time to study. My grades are slipping.

When I tell her to be quiet or politely suggest she shouldn't spend so much money, she starts crying. Sometimes, she tears into me. I can't look the neighbors in the face because I know they hear us argue. Four weeks ago, I thought I loved her, but it's gotten to the point where I don't want to see her, I don't want to touch her, and I especially don't want to hear her.

I thought marriage would be fun. We would study together during the week and sleep in on the weekends. We would hold each other every night. We would discuss important issues, not argue about whose turn it is to wash the dishes.

Hellfire used to be the worst punishment I could imagine. That was before I married Becky.

∼

She wants to go see her parents this weekend.

"You just saw them a month ago."

"And I want to see them again. You promised I could visit them regularly."

"Yeah, like a couple times a year."

"I want to go every month."

I should have insisted on details before I signed that contract. "Go ahead. You can take my car. I'll manage for the weekend." A little quiet will be nice.

"No, you have to come, too."

"Why?"

"Because you're my husband, and you want to be with me. That's why you married me, isn't it? How would it look if I went home without you?"

I can't remember why I married her. I must have been insane. "We don't have to be together all the time."

"We're newlyweds." She blows in my ear. "Come on, Baby. It will be fun."

It's no use fighting her. If I try, she'll nag me day and night. And I do like the romance. That's the only good part about being married.

∼

When I get home from school on Friday, she's packed and ready to go. "Where were you? At this rate, we'll never get there."

"I was at the prayer." The one near campus. I haven't been back to Darul Islaam since Faruq mentioned the hundred lashes.

"Do you have to go every Friday? My parents don't always go to church, but they're still good Christians."

"Islam is different. Do we have to get into this now? I thought you were in a hurry."

"I am. The suitcases are packed. Take them down to the car."

"I need to pack my stuff."

"I did it for you."

Great. "I need to eat first."

"You can eat on the way. Now let's go!" she screams. She never screamed before we were married.

∼

We pull up to the house sometime after midnight. I'm beat. Becky uses her key. We walk quietly to her room. I crawl into bed. She changes into something frilly and whispers, "Do you remember that time you came to see me?"

I groan and roll over. A second later, I'm sound asleep.

~

I wake up with the sun in my eyes. Why did she raise the shades?

I didn't pray. My prayers have been spotty this last month. She doesn't like me to pray because then I can't listen to her. She absolutely hates it when I try to read the Qur'an. She says religion shouldn't get in the way of our relationship. I probably won't pray all weekend. It's too much of a hassle.

When I walk into the kitchen, Artie corners me. "It's about time you got up. I don't tolerate laziness in my household." I thought Artie tolerated pretty much anything.

Eileen points to my plate on the table. "The food is cold. We ate hours ago. You can heat it in the microwave." The food is pancakes and sausages. I told them I don't eat pork, but they don't seem to hear me.

I blink at the plate. I'll skip breakfast. "Where's Becky?"

"She took Denny to soccer practice and Charlie to the library on her way to visiting her friends. They'll be back in a few hours."

Great. My wife is gone, and she took my car. I'm stuck here with my in-laws, who don't seem to love me nearly as well as they used to.

I should study, but I forgot my textbooks. I have a test on Tuesday.

I make coffee and sit on the family room couch with Artie. He's watching golf.

~

I'm dozing when Becky walks in, giggling. It's been three weeks since I heard her laugh.

"Mom, I went to the mall, and you'll never guess who I ran into. Paula Parker. You know, the one who always brags. She was supposed to be going to college in Boston, and all last year she emailed me about her sexy new boyfriend. Guess what she's doing now? Selling shoes. Can you believe it? She must have flunked out of school. I don't know what happened to the boyfriend. Maybe she made him up."

"That Paula always did have an active imagination."

"You should have seen the look on her face when I told her I'm married. When I showed her a picture of Isaiah, she practically drooled all over it. And *I* still have my scholarship."

She drooled? I doubt that. I'm not scary-looking, but I've never been the type of guy girls drool over.

My wife jabbers with her mother for another fifteen minutes or so before remembering me, her quasi-handsome husband. "Hi, Baby," she says, kissing my cheek. "Are you having fun? I didn't know you liked golf."

I hate golf. "I'm spending quality time with your father." I don't think he likes golf either. He's snoring.

"Anyway, I called my best friend Brandy, and we decided to meet for dinner at Leonardo's. Their lasagna is fantastic. You don't mind, Mom, do you? I want to show off my husband." She hugs my shoulders. "You did bring something nice to wear, didn't you, Baby?"

"I don't know. You packed me for me, remember?"

"That's right. Okay, I know how to handle this. Brandy will be so jealous."

After lunch, Becky wants to show me around town. We see her high school, her middle school, her grade school, her daycare center, and the hospital where she was born. I'm glad we don't live any closer. I'd die of boredom.

Our last stop is the mall. "Didn't you just come here this morning?"

"You need new clothes. All you wear are jeans and those robe things."

"We have to save our money, Becky. I don't need fancy clothes."

"I want you to make a good impression." She pouts. "Why won't you let me buy clothes for the man I love?"

I hate when she does that. We go to three different stores before she's satisfied with my new wardrobe. "You'll look so handsome in these."

I thought I already was handsome, at least to Paula Parker.

～

She makes me wear my new suit to the restaurant. The tie feels like a noose around my neck.

The first thing I notice is the bar. I shouldn't be here. I don't pray much these days, but I am still a Muslim.

"Could we eat somewhere else? Someplace that doesn't serve alcohol?"

"Don't be silly. All the good restaurants have bars. I told Brandy we'd meet her here. Wait until you taste their food. You'll be glad we came."

Two minutes later, Becky screams and runs toward a very nice looking blonde. "Brandy! I missed you." They hug for a minute or two and talk about which one is skinnier and which one got her hair done. Then Becky puts her arm around my waist. "You remember Isaiah. My husband." She puts too much emphasis on that last word.

Brandy smiles sweetly. "How are you, Isaiah? Nice to see you again." A tall, curly-headed guy walks in behind her.

"Brent," says Becky. "Are you two still together?"

"Yeah," says Brandy, "I can't get rid of him."

The food is good—I can say that much—but, otherwise, the evening is a complete waste. And Brent orders wine. I shouldn't be here.

Brent and I spend the entire evening listening to the girls talk. Once or twice, I try to get a conversation going with him. "So, Brent, are you into football?"

Becky interrupts. "We have the nicest little apartment. Isn't that right, Baby? You'll have to come visit us. Isaiah grew up in Chicago. You wouldn't mind showing Brandy and Brent around, would you?

"Whatever you say, Becky."

～

There is one thing about my wife I really cannot figure out. As we drive back from the restaurant, I ask her. "When we first met, you talked about history and literature. Now, you act like any other silly girl. What happened?"

"I'm not silly. How could you say that?"

Ripples

I'd better be careful or all night she'll tell me how unsilly she is.

"What I mean is, why don't we talk about serious things anymore?"

"Because we're married now. We don't always have to be serious."

That made no sense to me at all, but, if I'm smart, I'll drop it.

Of course, when we get back to the house, she has to tell her mother all about the evening. What she said. What Brandy said. What Brandy was wearing. What we ate. My mother and Ruth never had conversations like that.

When they finish analyzing the evening, we go back to our room. Becky kisses me. I caress her. This is nice.

∼

In the morning, Artie and Eileen insist we all go to church together.

"I don't want to go to church," I protest. "I'm a Muslim."

"You're part of this family now," says Artie. "You'll come with us."

I haven't been to church in nearly a year. Not since my father declared me dead. Maybe they think they can convert me back to Christianity, but I know the Bible better than they do. I get dressed and go, just to keep peace in the family.

∼

The service was different. A lot of singing. A lot of sitting and standing. Not much excitement. Artie snored during the sermon. There was a lot of pomp, but I didn't feel the spirit.

I need to get back to Chicago—I have an early morning class—but we don't leave until late afternoon. I keep telling my wife to hurry, but she has to call more friends and visit her grandmother. We sit down to a large dinner. The roast chicken is delicious. I'm getting sleepy.

Becky tells Charlie to put our things in the car. I'm still sitting at the table, trying to stay awake.

"Let's go, Baby. We're running late."

Now she wants to leave. I hand her the keys. "You drive. I need a nap."

∼

When I wake up, we're sitting in a parking lot somewhere. Becky is gone. It's dark. I clear my mind and focus on the neon lights of the grocery store.

She comes back five or ten minutes later with a full cart.

"Where are we?"

"Near Madison. We'll be home in a few hours."

"Why did you stop?"

"We need groceries. Why else would I go to a grocery store?"

"Couldn't that wait? I have a class in the morning."

"Don't worry, Baby. You'll be fine. You always get good grades."

Not lately. I got a C on my medieval history test, and I haven't yet started the paper due on Wednesday. "Let me drive." I grab the keys from her.

"You don't have to be that way." She gets out, slamming the car door, and stomps to the passenger side.

I climb behind the wheel, pull back onto the highway, and push down on the accelerator. We need to get back to Chicago.

"Slow down, Isaiah. We'll have an accident."

"I know what I'm doing."

"What if we crash? How will you go to your classes if we crash?"

"Will you just shut up?"

That buys a minute of silence. Until she starts crying. "Don't talk to me that way. What did I ever do to you?"

"Do you really want me to tell you?"

"What is that supposed to mean?"

"You never shut up. You talk and talk, all day long. Sometimes I would like a little peace."

"It never bothered you before."

"Wait, I'm not finished. You're bossy. You pack my clothes. You tell me what to wear and where to go. I'm an adult."

"I'm your wife. That's my job." Her tears flow. I hope we have enough tissues.

"Being my wife isn't a job. It's your life."

"There's a depressing thought. Will I always have put up with your moodiness?"

"My mood is fine."

"Sometimes, you want to be close. Other times, you won't come near me. I try to get you involved in our marriage, but you resist. It's like you're my child."

"That's what I mean. You're bossy."

"*I'm* not finished. You keep saying you're a Muslim. You can't do this, and you can't do that. But when it suits you, Islam flies right out the window. If you are a Muslim, I don't see you acting like one."

"How would you know? You seduced me in your dorm room."

"I seduced you? That's not how I remember it."

"How many other guys have you been with?"

"Two. So?"

"So you had it all planned out. I was stupid enough to fall for it."

"Don't act so innocent. How many girls have you been with?"

"No one, besides you. I'm a Muslim."

"Don't start with that holier than thou crap. You are such a hypocrite."

"You're an expert on hypocrisy. You dragged me to church and a bar. I can't even pray around you and that family of yours."

"I never stopped you from praying."

"You didn't? Try every day since we got married. On top of that, you expected me to sit in church with your family—your mother singing hymns with that screeching voice of hers and your father snoring. That was a lot of fun."

"Don't you dare start in on my family. You're lucky they put up with you. And what about your family? Have I met your parents? Where are they? Do they even know we're married?"

"Your parents don't like me? They fell all over themselves when I came to visit last summer. And leave my parents out of this. They moved away. That's all you need to know."

"Why are you so secretive? I'm your wife. I need to know everything about you."

"So you can blab it to your friends? I can't trust that big mouth of yours."

"My big mouth? What else do you think is big? My butt, my hips, what?"

"Just your mouth. Your mouth is so big, there's no room for anything else."

"Do you want to hear my big mouth? Do you?" She screams. A high-pitched, ear-splitting scream. I feel like slapping her. I drive faster. The speedometer hits ninety.

"Slow down before you get us both killed."

"That doesn't sound like such a bad idea right now."

"Let me out of this car. If you want to kill yourself, go ahead, but I don't want to drive one more mile with you."

"Sorry. You're stuck with me."

"Let me out, Isaiah. I'm serious."

We're approaching Milwaukee. I take the next exit and find a well-lit parking lot. "Okay. Get out."

"You're leaving me here in the middle of nowhere?"

"I'm sure you can find your way home. Get out of my car."

She doesn't budge.

"Are you going to get out, or do I have to carry you out?"

"You have to carry me."

We sit. Five minutes. Ten.

"Are you going to slow down?"

"No. Are you getting out?"

"Give me some cash."

"What?"

"You can't expect me to get back to Chicago without money. Give me some cash."

"What happened to the cash I gave you from my last paycheck?"

"I spent it."

"You spent all that money in three days? I don't believe you."

"Most of it went for your new clothes. You should be grateful."

"I didn't want new clothes."

"So, you'd rather go around looking like a foreigner?"

"Stop trying to change me."

"I have to take care of you. You're my husband."

I'm sick of her. I bang the steering wheel. "Get out!"

"Give me some cash."

I pull a few bills from my wallet and throw them at her. "There."

She unbuckles her seat belt. "I'll see you in Chicago. Try not to get yourself killed on the way." She slams the door and walks away.

I get back on the highway. Peace and quiet. Finally.

Ripples

∼

I'm stopped by the highway patrol twenty miles from home. He asks for my license, registration, insurance, all that.

"You were going ninety-five back there."

"Yes, sir."

He lectures me about driving carefully before giving me a ticket I can't afford to pay. "You have to slow down if you ever expect to make it home." He gets in his car and takes off, looking for another offender.

Home. I wonder where Becky is. A pang of guilt runs through me. I call her cell.

She answers on the first ring. "Where are you, Baby?"

"I'm almost home. Do you want me to come get you?"

"Yes." She sounds frightened.

I turn around at the next exit.

∼

We walk into the apartment at 4:00 AM and fall into bed.

I wake up at noon. We missed our morning classes. My next class is at two. I fall back into my pillow.

She wakes up five minutes later and reaches for me. "Our first fight," she says softly.

I have the feeling it was something more.

Jamilah Kolocotronis

Isaiah: Part Three

We walk on eggshells. She's quiet, though I feel her watching me. I concentrate on my studies and pay very little attention to her. It's better that way. If I say one wrong word, our marriage will be finished.

On Thursday night, while I'm studying for my history test, she comes over and runs her fingers through my hair. I look up.

"Why don't you take a break?" she whispers.

I take her hand and lead her to our bedroom.

But, in the morning, it feels wrong. Is this all we have together? Will we spend the rest of our marriage in fear of the next blowup?

∼

She is trying. All week, she has kept her mouth shut. I should do my part.

On Saturday morning, I bring her coffee and bagel into the bedroom and wake her with a kiss. In the afternoon, we go to the lake and walk along the shore.

"Look at that family, Baby. That will be us someday."

The father carries a boy on his shoulders and holds his daughter's hand. The mother walks alongside him, her arm around his waist. She carries a picnic lunch. They look perfect. That will never be us. I nod and look out across the lake.

We go home and make love. There has to be more to marriage.

∼

On Sunday morning, she wakes up first, which is unusual, and brings me coffee, toast, and eggs. "Good morning, Baby. Did you sleep well?"

I nod, concentrating on breakfast.

"Thank you for yesterday. It was wonderful."

I stroke her arm. "Would you like to come back to bed?"

"No, I want you to eat your breakfast so we can get started on the day. I read about the nicest little museum up in Wisconsin. It's not too far. We can eat lunch up there and take a leisurely drive back." She strokes my cheek. "After that, I'll be ready for romance."

I sip my coffee. "What are you talking about? Do you realize midterms are coming? I hardly see you study."

"I can study later. Today, I want to make time for us."

"I'm sorry, Becky. I don't have that kind of time. I need to pull up my grades."

"Just one day, Baby. You can give me that."

"I really can't. I'm swamped. And I need to be at work at two."

"You didn't tell me you had to work today."

"Of course I have to work. How else do you think we're going to eat? I can't keep borrowing from my uncle."

"But what about us?"

"What about us? We have our whole lives to spend together. Right now, I need to get through school."

"Is school all you ever think about? Don't you ever think about me?"

"Of course, I do. What kind of question is that?"

"I ask you to spend one day with me, and you can't even do that."

"Why do you always have to make such a big deal out of everything?"

"This is a big deal. We're talking about our marriage."

"I thought we were talking about driving to Wisconsin."

"You never have any time for me. When I try to get close, you pull away. That's not how a marriage works."

"How is a marriage supposed to work, anyway? Is there a book I need to read? I thought being married would be fun. I didn't know I would have to work at it."

"It would be fun if you would make the effort."

"What do you need from me? I have my studies and my job. Isn't that enough?"

"But you're not trying to make me happy."

"Make you happy? I thought you were happy just being married to me." I raise my voice a tone. "'Oh, Brandy, this is my husband. Isn't he handsome?' It's all an act, isn't it?"

"What are you talking about? I love you, Baby."

"You love to boss me around and plan my life for me. You love to show me off and make your girlfriends jealous. But you can't love me. You don't know me."

"I want to know you. You won't let me."

"I need my space, but you are always in my face."

"In your face?" She leans closer. "Like this?"

I push her away. "Leave me alone."

She stares at me a second before running out of the room. A few seconds later, the apartment door slams.

She'll be back. This is just more of her theatrics.

∼

It's been five hours. She won't answer her cell. She took my car. I had to call in sick. One more strike, and I'm out of there.

∼

It's dark outside. Where could she be? I try to study, but I can't focus. Has she gone to Minnesota? How will I know? I can't call them and admit we were fighting.

I bang my head against the wall. Becky, where are you?

∼

It's midnight. I need to sleep. She'll come back soon. She has to. I need my car to get to classes tomorrow.

I lie down and close my eyes. Images flash through my mind. She could be hurt.

∼

It's still about an hour before sunrise. I haven't slept. I should pray. I step into the shower and wash up. She'll come into the bathroom, put her arms around me, and apologize for making me worry.

∼

Ripples

I need to get to class. I'll have to take the L. I grab a paper and write a short note. *I'm at school. Call me.* I know she'll be here by the time I come home.

I look for her on campus, but she's nowhere. I sit in my classes and take notes. My mind is far away.

∼

The note is still on the kitchen table where I left it. This isn't funny. I'd better call Eileen and Artie to see if she's there.

But what if she isn't? They'll give me the third degree. I don't need that. I'll call Uncle Brad instead.

Aunt Beth answers. "Hello, Isaiah. Is something wrong?"

"It's Becky. We had a fight yesterday. She walked out, and I don't know where she is. I'm starting to get worried."

"It took you this long to worry?"

"Let me talk to Uncle Brad. I need to know what to do."

"What have you done to find her?"

"I can't go looking for her. She took my car."

"Have you called the police?"

"They wouldn't take me seriously. It was just an argument."

"What if something happened to her?"

"Nothing will happen to Becky. She's tough."

"All right, Isaiah. Here's Brad."

Why was she hassling me?

"Assalaamu alaikum." My uncle won't give me the runaround. "Can you help me? Becky is missing, and I don't know where to turn."

"She's here. She came to our house yesterday. Why did it take you so long to call?"

Why is he giving me a hard time? "Could you tell my wife to come home? Tell her the game is over."

"I heard every word." Becky is crying. "You're right. It's over."

"So, come back home, and forget this nonsense."

"No, Isaiah. I want a divorce."

She wants what? I slam the phone on the table.

129

Jamilah Kolocotronis

Kyle: Part One

Things are picking up just a little. I'm surviving.

Though I am getting real tired of all the idiots I have to deal with. Yesterday, I stopped by an auto parts store to buy oil for my car. When I tried to get the attention of a salesman, he completely ignored me. Finally, I shouted, "Hey, when are you going to help me?"

He stopped flirting with the cashier. "Can't you see I'm busy?"

"I need oil for my car."

"You don't drive, do you?" Idiot. I gave him the finger before peeling out of that parking lot.

Work is okay. They sent me five new volunteers to train this morning. Like it takes a lot of skill to stuff envelopes. Why are they still stuffing envelopes anyway? These people need to get with the twenty-first century.

I'm sleepy. I can't sleep most nights. I depend on the TV to sedate me. I wish I could have one in my room, like I did when I was a kid, but my parents are into all this family togetherness now and won't allow blissful isolation.

~

Faiqa comes again on Tuesday. "Hello, Kyle. Do you have work for me today?"

"Always. How is your phone voice?" As nice as your in-person voice?

"I can handle myself. What do you have?"

"We're holding a big fundraising dinner, and ticket sales are slow. You'll need to call some of our past supporters and convince them to come. What do you think?"

"Give me the list and a phone so I can get started."

I like her spirit. She uses the phone on my desk while I type. Very persuasive. I'll need to give her a complimentary ticket.

She works for two hours, sells twenty-two tickets over the phone, and has seven more definite maybes. Impressive.

"I need to go now," she says, standing. She looks at the picture. "How long has it been?"

Ripples

"Almost two years."

"I can come back in a few days to pursue those definite maybes if you like."

"Don't feel sorry for me."

"I don't. I'll see you on Friday."

Finally, I have something to look forward to.

∽

When she walks in on Friday, she says, "I can't stay long. My mother wants me to go with her to Friday prayer."

"My dad goes to Friday prayers. I don't know which mosque."

"Your father is a Muslim?"

"He converted a few years ago."

"What about the rest of your family?"

"My little brother became a Muslim a few months ago. My mom is thinking about it—sometimes I catch her reading the Qur'an when she thinks no one is looking. And I have an uncle who became a Muslim before I was born." And then there's Isaiah, but his faith is probably as shaky as his marriage.

"What about you?"

I snicker. "I'm not religious. This life is hard enough. I don't have the energy to think about anything else."

"Aren't you a Christian?"

"Not really. I never bought into it."

"Don't you wonder about your girlfriend and the baby? You must think about death."

"I think about it all the time, but there's nothing I can do about it."

She nods and picks up the phone. "I need to make these calls."

She sells five more tickets. If the last two holdouts won't buy after her pitch, they won't buy from anyone.

Before she leaves, I tell her, "I have a ticket for you, in appreciation for your help."

"Okay, thanks. I'll see you next week."

There can never be anything romantic between Faiqa and me. That's obvious. It's not just my disability. She's a Muslim girl. She would never go for a guy like me. But it's nice to talk with someone who's smart and not afraid to say what she thinks.

I finish the proposal and send it out. I haven't told anyone about my program. If it comes through, they will have to take me seriously.

∽

Faiqa comes every Tuesday, and sometimes on Fridays. Tuesday has become my favorite day of the week.

She walked in this morning and handed me a book. "I thought you might be interested in this."

I glanced at the cover. Something about Islam. "You don't think you can convert me, do you? They've all tried—my dad, my uncle, my cousins, even my little brother. I'm inconvertible."

"Aren't you curious?"

"Is that what you call it? My dad got so curious, he stayed away from us for over a year. My curious cousin is married and miserable. Curiosity killed the cat. I choose life."

She laughed. "You won't even look at it?"

"Not a chance."

"What if I leave it here on your desk?"

"It will get very dusty."

"Suit yourself." She put the book back in her bag. "What do you have for me today?"

"More envelopes."

She's worked quietly on those envelopes for the last two hours. Sometimes I glance at her. I don't feel lonely when she's here.

On her way out, she tries again. "Are you sure you won't read it?"

"Positive."

"Okay. I'll see you next Tuesday."

"I'm looking forward to it." *More than you can imagine.*

Ripples

Kyle: Part Two

Dad, Matt, and I put on our suits. Mom wears a new gown—light blue and modest. Tonight is special.
Dad smiles at Mom. "You look beautiful."
She blushes. They kiss. It's great to have parents who love each other again.
We ask Becky to come with us, but she says she'd rather stay here. She's been at our house all week. That marriage never had a chance.

∼

The hall looks great. White tablecloths. Flowers on every table. Helium balloons along the walls. A string quartet plays Bach. The donors mill around, laughing and conversing.
Faiqa looks fantastic in her long, peach-colored dress. "Are you ready to get to work, Kyle?"
"What work? All I need to do is sit here and look good."
"You do look good." She smiles. "They're here, but that's only half the battle. Now we need to soften them up. Let's go. I'll show you how it's done."
I don't need lessons in schmoozing, but I would go anywhere with Faiqa. "Your table is over there, Dad. I'll be back."
We spot a group of four. The women wear expensive jewelry and stylish faux furs. The men stand tall and confident. Faiqa approaches. I follow.
"Philip," Faiqa says, "It's so nice to see you here. You come to every one of our functions. I truly admire your dedication. And, Rita, you look stunning. Your gown is absolutely beautiful."
She's good.
"Thank you, Faiqa. We wouldn't miss this. Hope Center is doing such wonderful work."
"They certainly are. I want you to meet one of our best workers. This is Kyle."
"Hello, it is so nice to meet you. Of course, you know the important work we do could not continue without your assistance."

"That is so true," says Faiqa. "Kyle, did you know Rita helped us start the clinic? We treat so many sick and injured every day, and all because of Rita's generosity."

"I love to help," says Rita. "Someone needs to step forward."

"Very true, Rita," I say. "I wish everyone had your sense of civic responsibility."

We wrap up the conversation with more chitchat, strongly laced with immoderate praise. On our way to the next victims, I ask Faiqa, "How did you know so much about them?"

She smiles. "I did my homework."

I didn't, but, while Faiqa lays the trap, I listen closely, looking for an opening into their bank accounts. It's for a good cause.

Ripples

Jennifer: Part One

If you ask me, Becky didn't appear to be a happy bride. I know how they got themselves into this mess. They both looked like they were being punished.

∼

In one week, my baby will be a year old. I'm planning a family dinner to celebrate. I've made all my lists. When Nuruddin comes home, I ask him to watch the baby so I can go shopping.

"What do you need?"

"Ahmed's birthday is next week. I want to buy him a couple more presents, and we need decorations and candles. I've invited the family for dinner. And I can't forget to order his birthday cake." I pick up my purse and the shopping list.

"You're ordering a birthday cake?"

"I thought about making one, but I have so many other things to do. I'll leave the baking to the professionals."

"That's not what I mean. Why are doing all this?"

"It's his first birthday. How does your family celebrate?"

"We never have birthday parties. It's un-Islamic."

"How can it be un-Islamic to celebrate my son's birth?"

"It's not done. You can invite your family for dinner, but forget the cake and decorations. We are a Muslim family."

"But I'm not a Muslim, and I want to celebrate my son's birthday."

"Jenny, you agreed to raise Ahmed as a Muslim."

"You can take him to the mosque, but what does Islam have to do with planning a birthday party?"

"Islam touches everything in our lives. I thought you knew that."

"I know Dad is strict, but my mother always celebrated our birthdays."

"Your mother is not a Muslim."

"Neither am I."

"I am. As the head of this family, I demand you respect the teachings of Islam."

135

I drop my purse and grab a tissue as a tear smudges my list. "Why are you being so rigid? It's just a birthday cake."

"It's not part of Islam."

"But it's part of who I am. You have to respect my ways, too."

He walks away. I hate when he does that.

"Don't do this to me, Nuruddin. I'm not finished."

"I'm too angry," he says in a low voice.

We spend the rest of the night in silence, broken only by his soft recitation of the Qur'an. I'm so irritated I could scream, but I know it won't do any good. Two months after we married, we argued about my favorite red dress. He said it was too tight. I said I had the right to dress any way I pleased. When he turned away, I went after him, shouting and screaming. He walked out of the apartment and didn't return for hours. We never said another word about it. I gave that dress to a charity. It reminded me of one of the worst nights of my life.

I ignore him and take care of my Ahmed while fighting the argument in my head. He is so wrong. And this is much more important than a silly red dress. I won't say anything else tonight, but this argument is far from over.

~

We're still not talking in the morning. I want to kiss and make up, but this is too important for me to compromise. Ahmed's first birthday should be one of those special moments I will always remember.

Nuruddin drinks his coffee and walks out without a word. Ahmed wakes up crying. I get him dressed and drive over to Mom's condo.

"What's wrong?" she asks. She can always read my moods.

"I didn't sleep well." Which is true.

"Are you worried about something?"

"Nuruddin and I had a fight, okay? But I don't want to talk about it."

She sighs. "If you say so."

She shows me her latest paintings. I wish I had her talent.

We chat and gossip over coffee and cheesecake. I glance at the time. "I'd better go." I quickly finish my cheesecake.

"Are you ready to talk about it yet?"

Ripples

"Don't you teach a class in the afternoon?"

"Not today. I have all the time in the world." She reaches over and brushes back my hair, like she did when I was little. "What's wrong, Jenny?"

"Nothing's wrong."

"You haven't tried to lie to me for a long time. It must be important."

"Nuruddin won't let Ahmed have a birthday cake. Can you believe it?"

"A birthday cake? Why in the world not?"

"He says it's un-Islamic. And don't say you warned me, Mom. I love being married to him—most of the time. I don't know why he's acting this way."

"No wonder you're upset. After all the years he's lived in this country, he should understand how much this means to you."

"But Dad never celebrated birthdays."

"I know. I always gave you bigger parties and more presents to make up for your father's neglect. And that's what we'll do for Ahmed."

"What do you mean?"

"We'll have Ahmed's birthday party here at the condo. Nuruddin never needs to know."

"I never keep secrets from him."

"But what he doesn't know won't hurt him. Right?"

Ahmed toddles over to me and pats my leg. "Mama," he says haltingly.

I pick him up and cuddle him. "Your first word! Oh, my precious baby."

"Don't you think your precious baby deserves a birthday party?"

"He sure does."

"I'll take care of everything. Bring Ahmed here at two on Saturday. Tell that husband of yours you're going shopping or something. Oh, I can't wait."

I can't, either. He'll look so sweet in his little party hat. We'll have to take plenty of pictures. Too bad I can't show them to Nuruddin. It's his loss.

∽

I bathe Ahmed and dress him in his best play outfit.

"Where are you going?" Nuruddin asks as I pick up my purse.

"Mom and I are going shopping. I'll be back by six at the latest."

"Do you think you should take Ahmed out in this heat?"

"Don't worry. We'll be in air-conditioning."

"I would like you to stay home, Jenny."

"I already arranged things with Mom. She doesn't have much time during the week, and I miss our shopping trips."

"Leave the baby at home then."

Think, Jenny. "Mom wants to buy him new shoes. You know she likes to spoil him."

He sighs. "Don't be too late." He kisses my cheek. "I'll miss you."

I hug him. This is wrong. I shouldn't lie. But I can just imagine the party Mom has planned. "Me, too."

∼

When I walk in, they shout out, "Happy Birthday, Ahmed!" and launch into song. Ahmed smiles and babbles. He loves the attention.

It's a great party. Ahmed digs into the cake, smearing it all over his face and hands. Icing falls to his diaper—Mom reminded me to take off his outfit. He wears a sweet party hat. Everyone blows horns and claps as he tears into his presents. There are so many. Mom says she'll keep them at her place. I can take home one or two at a time without raising suspicion.

I wish my stepmom Aisha and Raheema, my sister-in-law, were here, but I couldn't let them know. That's okay. I have my friends from high school and college, and two of my neighbors. And my Aunt Kimberly—Mom's sister. Grandma and Grandpa Layton came, too. They bought Ahmed the cutest outfits, along with a wagon and a riding toy. He's their first great grandson.

We gossip while nibbling on the buffet Mom arranged. We joke and laugh over coffee and cake. I haven't had a day like this since I married Nuruddin. I need to get out more often.

Aunt Kimberly is telling a funny story about going through customs in Paris when my phone rings. I answer, giggling. "Hello?"

"Jenny, you should have been home an hour ago."

Ripples

I should have checked my caller ID. I motion for everyone to be quiet. "I was just about to leave. Mom and I were just chatting over coffee, and I just lost track of the time. I'm just coming home right now." My heart is beating fast. I wonder how much he heard.

"Make sure you do."

I hang up. "That was Nuruddin. I need to go."

"Why?" says Aunt Kimberly. "Don't let your husband tell you what to do."

"Yeah," says Clarissa, a college friend. "Stand up for yourself. You can go home whenever you want."

That sounds like a good idea for a second or two, until I remember that Aunt Kimberly has been divorced three times, and Clarissa says she hates men. "No, I'd better go."

Nuruddin's call put an end to the festivities. Everyone watches quietly while Mom helps me get Ahmed ready. Clarissa whispers to Kayla. I can imagine what they're saying. Poor Jennifer is enslaved to that sexist Muslim.

By the time I walk into our apartment, I am fed up. He didn't have to call and embarrass me. Aunt Kimberly was right. I should have stayed.

He's waiting for me by the door. "You're late."

"You're not my father. You can't boss me."

"Did you enjoy stabbing me in the back?"

"What?"

"Your friend Shelby called. She couldn't remember if the party would be here or at your mother's place. Did you have fun? Was it worth it?"

I'm going to strangle Shelby. "I had to go behind your back. You were acting like a dictator."

"A wife must obey her husband."

"Oh, really? What century were you born in?"

"That is Islam."

"I'm not a Muslim."

"You married a Muslim."

"I married a man, not a religion."

"Islam is my way of life. You knew that when you married me. You will not disobey me again."

"What are you going to do? Take me over your knee and spank me?"

"Why did you lie to me?"

"I had to. You were being so unreasonable."

"You still don't know how strongly I feel about this."

"It's just a party. A little cake and ice cream never killed anyone."

"My son will grow up to be a Muslim, and I can't let you pollute his mind."

"Pollute his mind? I didn't know I married a fanatic."

"I am his father, and I say how he will be raised."

"And I am his mother. I thought you respected me."

"Until today, I have respected you very much, but you plotted behind my back. How can I trust you?"

"All I did was have a stupid birthday party for my son."

"You're right. It was very stupid!" he shouts. "Don't you ever do this again. Don't lie to me, and don't take my son away from Islam."

"I will do whatever I please."

He charges toward me, stopping two feet away. "You will not shame me!" he screams. He grabs a lamp and throws it to the floor.

Ahmed shrieks. I run into the bedroom and cry with my baby.

When Ahmed settles down, I cry quietly, my face in my pillow. I hear Nuruddin in the living room, softly reciting the Qur'an.

∼

We've barely talked or even looked at each other all week. I'm starting to wonder if we can make this marriage work. If we let a silly birthday party come between us, how can we handle everything else?

When Dad found out about the party, he lectured me. "You must obey your husband, Jennifer. Undermining him weakens your marriage."

I looked to Aisha for support, but she echoed Dad's comments. "If you want a healthy marriage, you need to communicate with Nuruddin, not go behind his back. It's not only a question of obedience. We're talking about respect. How would you feel if Nuruddin lied to you?"

All night, while staring at his empty pillow, I've thought about what she said. If Nuruddin lied to me I would be angry and hurt, and I would have a hard time trusting him. Maybe I did go too far.

Ripples

But he shouldn't have been so rigid. If he had listened to me, rather than making his own dictatorial decision, I wouldn't have needed to lie to him.

The bottom line is that I miss my husband. Tomorrow, I'll try to talk with him. No screaming or crying. I'll be rational and unemotional. I hope he's ready to listen.

∼

He's sitting on the couch, in his bathrobe, reading the Qur'an. I sit next to him.

"Can we talk about this?"

He keeps reading.

"Nuruddin, we need to fix this."

He looks up. "You're the one who broke it."

"Okay, I shouldn't have lied to you. There. I apologized."

"I need a wife I can trust, and I need my son to be raised as a Muslim. Do you think you can handle that?"

Rational and unemotional. I bite my bottom lip. "When he's older, you can take him to the mosque and teach him how to pray. I don't have a problem with that. But I don't want Islam to rule our lives. I'm an American, and so is Ahmed. I have the right to teach him about my culture, too."

"Aren't you the daughter of Joshua Adams? Everything your father does, every breath he takes, is for the sake of Allah. He doesn't restrict his practice of Islam to the masjid. Haven't you learned anything from him?"

"My father taught me to be tolerant of others. He lives Islam completely, but he never forced me to be like him.

"And I'm also my mother's daughter. You know how much she's helped me. She'll watch Ahmed so I can go back to school, and she's always there when I need her. I told her I wanted Ahmed to have a birthday party, and she offered to throw him one. You should be grateful."

"I am grateful to Allah. He is the One who gives me all I need."

Rational and unemotional? Forget it. "I'm trying to discuss things, and you keep throwing out religious platitudes!" I shout. "How can I get through to you?"

"I need to go to work."

"How long will this last? Why don't you ever consider how I feel?" I don't try to stop the tears.

He touches my hand. "I know how you feel, Jenny, but we can't live our lives based on feelings. Allah sent laws to guide our lives. When we don't follow them, we invite trouble. You lied to me, and you disobeyed me."

"Who died and made you king?" I want to scream. But, before I open my mouth, I study my husband's face. He has deep circles under his bloodshot eyes. His hair looks like it hasn't been combed in days. The brightness is gone.

Why should I obey my husband? I have rights, too. Why should he have the last word? If I give in to him, won't I be betraying every woman who struggled for her rights? Won't I be showing my son that women are to be dominated?

But this isn't working. I can stand up for my rights and protest loud and clear, but, in the end, I will be standing alone. I want my happy family back.

I don't understand why I should obey him. It doesn't seem worth arguing over. Not now. I touch his hand. "I'm sorry."

He reaches for me. It is so good to be back in his arms.

Ripples

Jennifer: Part Four

It's been a week. We're close again, but I'm still struggling with what it means to be married to Nuruddin. What are my rights as his wife? Did I lose myself when I married him?

∽

I'm going back to school tomorrow. I stand in front of the closet for an hour, trying to decide what to wear. My best outfits are still a little snug on me. I've worn sweat pants most of the time since Ahmed was born.

Nuruddin comes over and kisses me on the neck. "You look beautiful no matter what you wear."

"Don't you think this dress makes me look fat?"

"Are you going to school or a fashion show?"

"I do look fat, don't I?"

"Ahmed and I think you're beautiful. It doesn't matter what anyone else thinks." He kisses me again.

I am fat. I'll stick with the sweat pants.

∽

On Monday morning, I take Ahmed to Mom's place.

"Look at my sweet grandson. We'll have so much fun together."

"Thanks for watching him, Mom. Are you sure it won't interfere with your work?"

"I set my own schedule now, remember? I told the nursing home I won't be able to come in the mornings, and they're fine with that. The school in Elmhurst wants me to work with the kids after lunch. Oh, and did I show you my most recent work?"

"No, I don't think so. But I need to get going. I don't want to be late."

"It won't take long." She goes to her easel and produces an abstract consisting of bright colors and jagged edges.

"That's great. What do you call it?"

"'Marriage.'" She smiles. "I'm glad you like it. You'd better get going."

"Okay, Mom. Thanks again."

I know she doesn't mind babysitting. She loves Ahmed as much as I do. I mean, who wouldn't?

Marriage. Bright colors and jagged edges. That says it all.

∽

I slide into a seat just as the professor walks into the room. I turn on my old notebook and get ready to type.

She's talking about the responsibility of being a journalist. It's very interesting, but, halfway through class, I lose my concentration. I miss Ahmed.

Before my next class, I call Mom. "How is he? Is everything okay?"

"He's fine, Jenny. I do know a thing or two about babies."

"I know, but I've never been away from him this long."

"He's just finished eating. I'll give him a bath in a few minutes. After that, we'll go for a little walk. Do you approve?"

I laugh. "Sure, Mom. I'd better get to class."

"Yes, you'd better. Stop worrying."

I make it through another class. As soon as the professor dismisses us, I race out the door.

Mom has Ahmed ready to go. "I need to leave for the nursing home soon. He was perfect."

"Great." I grab my baby and hold him close, breathing in his sweetness. He pulls my hair and giggles. "We'll see you tomorrow, then. Have a good time with the old people."

"I always do."

∽

When Nuruddin comes home, I'm in the kitchen. He kisses my cheek. "I have a surprise for you."

"What? Where is it?"

"Come here." He takes my hand and leads me into the living room. A luscious chocolate cake sits on the coffee table. "For my beautiful wife," he says. "Now you have your cake."

Ripples

I laugh. He still doesn't understand, but he tried. We kiss. Marriage to Nuruddin isn't always easy, but I can't imagine my life without him.

Tough Choices

Life is the sum of all your choices.

—Albert Camus

Isaiah: Part One

I haven't talked to my wife all week. But I do miss her. The apartment is too quiet, and the bed is too large.

Uncle Brad and Aunt Beth came over a few days ago, gathering her books and clothes while I watched helplessly. Before leaving, my uncle sat with me at the kitchen table.

"Do you want to end your marriage?"

"I don't know."

"Tell me what you do know."

"We fight almost all the time. Sometimes I can barely stand to look at her."

"Five weeks ago, you were madly in love with her."

Has it only been five weeks? "I didn't know how hard it would be to live with her." Almost as hard as living without her.

He stood. "I have never known you to give up so easily."

I laughed. "You don't know Becky."

"I think I do. She's stayed in our spare room for a week now, and she's a very nice girl. Almost as nice as your Aunt Beth."

"She's nothing like Aunt Beth. She's bossy and controlling and always wants my attention. Doesn't she realize I have my own life to worry about?"

"If you keep acting this way, your own life will be all you have to worry about."

They leave. I slam the door behind them. No one understands me.

∼

I have all the time I need to concentrate on my studies, but I can't focus. What right does she have to walk out on me?

I'm trying to prepare for an economics test, but I keep reading the same sentences over and over. I get up to fix myself a sandwich. That's practically all I've eaten since Becky left. Mom never taught me how to cook.

"Assalaamu alaikum, Isaiah." Uncle Joshua knocks. I put down my sandwich and let him in. Aunt Aisha and Becky are with him.

"Walaikum assalaam. What are you doing here?"

"We need to talk."

"All the talk in the world won't fix this."

My wife pipes up. "I told you. There's no reasoning with him."

My uncle grabs my shoulder. "Sit down, Isaiah. Lose the attitude."

We sit.

"You need to work on your marriage," says my aunt. "Don't do something you will both regret."

Like getting married in the first place? "It won't work," I mumble.

"Why won't it work?" my uncle asks.

"He won't talk to me," says Becky.

"And she talks all the time."

"You used to like listening to me."

"That was before I had to live with you."

"That's what marriage is about," says Aunt Aisha. "Living together and caring for each other in spite of the little irritations."

"But I didn't know marriage meant surrendering."

Becky snaps. "What have you given up?"

"You hound me day and night. I need my privacy."

"Becky, what bothers you most about Isaiah?" Uncle Joshua asks.

She spends fifteen minutes detailing my faults. I'm self-centered and secretive. I don't try to get along with her parents. I complain too much and help too little. And I'm only a Muslim when it suits me. I really needed her to say that to my uncle.

Now, it's my turn. She's bossy and likes to show off. She talks all the time and rarely gives me a minute's peace. She spends too much money and refuses to get a job. Her parents don't like me. And, because of her, I may actually flunk a class for the first time in my life.

I don't know how to say what else is bothering me. She's been with two other guys. I can't get it out of my mind.

Uncle Joshua shakes his head. "I wish you had come to me earlier, Isaiah, before you married Becky. I'm not sure the two of you should have married in the first place, but now you need to make the best of it. You can start by being kind."

"I am kind," says Becky. "I want to take care of him, but he pushes me away."

"He's a grown man," says Aunt Aisha. "He needs you to be his friend, not his mother."

Ripples

Somebody finally understands. "And when I try to treat her nicely, she thinks she can walk all over me."

Uncle Joshua grasps my aunt's hand. "You can never be too kind to your wife."

"Marriage means working together," says Aunt Aisha. "It isn't always easy, but the rewards are tremendous." She squeezes my uncle's hand. "Both in this life and the next."

"Marriage means caring. Whatever you do, you have to consider how it will affect the other person. If you really respect one another, your other problems will seem minor." Uncle Joshua pulls my aunt close to him.

"That sounds easy, but you haven't tried living with Becky."

"No more put-downs. Respect your wife. Apologize."

"Sorry," I mumble.

"Where do we go from here?" Becky asks.

"You don't go anywhere," says Aunt Aisha. "You stay together and work things out."

"We've tried that. All we do is fight."

Aunt Aisha smiles. "Remember to respect her, and she'll respect you. That's the way to end the fighting."

Uncle Joshua stands. "We need to go. If you need help, call us. Whatever you do, don't walk out. That won't solve anything."

They leave. We look at each other. I don't know whether to scream at her or kiss her.

"Let's try again," she says softly, coming closer.

I have missed her. Maybe we can make this work.

Jamilah Kolocotronis

Isaiah: Part Two

It's been three days, and things are good, but we're both being careful. Aunt Aisha said we need to work together, but I didn't know it would be this much work. I feel like one wrong step will trigger an explosion. This isn't how it should be.

We struggle to be respectful and kind. We're not husband and wife. We're actors, diligently playing our roles. We say *please* and *thank you*, and not much of anything else. In the bedroom, we drop our masks and desperately grope, but it's not enough.

∽

On Friday morning, I break the silence. "I'll be late today. I'm going to pray at Darul Islaam. I'll meet you on campus at around four."

"Why so late?"

"I need to talk with Faruq." I lightly touch her hand. "Something's wrong between us. He can tell me how to fix it."

"Nothing's wrong, Baby. Everything will be good again."

"Stop pretending. You know we're in trouble."

She cries. "I'm trying so hard."

"I know you are, and I am, too, but it shouldn't be this much work."

"Don't you love me?"

"Of course, I do." I can't discuss this when she's crying. "Forget about it. We need to get to class."

She won't forget. All the way to campus, she keeps it up. "I'm trying to be a good wife."

"It's not you. It's probably me. I don't know. Let me talk with Faruq. I think he can help."

I drop her off near her class. "I'll see you later."

"I'll see you." She sounds like she's ready to cry again.

I should reach over and hug her, but I don't feel like it.

∽

Ripples

Faruq is in the front row. The sermon is about to start. I pray and sit down to listen.

Today's sermon is about repentance. Very appropriate.

After the prayer, I sit next to him. He ignores me. I try anyway. "Assalaamu alaikum. Listen, Faruq, maybe you were right."

He looks up, eyebrows raised. "Maybe?"

"Our marriage is a mess. Can you help me?"

He glares at me, pointing his finger. "This is your last chance."

When I tell him about the problems Becky and I are having, he says, "What did you expect? Marriage isn't easy to begin with, and you started off on the wrong foot. I'm surprised you are still together."

I think that's the common opinion. "What should I do?"

"I told you. Accept your punishment. Purify yourself. You have committed a major sin. The Prophet, peace and blessings be upon him, warned of the consequences of fornication in this life and the next. Poverty. The wrath of Allah. Hellfire. Is that what you want?"

"I don't want to be beaten. I can't stand it." My mind flashes to my father and his belt.

"The Prophet was a gentle man. When he needed to punish someone, he chose a whip which was neither too thin nor too thick. He told the man to keep his clothes on. Some say one hundred lashes will kill a person, but not if it's done in the way of the Prophet."

"What happens if I let you beat me? Will things get better?"

"If you repent to Allah sincerely, your life will improve. Receiving your punishment is part of your repentance."

"How will it be different than what my father did to me?"

"I won't do it out of anger."

"I don't know. I want to change things, but not like that. If you cared for me, how could you hit me?"

"Allah said in the Qur'an, 'The woman and the man guilty of adultery or fornication—flog each of them with a hundred stripes; let not compassion move you in their case, in a matter prescribed by Allah, if you believe in Allah and the Last Day; and let a party of the Believers witness their punishment.' These are the words of our Creator. If you do this, Isaiah, Allah will forgive you, and your life will be right."

"People have to witness it?"

"We can't do it in public. It's against the laws of this land. Come to my apartment tomorrow at five. My two oldest sons will witness. The purpose of Islamic punishment is twofold—to purify the offender and to serve as a reminder to others. If you fulfill your obligation to Allah and help two young men stay on the right path, you will be rewarded."

"Do you have to worry about your own sons?"

He raises his palms. "I do my best to teach them Islam, but they're human."

I've never seen Faruq this human before. "I need to go. My wife is waiting for me. I'll see you tomorrow."

"Insha Allah."

∼

She badgers me. "Why did you need to talk with Faruq? What did he say?"

"I need to go back there tomorrow."

"Why?"

"I don't want to talk about it."

"You can tell me. I'm your wife. We shouldn't have any secrets. Don't you trust me? What's wrong, Baby?"

She goes on and on. When we get home, I open my history text and try to ignore her.

Sometime during the evening, she gives up and calls her mother. I listen to her end of the conversation. "I don't know what's wrong with him, Mom. He won't tell me anything. Shouldn't husbands and wives share everything?"

When she hangs up, I say, "Do you have to discuss our marriage with your mother?"

"Most people actually talk to their parents." She walks away and shuts the bedroom door. It's nice to have a little quiet.

We go to bed at the same time, but we're not together. Right now, I want to be left alone.

∼

Ripples

In the morning, we continue moving in our separate spheres. I read most of the day. She studies a little and spends the rest of her time on the phone.

At 4:30 AM, I grab my jacket. "I need to go."

"Where are you going?"

"This is something I need to do." I walk away.

"Isaiah. Come back. Don't walk out on me."

Her voice echoes through the hall.

∽

I'm about to climb into my car when I hear a familiar voice calling me.

"Isaiah. Assalaamu alaikum."

"Walaikum assalaam." I smile and try to act natural. He doesn't need to know where I'm going.

My uncle walks over and gives me a quick hug. "Do you have a few minutes? I was just coming to visit you. How's everything going?"

"Everything's fine." I pull away. "I need to go. You can come back later."

"What's wrong, Isaiah?"

"Nothing's wrong." My ear itches but I resist pulling on it.

"Have you been fighting with your wife? You're not walking out on her, are you?"

No, not really. "Everything's okay, Uncle Joshua. There's just something I have to take care of." I hesitate. "Um, Becky asked me to pick up something from the store."

"Don't lie to me, man."

"I need to go. I'm running late."

"Late for what?"

He's pushing too hard. "Can't you just mind your own business and leave me alone?" I shout.

"I can but I won't. Something is going on and I'm not leaving until you tell me." He walks over to the passenger side and opens the door. "Let's sit down."

Why won't he just go away? I have to do this and I don't need him bothering me.

He leans over to the driver's side and opens the door. "Come on, Isaiah. Have a seat."

I roll my eyes and plop behind the wheel.

"This must be important." He leans back. "Whenever you're ready. I have all night."

I stare through the windshield. Faruq is expecting me. I need to get this over with. What can I say to get rid of my uncle? "There's nothing to talk about. I need to go meet somebody. We're, um, going to study together for a history test."

Uncle Joshua stares at me until I turn away. "Try again."

I need to stay calm. "Seriously. The guy's name is, um, Tony. He needs my help."

"I'm not buying it, Isaiah."

We can keep dancing around like this all night. I fidget, my fingers beating out a rhythm on the steering wheel. What can I say that he'll believe?

"You can feed me stories all night or you can tell me the truth. And remember, you'll never be as good a liar as I used to be."

I remember hearing about all the trouble Uncle Joshua got into when he was young. Maybe he will understand. I'd better go ahead and tell him because it's the only way he'll leave me alone.

"Okay, there's this guy named Faruq over at Masjid Darul Islaam. He helped me take shahadah and taught me how to pray. Anyway, when he found out what Becky and I did—before we were married, I mean—he said I needed to get lashed. At first, I refused, but I'm about to lose my marriage, and I don't know what else to do. I have to accept my punishment so Allah will forgive me and my life will be good again." The words come pouring out. It feels good to tell someone.

Uncle Joshua is quiet. He looks at me for a minute then stares at a nearby streetlight. I wait.

"Faruq is right," he says. "That is the punishment for fornication."

"That's where I'm going—over to Faruq's place. I have to do this."

"Did you tell Becky what you're planning to do?"

I shake my head. "She wouldn't understand."

"Even though Faruq is right, you shouldn't do it."

Ripples

"What do you mean? I have to do it."

He faces me. "What you did was wrong. You know that. The punishment prescribed by Allah is to be lashed one hundred times, but this isn't the way to go about it. We're not living in an Islamic country, and what Faruq wants to do to you is called assault. He could get into a lot of trouble."

"Not if I don't say anything."

"Even if we were in an Islamic country, one man can't hand out the punishment. It would need to go through a court of law."

"That doesn't make any sense. There's no court in the world that would convict me."

"There is no court in this country that would convict you. That's true. Now you know what it means to be a minority."

"So, what am I supposed to do? I have this sin hanging over me, and I'm going to Hell." So is my marriage. I feel like crying but I can't do that in front of my uncle.

Uncle Joshua reaches for me. Before I know it, he's holding me against his chest and I am crying. He strokes my head. "Let it out, Isaiah," he says softly.

∼

When I'm calm, I pull back and wipe my eyes with my sleeves. "So, what should I do? Do they whip people in Pakistan? Maybe you could send me to Pakistan." I feel like a ten-year-old again, lost and looking for direction.

"Let's go see Faruq. I want to talk with him."

"Don't fight with him. Faruq is a good Muslim. He doesn't want to hurt me."

"I know. I just think we need to talk."

Uncle Joshua and I are silent as I drive to Faruq's apartment. I'd better let Uncle Joshua do the talking. This is all his idea.

I knock. "Assalaamu alaikum."

He quickly opens the door. "Walaikum assalaam. You're late." Faruq stops. He stares at my uncle, who offers his right hand and puts his left arm around my shoulders.

"Assalaamu alaikum. I want to talk with you about my nephew."

Faruq glances at me and looks back at my uncle. "*Walaikum as-salaam.* Come in, Brother."

We sit on the green cushions—I slouch in the middle with Faruq and Uncle Joshua on either side of me. My uncle talks over my head.

"I came to visit Isaiah and, *alhamdulillah*, I caught him just before he left. After a little prodding, he told me where he was going and why. Brother Faruq, I admire your conviction, but I don't think you should do this."

Faruq shakes his head. "Isaiah told me about his liberal uncle. I reminded him we must first obey Allah."

Uncle Joshua smiles. "You probably mean my brother. I was educated in Pakistan, and I'm very familiar with the Shari'ah. I agree that, according to the Qur'an, Isaiah should be lashed for his sin. But we don't live in Makkah or Islamabad. We live in Chicago."

"We must follow the word of Allah, no matter where we live."

"Yes, as much as we can. But, in this country, when we try to practice huddud, punishing according to the Shari'ah, we are also breaking the law."

"I don't follow the law of this land."

"Do you think the punishment should be carried out by one man, without a judge or due process? We must follow a certain procedure. That is Islam."

"Isaiah confessed to his sin. He asked me to punish him."

Uncle Joshua nods. "That's the first step, isn't it? He is ready to repent. And, if I hadn't stopped him, he would have received the lashing by now. But it won't work. Not here and not now."

Faruq frowns. "We can't turn our backs on the commands of Allah."

Uncle Joshua touches my shoulder. "This is my nephew. I've seen him grow from an infant to the young man he is now. And I know you care for him, but you couldn't possibly love him the way I do."

"Allah said, 'Let not compassion move you.'"

"I know the ayah. If things were different—if we had an Islamic judge, an Islamic court—I wouldn't stand in the way. But we can't take the law into our own hands."

Faruq closes his eyes and softly mutters. "Astagfirullah. Astagfirullah. Astagfirullah."

Fear grips me. "What should I do?" I don't want this hanging over me for the rest of my life. I don't want to go to Hell.

"You need to repent, Isaiah. Fast and pray and ask Allah to forgive you. Be sincere. Change yourself from the inside. If you're sincere, Allah will help you."

I look at Faruq, who is staring at the floor. I've never seen him so uncertain.

After a few minutes, he looks up. "Your uncle is right. By Allah, I don't like it, but he's right."

"What about the lashing?" I was almost ready for it.

"Repent, as your uncle said. Turn your heart completely to Allah, my young brother."

Faruq is quieter than I've ever seen him. He excuses himself and returns with tea. He and Uncle Joshua talk quietly about the days when Islam spread peacefully across the earth and Muslims were united. I listen and learn.

Before we leave, Faruq gently hugs me. "You're a strong young man, and I respect your courage. Now you need a new name. Isaiah is a good name for a Christian, but you're not a Christian, are you?"

"I've thought about changing my name, but I haven't found one which feels right."

"I've decided to call you Saifullah."

Uncle Joshua smiles. "I think that fits you."

I like the sound. "What does it mean?"

"The Sword of Allah. You will grow in strength and fight for what is right."

The Sword of Allah. I feel stronger already.

~

It's late. Uncle Joshua says goodbye in the parking lot.

"You need to go talk with your wife. Your first act of repentance should be in your kindness to her." He hugs me. "I also respect your courage, Saifullah."

"Don't call me that around the family."

"It will be between us."

When I walk into the apartment, Becky tries to ignore me. She manages to stay quiet for two minutes before the questions start. "Where were you? What happened?"

"I can't talk now." I grab a towel and head for the shower. The first step of my repentance will be to clean myself and pray.

"Isaiah, are you okay in there?" She knocks repeatedly.

I don't answer. I step out and dry myself, and when I'm dressed, I bow down to Allah, asking Him to forgive me.

Becky is waiting, sitting on the edge of the couch and watching me.

I turn around. "I need to tell you something."

"Please, Baby. I want to help you."

I sit with her on the couch, hold her hand, and meet her gaze. "A few months before I met you, I almost killed my father. I wanted to put an end to it."

"You did what?" She pulls away.

"Listen. Be patient. It's a long story."

When I'm finished, she says, "He did that to you? What kind of father would beat his son? Why didn't your mother stop him? No wonder you don't want to see them."

"I don't want to see him. I worry about the others."

"Show me your back." She removes my shirt and gently traces the scars. "I asked you once how you got these. You wouldn't tell me. My poor baby." She massages me with a soothing lotion.

I kiss her hand. "I love you."

"It took you long enough to say it."

"I wanted to make sure I really meant it."

She strokes my head. "I love you, too."

Ripples

Kyle: Part One

We surpassed our goal at the fundraiser. I wonder how much extra was raised by the personal contacts Faiqa and I made.

I enjoyed myself. For one night, people looked me in the eye and talked past the wheelchair. I won't deceive myself. They won't invite me to their homes. None of those men would let me marry his daughter. But, for one night, they threw me a few bones and pulled me into their circles. Sometimes, I'm learning, that's all I can expect.

∼

Uncle Joshua drops by my office on Tuesday morning. "How you doing, Kyle?"

"I'm good. The dinner was a success. Did you hear?"

"Yes. Now we won't have to cut our programs."

"I didn't see you there."

"They served alcohol. Aisha and I aren't comfortable with that."

I wonder why it didn't bother Faiqa or Dad. "Anyway," he continues, "I have some mail for you. The office sent it to me by mistake."

I glance at the address. Did I get the grant? I cross my fingers and rip open the envelope. "Yes!"

"What's up?"

"I've been working on a drug awareness program. I went through two or three programs before ninth grade, and I know what will work. So, I wrote the proposal and applied for a grant. I got it."

He smiles and shakes my hand. "That's great."

"I'm going to make a real difference here at Hope Center."

My uncle frowns. "I admire your initiative, and your program must be good because you got the funding, but you went about it the wrong way."

"I didn't do anything wrong."

"Organizations run on politics. New programs must be approved by the board of directors. Initiative and independence are great, but they're often discouraged in the workplace. Before you can go through with this, you will have to submit everything to the board."

161

"That's not right. I'm just trying to keep kids from screwing up their lives."

"You have to jump through the hoops. That's life." He sighs. "That's why Umar and I opened our own agency. Minimum oversight, maximum results."

"Do you want to do it again? I could work with you."

"I don't have the energy to start over. And that would take months to set up. You need to get moving on this, or you'll lose the funding. Prepare a package for the board. They meet next Tuesday. You have a week to get ready."

"Yeah."

He pats my shoulder. "For what it's worth, I'm very impressed. Send me a copy of your proposal. I'll help you refine the details. I know what the board is looking for."

"Sure, I'll send it." Like it's going to make a difference.

"I need to get back to work. Send me your document as soon as you can."

∽

When Faiqa walks in an hour later, I'm still sulking. "What's wrong?" she asks.

"I have a great idea for a drug awareness program. I wrote a proposal and received a grant, but I need to have it approved by the board. What do they know?"

"Tell me about your program."

I show her my proposal and explain how it will work, why it's better than many other programs, and why I'm so sure of it. "I know a thing or two about drugs."

"Can you send me a copy? I'd like to study it."

"Just don't go stealing my ideas."

∽

Uncle Joshua helped me revise my proposal. He says they'll accept it. I hope he's right.

Ripples

I wanted to go to their meeting, but Uncle Joshua said they'll ask me to come if they need my input. I sit at home and watch TV, trying to think about something else. I fall asleep in my chair.

~

I've just settled behind my desk when Warren walks in. "Kyle, I am very impressed with your work. I am pleased to inform you that the board has approved the program, and Hope Center is ready to assist you with both facilities and personnel."

Yes! "Thank you."

"I like the way you pulled all the elements together to create your program. Would you be interested in taking courses to help you develop your abilities?"

"Definitely."

"I'll let you know of upcoming seminars and workshops. Meanwhile, you need to keep taking those college classes." He smiles. "Keep up the good work."

I did it. I call Uncle Joshua. "Thanks."

"You have a solid program there. I think you'll do a lot of good."

I can't wait to tell Faiqa.

~

She walks in on Friday, smiling. "Congratulations. They like your program."

"How did you know?"

"Do you promise not to get mad?"

"Tell me."

"My father is on the board of directors. That's why I started volunteering here. He said they could use my help."

"So, you did it? It wasn't because of the quality of the program?"

"Of course, it was. I just put in a good word, that's all."

I look away. "I don't kiss up."

"You didn't. I saw a good program that might get bogged down in politics, and I helped it along a little. That's all."

"Thanks a lot. I guess you feel sorry for the crip."

"Don't say that, Kyle." She leans on my desk and looks into my eyes. "Listen to me. I started working here because of my father, but I kept coming because of you."

I want to tell her flattery won't get her anywhere, but it's been a long time since a woman said anything nice to me. "So, you think my program is good?"

"I think it's great. You'll help a lot of kids."

I want to help them stay out of wheelchairs.

Ripples

Jennifer: Part One

Michael left Chicago over a week ago. He's flying to the Middle East today—I wish I knew exactly where he's going. He said he would call before he shipped out. I wonder why I haven't heard from him.

∼

I woke up this morning feeling very satisfied with myself. I've finished my first week of classes, and everything is going smoothly. It's great to be productive again. I have classes four mornings and one evening a week, and I do my homework after Ahmed goes to sleep at night. When there's time, I drink coffee with Mom before class. I still miss my baby, but Mom was right. I love being back in school.

Nuruddin is asleep. I get up to start breakfast. I'm flipping pancakes when Mom calls.

"Are you busy, Jenny?" She's crying. "I'm coming over. I'll be there in a few minutes." She hangs up.

What was that about? I stare at the phone until the smell of burning pancakes brings me back to reality. The frantic beep of the smoke detector is followed by Ahmed's screams.

Nuruddin stumbles into the kitchen. "What happened?"

"I don't know." I drop the phone and the spatula and run to my crying baby.

By the time Mom arrives, I'm dressed, Ahmed is happy, and we're eating the burnt pancakes, smothered in syrup. She pounds at the door. "Jenny."

"I'll get it." Nuruddin is used to my mother's little crises, but, this time, I think it's serious.

She runs in shouting. "He's AWOL. Did you know that?"

"What are you talking about, Mom?"

"Someone from the army came to see us this morning. They say Michael deserted. They think we know where he is."

"Michael? He wouldn't do that. He's never run away from anything."

"That's what I told them. I don't know what could have happened."

"Have they found any signs of foul play?" my practical husband asks.

Mom sits down, her face in her hands. "I keep imagining him alone somewhere. He must be hurt."

I put my arms around her. "I'm sure he's okay." Though I'm not at all sure.

After she leaves, Nuruddin comforts me. "Don't worry. Trust in Allah."

"But bad things happen all the time. What if someone hurt Michael?" What if he's. . . I can't think about it.

"Trust in Allah that your brother is safe."

I wipe my eyes. "Do you mean that people who trust in Allah never have anything bad happen to them?"

He's quiet for a moment before shaking his head. "No. Allah allowed them to kill my brother."

We cry together for brothers lost. One forever. Where is Michael?

Ripples

Jennifer: Part Two

I'm so worried about my brother that I can barely concentrate. No one has heard from him for weeks. Mom and Peter flew to Brownsville yesterday to see what they can find.

This isn't like Michael. He's always so careful. Someone must have gotten to him. They say his car is missing. I keep imagining him lying somewhere, hurt and alone.

I try to stay focused on Ahmed. He's growing every day. His latest skill is climbing. I have to keep a close eye on him.

The baby is asleep, and Nuruddin and I have just gone to bed. He rolls onto his right side and begins snoring. I start a crossword puzzle. My nightly routine. I'm on my second clue when the phone rings.

"Jenny, we know where he is. He's okay." Mom sounds exhausted.

"Michael called?"

"We tracked down a friend of his from the mosque. He said Michael went to Mexico."

"Mexico?"

"Michael will call home soon. We'll come back early tomorrow. Do you have any idea why he would do this?"

"Yes, Mom, I do. We probably shouldn't discuss it on the phone. I'll talk to you tomorrow."

He's safe, and he won't have to fight. But Mexico? What will he do down there?

I interrupt Nuruddin's snoring. "Wake up. I need to tell you something."

"What's wrong?" he mutters.

"They found Michael. You'll never guess where he is."

~

I drive over to Mom's place right after breakfast. Jeremy is here, too. We throw out questions. "What did he say?" "Is he okay?" "When will he come back?"

"The man at the mosque said Michael left because he doesn't want to fight other Muslims. Where would he get an idea like that?"

Jeremy and I exchange glances. "I told him I wouldn't go," says Jeremy.

"And I said I was worried he might get killed. Nuruddin was trying to convince him, too."

"So, the three of you ganged up on him," says Peter, my stepdad. "The poor guy never had a chance."

"But Michael has very strong convictions," says Mom. "I can't see him changing his mind that easily. Going AWOL and disappearing into a strange country? That does not sound like your brother."

"It must have been bothering him. I know he doesn't want to fight any more than I do."

"No one wants to fight, Jeremy. It's what soldiers do. How will he survive down there in Mexico?"

As if on cue, the phone rings. Mom answers, gasps, and listens. After a minute, she hangs up.

"That was Michael. He couldn't talk long. I'm sure our phones are bugged. He's in a southern area of the country called Chiapas. He said he's staying at a mosque down there and told me not to worry."

"We know he's safe." Peter hugs Mom, who's crying again. "Is it possible he could walk into a mosque in a strange country and find someone to help him?"

Jeremy nods. "Yes, it's possible."

"Interesting," says Peter.

Together, we look for Chiapas on the map. "Here it is," says Peter. "Much further south than I had imagined. I wonder how he made it all that way."

∼

When Nuruddin comes home, I tell him about Michael.

"I knew your brother was too smart to allow himself to be used."

"But I don't know when I'll see him again."

"He's safe and living with Muslims. Don't worry."

"I miss him."

My husband pulls me close. "You'll always have me."

∼

Ripples

As we climb into bed, Nuruddin says, "I forgot to tell you. My father called today. They'll come at the end of next month."

"They're coming?"

"Isn't it great?"

I kept hoping it wouldn't happen. I'm still not ready.

"Baba said he wants to stay with your father. I asked him to stay here, but he knows we don't have much room." I've rarely seen Nuruddin this excited. "They can't wait to meet you."

Probably to see what's wrong with me. "What's your mother's name? You call her Mama, and Dad calls her Abdul-Qadir's wife. Can you believe it? We've been married for two years, and I don't even know her name."

"Nobody uses her name. She's always Mama. Her name is Fatima."

"That's pretty. Why doesn't anyone ever use it?"

"Because she's Mama."

"What about me? Will people forget my name, too?"

"No, I'm sure you'll remind them."

Before he goes to sleep, I ask Nuruddin, "Do you think they'll like me?"

"Of course, they will. Are you worried?"

"I'm not Pakistani. I'm not even a Muslim. Won't that bother them?"

He's quiet. I sit in our dimly lit room and wait for him to say something.

"Does it bother you?" I ask.

"I love you, Jenny," he says softly. "You're a good person."

"Would you love me more if I was a Muslim?"

"No, but I hope you'll think about it. It would be good for Ahmed."

"And if I never become a Muslim?"

"I will still love you."

"What about your parents?"

"My parents are very kind people. You are my wife and the mother of my son. They accept you. Stop worrying."

"Would they accept me more if I was a Muslim?"

"I love you. I know they'll love you, too." He kisses me. "Good night."

Three minutes later, he's snoring. I try to concentrate on my crossword puzzle, but my mind races. They'll hate me. I know it.

∼

Nuruddin's parents wouldn't be coming at all if it wasn't for Dad. It's his fault.

He finally settled that lawsuit from back when he was in prison. The out-of-court settlement wasn't as large as his lawyer wanted, but it was enough. Six figures. He gave each of us kids some money, paid off the house, and bought Aisha a new van. Then he told Abdul-Qadir to pack his suitcase. First, he's bringing Nuruddin's parents here. Next summer, he's sending them to Hajj.

They'll be here in twenty-five days. Every day, I get more nervous. I tried to talk to Dad about it last week. He laughed.

"You're worried about Abdul-Qadir? He is the most gentle, most accepting person I have ever met."

"But he might not like me."

"When I first met him, Jenny, I was barely a Muslim and a just a step past being messed up, but he took me into his home and gently taught me. And you are a wonderful young woman. I know he'll love you—almost as much as I do."

"But I'm not a Muslim, and I'm not ready to be a Muslim. What about that?"

He shook his head. "You don't know Abdul-Qadir."

He doesn't understand. And I can't go to Mom. She likes Nuruddin—who wouldn't? But, if I say anything, she'll tell me I shouldn't have married a Muslim boy whose parents live in a strange country on the other side of the world.

I'll try Aisha. I go over in the afternoon, and we have tea while little Maryam plays with Ahmed. She tries to treat him like one of her dolls. I watch her closely while telling Aisha about my worries.

"I understand," she says. "Do you know how afraid I was of meeting your Gramma?"

"Gramma? How could anyone be afraid of her?"

"I didn't know if she would accept me. Especially because I'm black. I didn't know how she would feel about that."

Ripples

I don't really think about people as being black, white, brown, or whatever. Nuruddin is dark, and so is our beautiful son. "But Gramma wasn't prejudiced."

"No, she wasn't. From the day we met, she always treated me well. Do you understand what I'm saying? It's perfectly natural to be afraid of meeting your husband's parents, but I know they'll love you."

I hug her. "You're a pretty cool step-mom."

She smiles. "I try."

Negotiating the Curves

Unless both sides win, no agreement can be permanent.

—Jimmy Carter

Isaiah: Part One

After I told Becky about my family, things started getting better. I hadn't realized how much my secrecy bothered her. I feel better, too, now that she knows. She wants to see pictures of them, but I didn't bring any when I left the house that night. I'll ask Uncle Brad.

Last night, I felt comfortable enough to talk with her about the two guys before me. "Did you love them?" I asked.

She touched my face. "I never loved anyone except you."

"Why did you do it then?"

"It was in high school. Everybody did it. The first one was at a party. I got drunk. I dated the other guy for a couple months before I realized he was a jerk. Don't worry about it, Baby."

"Do you ever think about them?"

"Why should I, when I have you?"

I didn't answer. She put her arms around me. I fell asleep listening to her heartbeat.

∼

I go to Darul Islaam every Friday. Today, after the prayer, Faruq says, "My family would like to invite your family for dinner."

"I don't know if Becky will come."

"Be at my apartment at six. You'll eat there with my sons and me. My oldest daughter will escort your wife to the women's dinner."

She'll love that. "I'll try to convince her."

"Remember, you're the head of the household."

Has anyone told Becky that?

∼

Her reaction is predictable. "What do you mean, I'll eat with the women?"

"Some Muslims think men and women should be separated."

"Where do Muslim babies come from?"

"Ask one of Faruq's wives. I'm sure she can tell you."

"'One' of his wives? How many does he have?"

"Two."

"Is that something all Muslim men have to do? Do you want a second wife now?"

"No, Becky, I think one wife is enough for me." More than enough, some days.

We have a long talk. Finally, she agrees. I'd like to say I asserted my authority, and she quietly submitted. The truth is, I promised we'll go to Minnesota next weekend,

∼

She wears a dress for the dinner, which is a nice change from her jeans. It's a little short for Faruq's family, but it's the best she can do.

We need to leave. I don't want to be late.

"Are you ready, Becky?"

"Just a minute. I need to put on my make-up."

"No, don't. Muslim women don't wear make-up outside their homes."

"How can they possibly go out without make-up?"

"Ask them."

"What are their names?"

"Faruq calls them Umm Muhammad and Umm Yahya. They're the mothers of his oldest sons, Muhammad and Yahya."

"But they're more than wives and mothers. What are their names?"

"You'll have to ask them."

"Don't you know anything?"

I bristle. "I've never met Faruq's wives, I don't know their names, and that's the way he prefers it."

"Okay. You have a strange friend."

I don't respond. I'm learning I don't always have to prove I'm right.

When we arrive at Faruq's apartment, a young woman greets us in the hallway. "You must be Becky," she says, hugging my wife. "Let's go."

Becky looks at me with a mixture of irritation and fear. She'll survive this. I knock.

Ripples

"Assalaamu alaikum," says Faruq. "We were just about to leave for the masjid."

I've tried hard, these last couple of weeks, to keep up my five daily prayers. I still miss some occasionally, but I'm improving. I stand shoulder to shoulder between Faruq and Muhammad.

As we walk back to the apartment, I'm struck by the aroma in the hallway. Faruq opens the door. On the floor is a large platter of rice and lamb.

"Come in. The food is ready."

We wash our hands and take our places around the platter. When I was eight, I tried eating with my hands. I got beaten for making a mess.

We eat and talk. Faruq has five sons—Muhammad, Bilal, and Ali in one family, Yahya and Suleiman in the other—and four daughters. All of the children are home schooled. His boys cite both Islamic history and scientific theory with ease. I wonder how Mom's home schooling efforts are going.

Our conversation meanders from Islamic ethics to weaknesses in the Muslim ummah. I tell them about my cousin Michael's defection to Mexico.

"Masha Allah. We need more Muslims like him. Right, boys?"

"Your cousin is very brave," says Yahya.

"When I'm drafted, I won't run away. I'll fight," twelve-year-old Bilal states proudly.

"Life isn't that easy," I say. "You might get killed."

"Then I will die for the sake of Allah."

"I don't know what I'll do if I'm drafted. I have a family to take care of." I couldn't abandon Becky, either by leaving or dying. She'd never forgive me.

"I want to be like Hamza. Tell us the story, Baba."

"All right, Ali." Faruq tells about the courage of Hamza with details and emotion. I listen, engrossed.

Faruq is the head of his household, but he doesn't act like a king the way my father does. He listens to his sons, and they're comfortable with him.

I've been here for three hours, lost in Faruq's stories, when I remember Becky. I wonder how she's managing. I wait to hear how the Conquest of Makkah turned out before interrupting.

"I need to go, Faruq. It's getting late."

"It is. Suleiman, go to Mama and ask for the brother's wife." While we wait, he takes me aside. "You need to teach her Islam. That would be the best thing to come out of this marriage."

"It's not easy."

"No, it's not. Would you believe that my first wife and I weren't Muslims when we married?"

"Seriously?" I can't imagine Faruq not being a Muslim.

"We were eighteen. By the time I turned twenty-five, I felt very restless. We fought often and nearly divorced. Then, one day, the World Trade Center towers were brought down, and Muslims were accused of doing it. When Muslims came on TV saying Islam was a religion of peace, I became curious. I went online and sought out Muslims in chat groups. My cyberspace friends persuaded me to read the Qur'an. I converted six months later. I immediately began teaching my wife about Islam. After two weeks, she made shahadah."

I don't like asking personal questions, but I've always wondered. "When did you marry again? And why?"

"I had been a Muslim for five years when a woman in our masjid lost her husband in a carjacking. She was alone with two young daughters. After praying about it, and consulting my wife, I asked the woman to marry me so I could take care of them."

"Do your wives live together?"

"No. Each has her own home. I stay here and visit each one." He smiles. "You're not thinking about taking a second wife, are you? I think you have your hands full."

She knocks. "Isaiah, are you there?"

"My boss. I'd better go."

"Your wife is not your boss. She is your responsibility. Guide her, and treat her well, and your family will be successful."

"Isaiah? Don't leave me waiting out here alone."

Yes, boss. "I'll try."

~

She starts up as soon as I step out of the apartment. "You wouldn't believe—"

Ripples

I raise my hand. "Please don't."

So she waits until we get in the car. "They're nice, but strange. They both cover their faces when they go out. Can you imagine? The one who calls herself Umm Muhammad was nice, but Umm Yahya kept preaching to me about Islam. I felt sorry for those girls, too. One of them is my age, but you wouldn't know it, because she keeps herself all covered. She said they're arranging for her to be married soon. She doesn't know the boy. She sounded happy about it, but I can't imagine why.

"I asked his wives what their names are. They wouldn't tell me. And I asked why Muslim women don't wear make-up. Umm Yahya said she keeps her beauty only for her husband. When I asked about two women being married to the same man, they laughed. Umm Muhammad told me she's happy to have a sister to share her life, and Umm Yahya talked about how grateful she was.

"The children seemed happy. The home was beautifully decorated. I enjoyed being with them, but I don't understand them."

"They probably don't understand you, either."

"Why not? I'm normal. They're the strange ones."

"Define normal."

"You know. Like everyone else."

"In those novels you study, is the main character usually like everyone else?"

She thinks a moment. "No, I guess not."

"Even your hero, Martin Luther, made a name for himself because he was different."

"He's not my hero. Though I do respect him for the way he challenged authority."

"He wasn't like everyone else. By the way, Muhammad also stood up for what was right, against tremendous odds."

"He did?"

"So, what do you think? If Faruq invites us again, will you go?"

"They were nice, and the food was delicious. I think I ate too much. But I missed you."

"I missed you, too."

Jamilah Kolocotronis

Isaiah: Part Two

The year is almost over. I wake up on a gray Saturday in late December and review my last twelve months. Fighting with my father. Becoming a Muslim. Marrying Becky—and nearly divorcing her. No wonder I'm tired.

I've made it through two more trips to Minnesota, not counting Thanksgiving dinner with Artie, Eileen, and about thirty relatives. There's one more challenge for the year. Christmas.

Of course, we're supposed to go to Minnesota for the big day. It doesn't matter how many times I explain to Becky that I'm a Muslim and don't celebrate Christmas. When I tell her to go alone, she ends up crying, and I end up apologizing. When I suggest we both stay in Chicago, she screams about how I never liked her family. Faruq keeps telling me I'm the head of the house, but he never tried living with Becky.

So, we're driving up to Minnesota for Christmas. I'll take my Qur'an and prayer rug and stay on the sidelines. Hopefully, they'll be so wrapped up in their own family traditions that they won't pay attention to me.

Our family celebrated Christmas, but we kept it simple. My father detested the commercialization of the holiday. Every day throughout December, we heard his lectures about Santa Claus, reindeer, and people who go into debt buying gifts. We would go to church on Christmas morning. In the afternoon, Uncle Brad and Aunt Beth would come for dinner. Last Christmas, they went on vacation, and it was only us. Mom and Dad didn't believe in buying tons of presents, either. A book or an educational game, or maybe a computer for the family. And clothes. Always clothes.

The Wagners, on the other hand, go crazy over holidays. They did on Thanksgiving, anyway. A huge inflatable turkey in the front yard. Autumn decorations all over the house. On the day after, Eileen dragged Becky out of the house at 3:00 AM to go shopping. I can only imagine what they'll do with Christmas.

We leave on the twenty-third. Becky insists we be there for all of the family traditions, which start tomorrow.

Ripples

I spot their house three blocks away. It's the brightest one in the area. I wonder how Artie can afford that kind of electric bill.

They have it all. A million lights, most of them blinking. Santa Claus and his reindeer. A twenty-foot inflatable snowman. Styrofoam candy canes. Electric candles in all the windows. And, way over in the corner of the yard, a crèche portraying Mary, Joseph, the Wise Men, and an assortment of animals huddled around a manger.

Becky claps her hands. "It's good to be home." She leaps out of the car and runs to the front door. The doorbell plays "Jingle Bells." They perform their Wagner greeting, which is hugging and kissing everyone in sight. I stand by the car until I think it's safe.

When I walk in, Artie puts a red and green plastic cup in my hand. "Merry Christmas, Isaiah. Have some eggnog."

I've never tasted eggnog. I sniff the concoction. "Is this spiked?"

"Absolutely. Drink up."

I put the cup on a table and carry the suitcases to our room. I'd like to stay in here with the luggage, but I need to use the bathroom. As soon as I walk out into the hall, Becky holds something over my head. "You have to kiss me, Baby. We're under the mistletoe."

I give her a quick kiss and head for the bathroom. When I come out, my father-in-law hands me the eggnog. "You forgot something."

"No, Artie, you did. I don't drink."

"Make an exception. It's Christmas. Time to celebrate."

"Excuse me. I need to pray." I slip by him, go back into the room, and lay out my prayer rug. It's hard to concentrate with the Christmas music playing in the living room. Before venturing back out into the fray, I read *Surah al Ikhlas*. "Say: He is Allah, the One and Only. Allah, the Eternal, Absolute; He begets not, nor is He begotten. And there is none like unto Him." That should help me get through these next few days.

I venture out, only to be attacked by Becky and the mistletoe again. That's not too bad, but then Brandy gets hold of it. "You have to kiss me, Isaiah."

"Sorry. I only kiss my wife." I dart away.

Finally, they turn off the music, and everyone goes to bed. I crawl under the covers, mumbling. "I'm glad that's over."

"I can't wait until tomorrow," my wife bubbles. "That's when the excitement really begins."

∼

I wake up before sunrise, make my prayers, and read the Qur'an. After thirty minutes, I feel peaceful and ready to handle anything.

Until Becky wakes up. "Good, you're ready."

"Ready for what?"

"The Wagner family Christmas traditions. Today's the most important day of the year. We have an early breakfast. Then the women bake Christmas cookies while the men decorate the tree. After lunch, we visit the nursing home. Then we come home and sing Christmas carols with our neighbors. Tonight, we'll go to my grandmother's house, where we'll exchange presents and have our big Christmas dinner. I can practically taste Grandma's ham."

How do I say this? "Um, Becky, I don't celebrate Christmas. And today is Friday. I need to go to the mosque."

"The mosque? On Christmas Eve?"

"It's not Christmas Eve for Muslims. It's just another Friday."

"But you're part of this family now. You need to practice our traditions."

Head of the household. "I'll go to your grandmother's house, and after the Friday prayer I'll go to the nursing home, but I will not decorate the tree or sing Christmas songs. I don't celebrate Christmas."

"How can you say that? You grew up in this country. You were a Christian."

"Even my father, the preacher, didn't believe in commercializing Christmas. It was a simple day of family and worship."

"That's tomorrow. We'll attend church, open our family presents, have a big dinner at home, and go to the movies."

She's not listening. "I'm a Muslim now. I need to go to the Friday prayer. And I do not celebrate Christmas."

"But, Baby, this is our first Christmas together."

How can somebody so intelligent be so thick-headed? "Let's eat breakfast. I'll explain it to your parents."

"No, Isaiah, don't say anything."

Ripples

"They have to know."

"You'll ruin the holidays." She grabs my arm. I pull loose and head for the kitchen.

They're eating breakfast. "Where's Becky?" says Eileen. "She knows how special today is."

"She'll be out soon."

"I'm looking forward to your help with the tree this year, Isaiah. Charlie's still a little too short to reach those higher branches, and I can't stretch like I used to."

"I can't help you, Artie. I don't celebrate Christmas."

"Oh, that's silly," says Eileen. "Everyone celebrates Christmas."

"Not Muslims. I can help you around the house, but I won't do the Christmas tree."

Artie pushes his plate away. "I don't know what's wrong with you. Since the day you met my daughter, you have turned this family upside down. I never thought my own son-in-law would disrespect me. And on the day before Christmas." He stomps out the back door.

Denny whispers. "You just spoiled our entire Christmas."

"All I said was. . ."

"Don't worry about it," says Eileen. "Artie will cool down. But, Isaiah, you must be joking. After all, you grew up Christian. Don't you miss the Christmas traditions?"

I spend the next hour explaining. Eileen agrees to let me do things my way. I'll carry boxes of decorations for Artie and clean up the kitchen while they bake. I'll go to the mosque and meet them at the nursing home. While they sing carols, I'll have the house to myself. And we'll all go see Grandma tonight.

Becky listens. I think she finally understands.

∽

I've made it through my first Christmas as a Muslim. I even managed to avoid Grandma's ham—she let me eat leftover chicken instead.

Yesterday, during the gift exchange, I accepted the presents Eileen bought for me and silently pledged to buy them each something for Eid.

Jamilah Kolocotronis

Isaiah: Part Three

We made it safely back from Minnesota. I drove sixty-five the entire way, watching other cars speed past. And Becky hasn't nagged me once since I made my stand.

We have one more week of winter break. It's nice to have time to relax together. I want to spend most of the week at home. She does coax me out for ice skating on a Wednesday afternoon. I make a fool of myself, slipping all over the ice, while she floats gracefully around the rink.

As we relax after dinner, she says, "That was nice. I love skating."

"My father doesn't believe in wasting time on amusement."

"No wonder you're so boring."

"What?"

"I'm teasing." She gives me a peck. "Where are you taking me on New Year's Eve?"

"Can't we stay home?"

"But everybody goes out to celebrate."

"My family never did."

"Your family never did many things. Where are you taking me?"

"What are we supposed to do if we go out?"

"Party. Eat, drink, and be merry."

"I don't drink. You know that."

"You can be the designated driver. You wouldn't begrudge me a little champagne."

Head of the household. "No, Becky. If I believe alcohol is bad for me, why would I want it for the woman I love?"

That keeps her quiet until morning. "So, how are we going to celebrate New Year's?"

"Why don't we curl up on the couch and...." I pull her close.

"We always do that. I want the night to be special."

"If I take you to a movie, will you be satisfied?"

"Not unless we have dinner out, too. And no fast food."

"We can't afford much more than that. Okay, dinner and a movie. Then we'll come home and celebrate."

We go to see a romantic comedy and wrap up the evening at a pizzeria. The best part of the evening is being with her.

A new year. A fresh start.

184

Ripples

Kyle: Part One

I woke up in my bed this morning, and I was smiling. I felt at peace for the first time since. . .well, since Dad took off on his middle-age crisis trip, I guess.

While I was getting dressed, I realized that I didn't dream about Amy last night. We always meet in my dreams, but I missed our rendezvous. I was struck by guilt for leaving her waiting. She must have wondered why I didn't come.

I will always love her. Nothing has changed. It was just one night.

∼

Faiqa shows up with a smile on her face. "How are you today, Kyle?"

"I'm good." I'm great, really, but I don't have the right to be this happy.

She picks up Amy's picture. "What made you fall in love with her?"

"I don't know. Maybe it was her smile. Or how she always made me feel better. She was very caring."

"I can tell." She puts the picture back in its place. "Are you ready to start planning for the program?"

"I've thought about it all morning." When I wasn't thinking of you.

"I made a list. Why don't you go over it and see if I missed anything?"

She sits close to me. I glance at her. She was the girl in my dreams last night.

Kyle: Part Two

I've signed up for four classes next semester. It will be hard to manage along with work, but I need to finish.

Faiqa still stuffs envelopes when the need arises. The rest of the time, she helps me develop my ideas. She's also working on a system to bring us into the twenty-first century so we can eliminate the envelopes.

We talk, laugh, and share ideas. I've always known nothing could develop between us—there are too many obstacles—but, one day, she asks me again. "Have you ever considered becoming a Muslim?"

I laugh. "Why would I want to do that?"

"I can't marry a man who isn't a Muslim."

I laugh harder. "Like you would really want to marry me."

"It's possible."

"You can't be serious. You're beautiful. You could have your pick of a thousand different guys. Why would you be interested in me?"

"You're not so bad looking yourself."

"From the waist up, maybe. But we don't want to talk about the rest of me."

She blushes. "No, we don't. I need to go. I'll see you on Friday."

∽

All Friday morning, she concentrates on her work, barely talking to me. Before leaving, though, she asks, "Would you consider studying Islam? For me? As a friend, I mean."

"Are you still carrying that book around?"

"Hmm. Let's see." She peeks in her bag. "Yes, here it is."

"Quite a coincidence."

"Will you read it?"

I shrug. She helped save my program, and her ideas are invaluable. The least I can do is read a book. "What do I have to lose?"

"Can you read it over the weekend and let me know what you think?"

"I don't have anything better planned."

"Enjoy your weekend," she says, walking out.

Ripples

I look at the cover and flip through the pages. A book about Islam. It won't change my mind, but it won't hurt.

~

I read the book. It was better than watching TV till I drop.

First, it talked about God. Big surprise there. I don't know what I believe. Is there a God? Isn't there? Does it matter?

There was a long section about Muhammad. I have no problem with him. I kind of wonder about all that talk of revelation, but, otherwise, he seems cool.

The next section dealt with what a Muslim should and shouldn't do. I knew most of that. Some of it makes sense to me, like not drinking, but some of it sounds too strict.

The last section was philosophical, comparing Islam with Western thought and tackling major issues. I carefully read the section on death. I know about predetermined lifespan and God's will, but I still don't understand why Amy and the baby died. And why I didn't die with them.

If I had any real guts, I think I would have killed myself a long time ago. I could stop hurting, and I would be with them. But I guess I'm too lazy. And there are still enough things I like about life. Pizza, kung fu movies, my car, my job. Faiqa.

On Tuesday, she asks if I read it.

"Yeah. It's okay, but I'm not sure if I believe in God. And it didn't tell me why Amy had to die."

"We each have a lifespan."

"I've heard the lifespan speech a hundred times. Tell me something new."

She keeps typing. After a couple minutes, she says, "We believe God controls the universe and everything in it. As Muslims, we recognize His wisdom. Being a Muslim means submitting to Allah and His will. That's the best answer I can give you."

"That's sounds more like a copout. I don't submit. No one tells me what to do."

"You used to play football. Did you listen to your coach?"

"Sure."

"Why?"

"Because he knew how to win. What does that have to do with anything?"

"Did the coach ever take someone out of the game?"

"All the time."

"Did he ever make a decision you didn't like?"

"Sometimes."

"But you followed him anyway because. . ."

"He knew more. But, if the coach took me out of the game, it was because I was having a lousy day, and the team could do better without me. Why would God take Amy? She was the best thing that ever happened to me."

"I don't know. Maybe we'll find out when we die."

"But you submit because you trust Allah."

"Yes, I do."

"It must be nice to feel so sure of something."

She nods. "It's very nice."

Ripples

Kyle: Part Three

Warren wants to start the program in January, when the kids are restless and all that Christmas charity disappears. We've decided to call it "Kids Who Care." After three months of preparation, we're almost ready.

We're targeting younger kids, ages eight to twelve. That's the time to get them. If you wait until they're teenagers, it's too late.

My program is different, because we don't spend all our time talking about drugs. Only twenty-five percent of our time is specifically geared toward that. The rest deals with behaviors. Addiction isn't about the drug. It's about the person doing the drug.

Dad's addictions started with his first cigarette when he was ten. He's back to smoking, too. There's no way Mom would let him smoke in the house, but his clothes reek. He knows it's not good for him. He says it helps him stay off the bottle. He's an addict.

I have little addictive behaviors. Nothing as serious as Dad's. Watching TV until I drop is one of them. And drinking coffee all day long. It makes me jittery, but I crave it.

Addiction starts with attitude. That's what the kids will work on. We'll spend three weeks out of every four promoting behaviors like honesty, responsibility, and selflessness. We won't lecture, either, or play cute little games. Every week, the kids will do things for others. Pick up litter at a city park. Encourage people to adopt pets from animal shelters. Read to people in nursing homes.

On the fourth Saturday, we'll have an assembly. We won't tell the kids about the different kinds of drugs. I was in a program like that, and it made me want to try the stuff. We'll talk to them about addictive behaviors—lying, stealing, self-centeredness—and do role plays. The high point will be the testimonials from teenagers and young adults who are willing to share their stories of a drunken dad or a drugged-out mom. The message is, addiction hurts.

Warren convinces me to tell my story first. Not my own drug and alcohol encounters. I'll tell them how it felt to have a dad too drunk to talk to me or help me with my homework. How he walked out on us because drinking was more important than we were. And I'll let them know how hard he's working to make it up.

We're hoping for a large turn-out. I've lined up community service projects for the first four months. Faiqa is in charge of recruiting volunteers. We're ready to go.

I need this program to succeed. I want to help the kids. And I have to be more than just an envelope-stuffing crip.

Ripples

Jennifer: Part One

My finals start next week, and I don't know how I'll get through them. Ahmed constantly demands my attention. Every time I pick up a textbook, he calls out or whines. If I don't respond, he crawls all over me or cries until I give him what he wants.

Nuruddin wants my attention, too. His parents are coming in less than three weeks. "We need to get ready."

"Can't it wait? I have to pass my exams."

"This is important, Jenny. I haven't seen my parents for four years."

"I know, but let me get through this first." I'm trying to be the obedient wife, but it's driving me crazy.

∼

Two more tests to go. I'm doing well. I just need to keep up my concentration.

On Wednesday afternoon, I come home, put Ahmed down for his nap, and sit on the couch to study. I'm thoroughly engrossed when there's a knock at the door. I keep reading.

"Jennifer, are you there?"

It's Aunt Kimberly. I drop my book and run to let her in.

"When did you get back?"

"This morning. Greece was wonderful. The food, the scenery. And the men. You need to go there someday."

"I want to hear all about it."

We're still talking when Nuruddin comes home. He walks in and says, "I had to skip lunch. I hope dinner is ready."

"Nuruddin, how are you?" Aunt Kimberly gives him one of her hugs.

He winces. "It's nice to see you. When will dinner be ready, Jenny?"

"I haven't started cooking. I didn't realize it was so late."

"I have an idea," says my aunt. "Why don't we all go out to eat? I know a wonderful Greek restaurant."

My husband frowns. "Thank you, but I had a long day at work, and I expect to come home to a hot meal."

"You had a long day? This is finals week, remember? I go to classes and take care of Ahmed. Why should I be your servant?"

"You're my wife. It's your duty to cook for me."

Aunt Kimberly grabs her purse—a wonderful handmade bag she bought in Kenya. "I just remembered. I'm meeting someone for dinner. I don't want to keep him waiting. Take care, Jennifer. I know you'll do well on those finals." She hugs me, whispering. "Don't let your husband push you around." She gives Ahmed a kiss and flies out the door.

I'm so angry I feel like hitting someone. "Do you see what you did? That was no way to treat my aunt. Get dinner yourself!" I stomp into the bedroom, slamming the door. Ahmed is screaming. Let his father take care of him.

Ripples

Jennifer: Part Two

We muddled through the night. Nuruddin took the baby to the restaurant on the corner, bringing home curry and rice in disposable containers. I ate after they were asleep. In the morning, we acted as if nothing had happened, but I'm scared. We fight too much, and it's always over the same thing.

Why doesn't he respect me? Was Mom right when she said I shouldn't marry a Muslim?

∼

I just finished my last final. It feels so good to get those exams out of the way. I'm exhausted. I get Ahmed from Mom's place, eat a little lunch, and lie down when he takes his nap.

I wake up to voices. Ahmed is screaming. That's nothing new. But I also hear Nuruddin.

"Shh, don't make too much noise. Let Mama sleep."

I lie in bed, still tired, and listen while Nuruddin changes the baby's diaper and plays with him. When my husband walks into the bedroom, I pretend to be asleep. He kisses me.

"Wake up, Jenny."

I slowly open my eyes and look around. Candles are burning on the dresser, and dinner is sitting on the tray beside me.

"Did you have a good sleep?"

"Yes, very good. What's all this?"

"Congratulations on finishing your finals. I love you."

We kiss. Suddenly, I notice how quiet it is. "Where's Ahmed?"

"That woman downstairs is watching him. Mrs. Porter. We're alone."

After I eat, he massages my shoulders. The tension escapes.

Just when I think I can't stand him anymore, he does something wonderful. I can't imagine my life without him.

∼

On New Year's Eve, Mrs. Porter watches Ahmed while we cuddle and talk about our dreams. He's working hard. I'll graduate soon. We'll move to a house. Our life will be perfect.

Ripples

Jennifer: Part Three

His parents are coming in ten days. I want to impress his mother with my culinary skills. I put Ahmed in his stroller and walk to the Pakistani grocery. I'll make biriyani for Nuruddin tonight.

By the time he comes home, the food is ready. "I smelled it all the way down the hall. I can't wait to eat."

During dinner, I watch for his reaction. He looks happy, but doesn't say anything. I have to ask. "What do you think? Is it as good as your mother's?"

He laughs. "Mama started cooking when she was six years old. By the time she married Baba, at sixteen, she made the best biriyani in the city. If cooking was an Olympic sport, she would have a gold medal."

"So it's not as good as hers, is it?"

"It's very good. I love it. But Mama is a champion cook."

I hadn't realized she was such a formidable opponent.

After dinner, Nuruddin offers to clean up and take care of Ahmed. I sit at the computer and work on a short story. It's coming along, but very slowly. I force myself to write a paragraph and stop to read it. I delete what I've written and start over.

I'm still typing when Nuruddin comes over and rubs my shoulders. "Ooh. That feels good."

"I can't wait to see Mama and Baba. You'll love them."

But how will they feel about me?

Meeting the Challenge

Twenty years from now, you will be more disappointed by the things you didn't do than by the ones you did do. So throw off the bowlines. Sail away from the safe harbor. Catch the trade winds in your sails. Explore. Dream. Discover.

—Mark Twain

Isaiah

We've fallen into a comfortable routine. Classes and work during the day. Studying and togetherness at night. And not so much fighting. She's learning to tolerate my idiosyncrasies, and I'm trying to be more attentive. There are times when I wonder how we've made it this far. The truth is, she completes me.

We're still working on the whole power thing. She's used to getting her way—Artie and Eileen never said no to her—and my father groomed me to be a leader. I hate him and the way he pushed me, but sometimes those old lessons rear their ugly heads.

Be the head of the household, Faruq says. My father is. I was afraid of him, but I can't say I ever really loved him. Faruq's approach is softer. I need to find my style. I did stand up for myself on that last trip to Minnesota, and it felt good.

∼

Today is Mom's birthday. We always did something special. Ruth and I are both gone now, and my father is probably too busy with his church to pay attention. I hope he's taking care of Mom.

I could call my Aunt Debbie and ask for their address and phone number. I know she'd give them to me. But, as much as I miss Mom, I still don't want to have anything to do with my father.

We're in different worlds now. They know nothing about my life. If I do ever see them again, will we be able to speak the same language?

Jamilah Kolocotronis

Kyle: Part One

We've advertised the program for the last two months. I delivered flyers to area schools, sent press releases to the Tribune and Sun-Times, and persuaded area businesses to contribute treats and refreshments for opening day. The mayor and city council members are coming to show their support. I want to make sure everyone pays attention.

Saturday is the big day. We're going all out—clowns, balloons, t-shirts, gift bags. We'll have to settle the kids down long enough for the politicians to speak. I'll finish the program with my own story, and we'll wrap up with a rally.

On the night before, I tell Dad what I plan to say.

"Do you really need to do that?" he says quietly.

"It's what I went through. Could you be there with me? I want them to see how you've turned your life around."

He rubs the back of his neck. "Saturdays are always busy. They may need me at the garage."

"Just for an hour, Dad. To make up for all those other times." I hate to pull the guilt trip, but I really need him there.

Tears run down his cheeks. He hugs me. "I'm sorry, Kyle. I want to make it up to you."

"I know, Dad. And I'm proud of you for trying so hard."

∼

They all come for my big day. Even Isaiah and that talkative wife of his.

Uncle Joshua greets me at the door. "Are you ready?" he grins. Why is he always so happy?

The kids are here. Hundreds of them. We may need more volunteers.

I wheel up to the stage—I made sure they put in the ramp—and take the microphone. "Are you ready?"

A few kids settle down.

"I said, 'Are you ready?'" A little more forcefully. Some kids are still talking.

"If you're ready, say yes."

Ripples

"Yes," they reply.

"You guys can do better than that. Say yes."

"Yes."

"C'mon, I can barely hear you. Say yes!"

"Yes!"

"That's more like it." I have them now. "My name is Kyle, and I'm glad you're here. We have treats and surprises for you, but, first up, we have some important people who want to greet you. Will you listen? Say yes."

"Yes!"

"That's the spirit. You're great kids. Now a few words from our mayor."

Thankfully, the politicians keep their speeches short and dynamic. I'm about to take the mike when a board member approaches. "I'd like to say something, Kyle," he whispers.

He takes a few minutes to repeat what has already been said. Who is this guy? He calls himself Gil. The kids are getting restless, and I'm afraid of losing the momentum.

Finally, he steps aside, and I go to the mike. "If you're ready to listen, say yes."

"Yes!"

We haven't lost them.

"I'm sure you noticed this chair I'm sitting in. I can't walk anymore because I did something stupid. I got drunk and climbed into a car with a drunk driver. Was that smart or stupid? Say stupid."

"Stupid!" they scream. Kids love that word.

"Real stupid. Sometimes even smart people do stupid things. Now, raise your hands if someone in your family drinks or uses drugs."

Way too many hands go up. And that's only the kids who feel comfortable enough to admit it.

"Remember what I said. Even smart people do stupid things. Can you say it?"

They try, but it's a little weak. We'll work on that later.

"I want to tell you about my dad. He's real smart, one of the smartest people I know, but, when I was your age, he was a drunk. He wasn't mean. He just didn't pay much attention to me. For a long time, the bottle was more important than his family.

"But, he beat his addiction, and I'm proud of him. I'm going to ask my dad to come up here, and I want you all to cheer for him. Can you do it? Ready, set, cheer!"

Dad stands off to the side, rubbing his neck. He doesn't like to be in the spotlight, especially when it comes to his addiction, but this is important to me, and he knows it. Mom knows it, too. She takes his hand and walks with him up to the mike.

The kids are still cheering. As their noise dies down, I yell, "Louder!"

After a minute, I hold up my hands, signaling them to settle down. The volunteers, led by Faiqa, help out on the floor.

"My dad hasn't had a drink for more than two years, and I think that's great. He is the best dad in the world." I didn't mean to say that. I choke back my emotions. "Are we ready to fight addiction? Say yes."

"Yes."

"Are we ready to help others? Say yes."

"Yes."

"Are we ready to care? I want a big yes."

"Yes!"

"You guys are great. I'll turn you over to your team leaders now, and next week we'll get down to business. Are we ready? Give me your loudest."

"Yes!"

The volunteers go into action, each with his or her own team of kids. Faiqa helped coordinate it all. I take a deep breath. Dad puts his hand on my shoulder. I look up.

"I'm proud of you, too," he says. I see a couple of tears. He never cries in public.

Gil comes up on my right. "Kyle. I've heard some great things about you from my daughter, Faiqa."

He's Faiqa's father? He doesn't have an accent. She said her father was Egyptian.

I study him. He's six foot, easily, and has a strong build. His short black beard is neatly trimmed. "Very impressive," he says. "This is an important day."

"Yes, sir, it is."

A reporter from Channel Three interrupts. "Are you ready for an interview, Kyle?"

"Sure. That would be great."

They start the camera and ask me about the program. I try to keep up the energy I had with the kids.

When I'm finished, a reporter from the Tribune comes over. "Tell me how you ended up in that wheelchair."

"Do you remember, a couple of years back, when five teenagers died after their car ran into a tree? There was one survivor. That's me."

He perks up and asks more questions, going back to my childhood. I tell him about my academic and football successes and my addictions to alcohol and pot. I also tried heroin twice, not long before the accident.

He asks what I remember about the accident. I describe speeding down the road, trying to see how fast Steve's new car would go. I remember becoming airborne, whooping it up. I don't remember the impact. The next thing I knew, I was waking up in the hospital, and Mom was telling me they were dead.

He urges me on, so I tell him about my four months in rehab and adjusting to life in the chair. I give him a couple funny stories. Like the time I got pulled over for speeding. I told the cop I couldn't step out of the car. He didn't believe me. I was afraid he might pull his gun, so I slowly reached up for my wheelchair. Then I asked him to step aside so I could open the door and set it up. He let me go with a warning.

I tell him about Amy, too—how much I miss her, and how it was my fault. I don't tell him I still feel guilty for being alive.

We talk for over an hour. He asks for my phone number. "I may have follow-up questions. If my editor agrees, I'd like to turn this into a week-long series. We'll send a photographer out to get pictures of you at work and home. Is that okay with you?"

"Sounds good."

"I'll talk to you later, Kyle. You have something special going on here. Keep it up."

He leaves, and I look around. I've been totally involved in the interview. Everyone is gone now, except for Matt, Mom, and Dad.

I go over and touch Dad's arm. "I know that was hard for you."

He nods. "Yeah. But I lived through it." He takes a deep breath. "All of Chicago knows I'm an alcoholic."

"All of Chicago knows you're a great dad."

He hugs me. I don't ever remember feeling this close to him.

Jamilah Kolocotronis

Kyle: Part Two

My story is plastered on the front page of the Sunday Tribune. "Survivor." There's a picture of me on stage with Dad. An insert promises installments throughout the week.

A survivor. Is that what I am?

On Monday morning, when the second installment comes out, five high schools call and ask me to talk to their students. By Friday, I'm booked at twenty-two schools. I'll be busy through March.

It's a great week. Until Friday afternoon, when Faiqa's father walks in.

"Hello, Mr. Hammadi."

"Hello, Kyle. You're doing a great job. I'm not here about the program, though."

What's up?

"I know you and my daughter have become good friends. I've told her to stop coming to your office. She will continue to assist with the program."

What? "Why?"

"We're Muslims. It's not allowed for a man and a woman to be friends. I grew up in this country, and I know what can come from such a friendship."

That's why he doesn't have an accent. "Look at me. I'm in a wheelchair. I won't do anything to your daughter." Not that I haven't thought of it.

"Even so, it's not a good idea. You're not a Muslim. You have a past." Great. I had to open my mouth to that reporter. "It's better to stop it now, before my daughter becomes too attached to you."

What am I, a lost puppy? "Would it make a difference if I were a Muslim?"

He pulls on his beard. "There are other considerations, Kyle. You know that."

"I know. But would it make a difference?"

He avoids looking at my chair, concentrating instead on the calendar hanging over my desk. "It might," he says finally. "Have you seriously thought of converting?"

"I've thought about it a little." For all of five seconds now.

Ripples

He stands and raps on my desk. "If you become a Muslim, you know how to reach me. Then we'll talk."

He walks out, and I sink into my chair. I have to see her. I didn't realize until a minute ago how important she is to me.

The only way I can see her again is if I'm willing to marry her. Am I? That's a stupid question. If she's willing to marry me, and if her father allows it, I will be very, very lucky.

I call Dr. Brooks' office to make an appointment. I never asked him about intimacy in my condition. It never seemed pertinent. Now I want to know if I could be a husband. Maybe even a father. A guy can dream.

Next, I go on the computer and order eighteen books about Islam. One way or another, I need to become a Muslim.

Jamilah Kolocotronis

Jennifer: Part One

Eight days before Nuruddin's parents arrive, I decide to test my cooking skills on the family. I'll invite Dad and Aisha, Mom and Peter, Jeremy and Raheema, and Umar and Safa. When I tell Nuruddin my plan he says, "They won't all fit in here."

"It's only eight people."

"You forgot the children."

He's right. I call Aisha and ask if I can make dinner at their house. "You don't have to worry about anything. I'll take care of the shopping, cooking, and cleaning."

"That sounds great, Jenny." She laughs. "You're welcome to do that every day."

Aisha hates to cook. I don't know why. I love it.

∼

In the morning, I buy my supplies. Ahmed cooperates. He doesn't fuss in the store, and he waits until we get home before pooping in his diaper. This is going well.

After Ahmed wakes up from his nap, I go to Dad and Aisha's house while everyone is at work and school. I put Ahmed in the playpen and start chopping the onions. Five minutes later, he's screaming. I play with him, check his diaper, and put him back. He cries again. I feel his forehead. He may be warm. I run my finger over his gums. He has teeth coming in. I give him medicine and hand him a teething ring. Two minutes later, he's calling for me.

I strap him to me and continue cutting the onions. He's happier now, but he wants to play with my hair, my eyes, my mouth. He grabs at my arm. He begs me to let him play on the floor, but I'm afraid he'll put something in his mouth. He wiggles and fusses, finally erupting into another scream. By the time the onions are diced, I'm crying.

I walk and sing to him. His eyes close. I carefully place him in the playpen and tiptoe away.

He sleeps long enough for me to get the biriyani started. But, just as I'm preparing the dough for the nan, a Pakistani bread, he starts up again. He stops the second I pick him up. Maybe I have spoiled him.

Ripples

When Aisha comes home, the biriyani is halfway done, but I haven't started anything else. I'm sitting on the couch, feeding Ahmed a banana and crying.

She looks at the mess I left in the kitchen. "Give me that precious boy."

Aisha spoils Ahmed while I work up a sweat in the kitchen. Freedom. I love my sweet baby, but it's great to have a few minutes on my own.

By the time Dad comes, I'm really cooking. The chicken yakhni, or soup, is simmering, and I'm working on the pokara, an appetizer made with potatoes. He stands in the doorway and takes a deep breath. "Something smells good in here."

When Mom and Peter walk in, everything is perfect. The food is almost ready, and the kitchen is spotless. Mom squeezes my shoulder. "Do you need any help, Jenny?"

"No, I have it under control."

She looks around. "Great job."

Just what I needed to hear.

Safa walks in. "Jennifer, the house smells wonderful. I can't wait to taste your cooking."

Jeremy and Raheema come next. "Listen to this," says Raheema. She looks at Nadia. "What's your name?"

"Nadia," my niece says carefully.

"How old are you?"

"I'm two."

"And who is the prettiest girl in Chicago?" my brother interrupts.

"I am, Baba."

Raheema looks at him. "When did you teach her that?"

Jeremy laughs and picks up his daughter. "She is the prettiest girl in the whole entire world." He plants raspberries on her tummy while she giggles.

It's funny to see Jeremy acting so silly. Kids do that to you.

Nuruddin comes last. I don't hear him. He grabs me from behind and kisses my neck.

"How's my Pakistani cook?"

I'm in the middle of preparing the gulab jaman, a dessert. I pull away.

207

"It smells just like my mother's cooking."

"Really?" I turn around.

"Yes." He kisses me. I hope he's right.

He helps me set the table, and they all come in to eat. I glance around nervously, waiting for their reactions.

Peter is first. "This is great, Jennifer. You are quite the cook."

The rest follow. Wonderful. Delicious. The best I've ever tasted. Even Safa, the master cook, says she loves it. I soak up the compliments before taking a bite. Not bad.

Nuruddin reaches under the table, squeezes my knee, and whispers, "They will love you."

Ripples

Jennifer: Part Two

Their plane lands in two hours. I finally got Ahmed to go down for a nap so I could shower. Nuruddin bought me a new shalwar khamis for the occasion—a long lavender and white tunic with loose-fitting pants. I put my hair up in a bun and take a few minutes to make sure everything in the apartment is perfect. Ahmed will wake up soon. I should have just enough time to feed him before going to the airport.

~

"They're here!" Nuruddin shouts as their plane taxis into the gate. His voice startles Ahmed, who fusses.
"It's okay, honey." I bounce as I walk with him. He begs to go down, but who knows what he could find on that floor? "Please, Ahmed, settle down."
I rummage through the diaper bag. I try a rattle. He throws it on the floor. Then a cookie. He throws that, too. I give up and pull out his pacifier. He's too old for it, but he's quiet. I breathe deeply and glance up. They're here.
They're so small. The way Nuruddin and my father talk about them, they've always seemed larger than life. But Abdul-Qadir is just a thin, little, old man. And Fatima—Mama—only comes up to my shoulder. She's dressed completely in black.
Nuruddin smiles and laughs. He hugs and kisses them. Mama cries and holds on to him. I don't know what to do. I watch.
Finally, Nuruddin turns to me. "Mama, Baba, this is Jennifer."
Mama grabs me so hard I nearly fall over. She hugs me and lifts up her veil to kiss me, her saliva wet on my cheek. I don't dare wipe it off, but it's kind of gross. Then Abdul-Qadir—I have to remember to call him Baba—grabs me and gives me a big hug. He's strong for an old man.
Mama smiles with her eyes and touches my face. "Pretty," she says. I know she doesn't speak much English. I'm glad she chose that word.
Abdul-Qadir—Baba—nods and grabs Nuruddin again. Mama joins in. It takes several minutes for them to let go so we can get their luggage.

Ahmed cries again in the car. I try the pacifier. He throws it down. He wants to be nursed, but he has to stay in the car seat. Mama stares at me. Nuruddin says something in Urdu. She shakes her head.

We pull up to Dad's house. My father comes running out to the car. He opens the door and practically yanks Baba out. "Assalaamu alaikum, Abdul-Qadir," he says, smothering him with a hug. Abdul-Qadir looks so fragile. I hope he doesn't break.

Nuruddin helps his mother out of the car and walks with her into the house. Dad walks with Abdul-Qadir. I stand alone on the sidewalk, holding my crying baby. "Hey, remember me?" I want to say. I walk behind them, unnoticed.

Ismail and Mahmoud are here, too, with their families. Mahmoud's wife, Haleema, hugs Mama and talks with her in Urdu. Mama smiles and speaks in animated tones. A few times I hear my name. What are they saying?

All evening, I take care of Ahmed, invisible to everyone except my son. I'm trying to stay calm, but it's not easy.

I wait until we're on our way home. "I'm glad everyone had such a nice time," I say in the most sarcastic tone I can muster.

"*Alhamdulillah*, it was great. I didn't realize how much I missed them."

"Did you miss me?"

"Miss you?" He keeps his eyes on the road. "You're here."

"I'm glad you noticed."

He looks over while we wait at a red light. "What are you talking about?"

"You didn't talk to me all night. No one did. Half of the time you were all speaking in Urdu, even Dad, and I didn't know what anyone was saying. I tried so hard, and no one even looked at me." My tears distort the passing street lights.

"I haven't seen them for four years!" he shouts. "What did you want me to do? They're my parents."

"I'm your wife."

"I see you every day."

"Are you tired of me? Is that what you're trying to say?"

He goes silent. I hate when he does that. "Answer me. Don't you love me anymore?" I cry. He ignores me.

Ripples

He pulls up to our building. I get our sleeping baby from the back seat and start to say something. He gives me one of those looks. He hates when I complain in public. I hold it until we walk into the apartment.

"Do they have a Pakistani girl picked out for you? Would you rather have someone who can speak your language and cook like Mama and, and...?" Ahmed's screaming interrupts my rant. I go into the bedroom to nurse him back to sleep.

Nuruddin doesn't come. Thirty minutes later, I find him asleep on the couch. Good. I hope he wakes up with a backache.

∼

Ahmed's fussing wakes me. The sun has risen. Nuruddin missed his prayers. If he had a Pakistani wife, she would pray with him. Is that why he doesn't love me?

I sit in the easy chair and feed Ahmed. While he nurses, I study my husband. His thick, black hair. His strong arms. His cute little mouth. When we met, I thought he was the best looking guy I had ever seen. I couldn't wait to marry him. Most of the time, he treats me well. So, why doesn't he love me anymore?

I sigh and look down at my baby. He has his father's hair, his father's mouth, his father's dark eyes. He'll grow up to be very handsome. And, one day, a woman will come along and try to take my son from me, but I won't let her. I kiss his forehead and breathe in his sweet baby smell. Ahmed is mine, and he always will be.

Is that how Mama feels about Nuruddin? She has so many other children to love. My parents have other children, too, but I always know how much they love me.

Maybe I was a little unfair. He hasn't seen them for a long time. They are his parents. He used to be their baby.

"Nuruddin. Nuruddin," I say softly. "You need to pray."

He opens his eyes, grunts, and stumbles to the bathroom.

Ten minutes later, he sits on the arm of the chair. "How's our Ahmed this morning?" The baby stops nursing and reaches for him.

I look up. "I'm sorry."

He strokes my head. "I know, Jenny."

After breakfast, we drive over to Dad's house. Baba and Mama are napping in the family room. Dad and Aisha fixed it up for them so they wouldn't have to climb the stairs.

Nuruddin helps Dad with the yard work. Dad's arm never did heal properly after that fight in prison. He says it bothers him more now because he's old. I don't want Dad to get old.

Aisha and Maryam play with Ahmed while I work in the kitchen. I bought everything on Thursday and stored it in their house. If I time it right, I should have a nice Pakistani meal on the table by the time Baba and Mama wake up.

I know the recipes by heart now. I dice the onions, peel the garlic, mix the spices, and chop up the chicken, losing myself in the rhythm of my work. While I stuff the samosas, I daydream about how pleased they will be. They'll have to love me.

"No." I jump at the interruption. Mama is standing in the kitchen door, watching me. "No," she says again, walking over and taking the dough from me.

I'm too surprised to protest. I watch as she deftly shapes the dough, stuffs it, and places the samosa quickly and expertly into the heated oil. She takes more dough.

"Look," she says. She shapes the dough slowly, making sure I follow her. After depositing the second samosa, she turns to me and says, "You."

I try to duplicate her movements. She stops me and smoothes the dough before placing the samosa into the pan. Then she motions for me to continue while she helps me stuff and fry.

We're working side by side in front of the stove when Nuruddin walks through the back door. He puts his arms around both of us and kisses us each on the cheek. First, his mother, then me. She still gets top billing. I'll have to live with that.

Taking Chances

*Living at risk is jumping off the cliff
and building your wings on the way down.*

—Ray Bradbury

Isaiah: Part One

A year ago today, I tried to kill my father, and he pronounced me dead.
All day, I feel restless, bothered. I pray and read the Qur'an, but the feeling won't go away. I grab my car keys. "I won't be gone long."
Becky looks up from her book. "Where are you going?"
I shut the door and climb into my car. After an hour by the lake, I'm ready to go back.
She closes her book. "What's wrong, Baby?"
"Nothing." I stretch out on the couch, my head in her lap, and close my eyes.
She leaves me alone. We're learning.
It's February. Spring break is a month away. I need to do this. I sit up. "I'm ready to talk now."
She puts her book down. "What is it?"
"You know about the fight with my father. It was a year ago tonight. And I need to see them. Not my father—I don't care if I never see him again—but I miss my mother— and my brothers and sisters." Except for Jacob, the little weasel. Half of my beatings were because he'd ratted on me. "I know you wanted to head north for spring break, but I need to go to Arkansas."
"That's what's bothering you? Let's go. I can't wait to meet them."
She may change her mind once we get there.

~

They live in Pine Creek, Arkansas, about twenty miles north of Little Rock. There can't be more than five thousand people in that town. I wonder how Becky will manage without a shopping mall.
Mom used to take us down there every summer. We stayed on my aunt's farm. They had chickens, goats, and a few dairy cows. Uncle Ken grew corn. Aunt Debbie grew almost everything else. Tomatoes, cucumbers, lettuce, you name it. We'd have a feast all summer long. A couple of years ago, they sold the farm and moved into town. Uncle Ken opened a store. Aunt Debbie is a substitute teacher at the high school.

We leave in two weeks. I'm more anxious every day—struggling to concentrate on my studies and snapping at Becky.

She understands. "I'm sure they miss you just as much as you miss them."

I don't know about that.

Ripples

Isaiah: Part Two

On Saturday morning, we eat a quick breakfast and hit the road. I thought we would drive non-stop, but Becky wants to stop in St. Louis. "I've only been here once, when I was a little girl."
"We'll stop for lunch. But no shopping."
"Shouldn't you take presents for your family?"
"I don't know if they'll even talk to me."
"What about your Aunt Debbie? What does she like?"
"She always enjoyed taking care of her chickens and working out in her garden."
"We're not taking a chicken. What's her favorite color?"
"How am I supposed to know?"

She pats my cheek. "You're impossible, Baby. Okay, I'll wait until we get down there. Once I meet her, I'll know what to get."

It's getting dark when we see the sign for Springfield. We could drive straight through the night, but there's no rush. We check into a nice motel and relax. It's good to be somewhere besides Chicago or Minnesota for a change.

We take our time in the morning. I get up early to pray and go to the lobby for the motel's continental breakfast. Becky sleeps late. I bring her breakfast in bed. It's after eleven when we take off.

I first noticed it south of St. Louis. Now, as we drive into Arkansas, the view takes me away. I'd forgotten how beautiful it is down here. More trees than I've ever seen. The road winds and curves through the hills. The sky is clear, and the world is peaceful. Becky scoots closer to me as I navigate the winding two-lane highway.

∼

We pull up to Aunt Debbie's house at around one. I run up to the front door and ring the bell. No answer. Where could she be?

It's Sunday, isn't it? They're at church. They'll be back soon. We sit in the car and wait.

I remember Sundays. Mom made us take baths the night before. After breakfast, we put on our best clothes. Dad left first to prepare for the service. Mom put us all in her van, reminding us to be on our best

217

behavior. We had Sunday school before going upstairs for the service. Afterward, Mom and Dad stood together, greeting the people. We were always the last to leave. When we finally got home, we ate roast beef and mashed potatoes. In the afternoon, we took naps, did our homework, and got ready for another week of school.

We've been here for about twenty minutes when Uncle Ken pulls his truck into the driveway. My aunt climbs out of the black pick-up and peers at my car.

I climb out and call. "Hi, Aunt Debbie."

"Isaiah?" She comes running. "It is so good to see you."

We hug. It's been a long time.

"Look at you. You've grown." Another hug. "You don't know how much I've worried over you."

For another minute, it's just Aunt Debbie and me. My second mother. She and Mom don't look much alike—Aunt Debbie is more on the plump side, and her hair is a lighter brown—but they both have good hearts.

She steps back and laughs. "Look at the two of us. Come inside. I've got Sunday dinner waiting. Do you still like chicken and dumplings?"

"I do when you make them. Um, Aunt Debbie, there's someone I'd like you to meet." I open the passenger door. "This is my wife, Becky."

"Your wife? You're married?" She grabs Becky's arm and pulls her out of the car, hugging her tightly. "What's your name, sweetie?"

"I just told you. This is Becky."

"You did tell me, didn't you? What a surprise." Aunt Debbie laughs again. "Welcome to my home, Becky."

Uncle Ken ambles toward us. "Did I hear right? You're married? Do your parents know about this?"

"Not yet. I brought Becky here to meet them."

He slaps me on the back, same as always. "It's good to see you, Isaiah. Welcome to the family, Becky." Another hug.

"You must be hungry," says Aunt Debbie. "Let's eat."

She leads us to the kitchen. It looks exactly like the one on the farm. Red gingham table cloth, fruit plaques on the wall, her big apple cookie jar sitting on the counter. I bet it's full of homemade cookies. Just to be sure, I peek.

Aunt Becky slaps my hand. "No cookies before dinner."

Ripples

She puts two more plates on the table and tells Uncle Ken to bring more chairs. "Pull up a seat. I hope you're hungry."

Becky quietly looks around. This isn't Minnesota.

It's been a while since breakfast. I reach for the salad. Uncle Ken coughs. Aunt Debbie says, "Isaiah, we need to say grace first."

"Of course." I pull my hand back.

"Would you please say the grace for us?"

I wish she hadn't asked. I pause. "We eat this food in the name of God, the Most Gracious, the Most Merciful. Amen."

"That's an interesting prayer," says my aunt, passing the homemade salad dressing. "I've never heard it before."

"I learned it recently."

"Are you still in the same church, or have you gone somewhere else since your folks left?"

I'll have to tell them eventually. After lunch, I need to find a corner to say my prayers. "I've gone somewhere else."

"Is it one of those big churches, with the pipe organ blaring? I don't think I could stand all that noise."

"I don't go to church, Aunt Debbie. I go to the mosque."

She drops her fork. "Tell me you didn't. That is just what your parents were afraid of. I told my sister you were smarter than that."

"I've been a Muslim for nearly a year now."

"What about you, Becky? Are you a Muslim, too?"

"No, I'm Lutheran."

"I hope you bring up your children in the church. Make sure you see to that. Isaiah, how could you turn your back on your Lord and Savior?"

I'm trying to decide on an answer when Uncle Ken speaks up. "I won't have any dissension at my dinner table, especially not on Sunday. It's not good for a person's digestion. How is the weather up in Chicago? Have you all had much snow this year?"

By the time dinner is finished, we have thoroughly exhausted the subject of weather. Aunt Debbie brings a pineapple upside down cake to the table and updates me on my cousins.

"Jack is nearly done with medical school. He hopes to get his internship in Little Rock. And Willy," she shakes her head. "Well, Willy is still Willy. It does look like he'll make it through high school. He plans

219

to go to the technical college in the fall. Says he wants to be an auto mechanic." She sighs.

"It's good, honest work," says Uncle Ken. "How are your studies, Isaiah?"

"They're great. I've always found history to be fascinating. Don't worry. I'm keeping my grades up."

"That's fine, but why didn't you go to the Bible college like your father wanted?"

"I want to learn more."

"It seems to me that learning the Bible would be enough for anyone."

Faruq says the same thing about the Qur'an. I grab my wife's hand. "If I hadn't gone to Loyola, I wouldn't have met Becky."

"So you say. We're finished eating now, so would you mind explaining what's going on? I could hardly believe what your father told us about your rebellion, but I never should have doubted him. Chris Adams always speaks the truth."

He's right about that. My father couldn't tell a lie if you paid him. "There are two sides to every story. Did he tell you what happened that night?"

"Your mother told us you were arguing with your father because you didn't like his rules. When he refused to budge, you packed your suitcase and walked out. I couldn't understand why you would leave. You've always been such a good boy."

Mom, on the other hand, will lie to protect Dad. I won't expose her. "There was a little more to it."

"Your father is a man of God, and he always did his best by you. If you didn't like his rules, that was no cause to run away like you did. You broke your mother's heart."

"Is she okay?"

"She's fine," says Aunt Debbie, "But I see a sadness in her. I hope you came here to repent and ask for your father's forgiveness."

Becky and I exchange looks. I hope she has the good sense to stay quiet. I change the subject. "Where is Willy? I thought he'd be here."

"He left early this morning to work on a car at a friend's house," says Aunt Debbie. "I thought I would see him at church. He should be along soon."

Ripples

"You didn't answer me," says Uncle Ken. "Why did you run away?"

"You can tell them," my wife volunteers. "They're your family."

"What is it you need to tell us?"

I hesitate. "There are things about my father you don't know."

"I admire your father. He has dedicated his entire life to serving the Lord. You're lucky to be his son."

It spills out. "I'm lucky? Are you serious? Do you know what he did to me?"

I guess I was shouting. Uncle Ken stares at me. Aunt Debbie's mouth drops open.

I lower my voice. "He beat me. Did you know that?"

Uncle Ken shakes his head. "No, Isaiah, your father never beat you. He corrected you, that's all. He did it because he loves you."

"I had bruises. I still have scars from my worst beatings. Including the one he gave me that night."

"Do you mean the night you ran away?" Aunt Debbie whispers.

"I mean the night I tried to kill him. I would have, too, if Mom hadn't stopped me." The words tumble out. "It wasn't just an argument. He beat me for reading the Qur'an. I fought back. I couldn't take it anymore."

They're staring. Uncle Ken keeps shaking his head.

"Do you remember the summers I spent at your place? Didn't you ever wonder why I always wore a t-shirt, even when we went swimming? I had to hide the bruises."

"No," says Uncle Ken. "Chris Adams is a good man. If he hit you, he had his reasons. It couldn't have been as bad as you say."

"He had a reason. It's in the Bible. The Book of Proverbs."

"That's right. Your father is a man of God. He hit you to keep you on the straight path."

"Did you ever beat your sons, Uncle Ken?"

Aunt Debbie answers. "We talked about it when Jack was little, but neither one of us could bring ourselves to whip him. Not even when he brought those frogs into the house."

"And Jack is in medical school. Would beating him have made him more successful?"

"No," says Uncle Ken, "But I probably should have hit Willy. That boy has caused us nothing but trouble."

221

"But he's happy, and he loves you. Look at me, Uncle Ken. I haven't seen my mother in over a year, and I tried to kill my father. Does that sound like a happy family?"

"If you respected your father and did what he said, I expect that your life would be a whole lot easier."

"I give up." I walk away, the screen door slamming behind me.

Becky comes out a minute later and massages my shoulders. "Do you want to go back to Chicago?"

Yes. They'll never understand. "No, I need to do this."

Ripples

Melinda

Our phone rings while I'm cleaning up from Sunday dinner. I wipe my hands. "Hello?"

"Melinda, Isaiah just showed up on our doorstep. He wants to see you."

"Isaiah is here? When did he come?"

"He was waiting here when we came back from church. Are you free?"

Chris is taking a nap. He'll sleep for another hour or two. "I'll be right there."

I wish Ruth were here, but she and Andrew drove into Little Rock. I find Jacob reading in the living room. "I need you to finish the kitchen for me. I'll be back."

"Where are you going?"

"If your father wakes up, tell him I went to see your Aunt Debbie. I won't be long."

I grab my keys and rush out the door.

Oh, Isaiah, I've missed you. I hope there won't be trouble.

Jamilah Kolocotronis

Isaiah: Part Three

A familiar car pulls up. Before she can open the door, I run to hug her.

"Isaiah," she says. "I've missed you."

I remember her scent and the way she held me when I was upset. "I love you, Mom."

She hugs me tight. "Debbie called and told me you were here. Let's go inside. We can talk."

"Does he know?"

"No."

My mother and I walk onto the porch. Becky stands. I take her hand. "Mom, this is my wife, Becky."

"Oh." I guess Aunt Debbie didn't tell her about that. "It's nice to meet you," she says quietly, taking Becky's hand.

Aunt Debbie is waiting for us at the kitchen table. "I don't understand everything you've said, but you don't need to run away. We're your family, and we'll always stand by you."

I don't think Uncle Ken will. "Thanks for calling Mom." I touch my mother's hand. "I had to come see you."

"It's been too long." She wipes her eyes.

"How is everyone? Are you okay?"

She tells me my brothers and sisters are doing well. "Ruth and Andrew are in town. She's expecting a baby any day now."

"That's great. I can't wait to see her."

I fill Mom in on my life—going to school, meeting and marrying Becky. Only the good. We can forget the bad.

Mom asks Becky a few questions about her family and her studies. Becky speaks softly, giving one word answers. She wasn't prepared for the reality of my family.

After an hour, Mom says, "I need to go."

"He doesn't know where you are, does he?"

"He knows I'm at my sister's house. I need to get back. I'll try to come tomorrow so we can talk more."

Another hug, and she goes back to him.

I turn to Aunt Debbie. "We'd better go find a motel. I'll see you tomorrow."

"You're not staying in any motel. We have plenty of room."

"How will Uncle Ken feel about that?"

"We both respect your father, Isaiah, and we don't like to hear you say such hurtful things about him, but you're my sister's boy. I would never turn you away. Go get your things."

She leads us upstairs to Jack's room. It looks exactly as I remembered. Jack and I used to stay up late at night, exchanging ghost stories. I stretch out on the bottom bunk and stare at his posters—the same ones he put up in his room at the farmhouse ten years ago. His favorite supermodel. The Tennessee Titans. A few inspirational quotes to placate his parents. Becky briefly inspects the room before snuggling next to me.

~

In the morning, Becky says she wants to go shopping. Aunt Becky gives us directions to an outlet mall outside of Little Rock. I spend the day following my wife, reminding her not to spend too much.

"Your family is a little strange," she says on the way back. "They're nice, but they're so religious."

"That's how I grew up."

"Everybody talks about how good your father is. Do you think you could be wrong about him?"

"You've seen the scars."

"But I don't understand how a man who beats his child could be so well-loved and respected."

"Dad has two faces. To outsiders, he's pious and soft-spoken. At home, he was a tyrant."

"And that doesn't bother your mother?"

"If it does, she would never say it."

"Why haven't you gone to see them yet?"

"We'll go to the house tomorrow. I want you to meet my brothers and sisters, especially Ruth, but I don't want to see my father."

"You make everything so complicated. You're talking about your family."

"You see how different they are." I laugh. "Can you imagine Artie and Eileen coming down here?"

"That would be interesting."

It's nearly dark when we pull up to my aunt's house. Becky carries in the new dress she bought.

Dinner is on the table. "Isaiah, Becky, come in here, and eat my fried chicken."

Nobody fries chicken like Aunt Debbie. We wash our hands and dig in.

We're still eating when Mom comes. Uncle Ken brings in another chair.

"I couldn't come earlier. Your father stays home on Mondays, you know. He has a meeting over at the church tonight. I won't be able to stay long."

"I don't like it," says Uncle Ken. "You shouldn't sneak around behind your husband's back. I have half a mind to tell him what's going on."

"Please don't. I know you mean well, but there are some things you don't understand."

"I have been married to Debbie for over thirty years. Don't tell me I don't know what goes on in this family."

"You would be surprised. Both of you. Chris is a very private person."

"So, it's true what the boy is saying? His father beat him?"

"I never thought of it as beating. Chris wanted the children to behave, and I certainly agreed with that. Looking back, I admit that sometimes he took it too far. Especially with Isaiah. You always were such a handful."

"You know why I fought him that night, Mom, don't you?"

"What you did was wrong, but I've thought it over, and I suppose I understand what you've been through."

"What about Benjamin? Is he getting hit now that I'm gone?"

"Sometimes your father needs to punish him. I keep an eye on things to make sure it doesn't get out of hand."

Aunt Debbie reaches over and touches Mom's hand. "He hasn't hit you, has he, Melinda?"

"No, of course not. Chris is a good person. It's just that he worries about the children. He wants to make sure they grow up to be proper Christians."

Ripples

Uncle Ken looks at me. "Don't you have something to tell your mother?"

The doorbell rings. Uncle Ken gets it. I hear my father's voice, friendly at first, then low and threatening. He pushes past Uncle Ken and storms into the kitchen.

He stops. We stare. His face turns red. He clenches his fists. His classic warm-up.

"Melinda," he says, "You left the children by themselves."

"Ruth and Andrew are there."

"You need to go home."

Mom meets his glare. "I'll go home soon, but I want to see my son."

"Isaiah is dead. The sooner you learn to accept that, the easier it will be on all of us."

"I won't turn my back on him."

My father's gaze is hard. "You need to leave us alone," he says too quietly. "Don't cause any more trouble for this family."

I'm ready for another showdown, and so is he. But I have my wife and my mother, one on each side, gently restraining me. He has his pride. "We must keep up appearances." I don't know how often I've heard that.

"Don't worry, Chris." Mom soothes him. "I'll go home soon."

"Make sure you do." He rushes out, slamming the door behind him.

"He came to borrow my drill for repairs over at the church," says Uncle Ken. "He saw your car and asked what you were doing here."

"Don't worry about it," says Mom. She squeezes my hand. "You know he loves you."

"Are you sure about that?"

"He's hurt. He had so many hopes for you, and everything's changed. Is there something you were going to tell me?"

This will be harder than I thought. I can't find the words.

Becky jumps in. "Isaiah is a Muslim. He converted a year ago."

I don't know whether to thank her or strangle her. Anyway, it's done.

Mom is quiet. Finally, she says, "I love you, Isaiah, but I can't understand why you would turn your back on the Lord."

"I worship God. I pray."

"You have walked away from salvation. I wish I had the words. You used to be a good boy."

"I'm trying to be good."

"Your father is right. I need to go home. Come to the house tomorrow. We'll talk." She gives me a quick hug and walks out.

"You made your mother cry," says Uncle Ken. "Is that what your religion teaches?"

What am I supposed to say? "I need to pray."

∼

I wake up before sunrise for the morning prayer. On my way to the bathroom, I run into Willy, stumbling toward his room.

"Hey, Willy, how you doing?" I whisper loudly.

He spins around, nearly falling. "Hey, Isaiah, nice to see you."

I can smell his breath. Aunt Debbie and Uncle Ken have problems of their own.

∼

We find Aunt Debbie in the kitchen, wearing her new dress. "Thank you, Becky. I love it. How in the world did you know my size?"

"My mother taught me everything I need to know about shopping."

Everything except how to stop.

Aunt Debbie serves bacon, eggs, and biscuits.

Uncle Ken sits down and digs in. "I always say there's nothing like a good breakfast to start the day."

I eat my eggs. Aunt Debbie puts two slices of bacon on my plate. "They're nice and crispy, just the way you like them."

I'm glad the bacon's not touching my eggs. I'm hungry. "Thank you, but Muslims don't eat pork."

"That is the strangest thing. I don't understand why you would want to follow a foreign religion."

"There are many American-born Muslims."

"Not around here. You might see a few scarves or turbans in Memphis, or even Little Rock, and I'm sure they have them in places like New York and Chicago, but this is God's country."

I want to tell her Muslims worship God, too, but I don't think she'd understand.

Ripples

After Becky and I do the breakfast dishes, I ask Aunt Debbie for directions to Mom's house.

"Do you want me to go with you?"

"You can come if you like. What about your work?"

"If they haven't called by now, they won't need me today. Ken, do you need my help at the store?"

"I'll manage. Go on over to Melinda's."

They live only a mile from Aunt Debbie, right down the street from Dad's church. "Do you see those flowers out in front of the church? Your mother did all of that. She's a real woman of God."

My aunt doesn't finish the thought. It probably goes something like, *She's so pious. How did she end up with a son like you?*

It's a one-story yellow frame house, much smaller than the one we had in Chicago. Bikes lay out in the yard. There's only one car in the driveway. He's gone.

I jump out and walk quickly to the front door. A man answers. Tall, thin, and frowning. "What do you want?"

Andrew. I'd forgotten about him. "I'm here to see my mother."

"Why did you come? Haven't you caused enough trouble?"

"Is she here?"

"Your mother took Ruth to the doctor in Little Rock. They'll be back in a few hours."

"Can I come in?"

"I'm teaching the children. You interrupted our Bible lesson."

"Andrew." Aunt Debbie intervenes. "Isaiah is a member of this family. Don't make us stand out here."

"You're welcome any time, Aunt Debbie, but I know how Dad feels about him."

Andrew is the son Dad always wanted me to be.

"If that isn't the most ridiculous thing I've ever heard. You open that screen door right now. I'll deal with my brother-in-law."

"I can't do that. I have my orders. If you'll excuse me, I need to get back to my lesson." He shuts the door.

Becky speaks for all of us. "What kind of Christian closes the door on a member of his family?"

"I'm going to get to the bottom of this. Drive me over to the church, Isaiah."

"I'd rather not deal with him."

"Do as I say. I'm getting madder by the second, and you don't want to cross me."

Aunt Debbie never gets really mad. She's too kind. But I obey.

As soon as I pull into the gravel parking lot, Aunt Debbie hops out and stomps up the concrete steps, slamming the church door behind her. Becky and I stay in the car.

We wait. Five minutes. Ten. When my aunt comes out, she's still stomping. "Come inside!" she shouts, jerking my arm. "Becky, you come, too."

Like I said, Aunt Debbie never gets mad. I haven't seen her like this since Willy broke five pieces of her Sunday china with a poorly-aimed Frisbee.

I trudge up the church steps. I just want to see my brothers and sisters. I don't feel like dealing with my father.

It looks like a hundred other small churches. Twenty rows of pews. A box for the choir. A small pulpit in front. No decoration except for the large wooden cross.

She leads us through the sanctuary to Dad's office. He's sitting at his desk, his arms crossed.

"Will you leave it alone, Debbie? This is none of your business."

"Since when isn't family my business!" she yells. "I won't leave here until I see some kind of peace between you two."

"You'll be here for a very long time. All of you need to leave. I have work to do." He turns to Becky. "Who are you?"

She offers her hand. "I'm Becky Wagner-Adams. Your daughter-in-law."

He flinches, but quickly recovers. "You have a family now, Isaiah. Leave us alone."

My wife grabs his arm. "This isn't right, Reverend Adams. Christianity is about love. Why don't you love Isaiah?"

My father jerks away. "You don't know my son."

"I know him better than you do. Isaiah misses you. That's why we came here."

Her big mouth again. I grasp her hand. "Let's go, Becky."

"No. I'm with Aunt Debbie. We're not leaving until you work this out."

Ripples

"There is nothing to work out!" I shout. "Don't you see that?"

My father stands and looks in my direction, avoiding eye contact. "I will not have dissension and chaos in my sanctuary. Leave," he says, in that same quiet voice.

I close my eyes and quietly recite *Surah al-Fatihah*. I won't let him anger me.

"Let's go, Becky, Aunt Debbie. Allah commands us to respect our parents. I don't want to fight him."

He sinks into his chair. "You're a Muslim."

"I'm a believer."

He folds his hands and mumbles words of prayer to his lord. It's his way of ignoring sinners like me.

I walk outside and sit on the steps. Aunt Debbie and Becky join me a few minutes later.

"If we just talk to him," says my wife, "I think he'll understand."

"You don't understand, honey." My aunt pats Becky's hand. "When he's speaking to the Lord, he doesn't hear anything else. He's a very pious man."

That's one way of looking at it.

∼

After lunch, we go back to see Mom. Ruth comes to the door.

I try to hug her, but it's hard to get close. "Any day now?"

"Six more weeks. They say it's a boy. That beard looks good on you. Come on in."

"Andrew won't mind?"

"I'll take care of him. This must be Becky. I've heard about you." She hugs my wife.

Andrew is sitting on the couch. "You're back. You must enjoy causing misery."

"Lay off, okay?"

"Your father is a great man. There is no excuse for your disrespect. I won't tolerate it."

"Who made you boss?" Okay, I'm back to acting like a ten-year-old, but Andrew makes me crazy. What's worse, he's the father of my nephew.

231

"If you've come here to fight, you'd better leave. I won't allow you to upset my wife." He puts his arm around Ruth's shoulders and pulls her closer.

"Look, Andrew, I didn't come here to see you. Is my mother home? Where are Benjamin and Martha?"

"Mom took them for a walk in the woods behind the house for their science lesson," says Ruth. "They should be back soon. Jacob is in his room. I'll get him."

Peace and love in the family. I need to forget the past and be nice to my brother.

When Ruth leaves the room, Andrew gives me a dirty look. I decide to provoke him.

"How many Muslims have you converted over there?"

"I care about my fellow man. I don't want to see anyone living in darkness. My job is to bring the light of the Lord and the good news of salvation. The life there isn't easy, but I hope to find my reward in Heaven. My earthly reward is in every man and woman whose eyes are opened to the truth."

"I didn't ask for a sermon. How many?"

"Let's just say that, for every misguided American like you, I bring twenty Indonesians to the way of Christ."

"You must be proud of yourself."

"I don't do this for worldly gain, but only to bring hope to the hopeless."

"You should know about hopelessness."

Ruth comes between us. Jacob follows. I offer my hand. "How are you?"

"I'm good." He accepts the invitation, eyes to the floor. "I have to say something, Isaiah, and I have to say it now because I don't know when I'll see you again. I should have helped you that night. I didn't know how it would turn out."

I pat his shoulder. "I understand." He had to save his own skin. Jacob has always known how to survive. "Oh, and I'm sorry for grabbing the laptop."

"That's okay," he says. "Dad won't let us use the computer anymore."

Mom walks in with the kids. Benjamin runs to me. "Isaiah, you're back!"

Ripples

"For a little while. How are you, buddy?"

"I'm okay. Don't leave."

I hug him. I can't explain why I'm turning my back on him.

I reach for Martha. She pulls away and stares at me from behind Mom's skirt.

"Isaiah, come on into the kitchen," says Mom. "We need to talk."

Becky stays in the living room with Ruth. Benjamin and Jacob sit with us at the same old wooden table. Mom brings me a glass of milk and a plate of her brownies.

"Tell me more about Loyola."

"I love it. I'm constantly learning. It's fascinating."

"It is a Christian school," she says. "What about Becky? How did you two meet?"

"We ran into each other at Loyola. She's studying literature."

"And she's from Minnesota?"

"We go up there sometimes to see her family." Almost all the time.

"Are her parents good Christian people?"

"They go to church on Sundays. They're nice." And a little overbearing. "How do you like Arkansas?"

"The air is so fresh. We go for walks in the woods nearly every day. I don't miss the city."

"Do you miss me?"

"All the time. I wish there were another way, but you don't realize how much you've hurt your father." She looks at my brothers. "Jacob, go help Benjamin with his math."

She waits until they're gone. "I don't understand why you had to leave the church. We taught you to be a proper Christian. I keep going through it in my mind, trying to see where I went wrong."

"It wasn't you, Mom. I was curious."

"You've always been curious. It usually brought trouble."

"When Uncle Brad came back and became a Muslim, I wanted to know why. I asked him, but he told me to find out for myself. That's all I was doing. Dad didn't have to get upset. I wasn't planning to convert."

"What was he supposed to do?"

"I don't know, but, when Becky and I have kids, I know I won't beat them. I want my kids to like me."

"Your father isn't perfect, but everything he does is because he loves you."

"He loved me, you mean."

"He still loves you, but you've broken him in a way I thought no one could. When Becky and you do have children, you will see what I mean. I wish you could see it now."

"Why is he turning his back on me?"

"You abandoned your faith. The Christian faith is all he lives for, all either of us lives for. I wish I could understand why you did it."

"I wish I could make you understand. All I can say is, you would have to read the Qur'an."

"I don't need to go searching. I know where the truth lies."

I won't convince her, and it's useless to try. "Becky and I have to go back to Chicago soon. Can I call you? Will you write?"

"I'll do what I can, but I don't want to defy your father. I shouldn't have come to my sister's house without telling him. You can't imagine how much I've missed you."

I grasp her hand.

The front door creaks opens. He goes to the closet to hang up his jacket. "Melinda, is dinner ready?" She doesn't answer. He turns around and spots Becky.

"Why are you here?"

"I wanted to meet Isaiah's brothers and sisters."

He sees me in the kitchen and rushes toward me. "I told you to stay away."

"I came to see my family."

"You don't belong to this family anymore. I want you to get the hell out of my house."

"Chris. Stop."

"You always stand up for him, Melinda. That's what spoiled the boy. I'm the head of this family, and I say he must go."

"He's our son."

"Do you hear me?" he says in his quiet controlled voice. "Leave this house. Now."

"I need to see my mother. You can't tell me what to do."

He raises his hand. As he comes toward me, I wonder which one of us will come out of this alive. I brace myself.

Ripples

He stops, his hand in midair. I look up. His eyes are still full of hate, but Jacob is holding his arm. "No, Dad, don't hit him again."

Dad has never hit Jacob, and he won't do it now. He lowers his arm.

"You are tearing this family apart," he says in a low voice. "I don't want to see your face in here again."

Do I walk away, grateful that no one was killed, or do I stand up for myself? I meet his gaze and try to decide.

Mom grabs my shoulder. "You'd better leave, Isaiah. I'm sorry."

I study her face. She's crying, but there's a hardness in her eyes. Or is it despair?

I kiss her on the cheek. "I love you, Mom." I walk out, staring at their beige carpet. Becky follows.

Andrew shuts the door behind us. We wait in the driveway for Aunt Debbie, who must be giving Dad another piece of her mind. She comes out five minutes later.

"There's no talking to him. This is such a sad, sad situation."

∼

When we get back to the house, Becky and I head for our room and discuss our plans. At dinner, I tell them. "We're leaving in the morning. I have to go."

"Let me talk with him," says Uncle Ken. "Maybe I can straighten this out."

"Thanks, but it's no use. You were there, Aunt Debbie. You saw how it was."

They try to convince us to stay longer, but my mind is made up. I came to see Mom, Ruth, and the kids. I saw them. He'll make sure I don't get near them again.

Before we go to bed, I pull Uncle Ken aside. "You'd better keep an eye on Willy. He drinks. I caught him stumbling home this morning."

"I suspected that. Don't tell his mother. I'll take care of it."

He checks the doors and turns out the lights. I get ready for the night.

∼

I'm in the field behind the church. I recite the Qur'an while I wait, sitting on the hard ground with my back against the building. The wildlife emerges. A family of deer crosses the field. Mice run through the weeds. I grab a small one by the tail and study it. It frantically waves its little feet. I throw it against a rock. Its small body shatters. Alive one second, dead the next. I'm always amazed at the fragility of life.

It's pitch dark. Headlights cut through the bleakness, approaching from the west. The car comes to a stop. He steps out, unlocks the church door, and walks inside.

I know his routine. First, he prays. Hands folded. Head bowed. After the supplication, he goes to his office and reads through the sermon. He'll walk into the sanctuary and begin to preach, growing louder and firmer with every sentence. When he's done, he'll pray again. Before leaving, he'll inspect the sanctuary to make sure all is ready for the Wednesday night service.

I could go in now. While he's praying, he hears nothing. I could hit him and be done with it.

That would be too easy. I'll wait until he starts preaching. I'll walk in, the door creaking a little. He'll look up and wonder at the late night visitor.

I allow five minutes for the first prayer. Now he's in his office. He picks up his sermon and walks into the sanctuary. He stands at the pulpit. His voice rings out. "Good evening, brothers and sisters."

I make my entrance. He stops, embarrassed to be caught rehearsing. "Hello. May I help you?"

I walk slowly to the front. I'm twenty feet away. Now fifteen. Now ten. Moonlight catches my face. He drops the papers. His hands form into fists.

We face each other, waiting. Frozen. Mute. Seconds tick.

"What are you doing here?" he snarls. "Go away, Isaiah. Leave us alone."

"I'm not Isaiah. I am Saifullah. The Sword of Allah. I have come to seek vengeance in the name of my Lord. To rid the earth of those who reject Him."

"For God's sake, you must turn and walk away. Go back to Chicago and your Islam," he says with contempt.

Ripples

"But I came all this way to see you. Won't you kill the fatted calf for your prodigal son?" I inch closer.

"I had a son named Isaiah. He was a good boy. He wanted to be a missionary. He said he would travel the earth to preach the Gospel. He promised he would make me proud."

"He said those things because that's what you wanted to hear. He wanted to please you, but he never knew how. You never told him he was good. You only lectured and beat him. He thought if you were happy with him, you would stop, but you didn't. Not until the day he became stronger."

"You could have killed me."

"I know. I've come to finish what I started." I'm three feet away.

"No, Isaiah. Don't talk that way. You can still be good. Get down on your knees, and pray. Ask the Lord to rescue you from Satan's grip."

"I pray all the time. Allah answers my prayers because He loves me. I am smart, and I am special, but you never knew. You saw only my faults."

"I confess I was too quick with the belt. I was following God's command. I hoped you would grow up to be righteous."

"I am more righteous than you will ever be. You struggle with your pitiful faith and give your pitiful sermons in this pitiful little church because you don't know what righteousness is. You don't know what faith is. You stumble in the dark and brag that you know the way. I used to fear you. Now I despise you."

I'm standing six inches from him now. He backs away.

"What do you want from me, Isaiah?"

"I told you, I'm not Isaiah. I am The Sword. And I will cut you down." I slap him with the back of my hand. He stumbles and falls to his knees.

"That's better, but it's not enough. You must bow all the way down." I grab the back of his neck and push his head to the floor. "Say 'Allahu akbar.'"

He trembles. "Lord Jesus Christ, please save me."

I kick him. "Say '*Allahu akbar.*' Say, 'There is no god but Allah.' Say it."

"For God so loved the world," he whispers, "That he gave his only begotten Son, that whosoever believeth in him should not perish, but have everlasting life."

"That's wrong!" I kick him again and again until he is lying on his side. "I told you what to say."

"I won't."

"Allahu akbar." I kick his legs. "There is no god but Allah." I kick his chest.

"Jesus Christ is my only Lord and Savior."

"Do you dare to reject Allah?" I become The Sword as the rage consumes me. He pulls himself into a ball. I fall to the ground and beat him with my fists. Blood streams from his nose and mouth. He pleads with me. Finally, he falls silent. My job is done.

~

I bolt upright, taking in huge gulps of air. My t-shirt is drenched. Becky murmurs. I touch the wall, the mattress, the upper bunk. Everything feels real. What was that? What does it mean? What dark thoughts haunt my heart?

I'm restless, but I don't dare leave the security of the bed. "Becky, wake up," I plead. "I need you."

"What is it?" she mumbles.

"Hold me."

She rolls over and puts her arms around me. I pull her closer and hold her tighter.

"Hey, don't squeeze me. Go back to sleep. Whatever it was, you're okay now."

She strokes my head. I concentrate on the safety of her closeness.

Ripples

Isaiah: Part Four

I barely slept. I go downstairs and pour a cup of black coffee.

Aunt Debbie made French toast for breakfast. "Here, I know you can eat this. Not a bit of pork today."

"Thanks." Somebody in this family cares about me.

We say goodbye on the front porch. "Call me," says Aunt Debbie. "If you ever want to get a message to your mother, let me know."

Uncle Ken and I shake hands. "It was good to see you again, Isaiah, and nice to meet you, Becky. Don't be strangers." He pats my back. "Think about returning to the Lord." He glances at his watch. "I'd better go open up the store. Drive carefully."

∼

We didn't stay as long as I'd hoped, so we'll spend a few days in St. Louis. As we drive out of Arkansas, I remind Becky, "We need to stay on budget."

"When we get back to Chicago, I'm going to get a job. I need more spending money."

"Why? What do you need to buy?"

She pats my cheek. "Don't worry about it, Baby. It will be my money."

"But how much stuff do you need?"

She just laughs.

Kyle: Part One

I have spent the last six weeks studying Islam. I've read twenty-nine books and fifty-three articles. I've cornered Nuruddin, Jeremy, and Isaiah with my questions. I've visited eight different mosques.

I haven't seen Faiqa in almost two months, except for Saturdays when she's busy with kids and volunteers. I wonder if she's avoiding me.

∼

The board meets tonight. I work late. Fifteen minutes before the meeting, I go out to the hallway and read the bulletin board. A few minutes later, he walks in the door.

I look up, acting surprised to see him. "Oh, hello, Mr. Hammadi. How are you?"

"Good evening, Kyle. I keep hearing great things about your program."

"Thank you. How is Faiqa?"

"She's well. She has been concentrating on her studies."

No other guy in the picture. Good. "I've been learning about Islam. It's very interesting."

"Yes, it is. Do you have any questions?"

I'm ready for him. "I was wondering, how do you think the Islamic months should be determined? Through calculations, or through the actual sighting of the moon?"

"That's a good question. There are different viewpoints, of course. I'm inclined to say that—." Another board member rushes past. Mr. Hammadi looks at his watch.

"I need to go inside. We'll talk later." He shakes my hand before walking away.

Yes. I am on my way.

∼

He stops by my office two days later. "I've thought about our conversation. Are you seriously interested in Islam?"

Ripples

I nod seriously. "Yes, I am."

"Tell me, Kyle, what attracts you to Islam?"

Besides Faiqa? I have an answer he'll like. "You've read my story. I was never into religion, but after the accident, I knew I was missing something. I watched my father pray and read the Qur'an, and I could see how much happier he was." That part is true. "My father tried talking to me about Islam, but I wasn't interested. One night, though, I couldn't sleep, and I remembered my father talking about the peace Islam gives him. I realized how much I wanted to feel at peace.

"My education trained me to cautiously consider all aspects of an issue, scientifically, and without emotion. For the last several weeks, I have studied every facet of Islam. I have to tell you, I am impressed."

He nods. "Islam is impressive. Are you thinking of converting?"

"Yes, sir. I've thought about it for quite a while now."

"I see."

I'm ready to go for it. "I plan to go to the mosque tomorrow and make shahadah. I don't want to spend another week without committing myself to this beautiful religion."

"That's wonderful, Kyle. Which mosque will you be attending?"

"My father always goes to the Lincoln Mosque. I want to say my shahadah in front of him."

"The Lincoln Mosque? Is that the one on the north side, near Evanston?"

"Yes, that's it."

"Very good. That is excellent news." He offers his hand. "I need to go now. I'll talk with you later."

My plan is working perfectly.

Jamilah Kolocotronis

Kyle: Part Two

I leave the office at lunchtime and arrive at the mosque before the crowd. I find the imam and tell him I want to make shahadah today.

"Masha Allah. That is great news." He asks me a few questions and shows me where to wait for my big moment.

I sit in back to listen to the sermon and watch them pray. Dad is in the front. I didn't tell him. Soon, I'll be praying, too. Can I do it? Sure. I can do anything that brings me closer to marrying Faiqa.

After the prayer, the imam stands. "We have a young man here today who has announced his intention to make shahadah. Would you come up here, please?"

I slowly wheel toward the front, all eyes on me. I glance over at Dad. His face says it all.

The imam gives me the words in English and Arabic. I pronounce them perfectly. I practiced.

Someone shouts. The entire congregation responds. They sound like they're ready to go to war, but I know that's how Muslims respond to good news. I read it in a book.

Suddenly, I'm surrounded. Guys keep coming over, shaking my hand and hugging me. Someone slips me money. A nice fringe benefit.

Dad slowly makes his way through the crowd. "Kyle, you're a Muslim," he says softly, close to tears.

We hug. He's happy. Another fringe benefit.

The crowd thins. Dad and I meet Mr. Hammadi on our way out. I knew he would come. "Congratulations, Kyle. Assalaamu alaikum."

"Walaikum assalaam." Like I said, I've been studying.

~

The minute I come in after work, Matt runs up. "Hey, assalaamu alaikum."

"Walaikum assalaam."

Mom is in the kitchen. I wonder if she knows. I go to my room and relax until dinner.

Ripples

She waits until we're finished eating. "Kyle, your father tells me you went to the mosque today."

It's hard to read her face. "I became a Muslim."

"Is that what you think is best?"

It depends. Do you mean, what is the truth, or what is best for my life? "Yeah, it's good." I'll be able to marry Faiqa. What can be better than that?

"If you're sincere about this, I support you."

And, if I'm not sincere? She has always been able to read my face. But she just nods and takes her plate to the sink.

Jamilah Kolocotronis

Kyle: Part Three

Two weeks pass, and I put on a good show. I pray five times a day. I speak Arabic as often as possible. I buy some of those Pakistani clothes and wear them to work every day. I spend part of my lunch hour reading the Qur'an. I am a Muslim.

Faiqa and her father walk in on Friday morning. "Assalaamu alaikum," he says.

"Walaikum assalaam wa rahmatullahi wa barakatu," I reply. I'm getting good at this.

"How are you, Kyle?"

"Alhamdulillah. *Kef halek*?"

"I'm fine. I told Faiqa about your conversion. She wanted to come see you."

She smiles. I lower my eyes, concentrating on a paper on my desk.

"It's nice to see you again, Sister. How are you?"

"I was surprised to hear you had converted. Do you like being a Muslim?"

"Masha Allah, I should have made shahadah long ago. I am so much happier now." Especially since you're here.

"That's nice."

"We must go," says Mr. Hammadi. "Faiqa insisted on coming to give you her salaams."

She likes me, too. I knew it. "I'm very glad you could come." I pretend to stare at the desk while sneaking a peek at her smile.

"We'll let you get back to your work. Assalaamu alaikum."

"Walaikum assalaam wa rahmatullah." I don't have to overdo it every time.

They turn to leave. I stare at Faiqa as she walks away.

∼

Two more weeks. I continue to be a model Muslim. I see Mr. Hammadi much more often now.

The time is right. I send him an email, saying I need to speak with him about an important matter. He arranges to meet me on Friday afternoon.

Ripples

We exchange greetings, and he sits down. "You have something to discuss?"

This is it. Everything I have done for the last fourteen weeks has led up to this moment. I can't blow it.

"Yes, sir. I have enjoyed getting to know your daughter these last several months. She is very intelligent, has a good sense of humor, and she's caring. I have never met a woman like Faiqa. I know I don't have very much to offer," I begin. A little humility won't hurt, as long as I don't overdo it. "But I care for your daughter. I know I could love her, for the sake of Allah, if she would be willing to love me in return, and I would like to express my interest in marrying her." I said it.

He frowns. "I don't know, Kyle. You are a bright young man, and you appear to be a committed Muslim, but are you prepared for the responsibility of a family?"

"I know what you're thinking. You can say it. I'm a paraplegic. I've spoken with my doctor, and he said there are many men in my condition who are husbands and even fathers."

"Would you be able to support a family? I know your salary is rather meager."

"I've been saving. In addition to this job, I'm being paid for my speaking engagements. In two years, I'll finish college and find a better-paying job. Even now, between my savings and my speaking income, I would be able to support Faiqa."

He doesn't look happy, but he hasn't screamed at me. I wait while he considers the options. A low-income paraplegic convert. Not quite what he envisioned for his only daughter.

But I've watched him closely. He prides himself on being progressive. He won't automatically dismiss me. It would be against his liberal nature.

I wait long minutes while he silently debates my proposal. Finally, he looks up. "That is an interesting proposition. I will think about it and get back to you."

I have a chance. "Good. I'll look forward to hearing from you." I give him my best smile.

It's all business. No hearts and flowers. From my reading, I've learned the romance comes later.

He walks out, tugging on his beard. I get back to work. And I pray.

245

Allah, I say, make it happen. I mean, I'm putting in all this effort. I should get something from it.

Ripples

Kyle: Part Four

He's making me sweat. Two weeks without a word. I think about staying late and catching him before a meeting, but I don't want to look too anxious.

If this doesn't work, I'll find another girl. I am very lonely. I could probably pick up someone in a bar—some of those girls are pretty desperate—but I'm supposed to be a Muslim now. I'll figure something out.

On Saturday morning, I'm sitting in front of the TV in my bathrobe when the bell rings. A minute later, Mr. Hammadi walks in with Dad.

"Assalaamu alaikum, Kyle."

I adjust my robe and run my hands through my hair. "Oh, walaikum assalaam, sir." He wasn't supposed to see me like this.

"Turn off the TV," says Dad. "We need to talk."

"Yeah, uh, yes, of course." I click the remote and quickly review my lines. I can't let him see me rattled.

Mom walks in, unflappable as always. "Can I get you some tea?"

"Yes," says Mr. Hammadi, "Tea would be fine." He turns to Dad. "I don't have to tell you how impressed I am with your son. He's bright and ambitious. He's going places."

Dad smiles and nods. "Yes," he says. "Kyle has always kept us on our toes."

"He took me by surprise, though, when he asked to marry my daughter. Has he spoken with you about it?"

I haven't told my parents anything important about my life since I was ten—not until after the fact—but Dad won't betray me. "Faiqa is a very special girl," he says.

"I know both you and Kyle are new to Islam. I myself didn't follow the traditions in marrying Faiqa's mother. We're in America, and we must adapt." I know there's a 'but' coming.

"But Faiqa is my daughter. Marriage is a very important commitment and must be approached seriously. So, I have a proposition of my own."

More hoops to jump through. Well, I used to be an athlete.

"As I said, I'm impressed with Kyle's behavior, his attitude, and his ability to achieve, but, until a couple of weeks ago, I hadn't looked at him as a future son-in-law. In Islam, we have a period of engagement. This gives the man and the woman time to get to know one another, and also provides an opportunity for the family to consider the match. Our form of engagement does not necessarily lead to marriage. It is more like a courtship. Always supervised, of course. If you are sincerely interested in my daughter, Kyle, that is the path you must follow."

"That sounds good." Engaged. Now we're getting somewhere.

"Muslims also recognize that two people do not simply marry one another. They marry into each other's families. The engagement period will help us all become acquainted. Toward that end, Mr. Adams, I would like to invite your family to our house for dinner tomorrow night."

Mom brings the tea and pound cake—I wish she had baked when I was young—and they sit together to discuss the possibilities. I'm only a bystander.

I just said a few words to Amy's parents before we started dating. Later, they chatted with me, and I got to know them. I think they met my parents once, when they came to pick Amy up from my house. They never ate dinner together. Everything will be different with Faiqa.

Tomorrow night. I can't wait to see her again.

∼

They live in Evanston, near our old neighborhood, but I never saw Faiqa when I was growing up. Her parents sent her to a private all-girls' school.

Their house is large, nearly a mansion. Huge front lawn, columns, and tall plate-glass windows. I ring the bell. Mr. Hammadi greets us. I look around.

Freshly polished hardwood floors. A chandelier in the front hallway. He leads us into a room with plush couches and a floor-to-ceiling fireplace. I knew he did well, but I didn't expect this. How can I ever measure up?

"Sit down, please. Make yourselves comfortable."

A woman appears from the other side of the fireplace. "Assalaamu alaikum. I'm Faiqa's mother, Hannah."

Ripples

Mom exchanges a brief hug with Hannah and gives her a plant. "Hello, Hannah. I'm Beth. It's nice to meet you."

"Oh, these flowers are beautiful, Beth. Thank you."

"Dinner will be ready soon," says Mr. Hammadi. "We can talk first."

Faiqa isn't here. Her brother—I guess that's who he is—comes over and shakes my hand.

"Kyle, how you doing, man?" He's taller than Faiqa and has their father's curly black hair. Faiqa looks like her mother—slender, brown hair, brown eyes, a cute little nose.

"I'm good. How about you?" I know his name, but I'm so nervous I can't remember.

"Faisal, go help your mother in the kitchen, and tell your sister to come in here."

"Sure, Dad." He looks back at me. "See you later."

Matt gawks at the opulence. I try not to stare. Mom goes to the kitchen to help Hannah while Dad and Mr. Hammadi chat about the traffic. I keep looking for Faiqa.

Finally, she walks in and sits by her father. "Assalaamu alaikum, Kyle." She smiles.

∼

Dinner was great. Hannah cooked Egyptian. Lamb and rice. Stuffed eggplant. Chickpeas. Pita bread. And an all-American strawberry pie with Egyptian coffee for dessert. I wonder if Faiqa can cook.

During dinner, Hannah and Faisal asked me about my life, my plans for the future, everything. Mr. Hammadi listened. I kept waiting for him to say something about the engagement.

Mom and Dad are ready to leave. Mom makes a date to go shopping with Hannah, and Dad invites them all over to our house next Saturday. They might as well see how the other half lives.

Before going out into the night, I glance back at Faiqa. I wish I knew where I stood.

249

Jamilah Kolocotronis

Kyle: Part Five

I'm getting settled behind my desk on Tuesday morning when Faiqa walks in.

"Assalaamu alaikum. You look tired. Did you sleep well?"

No, I couldn't sleep because I was thinking of you. The truth, but it sounds ridiculous. "Yeah, I slept okay. What about you?"

"Dad said I can start working here again. He said we can use this time to get to know one another, as long as," she imitates his deep voice, "'You don't get too close, and the office door remains open.'" She laughs. "He is so funny sometimes."

Intimidating. Dominating. Fearsome. Funny is not a word I would use to describe Mr. Hammadi.

"What do you have for me today?"

We talk while she works on our latest mailing campaign, and I try my shot at another proposal. This one is an extension of Uncle Joshua's work to help boys without fathers. We talk about little things. She has a cat named Shadow. Her father says he'll buy her a new car when she graduates next year. Faisal is checking out law schools.

"Who's older, Faisal or you?"

"We're twins. Fraternal, of course. He's my best friend."

I'd better stay on Faisal's good side.

"So, you want to marry me?" she says, labeling another envelope.

"What do you think?"

"I'll let you know."

Before leaving, she looks at Amy's picture and frowns. "Are you planning to keep that there?"

"Is it a problem?"

"After we're married, you'll need to put my picture on your desk. See you later."

She walks away. I pick up the picture and stare at Amy. "Sorry, Babe," I say finally, "But I have to get on with my life. You understand, don't you?" I kiss her one last time and put her picture in my top desk drawer.

Ripples

Jennifer: Part One

Next week, Nuruddin's parents have to fly back to Pakistan. These last two months have gone by too quickly.

We've just finished eating at Dad's house. Mama and I cooked dinner together. I've learned so much from her.

The kitchen is clean, and we're relaxing. I watch Mama play with Ahmed as he climbs over the furniture. She laughs at his antics.

Baba walks over to me. "Come outside, Jenny. I want to talk."

He motions to the front porch swing. "Sit here." He sits next to me and takes my right hand between his palms.

"You're a good girl. My son is happy. You're a good mother."

Why do I feel that there's a 'but' coming?

"Jenny, why are you not a Muslim?"

I've tried so hard, but none of it matters. I look down.

"Look at me," he says. "What is wrong?" He gently wipes away a tear. "Don't cry," he says softly.

"I want you to like me."

"I like you, but I want to know. Why are you not a Muslim?"

I remember the Abdul-Qadir Dad always talked about. A kind and gentle man. He's not being mean. He just wants to know.

"I don't know. Islam is nice. It makes Dad and Aisha happy, and my brothers. I guess I'm not ready. I don't want to wear a scarf. I don't think I could pray all the time. I know I couldn't fast for a month. And," I look down again, "If I did want to be a Muslim, I don't know how I could tell my mother."

"Your brothers are Muslims. Does she abuse them?"

"No, of course not. But she depends on me."

"What do you mean?"

"I guess she needs me to be like her."

He nods. "Do you believe in God?"

I don't go to either the church or the mosque—I almost never have—but I pray. I only have to look at Ahmed's sweet face to remember God. "Yes, I do."

"Good." He pats my hand. "You are a good girl."

251

Jamilah Kolocotronis

Jennifer: Part Two

They left on Wednesday afternoon. I hated to see them go. I know why Dad loves them.

At the airport, Mama raised her veil and kissed me. Then she kissed Ahmed and held him while he squirmed. Her last kiss was for Nuruddin.

Baba hugged me and whispered "Read." I knew what he meant. Before they went through the gate, he said, "I love you, Jenny."

We watched as they walked through security and into the boarding area. We waited at the airport until their plane took off.

Nuruddin has been quiet these last two days. I know he misses them. I miss them, too.

They will spend the next few months in Pakistan, getting ready for their trip to Makkah.

∽

I'm studying for a test when there's a knock. "Jennifer, it's your mother."

I jump up to let her in. "What's up?" Something is always up with Mom.

"Michael just called."

"How is he?"

"He's helping farmers with their irrigation systems. It doesn't pay much, but he says he's happy." She shakes her head. "I always imagined your brother living in a New York penthouse, not sweating on a Mexican farm."

"At least he enjoys what he's doing."

She sighs, "I don't understand why he did this."

"He didn't want to fight."

"He had a duty to follow orders. Do you know how angry Grandpa Layton is? Your grandfather served his time in Vietnam even though the whole nation was against the war, because he knew it was his duty. He calls Michael a coward. We all had such high hopes for him."

"He's helping people. That's a good thing."

"He's supposed to be serving his country."

Ripples

I can't convince her that he's doing the right thing. Sometimes, I'm not sure who is right.

Jamilah Kolocotronis

Jennifer: Part Three

Nuruddin talks with his parents for about twenty minutes before handing me the phone.

I'm in the middle of writing a report for my political science class. "Just a minute. Let me finish this sentence."

"They're waiting, Jenny. It's long distance."

I take the phone, the words I was about to write flying out of my head. "Hello."

"Hello, Jenny. How are you?"

"I'm fine, Baba. How are you?"

"I'm always good, alhamdulillah. Do you pray?"

"Yes, Baba, I do." In my own way.

"Will you learn Islam? Your father will teach you."

I don't have time for that right now. Besides my daily assignments, I need to study for midterms. Maybe after my work load eases. But I won't ask Dad. I'm not ready to convert. Okay, I can study Islam when I'm not so busy. "Yes, Baba, I'll learn."

"Will you come here? To Pakistan?"

Come to Pakistan? I have two years of school left. I can't make that kind of trip while Ahmed is little. That is nowhere on my list of goals. But they did come all that way to see me. "I'll try, Baba."

"Good. We love you, Jenny. Mama wants to talk."

I wait a minute, and then her voice. "Jenny. How are you?" she says slowly.

I remember the hours we spent cooking together. "I'm good. How are you?"

There's a pause, then Baba's voice. "She says she misses you." I hear her rapidly speaking Urdu in the background.

"I miss her, too," I say. He translates.

"I will talk to Nuruddin now. God bless you, Jenny."

"God bless you, too." I hand the phone back to my husband and turn to the computer, but I've completely lost my concentration.

Learn about Islam? Go to Pakistan? I couldn't say no to him. I'll do those things one day. I did promise.

I stare at my report. I need to finish this. Where was I?

∽

Ripples

I had a test in my journalism class this morning. Ahmed is fussing. I can't wait to get home and relax with a cup of tea.

The phone starts ringing the minute I walk in the door. I don't want to talk. Not until I glance at the caller ID. Mexico.

I grab the phone. "Michael, is that you?"

"Jenny. It's great to hear your voice."

"How are you? What are you doing down there?"

"I'm building. Hurricane season is coming soon, and we're reinforcing the flood protection system. Tell Nuruddin he was right. I can't go into someone else's country with a gun in my hands."

"Are you okay? Where are you staying? Are you eating well?"

He laughs. "I'm great. The people here are very hospitable. I have a nice place to stay and all the food I can eat. Have you ever tried guava? It's fantastic."

"I worry about you, Michael. And I miss you."

"Don't worry. What about you? And how's my little nephew?"

"He runs and climbs everywhere. I can barely keep up. He's talking now, too. It's always Mama this, Mama that. Practically non-stop."

"Does he say 'Uncle Michael' yet?"

"How could he? He hasn't seen you in months. Can you come?"

"Not yet. You know that. I have to wait until things calm down. In fact, I can't talk long. I need to be careful."

"Even now?"

"Yes. I love you, Jenny. Kiss little Ahmed for me. Take care of yourself, okay?"

"You take care of yourself. You know I love you. I wish I could see you."

"When the time is right. I have to go now. Bye."

A click, and my brother is gone.

I give Ahmed ice cream and turn on the TV before collapsing with my tea. Why can't everything be the way it used to be?

~

Over three months ago, I wrote an essay for one of my writing classes, discussing the benefits and challenges of a multicultural marriage. My instructor loved it and encouraged me to get it published. I just received an email from the editor of a local magazine. My article will appear in their August issue.

I read the email four times before printing it out. I call Nuruddin. "I'm being published."

"That's great, Jenny." He sounds distracted.

"Are you busy?"

"I'm on my way to a meeting. Can I call you back?"

"I'll tell you about it when you get home."

"Okay." He hangs up.

My husband isn't impressed, so I call Mom. When she answers, I scream into the phone. "I'm being published!"

She wants to hear all the details. I know she'll tell everyone—even strangers.

"I am so proud of you, Jenny. I always knew you could do it. You are on your way."

Mom is never too busy to say just the right thing.

Ramadan

*Oh, you who believe! Fasting is prescribed to you
as it was prescribed to those before you,
that you many learn piety and righteousness.*

Qur'an, *Al-Baqarah* 2:183

Isaiah

As we drive into Chicago, I remind Becky that Ramadan is coming. "I need to fast for the next month. No food or drink during the day. Like last year."

"That sounds harsh. When my roommate fasted for Lent, she just gave up something like candy or soda. Why do Muslims have to make everything so difficult?"

I used to wonder about that, but I know the answer. Oddly, my father taught it to me. "When you want to get closer to God, you have to be willing to sacrifice."

"I think it's silly. Shouldn't it be enough just to believe?"

"But faith without works. . ."

"I know. But being a Lutheran is a whole lot easier."

"Anyway, I start on Monday."

∼

My second Ramadan, and my first one married. Five days now. It's going smoothly.

My first real challenge comes on Saturday morning. I wake up to eat and pray. I read Qur'an for about an hour. Then I crawl back into bed.

Becky snuggles close to me and blows in my ear. I'm about to reach for her. When I remember, I move to the other side of the bed.

"What do you think you're doing?"

"I can't. I'm fasting."

"I'm not trying to feed you, I'm trying to seduce you. Come on, Baby."

I sit on the edge of the bed. "I can't do that either. Not during the day."

"You have got to be kidding. That's actually part of your religion?"

"It's part of fasting. Food, drink, and. . .that."

"Do they actually talk about sex in those sermons at the mosque?"

"Sometimes. It's not an obsession, but Islam deals with all aspects of life."

She laughs. "No wonder so many people are converting. Maybe I should check this out."

I'm glad she's taking it well. When we first got married, she would have screamed.

~

Ramadan is half over. It's going so quickly. I get a little hungry in the afternoon, but it's nothing I can't handle.

Last night, we invited Jennifer and Nuruddin for dinner. Nuruddin and I broke fast and prayed together. Becky and Jennifer talked non-stop. I'm glad they get along.

On some nights, we've gone to Uncle Joshua's or Uncle Brad's. I think Becky feels more comfortable with them now that she's met my parents.

This afternoon, on the way home from school, she says, "We don't need to go up to Minnesota this month. I know how tired you are."

"You won't miss seeing your family?"

She squeezes my hand. "You are my family."

~

A few days before Eid, we go shopping. She picks out a nice long-sleeved yellow dress. It goes just below her knee. She helps me pick out a new Pakistani suit. "Black is definitely your color."

I buy presents for her family. A pen set for Artie, a movie for Eileen, a newly-released book for Charlie, and a football jersey for Denny. Becky won't tell me what they like. "You need to figure it out," she says. Maybe I should get to know them.

She wants to do a little shopping on her own. That gives me time to buy her a simple gold-colored bracelet. She doesn't wear much jewelry, but I think she'll like this.

Ripples

Kyle

In one week, I have to start fasting. I don't know how I'll manage. I mentioned it to Dr. Brooks at my last check-up, hoping he would say it was bad for my health.

"Good," he said. "You need to lose some of that weight." Great.

Our whole family will be fasting this year. Last week, Mom told Dad her secret. She's read some of my books about Islam and even finished the Qur'an. Every night at dinner, we discuss what Muslims believe. What has happened to this family?

Tonight, during dinner, Mom says, "I've made up my mind. I want to be a Muslim."

Dad holds her hand. "Are you sure?"

"I feel strange leaving the church, but Islam has saved our family. Now I understand why."

I don't know how she'll tell Grandma and Grandpa. They're tolerant, but still. Grandpa will probably shake his head and say, "It all started with the day Brad ran away from home." Which is true. After that, everything changed.

Mom plans to meet us at the masjid today and make the shahadah. She says she wants to wear a scarf, too, even though Hannah tells her it's not necessary. Aunt Aisha came over last night. I think they spent the whole time talking scarves. Before my aunt left, Mom modeled a scarf for us. She looked totally different.

∼

Faiqa comes early today to work on the automated system she's creating. No more stuffing envelopes. Now I'll have to find something else for the volunteers to do.

"I noticed the empty spot on your desk," she says. "Maybe this will help." She hands me a picture of herself in a silver frame. She's beautiful.

"What will your father say?"

"He won't mind. He likes you, Kyle. Stop worrying. Once you get through Ramadan, you're home free."

"It's a test, then?"

"You could say that. Nobody can fast for fifteen hours, he says, unless his faith is real."

Fifteen hours. Thanks for reminding me.

"We'll be there when your mother converts. It's exciting."

"Your dad has to let us get married. If he doesn't, Mom and Hannah will never forgive him."

She smiles. "Just make sure you keep my picture where you can see it."

I set it in the spot once reserved for Amy. Sorry, Babe. I've moved on. I have to.

∼

They're standing outside the masjid when I pull up. Mom, Dad, Hannah, Mr. Hammadi, Matt, Faisal. And Faiqa. "This is a great day," says Mr. Hammadi. "We are very happy that you're joining us in the family of Islam." One thing I've learned about my future father-in-law is that he's always good for a speech.

"We'd better go in now," says Hannah. I didn't recognize her at first in her green scarf. Faiqa is covered, too. She looks beautiful, as always.

Dad hugs Mom. "I'll see you inside."

I don't pay attention to the sermon. I'm thinking about my mother. She's always believed in God. When I was little, she read me Bible stories. She started studying Islam when she learned about Gramma and Walt's conversions. She hasn't bought pork for a long time. She loves what Islam has done for Dad. It was only natural.

But the changes. Four years ago, I was dating Amy. The star offensive lineman and the cheerleader. Dad was a senior engineer who drank too much. Mom was stressed out from work and trying to keep Dad and me in line. Matt was a goofy kid. Everyone is different. Except Matt, who is still goofy.

We pray. I wish I could kneel on the floor and touch my head to the ground. Not in this life.

The imam stands and invites Mom to the front. Hannah and Faiqa walk with her.

Is that my mother standing there in a long dress and scarf? The imam says the words, and she repeats them. Mr. Hammadi calls out

Ripples

"*Takbir!*" Everyone answers, "*Allahu akbar!*" Mom turns to face us all as the imam introduces "our new sister, Beth Monroe Adams." She looks first at the crowd, then at me. I see something in her eyes. She knows something I still don't understand.

We meet outside. "Let's go for lunch," says Mr. Hammadi. "This is a day to celebrate."

"I need to get back to work," I say.

Mr. Hammadi chuckles. "I'll talk to Warren. Meet us at The Grand Caravan. You know the place, don't you?"

"Sure. See you there."

Before climbing into my car, I reach for Mom. She hugs me tightly. "Look for the beauty, Kyle," she says.

What does she mean?

∽

My car likes to speed a little. I arrive before them and sit in the parking lot, waiting.

This is the Muslim area of town. Small meat shops, gift shops, and restaurants on every block. Jennifer and Nuruddin live near here.

The Grand Caravan occupies an entire corner and has its own large parking lot. I hate parking on the street. Most drivers don't slow down, even when they see me taking out my wheelchair. Some of them honk, like it's my fault or something. Which it is, in a way, but that's yesterday's news.

We go in. Mr. Hammadi calls for the owner, who sets us up in the banquet room. Faiqa's father has connections.

Faiqa and Hannah have taken off their scarves. Mom is wearing hers. She looks so different. Her face is shining.

∽

On Saturday afternoon, Aunt Aisha comes over and talks with Mom about prayer and fasting. When it's time to pray, Dad stands in front, and Matt and I take our places behind him. Mom stands in back. I don't believe we're doing this.

On Sunday night, we all go to the masjid. Ramadan starts tomorrow. When we get back, I stuff myself. I hope I can make it through the day.

∼

Matt shakes me. "Kyle, wake up. You need to eat."

I force my eyes open and glance at the clock. It's practically the middle of the night. "I'm not hungry."

"Get up. Mom made a big breakfast for our first *suhur*."

I groan and struggle into my chair. Mom prepared eggs, pancakes, hash browns, and cantaloupe. I wonder if she slept.

"Are you really going to fast, Mom?" Matt asks.

"I'm looking forward to it."

I sip my orange juice, too tired to enjoy the spread. How can anyone be excited about deprivation?

∼

It starts at midmorning. My energy lags. I grab my coffee mug. I remember and put it down. Tomorrow, I'll drink coffee in the morning.

At noon, my stomach growls. I can barely concentrate. By late afternoon, I'm having mild cramps. My mouth is dry. My head hurts. I don't know if I can make it. I wrap up my work and go home early for a nap.

Dad wakes me when he gets home. We pray. I go back to sleep. Dad, Mom, and Matt each pick up a copy of the Qur'an and read.

I'm dreaming about Faiqa when Matt interrupts. "Get up. It's time."

We break fast with water, dates, and a cheesecake. I drink greedily before digging into the cake.

"Slow down," says Dad. "You'll get a stomachache."

He's probably right, but I've waited for this moment all day.

After eating and praying, we drive to Uncle Joshua's house for dinner. I hope he made biriyani. I can't wait.

∼

I'm getting through Ramadan, day by day. By the fourth day, my stomach has calmed down, but I still look forward to sunset.

Ripples

I'm so tired. We wake up early to eat. At night, we go to the masjid and pray until we drop. Yesterday, the imam said we shouldn't watch TV during Ramadan. Who has the energy?

I only see Faiqa on Saturdays, and sometimes at the masjid in the evenings. I'm almost too tired to miss her.

I can't think clearly without my coffee. My work is suffering. I manage to slide by.

On Sundays, I sleep. On Saturday mornings, I'd like to rest, but I need to be with the kids. I fake a smile and do the best I can.

Sometimes, in my office, I think about cheating. I could order a sandwich or a pizza loaded with cheese. Who would notice?

But I guess it's a matter of pride. Matt can do it. So can Mom. I won't surrender.

∼

Ten days left. I'm almost there.

I watch Mom. She's going all the way. Wearing a scarf when she goes out. Praying five times a day. Fasting every day. Reading the Qur'an. She's learning to read Arabic. That's something I haven't tried yet.

Last week, she told Grandma, who took it calmly. She probably said, "As long as you're happy, Beth." Grandpa won't say much, either. He'll just frown.

I made the shahadah, too. I'm praying and calling myself a Muslim. Until these past few weeks, though, I never really thought about what being a Muslim means.

I converted for Faiqa, but I'm not fasting for her. No girl is worth this kind of suffering. There really is something to this.

∼

Three more days. After breaking fast, Dad asks me to spend the last three days with him at the masjid. I might as well. It's not like I'm getting anything done at the office.

∼

Being in the masjid is different. Someone's always praying or reading the Qur'an. In the morning, we sit in a circle and eat together. It's the same thing in the evening, when we eat from the same large platter. People talk about the spirit of Ramadan. Here, I can feel it.

On the last night, I decide to stay up. I read the Qur'an—in English, of course. I pray. But something's missing. When no one is looking, I climb out of my chair and throw myself on the floor. What I end up doing is more like modified push-ups. I touch my head to the carpet and talk to Allah. For the first time, I really think about Him. It's not about Faiqa, is it?

In the morning, we go home and get ready for Eid. Mom bought me a light blue Pakistani suit. I wash up and slip it on. Nice.

Ripples

Jennifer

Ramadan is coming soon. Nuruddin will be fasting all day, every day, for the next month. I don't understand how being hungry can make you more pious, but I've watched Dad do it for many years. He seems to get something from it.

The worst part of Ramadan, I think, is no marital relations during the day. The baby is older now, and Nuruddin and I finally have a little time to ourselves, but, even when Ahmed takes his nap on Saturday afternoons, I have to stay away from my husband. We haven't been married that long.

∽

We go to Dad's house for the first night of Ramadan. Uncle Brad and Aunt Beth walk in right behind us. Aunt Beth is wearing a scarf. I stare.

"Close your mouth, Jen. It makes you look uglier," says Kyle.

"Why is your mother's head covered?"

"She's a Muslim now. She converted three days ago."

"She did?" Uncle Brad's conversion was strange enough. And I know why Kyle did it. But Aunt Beth? She used to go to church all the time. Their whole family is Muslim. That's weird.

"What about you?" Kyle teases. "Do you plan to join us, or will you be the only family member in Hell?"

"You should talk, Mr. Piety. What do you think will happen when Faiqa finds out what you're up to?"

"Me? I'm as innocent as the fresh-driven snow."

"Don't get too close to my son. I don't want him to be corrupted."

"You can say it, Jen. You've always been jealous of me. Good looks, personality, brains. I can't help it if I struck the jackpot. Maybe you'll have better luck the next time around."

I can go on like this all day with my favorite cousin. Ruth and Isaiah are too serious. Whenever I need a laugh, I can always count on Kyle.

∽

267

Nuruddin needs to wake up early every morning to eat. On the night before Ramadan, he described how his mother always fixed a big meal for them.

I managed to get up the first two days, but, on the third day, I just can't open my eyes. When the alarm goes off, I poke him and tell him to eat something. Then I roll over and go back to sleep.

∼

Ramadan is half over. I've cooked breakfast for my husband four times. I haven't had to cook dinner all month because someone is always inviting us. Dad and Aisha, Umar and Safa, Jeremy and Raheema, Uncle Brad and Aunt Beth, Isaiah and Becky. And a Pakistani guy Nuruddin knows. I don't want to go there again. This guy's wife speaks perfect English, but they invited two other Pakistani couples, and all the women sat there and spoke in Urdu. I was completely invisible. It's not the first time that's happened, and I'm sure it won't be the last. I hate it.

On Friday and Saturday nights, Nuruddin insists on breaking fast at the mosque. I went with him one Friday. I sat there, in a roomful of chatting women and screaming kids. When it was time to eat, I swear one of the women actually pushed me out of the way. One group of women kept looking at me and shaking their heads. They were speaking in Arabic, but I know what they said. She's not fasting, why should she come here and eat our food? I couldn't find anyone who would treat me like a human being. When we got home, I described my ordeal to Nuruddin. In a loud voice. Now he goes alone.

∼

Eid is tomorrow. It went fast. I can't wait. I bought new toys for Ahmed and new clothes for all of us.

We're all going to the prayer tomorrow. Even though I'm not a Muslim, it's nice to be a part of something. And I like getting all dressed up. Besides, I have to show off my handsome son.

Eid

Isaiah: Part One

I kiss my wife. "Time to get ready for Eid," I whisper.
She reaches up and pulls me toward her. "Come back to bed, Baby."
I'm tempted, but I resist. "We don't want to be late for the prayer."
She showers and puts on her new yellow dress. She's beautiful.

∼

Kyle: Part One

I shower first because it takes me longer to get ready. We eat a light breakfast, and we're ready to go.
My first Ramadan is over. It wasn't too bad, not toward the end. Now I might get to marry Faiqa.

∼

Jennifer: Part One

I woke up early this morning and made a big breakfast for my husband. It's over now, and we can get back to a normal life.
I showered while Nuruddin ate. Then I bathed the baby and dressed him up in his little suit. He plays while I slip on a long yellow dress and thin matching scarf I found in a shop on Devon. I can't wait to show Nuruddin. He's in the shower.
It takes my handsome husband fifteen minutes to get dried off and dressed up. We're ready to celebrate. On our way out of the apartment, he grabs me. "You're beautiful."

∼

Isaiah: Part Two

We arrive at the hall. Becky grasps my hand. "So many people."
"You'll need to go to the women's section."

"I want to stay with you."

"My family will be there. Jennifer, Raheema, Aunt Aisha, Aunt Beth. Maybe you'll see Faruq's wives. And look at all the different cultures here. Think of this as a sociological study."

She smiles. "Being married to you is a sociological study."

~

Kyle: Part Two

I wheel into the room and glance back toward the women's section. I wonder if Faiqa is here yet. Next Eid, insha Allah, we'll be married. And, in a few more years, we'll have our own little baby to bring to the prayer.

"Kyle. Assalaamu alaikum." The voice of my future father-in-law. He comes up from behind and gives me a big hug.

"Walaikum assalaam, Mr. Hammadi. It's good to see you." Can I marry your daughter? Have you made up your mind? Ramadan is over now. What will it be?

Dad and Mr. Hammadi hug, and the two of them walk off together. It happens every time. Like I said, they have to let me marry Faiqa. They all get along so well, it would be a shame to break it up.

~

Jennifer: Part Two

So many people. No matter how many times I come to the prayer, I never get over it.

But I feel confident today. I'm one of the mothers. I imagine everyone's head turning as I walk past. Look at her beautiful child.

I find a place in the back of the women's section and sit down. I hope I can find someone to talk to. I wonder if the rest of the family is here yet.

Ahmed fusses. He wants to play, but he could get hurt or lost. I distract him with cookies and toys while scanning the crowd for a friendly face.

Ripples

~

Isaiah: Part Three

I look back, trying to spot Becky. I wonder what she thinks of all this.

~

Kyle: Part Three

Dad and Mr. Hammadi are still talking when the prayer is about to start. We all head up to the front and take our places.

~

Jennifer: Part Three

A friendly face. I see her first and rush to greet her.
"Aunt Beth. I love your dress. You look good in green."
"Look at you. So bright looking. Yellow is definitely your color. How's our little man?" Ahmed lunges at her. She raises her voice a pitch. "You're very handsome today, Mr. Ahmed."
Another woman walks up. She looks familiar, but I don't think we've been introduced. "Assalaamu alaikum, Hannah," says Aunt Beth. They hug. "I'd like you to meet my niece, Jennifer."
"Hello. It's nice to meet you." I'm suddenly shy.
"Jennifer, you have such a sweet little boy. What's his name?"
I like Hannah.
We're still getting acquainted when Raheema comes over, holding Nadia's hand. Then Aisha. Then Aunt Safa. Then Becky, wearing her own bright yellow dress. She looks overwhelmed. I know the feeling.
We're all talking when the prayer starts. Aunt Beth, Aisha, Aunt Safa, and Hannah hurry to the front. Becky stays with me. Raheema, too. "I have my period," she whispers.
I watch them pray. Practically my whole family is Muslim now. Except Mom, who once actually said she would rather eat glass. I wonder what they get from it.

Isaiah: Part Four

The sermon is about the family. I don't have Mom and Dad, but I do have something great with Becky.

I wonder if she'll ever consider becoming a Muslim. I won't force her. We've never even discussed it. She likes the traditions she grew up with, but she does like to learn. I'll wait and see if she brings it up.

We have two more years of school. Then I want to have children with her. I'll do everything right. I'll be the most loving father ever.

Kyle: Part Four

The sermon is about the Muslim family. My mind drifts, thinking about how it will be. Faiqa and me together.

Jennifer: Part Four

A lot of the women sit in the back and talk. That's strange. I actually wouldn't mind listening to the sermon. We find a place closer to the front so we can hear.

He's talking about the Muslim family. The Muslim mother, he says, is the glue holding the family together. She raises the children to worship Allah and reinforces her husband in his practice of Islam. She provides a peaceful home environment so her family can practice Islam whether they are in Makkah or Chicago.

The Muslim mother. Yes, that sounds like Mama. I'm a mother, too. Can I make a Muslim home for my family?

Isaiah: Part Five

After the prayer, I spot Faruq and his sons. We hug. "Eid Mubarak."

"Eid Kareem, Saifullah. What are your plans for the day?"

"I'll probably do something with my uncles. Or Becky and I may just go out to eat. How about you?"

"My family has prepared special treats. I hope you'll visit us. I can meet you at the masjid after Salatul Asr."

"I'll talk with Becky. We may come."

"Remember, you're the head of your household."

That's easy for him to say. "I'm trying."

"I need to go. I hope to see you later. Assalaamu alaikum, Brother."

I'm about to go looking for Becky when Kyle comes over. "Hey, Isaiah. Assalaamu alaikum."

"Walaikum assalaam. Where's everyone else?"

"I haven't seen Uncle Joshua or Jeremy yet. My dad and Matt are over on the other side."

I don't have my parents or siblings, but I have my wife, my uncles, my cousins, and Faruq. There are days when my life is so good that I'm afraid I'll stop missing them. This is one of them.

∼

Kyle: Part Five

The sermon's over, and everyone shakes hands and hugs. I work my way through the crowd, toward Isaiah. He's talking to some guy with a long beard. A fundamentalist. Must be Faruq.

When Faruq leaves, I go over and say salaam. Isaiah and I are Muslims. Who'd have believed it?

∼

Jennifer: Part Five

He ends the sermon, and everyone stands up and starts talking. Except for some of the women, who never stopped talking.

Raheema turns to me and gives me a big hug. "Eid Mubarak," she says. When we were little, she was my best friend. Now she's my sister-in-law, but I haven't felt this close to her for a long time.

Becky looks at me and says, "Now what?" This is her first time, isn't it?

"Now we greet everyone we know, and even people we don't know, and start looking for our husbands. It could take a while." I grab her hand. "Come with me."

Positives and Negatives

Life is a progress, and not a station.

—Ralph Waldo Emerson

Isaiah

We drive up to Minnesota two weeks after Eid. When I hand out the presents, Artie grunts. "Just what I need. Another pen." Eileen says, "Oh, yes, thank you Isaiah. This movie sounds very interesting" and puts it aside. Only Charlie and Denny are actually happy with their gifts. Two out of four.

This weekend is like every other in Minnesota. Becky spends most of Saturday shopping with her mother and hanging out with friends. On Saturday night, we meet Brandy and her boyfriend at a restaurant. Brandy holds up her left hand. "We're engaged!" I watch while my wife makes a fool of herself, jumping up and down with Brandy.

This time I chose the restaurant—a Middle-Eastern place I've discovered. Brandy's fiancé, Brett, complains. "No alcohol?"

"Try their gyros platter," I say. "It's great."

They grumble, but, after biting into her gyros, Brandy says, "I never knew about this place. We need to come here more often." One small victory.

~

I want Artie and Eileen to like me. The gifts didn't do it, so, on Sunday morning, I decide to try something drastic.

We're eating a pancake and scrambled egg breakfast. Everyone's quiet. I seize the moment. "Look, I know you don't really like me. Especially you, Artie." He doesn't protest. "But I love Becky, so I guess you're stuck with me. I'd like you to understand who I am." I hesitate. They're family, sort of, but do I really want to tell them?

Becky leans over and whispers. "Go ahead, Baby." She kisses me on the cheek.

Just the fortification I need. "You don't know much about me, really, and nothing about my family. There's a reason for that. I'm ashamed."

I tell them the whole story. Growing up with a father who found flaws in everything I did and used his belt to remind me of my imperfections. Getting to the point where I wanted to kill him. "He still won't talk to me. My mom takes his side."

Eileen hugs me. "I had no idea," she says, wiping away her tears.

I wait for Artie. After a minute, he nods. "My father had a belt like that. He didn't use it often, but I'll never forget."

∼

On the way home, Becky says, "Aren't you glad you opened up to them?"

"Maybe. I am glad you didn't tell them. You don't know how much that means to me."

We hold hands all the way back.

∼

On Monday evening, I call Aunt Debbie. "How is everything?"

"Everything is absolutely wonderful. Your sister had her baby yesterday morning. An eight-pound baby boy. They've named him David Aaron."

"That's great. How is Ruth?"

"Mother and baby are both healthy. You should see Andrew, acting like the proud father. And Chris. Do you know I haven't seen your father smile since they moved down here?"

"Can you send a picture? I want to see him."

"Your father or the baby?"

"The baby, of course." I don't know if I want to see my father's face again.

∼

I wake up suddenly. It's still dark. The nightmare returned. Waiting for him. Confronting him. Killing him.

I'm shaking. I wake Becky and ask her to hold me until it stops.

What does it mean? Am I capable of murder?

Ripples

Kyle

As the Eid crowd thins, we look for Mom, Hannah, and Faiqa. Jennifer is with them.

"What are you doing here, Jen? Didn't they tell you only Muslims are allowed?"

She stares at me. What's wrong? Maybe I crossed the line. I start over. "Eid Mubarak. The little guy is looking good."

"Better than you," she replies. She got me.

~

Mr. Hammadi invites our family to The Grand Caravan for lunch. The food is great, but I don't enjoy it. Ramadan is over. Can I marry Faiqa now?

A waitress clears the table. They keep talking. Even Faiqa chats away. Doesn't she care?

Dad and Mr. Hammadi argue over the bill. Faiqa's rich father wins. After paying, he stares at me until I look away.

"How was your first Ramadan, Kyle?"

This is it. I hide my hands under the table and flex them to help me relax. "It was good."

"You fasted without problem?"

"Sure. No problem at all." Except for being hungry, thirsty, and tired.

"Are you still interested in marrying my daughter?"

He's playing with me. I hope he doesn't notice the beads of sweat on my forehead. "Have you made a decision?"

"What do you think, Faiqa?"

"What?" She looks distracted.

"This boy says he wants to marry you. How do you feel about that?"

Boy? Excuse me?

"Whatever you say, Baba."

Faiqa, don't leave me hanging.

"And you, Hannah?"

"It's up to you, dear."

I know where he's going with this. Faisal also turns it back to dear old Dad.

He peers at me over his bifocals. "Let's review the facts. On the one hand, you work at a non-profit agency and don't earn much. You have a disability. You haven't completed your college education."

I thought he liked me.

"On the other hand, you are a practicing Muslim. You're very intelligent. You have a great deal of determination, and I think you're going places.

"So, on the one hand," he holds out his left palm, "Three negatives. On the other hand," he says, extending his right palm, "Three positives. Can you think of something to change this equation?"

This is no time to be shy. Not that I have a problem with that. "I care for your daughter. That should tip the balance."

"You care for Faiqa. Four positives." He lowers his right palm. "Any more negatives?"

"No, sir."

"In that case," he says, "I don't have any choice." He drops his left hand and extends his right. "Welcome to the family."

I accept his outstretched hand. "Do you mean. . .?"

"The positives outweigh the negatives. What more can I say? You may marry Faiqa."

"Yes!" I pump the air. Then I think better of it, and say, quietly, "Thank you."

Faiqa laughs.

"You knew, didn't you?"

They all start laughing. "All of you were in on it?"

Dad pats my arm. "We figured you could take it."

Man, it's true what they say. What goes around comes around. But I won't complain, because I've found my happiness. Nothing can go wrong now. I have Faiqa.

Ripples

Jennifer

Mom calls two days after Eid and softly says, "I just heard from Michael."

"How is he?" Why is Mom so quiet?

"You need to come over. Jeremy is on his way."

"Nuruddin will be home soon. We'll both come. Is everything okay?"

"Come quickly."

"What's wrong with Michael?"

"I'll tell you when you get here."

Nuruddin walks in twenty minutes later. Traffic. He kisses me. "What's for dinner?"

"We have to go to Mom's house. She heard from Michael. Something's wrong."

"Can't I eat first? It's been a long day. I barely had time for a sandwich."

"You can eat at Mom's place."

He frowns. "Let's go."

I grab Ahmed, who's playing happily with his blocks. He fusses. "Not you, too, baby."

∼

They're waiting for us—Mom and Peter, Jeremy and Raheema, Dad and Aisha. And a stranger.

"You took long enough," says Mom. "This man is Michael's friend. How do you say your name again?"

The stranger stands and shakes Nuruddin's hand. "Assalaamu alaikum. I'm Jamaluddin Menendez. I met Michael at the masjid in Brownsville, and I helped him get into Mexico. Three days ago, I received a package. He asked me to deliver it personally."

Mom takes over. "He sent each of us a letter and some photos." She holds up a picture of Michael standing next to a woman. Her skin is brown. I imagine her hair is black. It's covered by a scarf. "Look at her. She is your new sister-in-law."

"Michael's married?"

"Her name is Gabriela."

"How can Michael be married? When did this happen?"

"Two weeks ago," says Jamaluddin. "Her cousin gave me the package. He says they're very happy."

They do look happy, and she's pretty, but how could he be married? "He's planning to stay there?"

"That's what he says," Mom sighs. "If he comes back, he will be arrested for desertion. I don't understand. Why Michael? He has never been irresponsible."

"We talked about it many times," says Jamaluddin. "He realized he would be entering into a difficult situation in the Middle East. He said he didn't want to risk killing someone. That sounds like a very responsible decision to me."

"But just picking up and leaving his country and his family?" Mom gestures wildly. "That was a very dangerous thing to do."

"He had help. Once he made his decision, I contacted friends who took him to my village in Chiapas.

"I've known Gabriela for many years. We grew up together. I'm sure they will be happy."

"Can you get a message to my brother? Tell him how much I miss him."

"I'll try, insha Allah, but I'm sure he knows. It was a very difficult decision. In the end, he said, he wants to be a builder and not a destroyer."

Now he's building a whole new life for himself. I should be happy for him, but all I can think is, *When will I see you again?*

∼

We don't get home until late. Ahmed is sleeping. Nuruddin goes right to bed. He found leftovers in Mom's refrigerator.

She's very upset. She knows her other children can be difficult, but she has always depended on Michael to be stable and sensible.

Before going to sleep, I read my brother's letter for the tenth time and gaze at the picture. They look happy. But, Michael, what have you done?

Dreams and Nightmares

*Hold fast to dreams, for if dreams die,
life is a broken winged bird that cannot fly.*

—Langston Hughes

Isaiah: Part One

Last summer, I was making myself miserable over Becky. I'm glad that's all behind me.

Life is good, but the nightmare keeps coming, about once a week. It's always the same. Sitting behind the church. Walking into the sanctuary. Beating him, my heart full of rage.

On Friday, I try to tell Faruq. "I keep having this dream. It's awful. It starts—"

"Stop. The Prophet told us not to reveal our nightmares."

"I have to tell someone. It's driving me crazy."

"Have you told your wife?"

"Part of it. Some is too awful to mention."

"Nightmares are from Shaytan. Make *dua* before you sleep. Get up and pray. Read the Qur'an. Ask Allah to protect you."

"But it keeps returning."

"Shaytan is distracting you from remembering Allah."

"I need to tell you what I did."

He shakes his head. "Tell no one. Turn to Allah."

He doesn't understand.

Isaiah: Part Two

I talk to Aunt Debbie every Monday evening, right around eight. She says she waits for my call.

The last few times, Mom has been there. She asks if I'm eating well. She talks to Becky. Last week, she asked me to read the Bible again.

∼

When my aunt answers the phone, she says, "Hold on. I have someone special here who wants to talk to you."

"Hi, Isaiah. How are you?"

"Ruth! Are you okay? How's my little nephew?"

"He's right here. Can you hear him?"

I listen carefully. Little baby noises in the background.

"Is Andrew treating you well? Let me know. I'll come down there and take care of him."

"Andrew is good. I know you two never got along, but I hope you'll get to know him better."

That's not going to happen. "He doesn't mind you talking to me?"

"He left for Indonesia last week. David and I are flying out of Little Rock on Tuesday. We'll be back next summer."

"I need to see you before you go."

"Can you get down here in time?"

"We'll be there."

"You don't have to come, Isaiah. It's too far."

"To see my favorite sister and my little nephew? Tell Mom we're coming."

I hang up and tell Becky to get ready for another trip.

Ripples

Isaiah: Part Three

When I ask my boss for a few days off, he gives me a choice. Come in on Saturday, or I'm fired.

On Friday night, I give him my notice. There are other jobs.

Becky's boss was more understanding. She told him my sister is leaving soon for missionary work. A good and faithful Christian, he told her to have a safe trip.

∼

On Saturday, we eat a light breakfast and leave before sunrise. I want to get there before dark.

She drives first while I rest. I take over in St. Louis. We don't stop, except for a quick lunch. I pray in the car while she finishes her burger.

"I don't know what I'll say to my father," I say as we drive through Springfield.

"Don't worry about it. The right words will come to you."

"I don't care if I never see him again. I'm going for Ruth and the baby."

"I haven't given up on your family. You have to have faith, remember?"

Faith is one thing. Fixing my family will take a miracle.

∼

We pull up to Aunt Debbie's house as the sun sets and carry our luggage up the porch steps. Aunt Debbie runs out and hugs us. "The chicken and dumplings are ready. You must be exhausted after that long drive."

I stretch. My back hurts. Over six hundred miles in one day.

Becky hugs her. "I'm sorry we didn't bring you a gift. There wasn't much time to shop."

"Just seeing the two of you is enough for me. Come in out of this heat. Ken and Willy will get your suitcases."

I walk in the front door and hear a baby crying. I rush to the kitchen to see him.

"Settle down, David. Are you hungry? Is that better?"

She's engrossed in her son. I walk up quietly and kiss the top of her head.

"He's beautiful."

"You're here." She reaches out with one arm.

I bend down to hug her. "How are you?"

"I'm feeling good. The baby didn't wake up at all last night." She smiles. "Having a child is so amazing. You and Becky need to try it."

I pull up a chair. "We will, someday. Are you ready for your trip to Indonesia?"

"Almost. It's more complicated this time because of the baby. Mom has helped me get everything packed. We already shipped a few things over."

"Is this really what you want to do?"

"God created me to help others."

"Is that how Andrew feels about it?"

"He helps people in his own way."

By converting them. I don't want to argue with her. I nod.

Aunt Debbie hands me a plate full of food. "You need to eat. You're so thin."

I attack Aunt Debbie's chicken and remind myself to chew before opening my mouth. "You came to see me?"

"Aunt Debbie said you'd be here tonight."

"I hope you didn't wait long."

"Not long. Aunt Debbie wanted me to come even earlier so she could spoil David."

"That's nonsense." My aunt laughs. "You can't spoil a baby that tiny. He needs all the loving we can give him."

We catch up while I eat and she feeds the baby. David's birth. The kids' home schooling. Mom's garden. I don't ask about our father.

My stomach is full, and the baby is asleep. I study his face.

"He has your eyes," she says.

"And your nose." All he has from Andrew is his mouth. I hope he makes better use of it. "He's incredible. Will it be safe to take him all the way to Indonesia?"

Ripples

She laughs. "That's what everyone asks me. Millions of children are growing up in Indonesia, and David will have many advantages over them. The church provides us with a nice house, there's always plenty to eat, and we have good medical care. Think about the children who don't have that much."

Ruth always had a good heart. When we were kids, she constantly rescued stray animals, including two baby birds which had fallen from their nests. One died. She cried for a week.

"But he's so tiny. You'll be gone for an entire year?"

"That's the plan. We'll come back next summer and spend a few years here in the States. Andrew would like to teach at a Bible college and inspire young men the way Dad inspired him."

I nod and roll my eyes. "That's nice."

"Listen, Isaiah, you and Dad have to get past this. Both of you are being ridiculous."

"He doesn't know you came to see me, does he?"

"No, but it's not all his fault. I saw what you did to him."

"What was I supposed to do? I couldn't take it anymore."

"I'm not talking about that night. He's changed. He used to be so confident. Now he seems fragile somehow."

"What do you want me to do about it?"

"Have you ever thought of apologizing?"

"For what? Defending myself?"

"I told you, it's not just that night. You're different, and he doesn't know how to deal with it. Getting married without telling us. Becoming a Muslim. I won't tell you how to live your life, but I've had a little trouble myself with all these changes."

"So I have to apologize for being me?"

"No. For believing him when he said you were dead. You really don't know how much he loves you."

"If he ever loved me, I killed it by becoming a Muslim."

"Isaiah, I want you to look at my little David. I would do anything for him, even risk my own life to save his. I never imagined I could love someone this much. When David grows up, even if he does something I think is totally wrong, something I hate with every part of my being, I'll never stop loving him. That's what it means to have a child.

"Dad is strict and opinionated. He's also kind and warm-hearted. He taught you how to ride a bike, throw a baseball, and drive a car. Don't you think you owe him something?"

"I don't know."

"Think about it. I need to get back. Carry the diaper bag out to the car for me?"

Before she drives away, she says, "Sometimes, Isaiah, it really isn't about you."

I stand in the road and watch the car. Becky comes over. "I told you so."

"What?"

"This thing between you and your father. It's not all him. And, like Ruth said, it's not always about you."

"I don't want to hear it. Lay off."

I go back inside, run to the bedroom upstairs, and climb into the top bunk. I thought Ruth would understand.

I stare at Jack's poster, the one on the ceiling. It's a picture of the galaxy. I trace the constellations with my eyes. This is a good place to come when you want to discover the secrets of the universe or just get away from it all.

It's been a long day. I can barely keep my eyes open.

∼

When I wake up, the house is quiet. Becky sleeps in the lower bunk, softly muttering.

I wash up and spread my prayer rug in the living room downstairs.

After praying, I feel restless. I try reading the Qur'an. I can't concentrate. I lie down next to Becky, but, two minutes later, I'm up again. I put on my shoes and quietly slip out of the house.

All is quiet. No cars. No people. Only the stars. More stars than I ever saw in the Chicago sky. I walk, gazing at the stars and wondering at the secrets of the universe.

An owl hoots. A family of deer walks slowly across the street. Cats fight in the distance.

I notice the field. Then the church. The moon hangs low over the steeple. A single car sits in the parking lot.

Ripples

I walk up the concrete steps. The door softly creaks. The sanctuary is dark. Light emanates from his office.

I make my way slowly, silently down the aisle. He steps out of his office and turns on the reading light at the pulpit. He doesn't see me standing in the shadows.

He places his papers on the lectern and clears his throat. His voice rings out, "Good morning, brothers and sisters." Dress rehearsal for Sunday.

I step into the light. He stops, embarrassed. "Hello. May I help you?"

I stroll toward him. I'm twenty feet away. Now fifteen. Now ten. Moonlight peers through the window, catching my face. His hands form into fists.

We face each other, waiting. Frozen. Mute. Seconds tick.

"Why are you here?" he snarls quietly. "Go away, Isaiah. Leave us alone."

"I'm not Isaiah. My name is Saifullah. The Sword of Allah."

"Go back to Chicago and your Islam," he says with contempt.

"But I came all this way to see my sister. And you. Didn't you hear of the man who killed the fatted calf for his prodigal son? It's in the Bible." I inch closer.

He looks down. "I had a son named Isaiah. He was a good boy. He wanted to be a missionary. He said he would travel the earth preaching the Gospel. He promised to make me proud. He's dead now. I mourn for him."

"He said those things because that's what you wanted to hear. He wanted to please you, but he never knew how. You never told him he was good. You only lectured and beat him. He thought if you were happy with him, you would stop. But you didn't. Not until the day he became stronger."

"You could have killed me."

"I know. Sometimes I have terrible dreams in which I finish what I started." I'm three feet away.

"No, Isaiah. Don't talk that way. You can still be good. Satan has a hold of you. Pray, and ask the Lord to free you from Satan's grip."

"I pray all the time—at least five times every day. Sometimes Allah answers my prayers. He always listens. You never did. You never knew me. All you knew were my faults."

"I may have been too quick with the belt, but I was following God's command. I wanted you to grow up to be righteous."

"I'm trying to be righteous, but I have something evil inside of me. Something that makes me dream of killing my father."

"Come back to the Lord, Isaiah. Repent, and ask Jesus Christ to come into your heart."

"I worship Allah, the Lord of all the worlds. Jesus is a prophet of Allah. Nothing more." I'm six inches from him now. He backs away.

"Free yourself. You are in bondage, following a false god and a false prophet. Return to the Way and the Truth and the Life."

"The way is Islam. The truth is the Qur'an. All life comes from Allah."

"Give up your sinful ways, and turn to the one who was sent to die for you. He will open his arms and take you in as his lost lamb, if only you return to him."

"There is no God but Allah, and Muhammad is the Prophet of Allah."

"I won't have those words spoken in my church," he says in his low, angry voice. "Why do you insist on destroying yourself, Isaiah?"

"I told you, I'm not Isaiah. I am the Sword of Allah. And there are times when I want nothing more than to cut you down."

"My brothers have told me Islam is a religion of peace."

"It is."

"How can a religion of peace make you hate your father?"

"I don't hate you, though sometimes I think I should. I don't respect you, and Islam has nothing to do with it. You stood at that pulpit week after week, preaching about love and forgiveness, but you couldn't love me. You told me the beatings were for my own good, but there was nothing good about the cuts and bruises you inflicted. You can talk about how you put a roof over my head and guided me to be righteous, but you didn't show me love. That was all I ever needed from you."

"God is love. I gave you a good Christian home, sent you to a fine Christian school, and prepared you to enter the ministry. What did you do in return? You brought that book into my home. You put your hands around my throat."

Ripples

"That book? You mean the Qur'an, the revealed word of Allah. You don't know what happened that night."

"You wanted to kill me."

"I wanted to learn about Islam. Uncle Brad refused to teach me. I had to do it on my own. Do you realize if you hadn't beaten me that night, I might still be a Christian?"

He falls to his knees, faces the cross, and prays. He murmurs in whispers, fervent wishes to the one whom he calls savior. I'm uncomfortable, but I wait.

After several minutes, he turns to me, still on his knees. "For God so loved the world that He gave his only begotten Son—"

"That whosoever believeth in him shall not perish, but have everlasting life. I remember."

"So you're ready to repent and return to your Lord, Jesus Christ."

"No. I remember the verse. I no longer believe in it."

"You just said you might still be a Christian."

"If you hadn't beaten me and called me dead. It's too late now. On the night you cursed me, I decided to convert. I asked Uncle Brad to help me, but he refused."

"He refused? Why?"

"He said I wasn't ready, that I was converting only to get back at you. He was right."

"Faith cannot be based on revenge."

"I know that now. I found someone else who agreed to help me convert. Later, after I had made a few mistakes, he taught me the greatest lesson of all."

"What lesson can you learn from an infidel?"

My muscles tense, but I hold back. I need to put this into language he can understand. "I have a parable for you. Once there was a foolish young man. He became a Muslim to spite his father, and, even though he had his uncles and cousins around him, he felt very lonely. On the day his father refused to talk to him, he felt even lonelier because he knew that, in his father's eyes, he was truly dead.

"This young man was in college, and, one day, he met a beautiful girl. He tried to stay chaste, but the girl was beautiful, and he was lonely, so he surrendered to temptation. When his uncle learned of his sin, he told the young man to either marry the girl or never see her again. The young man couldn't imagine his life without her, so they married.

"He thought his problems had been solved, but they had only begun. He fought with his wife day and night. In despair, he turned to his friend, who offered a solution in accordance with the teachings of Islam. Be lashed one hundred times, in payment for his sins, and the burden of his wrongdoing would be lifted.

"Remembering the numerous beatings he had received at the hands of his father, the young man immediately rejected the idea. His marriage continued to deteriorate. Finally, in desperation, the young man agreed to the lashing.

"But the friend showed mercy to the young man. He advised him in his religion and sent him back home to his wife. The young man felt free for the first time in his life.

"Tell me, my father. Which man is better? The Christian who punished and dominated the young man, or the Muslim who lovingly accepted him?

"Remember the words of the Good Book. 'Therefore all things whatsoever ye would that men should do to you, do ye even so to them: for this is the law and the prophets.' The Book of Matthew, chapter seven, verse twelve. If you wanted respect from me, why did you treat me so cruelly?"

I wait for a response. He has fallen silent. My job is done.

He's still kneeling when I walk out of the sanctuary. The world is quiet, except for a train whistle blowing in the distance.

I crawl into bed with Becky and fall into a deep sleep.

Ripples

Kyle: Part One

One more month. Faiqa and her mother are busy making the arrangements for the wedding and reception—hotel, catering, flowers, and a thousand other details. They're inviting hundreds of people, including her grandmother, some aunts and uncles, and several cousins who will fly in from Egypt. I'll invite my aunts, uncles, cousins, Grandma and Grandpa, and a couple of people from work. Maybe thirty altogether. Have I missed anyone?

∼

Yesterday, I opened my desk drawer and saw Amy's picture. I haven't looked at it in weeks. We almost had it all. A marriage and a child.

But I'm becoming more honest with myself. Amy and I were both into drugs and alcohol. She swore she wouldn't touch anything while she was pregnant, but I'm not sure how long that would have lasted. Since her death, I've practically deified her. The reality wasn't as pretty. We didn't go to the movies or have picnics by the lake. That last year or so, all we did was get stoned. She was sober on the night of the accident. That's how I'll always remember her.

∼

Two more weeks. Mr. Hammadi is sparing no expense. I've heard that, in Islam, the groom and his parents should pay for the festivities, but my rich future father-in-law insists on splurging for the wedding of his only daughter.

We're meeting this evening to write up the marriage contract. Mr. Hammadi wanted to make a big deal out of it, but Faiqa persuaded him to keep it simple. Just the families.

We sit together with our parents. I look at my bride. "How is this supposed to work?"

"It's easy. I tell you what I expect, and you agree." She smiles.

"So, that's how it's going to be?"

"You'd better get used to it."

"What do you expect?"

"Two things. First, I know how much you want to be a father, but I'm not ready yet. I want to finish medical school."

"That will take years."

"How can I finish my studies if I'm worried about taking care of a baby?"

"It's better if you wait," says Mom. "A child is a tremendous responsibility."

"I understand how much this means to you," says Mr. Hammadi. "Are you ready for fatherhood?"

Probably not. And Faiqa has wanted to be a doctor since she was twelve. "Okay, but we will have children."

"Insha Allah." Faiqa smiles shyly.

Her other demand is easier. "Before we have children, you need to take me for Hajj. I've seen too many women postpone it. I want to go now while I'm young."

"That sounds great. Um, there's one thing I want, but I'm almost afraid to bring it up."

"What's that?"

"Would you start wearing a scarf, the way my mother does? You're so beautiful, and once we're married, I really don't want to share all that beauty with other guys."

"That's a chauvinistic remark. It's not like I go around wearing a bikini."

"I know. Don't get mad. Like I said, it's your choice." The imam says a husband should force his wife to cover, but I've decided to leave it up to her.

"In that case, I'll think about it. Good enough?"

"Sure." I hope she decides to wear it.

We also discuss the dowry. I can't imagine what to offer—her father is rich enough to buy her whatever she wants—but Faiqa says she wants two things. "All I need is a wedding ring and a trip to Egypt to visit my family members. The ones who can't make it for the wedding." How many relatives can one person have?

"You're getting off easy," says Faisal. "A lot of girls demand expensive jewelry, a new car, even thousands of dollars in cash. It will probably be years before I can afford to get married."

Ripples

Faiqa quietly smiles, and I remember how very lucky I am that she's marrying me.

We hash out a few more details, and it's done. We'll sign it during the wedding ceremony. I can't wait.

∼

One more week. I think everything is ready. Faiqa and her mother have picked out all the furniture for the apartment. They did let me choose the bedroom set.

I have a million little details to take care of. I'm packing up my stuff and getting it ready to take to the apartment. I need to change my address. I'll leave work for the volunteers to do while we're on our honeymoon. I can't forget to get the blood test. We'll pick up our marriage license on Thursday. I should make an appointment with Dr. Brooks so he can explain to Faiqa what it will mean to be married to me, but Mr. Hammadi would insist on chaperoning. I don't feel comfortable discussing all that in front of him.

Faiqa has her own to-do list. Every time we talk, she sounds distracted.

Marriage will be more complicated than I thought. I'm nervous and restless. I can barely sleep. Sometimes, I'm tempted to hop in my red car and escape.

But we'll get through it. Mom and Dad had a lot more obstacles than Faiqa and me, and they're still together. Even Isaiah is still married. If he can do it, so can I.

Kyle: Part Two

I'm getting married today. The ceremony is at four. I wish it was now. I can't wait.

And I can't sit still. I ask Faisal to come over. We play a video game. I can't concentrate. I've never been this lousy. My hands are twitching.

"Do you want to do something more active?" he says.

"What do you have in mind?"

"Let's go."

We climb in his car and end up at an outdoor basketball court. There must be twenty kids hustling for control. I remember when I could do that. Faisal works his way into the game and tosses me the ball. "Go for it."

I feel the texture of the ball. I try to remember. I dribble, but I'm out of practice. The ball rolls away from me. The other guys yell. "Forget it. Give us back our ball."

Faisal scoops it up. "No, man. Give him another chance."

I can do this. I bounce harder, stronger. I move closer. I shoot. Nothing but net.

"Yes!"

One of the kids scoops up the ball, and they continue showing off their moves.

Faisal runs over. "You did it, man."

"Dude, I used to tear them up on the court."

"You've seen the court over at our house, and I've got all that exercise equipment. Let's get you back into shape."

"My wife might want me to spend my time with her."

"I can handle her. I'm six minutes older."

We go out for pizza. When we get back to the house, I have two hours to get ready. I climb out of Faisal's car. "I'll see you later."

"I'll be there."

I eat, take a shower, and put myself together. Uncle Joshua gave me a new white wedding suit. I inspect myself in the mirror. Not bad.

I say goodbye to my empty room. My stuff is at the apartment. I have a suitcase packed and stowed in my trunk. Tomorrow morning, we fly to Los Angeles for our honeymoon.

Ripples

The ceremony starts in an hour. We wrote the Islamic wedding contract. We have our marriage license. Tonight, it becomes official, and Mr. Hammadi will finally let me go home with my wife.

I grab my car keys. "I'll meet you at the hotel," I call on my way out.

"We're right behind you," Mom says, adjusting her green scarf.

∼

It's almost time. People are trickling in. I don't know most of them. They're Mr. Hammadi's friends. We should get some nice wedding presents.

"Are you nervous?" Dad grins.

"Who, me? What gave you that idea?"

"I haven't seen you this jumpy since your team went to the state tournament."

I'm not just nervous about getting married. What if this is one gigantic joke? Everyone will be watching, Faiqa and I will be up there with the imam, and Mr. Hammadi will say, "You're not marrying my daughter. You're a crip."

Or Faiqa will look at me and say, "I can do much better than you."

I do my own version of pacing, rolling up and down the hall, until I feel a little calmer. Tomorrow at this time, we'll be in California, playing on the beach. She'll be mine.

I talk to some of the guests as they come in, even the ones I don't know. It takes my mind off things. Twenty minutes before the ceremony, Uncle Joshua walks in with his family. Jennifer is with him.

"Hey, Jen, how you doing?"

She glances at me. "Oh, I'm okay."

Come on. You can do better than that. "Where's that husband of yours? Did he finally get tired of you and go back to Pakistan?"

She stares at me, blinks, and runs away crying. Aunt Aisha goes after her.

"You don't know about Nuruddin?" says Uncle Joshua.

"No. What happened?"

He fills me in. "I know you two like to joke, but you really hit a raw spot this time."

I take off after Jen. Aunt Aisha is comforting her in a quiet hallway.

"Hey, Jen, I'm sorry. I didn't know. Will you forgive me?"

She doesn't look up. "Forget about it," she says between sobs. "You'd better get ready for your wedding."

"I'm ready. Just hoping she doesn't change her mind." The perfect chance for Jen to get back at me.

But all she says is, "She won't. Go on. I'll be there soon."

Aunt Aisha nods. "Don't worry, Kyle. We need a few more minutes."

"Okay. I'll see you later." I really put my foot in it this time.

I wonder where Isaiah is. He'd better not miss my big day.

There's a lot of commotion. It's time.

Dad and Mr. Hammadi are waiting for me. "Where were you? Faiqa is here."

"I had to take care of something. Do you want me to go in now?"

"Yes, and hurry," says Mr. Hammadi. "Faiqa is about to make her entrance."

The noise is getting louder. Somewhere between a song and a screech. It's the women. They're getting closer. Faiqa is in the middle of them.

They move into the room. I stare at Faiqa. I can barely recognize her with all the make-up and fancy clothes. She looks beautiful no matter what she wears.

The women keep up the noise. Mom and Hannah escort Faiqa to the front. The imam stands up, and the noise stops. This is it.

The imam gives a sermon about caring. He talks about the sacrifices and selflessness marriage requires. Then he asks Faiqa if she wants to marry me. I hold my breath.

She glances up and says softly, "Yes, I do." Mr. Hammadi repeats her answer in a loud voice.

I'm almost there. Now the imam is asking me. "I sure do," I say. Faiqa smiles.

We sign the marriage contract. The imam recites a short prayer. He finishes and smiles at us. "You're married. Mabruk."

The whole room erupts. The women with their special wedding chant. The men shouting "Allahu akbar!" What a noisy way to start our marriage.

Ripples

The rest of the evening is eating and talking. Sometimes I look at Faiqa and stare into her eyes. Most of the time, we're surrounded by people wishing us luck. Some of the women start dancing on one side of the room. Men dance on the other side. Faiqa's parents join in. My parents hold back. I've never seen them dance.

~

The evening has gone by in a whirl. It's late, and most of the guests are gone. I look around. Presents on the gift tables. Leftover food. Someone else will take care of it. I lean over and whisper to my wife. "Are you ready to go home?"

"I'm ready when you are." She smiles.

We say our goodbyes. Faiqa's parents hug me. Faisal shakes my hand. "Don't let her give you any trouble."

Mom hugs us both. She's crying. Dad hugs us, too. "Treat her well," he says.

We head for the car. "Just Married" is painted all over my car. Tin cans are tied in back. Faisal. We climb in.

~

I pull into the parking garage of our apartment building and kiss her hand. "Don't get out." I swing into my chair and go over to open her door. I take her hand. "Come sit in my lap."

She laughs. "What are you doing?"

"I want to carry you over the threshold."

She kisses me. In the hall. In the elevator. All the way up. I slowly wheel toward our apartment.

Finally, we make it inside. We're home. I never knew life could be this sweet.

Jennifer: Part One

These last couple months have been so busy. Nuruddin and I started house hunting. We hope to move when our lease expires in August. I can't wait.

I drop by Mom's place for lunch on a late May day. She's humming.

"You sure are happy."

"Peter said he'll go with me to Mexico. We leave in two weeks."

"I wish I could go." I have Ahmed to take care of, and Nuruddin has his job. And I've been so tired lately. A trip to Mexico sounds like too much effort.

∼

Ahmed and I are enjoying our summer. We go for a walk every day. At least once a week, I take him to the lake or the zoo. He can name most of the animals. He's so smart.

∼

I drive Mom, Peter, and Brianna to the airport. Jamaluddin told them they're being watched, so they booked their round-trip flight for Cuba. From there, they'll take another flight to Mexico City and go south to Chiapas by train. They won't be back until the middle of July. I don't know how I'll get by without Mom for an entire month.

While Mom and Peter check the luggage, I ask my little sister, Brianna, "Are you excited?"

"Yes. I've never been to another country."

I haven't either. "You're only eleven."

"My friend Morgan went to Europe last summer. She brags about it all the time. Now it's my turn to brag, because she's never been to Mexico."

"Will you tell Michael hi for me?"

"Okay."

She barely remembers Michael. I think she was only five when he went away to school. For her, this is just an adventure.

Ripples

Jennifer: Part Two

Nuruddin calls Mama and Baba the day before they leave for Makkah. He's animated and happy. He's always like that when he talks to them.

I'm watching Ahmed play with his new ball when Nuruddin passes the phone to me.

"Hello, Baba. How are you? You must be excited."

"Jenny, this is my dream. To go to Makkah and make the Hajj. Alhamdulillah. How are you? How is Ahmed?"

"Ahmed is good. He likes to jump."

Baba laughs. "I can almost see him."

"Are you ready to go?"

"I have been waiting for this all of my life. To be near the Ka'bah. I must do that before I die, insha Allah."

"It sounds interesting."

"One day, Jennifer, you will be going with Nuruddin to make the Hajj. Can you promise me you will do that? One day, you will be a Muslim."

He is so sincere. I can't say no to him. "Yes, Baba, I promise that I will be a Muslim one day." I don't know when. Someday, probably.

"Good. May Allah be with you and give you a good life. I love you, Jennifer."

"Yes, Baba. I love you, too."

Nuruddin takes the phone from me. I feel like I should have said something more, but I don't know what.

When he hangs up, my husband says, "You're ready to become a Muslim?"

"I don't know. It's possible."

"I heard you tell my father."

"He asked me, and that's what he wanted me to say. But I think I probably will. One day."

He squeezes my shoulders. "I can't wait for that day."

"I thought you said you would always love me, regardless."

"You know I do."

∼

My dreams are interrupted by the phone. It might wake the baby. Nuruddin answers.

He listens for a moment, then sits down on the bed. "*Inna ilahi wa inna ilahi rajiun,*" he says softly. I've heard that before. I think it's bad news.

After a few minutes, he hangs up and grabs my hand. "That was Kareem, the leader of Mama and Baba's Hajj group. He said. . . I mean, Baba. . ." He stops and stares.

"What happened? Is something wrong?"

"Kareem said they were walking around the Ka'bah. Baba stopped. A few seconds later, he collapsed. They tried to help him, but it was too late."

"Too late?"

"We all come from Allah, and to Allah we must all return." He pulls me close to him.

"No. Baba? That's not possible." How can he be gone? I hold on to my husband as we cry together.

∼

Ahmed's still asleep. I lie down, overwhelmed by the news. Nuruddin picks up the phone.

I doze, dreaming of Baba. He's close, but I can't reach him. Ahmed's cries wake me.

Nuruddin is still on the phone, speaking in Urdu. I kiss him and pick up the baby.

∼

Ahmed is playing. I'm putting on the coffee.

Nuruddin comes up behind me. "I need to go, Jenny."

"Go where?"

"Mama is there by herself. I need to get her and take her home."

I drop the carafe. It shatters. "You're going to Makkah?"

"I called the Saudi embassy. They'll give me an emergency visa. I must take care of my mother."

I'm too stunned to answer. Ahmed screams. I run to him.

Ripples

Nuruddin calls Dad. I force myself to finish fixing breakfast, though I'm not hungry.

I call my husband when the eggs are done. He kisses me. "I'm going to your father's house. He'll help me arrange things."

"Arrange what things? You can't just take off. What about Ahmed and me?"

"You have your parents. I need to take care of my mother." A quick kiss. "I'll see you later."

I don't understand what's happening. Losing Baba is bad enough. Now I'm going to lose my husband, too? What should I say? *Go on, honey. We'll be fine.* Maybe that is what I should say, but I can't.

When he comes back three hours later, Dad is with him. His eyes are red.

I'm sitting on the couch, watching Ahmed in his playpen. Dad sits next to me. "Nuruddin has to go, Jenny. You understand that, don't you? His mother is there without any family. She needs her son."

I will never completely have Nuruddin. "How long will you be gone?"

Dad and Nuruddin exchange looks. "I don't know," says Nuruddin. He looks away.

"Jennifer, Nuruddin may have to stay in Pakistan with his mother."

"What? Are you serious?"

"My oldest brother, Ahmed, is dead. Ibrahim lives in Islamabad, and he can barely afford to take care of his family. Baba sent me to America for my education, and now I must return to look after my mother."

"And what about your wife and child? Are you going to forget about us? Go, and marry a Pakistani wife!"

Dad grabs my shoulders. "Jennifer, listen to me."

I push him away.

"Jennifer."

"What?"

"Nuruddin must take care of his mother. That's Islam. If he can't come back for you, I'll take Ahmed and you to Pakistan. You will go to live with your mother-in-law in Karachi. Do you understand?"

"No, I don't understand. How can I?" Yesterday, my biggest problem was trying to get Ahmed potty-trained.

"Nuruddin will take his mother back to Pakistan. As soon as he's settled, you'll go, too."

"To Pakistan?"

"You knew we would go back someday," says Nuruddin.

"Yes. Someday." When Ahmed goes off to college, when we're ready to retire. But now? "You have a good job. I have at least a year of school left. Our life is here. And I don't speak Urdu. I don't know anyone there, except Mama, and she barely speaks English. How can I possibly live in Pakistan?"

"There's no choice, Jenny. You knew that on the day you married me."

On the day I married him, I had other things on my mind. How nice it would be to wake up in his arms. How much I wanted to have his child. The last thing I was thinking about was moving to Pakistan.

He did tell me. I just didn't take it seriously.

"Nuruddin has his ticket and the visa. He will leave this evening. Would you like me to take Ahmed back to the house so you two can spend some time alone?"

I don't want him to go, but there's nothing I can do. A moment alone would be nice. "Yeah. Just let me throw a few things into the diaper bag. You can get the car seat out of my car."

"No problem." Dad picks up the baby. "How's our Ahmed? Do you want to go on a trip?" Dad flies him around the room. I remember when he did that with my little brother Jamal. Now Dad can't lift his arms as high, and he has to sit down after a minute, but Ahmed still loves it.

I get him all packed up. Extra food, extra clothes, extra diapers, extra toys. "Are you sure you can handle it?" I say, handing Dad the heavy bag.

He laughs. "You're talking to an old pro." He walks out, making funny noises. I hear Ahmed's laughter echoing in the hallway.

They're gone. I look at my husband. "I know you have to go, but it's so hard."

He strokes my face. "I'll miss you, Jenny."

∽

Ripples

Dad and Ahmed come back five hours later. My baby is eating an ice cream cone. He's a mess. "Are you ready to go to the airport?" says Dad.

Nuruddin grabs Ahmed. "How can I leave you?" He smothers our son with kisses while Ahmed laughs and buries his face in Ahmed's soft cheek. After a moment, he looks up. "I'm ready." He wipes the ice cream off his face with a tissue. A speck remains on his nose.

I take the baby and clean him up. Dad and Nuruddin grab the luggage. I wish I had time to buy a gift for Mama.

We get to the airport two hours before the flight. After Nuruddin checks in, we have an hour to say goodbye. He takes Ahmed. Dad holds my hand. "You'll be okay, Jenny."

We sit on hard plastic seats and talk quietly until it's time for Nuruddin to leave. He holds me. "I'll send for you as soon as I can. I probably won't call for a few days. Don't worry. I love you, Jenny."

I don't want to let go. "I'm so sorry about Baba. Give Mama my love."

He hugs Dad. "Thank you for taking care of my family."

Dad puts his arm around my shoulders. "I think I can handle her for a few weeks."

The announcement comes. His flight is boarding.

"I need to go. Assalaamu alaikum, Dad. I love you, Jenny. I'll see you soon." He picks up his bags and walks away. I hold Ahmed very close.

I love you. Be safe.

~

Dad and I walk slowly back to the parking garage. "I'd like you and Ahmed to come stay with us."

"I'll be okay, Dad. I can manage."

"I'm sure you can, but I'll worry. You can stay in your old room. Jamal and I will bring your stuff over."

I'm so lonely right now, and it sounds good to be with family, but I want to stay in our apartment tonight. "Maybe tomorrow."

"Call me if you need anything. I don't care what time it is. If you hear a strange noise, or you feel lonely, just call, and I'll come right over."

"I'll do that."

He walks with me up to the apartment. "Lock your door. Don't open it for anyone."

"Don't worry."

"I'll see you tomorrow, Jenny." He kisses me on the cheek and waits while I engage the locks. I hear him walking away.

I'm tempted to fling the door open and call for him. "Daddy, come back. I need you." But I'm a grown woman now. I can take care of myself.

I sing Ahmed to sleep in our bed. I don't want to be alone.

Dreams and Nightmares Continue

*I have had dreams, and I have had nightmares.
I overcame the nightmares because of my dreams.*

—Jonas Salk

Isaiah

We sit down to a good, pork-free breakfast of fried eggs, fried potatoes, and biscuits with gravy. Aunt Debbie passes the salt and asks us to come to church with her.

"I'd like that," says Becky. "I've never been to a country church."

She can go. "I'll stay here and work around the house. Uncle Ken, what chores would you like me to do while you're gone?"

"As long as you're in this house, you are going to church. Now finish breakfast, and get into your Sunday clothes. We need to leave soon."

I don't have Sunday clothes. My best outfits are the tunics and baggy pants I bought when I first became a Muslim. I brought one pair to wear on the way back. I'm not doing this to be rebellious—I think I made my point very well last night.

"You're wearing that to church?" says Becky.

"These are the best clothes I brought. And it won't hurt to remind my father who I am."

"You should let me pack your suitcase, Baby." She shakes her head. "I don't know why you keep looking for trouble." She slips into her yellow dress.

Uncle Ken scowls when he sees me. "Are you trying to cause problems, boy?"

"Should I wear jeans and a t-shirt instead?"

He shakes his head. "Let's go."

∼

We're early. Some men are standing outside, talking about corn prices and herbicides. A group of women chatters. Until they see me. Everyone stops and gapes.

"I told you not to wear that," Becky whispers.

I decide to make the most of it. I smile broadly, raise both hands, and say, "Assalaamu alaikum. Masha Allah. Alhamdulillah. Allahu akbar."

I don't mean to mock the name of Allah, but I need to get past their gossiping tongues. Becky turns to the women. "He's new to this country. I'm teaching him about the Good Book. I'm praying he will accept Christ into his life."

Murmurs of approval rise from the crowd. "God bless you, honey," an old woman calls.

Uncle Ken glares at us, then smiles at the crowd. Aunt Debbie pretends not to notice. "How are you, Beverly?" she says to one of the old busybodies. "Is your arthritis still giving you problems?"

Becky and I walk into the church. My family is sitting in the front row, as usual. Dad must be in his office. I grab my wife's hand and lead her into the last pew. "Let's sit back here."

Slowly, the church fills up. As people walk past, they look at me and smile.

The gray-haired woman at the piano starts playing, and everyone stands, hymnals open. Becky motions for me to join them. "They're all looking at you."

I know this hymn—I know every hymn in the book—but I just stand and listen. Becky struggles to keep up. Her church has a different hymnal.

I'd forgotten how long these services are. There's more singing, performances from the choir, and some Bible readings before Dad stands up to give the sermon.

He's in the middle of talking about the importance of tithing when he sees me. He stops for a moment and fumbles with his notes. He clears his throat. Then he starts up again, exhorting one and all to give up their one-tenth to the Lord.

At the end of the service, the piano plays. Dad stands up in front with his preacher's voice. "This is the time to come forward and commit yourself to the Lord." He talks about being born again and starting life anew. It worked better in Chicago where there were more sinners. All eyes turn to me.

Dad keeps it up, his voice growing stronger. "Jesus will forgive you. You need only to ask. Come forward and give yourself over to the Lord." I heard his spiel so often over the years that I practically memorized it. I'm sure he hopes that, in spite of everything I said last night, I'll come up to be forgiven. A nice storybook ending. It won't happen.

He's gone on longer than usual. The strain is getting to him. He pauses twice to catch his breath. His face is red. If I were a good son,

Ripples

would I go up and make him happy? Maybe, but, in spite of my little performance outside, I'm trying to give up lying. I remain planted in the pew. Finally, he offers an emotional closing prayer and dismisses the congregation.

They file out slowly to the accompaniment of the piano. Normally, Dad would be out there ahead of the crowd, but he just sits behind the pulpit. After a minute or two, he rises and walks slowly down the aisle, avoiding my gaze.

Mom, Ruth, and the kids walk out behind him. They look surprised to see me, but they don't say anything. Everyone knows our family business stays behind closed doors.

We wait until the church is empty. The parishioners are walking to their cars. Mom, Ruth, and the kids must have gone back to the house. Uncle Ken and Aunt Becky are waiting inside the pickup. Dad stands alone.

As we walk out, I look at him. He returns my stare.

"Why did you come?" he says.

"Uncle Ken brought me."

"I thought you were ready to repent."

"I have repented for some things, but I'm not sorry I'm a Muslim."

"This is the work of Satan. You must resist."

"You will never understand the peace I feel when I bow down to Allah in prayer. You should stop tormenting yourself and search for the peace."

"'Peace I leave with you, my peace I give unto you; not as the world giveth, give I unto you. Let not your heart be troubled, neither let it be afraid.' Peace comes from the Holy Spirit, as prophesied by our Savior."

"The Gospel of John, chapter fourteen, verse twenty-seven. Muslims believe Jesus was predicting the coming of Prophet Muhammad. Muhammad is the *Parakleitos,* the advocate Jesus prophesied in that verse."

"Get thee behind me, Satan!"

He usually saves his theatrics for church. "I hoped, after last night, you would understand."

"I understand that, if you had died a physical death, I could bury you and visit your grave, but yours is a spiritual death, and now you torment me."

"Listen to yourself, Dad. This isn't an epic struggle between good and evil."

He takes off his glasses and rubs his eyes. "I lie awake at night, and I want to cry out, 'My God, my God, why have you forsaken me? Why did you allow my first-born son to be taken from me?'" His voice breaks. "I remind myself to be patient, as Job was. God has given me David to replace the son I lost. In his innocent face, I find hope."

I soften my tone. "You haven't lost me. I'm here, and always will be. I'm coming to the house later to see my mother, my sisters, and my brothers, and I will go to the airport on Tuesday to say goodbye to Ruth. I'm not dead, and you can't get rid of me."

He moans softly. "That is my cross to bear. To suffer the shame of a son who has chosen to follow the way of Satan. If you refuse to repent, there's nothing more I can do for you, but I will mourn you until my last breath."

He isn't listening. I touch his arm. "Goodbye, Dad. I'll see you later."

Becky and I climb into the pickup truck. I glance back at my father. He stands alone, his head bowed.

~

During Sunday dinner, Uncle Ken tears into both of us for our deception. "Don't you two have any respect for the church?"

"People were staring at me. What if I'd said, 'Oh, hi, I'm Reverend Adams' oldest son. You never heard of me? That's because I shamed my family and became a Muslim.' Instead, I just pretended I didn't know English."

He shakes his head. "I see your point, but I don't like it."

"Why didn't you come forward?" says Aunt Debbie. "Your father was begging for you to repent. You could have eased his heart."

"If I had gone forward, I wouldn't have meant it. I'm a Muslim. That won't change."

"Becky, talk some sense into your husband. Bring him back to Christ, as you said."

"Isaiah has the right to worship as he chooses. I can't tell him how to believe."

Ripples

"It's not right," says Uncle Ken. "I'm worried about Chris. He looks old these days. Did you see the way he walked out of the church? Like a man of seventy or more."

"He paints this as a struggle of Biblical proportions. Good versus evil. Why can't he simply accept that I've chosen a different way of life?"

"You still don't understand that, boy? From the day you were born, he set out to prepare you for the ministry. That's probably why he was so hard on you. He knew he, himself, wouldn't go far, but he thought you would set the world on fire."

"So, I didn't fulfill his dream. He still has Jacob and Benjamin."

"Benjamin has some potential. Jacob is a good boy, but too quiet. You, boy, you have a fire in your soul. You were supposed to use that in the service of your Lord, not let yourself be dragged into Hell."

"But, Uncle Ken, isn't it possible that Christianity isn't the only way? Why does everyone think being a Muslim automatically condemns me?"

"Unless you accept the Lord Jesus Christ as your personal savior, you are condemned. You know that in your heart. Or have you forgotten everything you were taught?"

No, I remember it all too well. "I follow different teachings now."

"I know." He wipes his mouth with his napkin and throws it on his half-eaten food. "I'm done here."

After he leaves, no one eats. Aunt Debbie throws the food in the trash. "Such a waste," she says more to herself.

I'm sure Uncle Ken would like to throw me out, but Aunt Becky always says blood is thicker than water. Even heathen blood.

I thought I would go see Mom after dinner—I haven't talked to her since coming back—but I'm tired. Becky comes upstairs with me. I stretch out. She picks up the Qur'an.

"What are you doing?"

"I want to see what it is about this book that gives you so much backbone." She reads. After a few minutes, she chuckles.

"You found something funny in there?"

"No. I was just trying to imagine you as an evangelist."

∼

In the morning, before he leaves to open the store, Uncle Ken takes another stab at educating me. "This is my second cup of coffee, and it isn't eight yet. I tossed and turned all night thinking about your father and you."

I shrug. "I don't know what to do about it."

"You know. Picture your father in the church yesterday, and you'll know exactly what you should do. What you should have done there in the church."

How will I ever reach Dad? I can't even make Uncle Ken understand.

Becky and I clean the kitchen before walking to their house, hand in hand. "What did you think of the Qur'an?"

"It's interesting. I'll keep reading."

I want to tell her about Islam, but it's better if she reads for herself.

We pass the church. No car. He stays home on Mondays. But I won't be intimidated. I walk up to the house.

Jacob answers. "Hey, Isaiah. It's nice to see you, but you shouldn't be here."

"I'll take my chances. Are you going to let us in?"

"Dad's in the shower. You can't stay long."

"I don't know why I should leave. This is my family."

He shrugs. "It's your funeral."

Mom is in the kitchen, taking biscuits out of the oven. I walk up behind her and touch her shoulder. She jumps.

"Isaiah," she whispers. "What are you doing here?"

"I miss my family. I want to come back."

"I want you back, but it won't work unless you first come back to Christ."

"Can I at least have a hug?"

Her hug is short and distracted. "I need to get this food on the table. You know your father likes a big breakfast. He'll be walking in here any minute. You need to leave."

"I don't understand."

She turns away from the stove. "You had better learn to understand. Do you realize what this is doing to your father? He barely sleeps at night. He gets headaches. His stomach is always upset. And he has

Ripples

dreams. He told me about your vicious dream of killing him. When your father dreams, he is embracing you and welcoming you back.

"He loves you, Isaiah. He wants to accept you, but you make it so difficult. You know what his faith means to him, and, yet, you continue to flaunt your rebellion. I always thought you had a kind heart. I never knew you could be so cruel."

His voice comes from another part of the house. "Melinda, where are my navy slacks?"

"They're in your closet. I'll be right there." She grabs my arm. "If you have any love for your father, you will leave. We'll see you at the airport."

I never could argue with her. "Okay, I'll see you then."

Becky is in the living room, holding David. I touch her shoulder. "We need to go."

"I thought you were going to stand up to him."

"It's not worth it."

She kisses the baby and carefully hands him back to Ruth. She'll make a good mother.

∼

We're stuck in this place for another day. I can't see my family. I'm tired of hanging around Aunt Debbie's house. We decide to walk into town.

It's hot. We step into the grocery store to buy ice cream. We haven't gone ten feet when a woman calls out. "Hello. We met at the church yesterday, remember?"

Becky slips back into her role. "Yes, how are you?"

"Oh, I'm fine, except for this heat. My feet are swollen up something terrible. But you don't want to hear about that. Has your friend opened his heart to the Gospel?"

"Not yet. I'm still trying to convince him."

"God bless you, dear, for bringing the truth to this poor man."

The cashier tells Becky she's praying for me. When we go back out into the sun, a man says, "Hotter than Hell today. I sure am glad I'm saved."

That's how it is all day long. Walking past the fire station. Sitting in the park. Waiting in line at the bakery. I feel like we've traveled into another dimension. The land that time forgot.

We walk back to the house, hot and tired. Aunt Debbie is in the kitchen. "Come in here, Isaiah," she calls. "You, too, Becky."

She's chopping carrots. "Where have you two been all day? I called your mother, and she said you left hours ago."

"We took a walk around town."

"What do you think? It's a little smaller than Chicago, isn't it?"

You could fit a thousand Pine Creeks into Chicago, with room to spare.

"It's nice," says Becky. "Here, we brought you a cake. I know how much you like chocolate."

"Well, isn't that sweet? Did you eat lunch over at Maeve's? It's the only restaurant in town, but the way Maeve cooks, we don't need anything else."

"No, we just had ice cream."

"I would feed you, but dinner will be ready in thirty minutes."

"Can I help you with anything?" says Becky.

"Sure, honey. Can you take over these carrots? After that, you can tear the lettuce and chop the celery."

I wander into the living room. Willy is watching some crime show. "Hey, how you doing? I haven't seen much of you lately."

"Thanks for telling my father. I got the scolding of my life. You shouldn't mess with people like that."

"Sorry. I thought he should know."

"By the way, I saw you and that wife of yours walking around downtown today while I was working over at the garage. One of the mechanics said you don't know any English. So, I said, 'You got to be kidding. Hell, that's my cousin. Reverend Adams' son. He went and joined some Moslems up there in Chicago.' I thought he should know. Understand what I mean?"

"Yeah, Willy. Thanks a lot."

I head back into the kitchen and help Becky fix the salad.

Uncle Ken walks in five minutes before dinner. He comes to the table frowning. "Some women came into my store this afternoon, gossiping as usual. I went about my work until I heard them mention Reverend Adams. Something about how he has another son who's a Muslim. The one who pretended to be a foreigner. This is a small town, and word travels fast. Your father is one of the most respected men in

Ripples

Pine Creek, and you have managed to taint his reputation in just two short days." He pounds the table with his fist.

"I want you to take your wife and your things and get out of my house. Chris Adams is my minister, my brother, and my friend, and I won't allow anyone to drag his good name through the mud."

"We can't just throw them out on the street, Ken. They're family."

"This boy sure doesn't act like family. You'd think he was brought up by wolves."

Willy snickers.

"Shut up, boy, if you know what's good for you, or you'll be out on the street, too."

"I won't tolerate it. You will not treat my nephew this way." Aunt Debbie puts her arm around Becky's shoulders. "You two can stay here as long as you like."

"This is my house!" Uncle Ken shouts. "I'm the one who puts a roof over your head."

"And who is it that washes your clothes, cooks your meals, and cleans your house? You can't talk to me that way, Ken Tanner."

"The hell I can't. This is my house, you are my wife, and I can talk any way I want."

Willy smirks. "I didn't know you could curse, Dad."

"I should have smacked you a long time ago."

I yell above the fracas. "Don't fight. We'll leave." I grab Becky's hand. "Let's get our things."

"You will stay right here," says Aunt Debbie. "I will not have my kin put out like stray cats. Ken, I don't like the problems between Chris and Isaiah any more than you do, but Chris brought some of it on himself. Melinda sat right here at this table and told me how Chris beat the boy. They'll move on tomorrow, after Ruth leaves. Tonight, they will stay in my home."

This is only the third time I've seen Aunt Debbie get angry. Life is full of surprises.

Uncle Ken runs his hands through his hair. "One more night. That's it."

"Now that that's settled," says Willy, "Let's eat."

This chicken is good, but my appetite's gone. How did everything become so complicated?

When he's finished, Willy stands up and heads for the living room.

"Get back here, and wash your plate." Aunt Debbie is still tense.

"No problem." On his way to the sink he whispers, "Gotcha."

Becky stays to help Aunt Debbie. I sneak up to Jack's room. I need to lay low for the next twelve hours.

Ripples

Kyle: Part One

My wife and I snuggle together on the plane and plan our week.
"First, we have to go to the beach," I say. "I love the ocean."
"Wait until we go to Egypt. We'll swim in the Mediterranean. Anyway, I want to spend some time touring the studios. Maybe we could go on one of those tours of celebrity homes."
"I didn't think you were into that kind of thing. Speaking of movies, Dad thinks we should go visit my Uncle Rob while we're out there. He used to be a screenwriter."
"You have an uncle in California?"
"A great uncle, yeah. One of his movies won an Oscar."
"Why didn't you invite him to the wedding?"
"I didn't think of it. I only remember seeing him once, and that was at my grandmother's memorial service. We're not like the Egyptians. How many of your relatives came to the wedding?"
"My grandmother, two uncles, five aunts, and twelve cousins. They flew all the way from Egypt. I'm sure your great-uncle would have flown in from California. Don't you have another uncle, too? I thought you said your dad has two brothers."
"Isaiah's dad moved down to Arkansas about a year ago. He doesn't like us because we're Muslims. I don't know why Isaiah and Becky didn't come to the wedding."
"Egyptians have large extended families. My mom's family is close, too. What happened to yours?"
"I have no idea. Welcome to the Adams family circus."

∼

Our hotel room has a great view of the beach. We settle in and get ready for our swim. Faiqa wears a modest suit. I pull on my knee-length trunks.

The ocean. I drive the rental car as close as I can and hop into my chair for a better view. Faiqa sits in my lap. There are some benefits to having a wheelchair.

She's seen the Pacific, the Atlantic, and probably the Indian and Arctic Oceans, too. This is only my second time. I stare. It's awesome.

"Keep going," says Faiqa. "You want to swim, don't you?"

When I'm close enough, I park my chair and use my arms to "walk" into the waves. I sit while Faiqa splashes me. I grab her and kiss her, the waves covering us in a blanket of froth.

All day, we play and swim. I love being in the water. The weightlessness. The freedom. I wish we could stay here forever.

When we go back to our room, we order room service and take turns feeding each other. At night, I hold her close.

On Tuesday, we do the whole Hollywood thing. The stars on the sidewalk, the celebrity mansions, even a studio tour. Afterward, she does a little shopping on Rodeo Drive. Mr. Hammadi gave her spending money.

I've never been into shopping, but I have fun following her and watching her try on expensive dresses. I grunt when she walks out in something revealing.

"What's wrong?"

"You're my wife, and you're beautiful. I don't want every guy gawking at you."

She finally settles on a more modest black dress.

On Wednesday, we decide to drive up north along the coast. On our way out of town, we'll stop and see Uncle Rob.

"Shouldn't you call him first?"

"He's retired. I think we'll catch him at home." The truth is, I don't want to interrupt our honeymoon with a visit to a relative. Especially one I don't know. But Faiqa insists. Family means a lot to her.

We drive up a curving road to his ranch house. Ocean view. Nice.

An old man answers the door.

"Hi. We're here to see Rob Hudson."

"That's me."

I didn't think he'd be so old. "I'm Kyle, Brad's son. This is my wife, Faiqa."

"Brad? How is he? Come in, please."

He leads us to the patio, which looks out over the ocean. "It's good to see you again, Kyle. What brings you and your wife out to California?"

"We're on our honeymoon."

"And you came to see your old uncle? Now that is special. Would you excuse me a moment?"

Ripples

When he comes back, we talk about Chicago and Dad. I tell him about our family's conversion.

"I know about your father," he says. "He emails me regularly. Do you mean to tell me your entire family has converted? What is it about Islam that attracted you?"

I describe what I felt that time in the masjid, when I climbed out of my chair and touched my head to the floor. He listens.

We've been here for thirty minutes maybe when the doorbell rings.

"I'll be right back."

As soon as he leaves, I whisper to my wife. "We came. Shouldn't we go now?"

"We can stay a little longer. Your uncle is very nice. I don't know why you never mentioned him."

"I told you. I barely know him."

He walks back in with a couple of guys in white coats who set up a table and return a few minutes later with food. It smells great.

"I thought we'd have a little picnic back here to celebrate your marriage. Everything is ready. Let's eat."

The food is fantastic. Shrimp, steak, rice, fried vegetables. I eat until I can barely move.

It's impolite to leave right after a meal. After Faiqa has told her life story, he tells us about himself. Why he left Chicago to try his hand at screenwriting. The movies he's written. The night he won the Oscar. His marriage and divorce. His daughter and her children. His novel which comes out next month. I never knew I had someone this interesting in my family.

Finally, he says, "I'm sure you two want to get going. I appreciate you spending your time with this old man."

"I've enjoyed every minute of it," says Faiqa. "Thank you so much for the wonderful meal." I nod. She can be the spokesperson for our family. I would have said something like, "Yeah, it's been nice."

He walks us out to the car. "It was so nice to see you. I need to come back to Chicago to visit everyone."

"Please do," says Faiqa. "You'll be welcome any time." I'm glad she doesn't invite him to stay in our apartment.

∼

We drive up along the coast for about an hour, enjoying the scenery. I pull into a public beach. We don't have our swimsuits. She sits on my lap, and we enjoy the beauty of the world.

When we get back to the hotel, I fall into bed. "I'm beat."

"I'll order room service."

California is beautiful, but the best moments are these. Being with my wife in the privacy of our room.

Ripples

Kyle: Part Two

The sun is in my eyes. I try to get up to close the curtain, but I can barely move. My body aches. "Faiqa," I whisper. "Faiqa, wake up."

"What's wrong?" She reaches for me and pulls back. "You're burning up."

"That would explain why I feel like death."

"Don't joke like that. I'll ask the front desk for some aspirin."

She pampers me with ice and hugs, but nothing works. I think my fever is getting worse. In my fog, I remember something Dr. Brooks said about getting immediate medical attention.

"I need to go to the doctor."

"Your doctor is in Chicago."

"You'll have to take me to the hospital. I must have an infection."

She helps me get dressed and tries to get me into my chair, but I'm too weak and too heavy to lift. "You have to call an ambulance."

"I'm scared."

"I'll be okay, honey." I want to reassure her with a hug, but I can't lift my arms.

They come. Faiqa brings them up to speed. They load me onto a stretcher. People stare as I'm wheeled through the hall. Faiqa walks beside me, clutching my hand.

They run the sirens. I wish they would turn those things off. It's not life or death, and the noise make my head hurt. Faiqa is bending over me, crying. I wipe away her tears. "Don't worry, honey. It's no big deal."

"No big deal?" She cries harder.

I know what's wrong before the doctor tells me. A urinary infection. I'm supposed to follow a strict routine, but I've let things go these last few days. "You have to be careful," he says.

I know. I know. "We're on our honeymoon."

"Take care of yourself. I'm sure your wife will appreciate it."

Faiqa's still clutching my hand. "Will he be okay?"

"He'll be fine. We'll keep him here for a few more hours. Then you can go back to your honeymoon."

Yeah, sure. I lie on the gurney in the emergency room, listening to someone scream, while the IV drips antibiotics into my system.

When they release me, Faiqa calls a cab. An aide wheels me out. We stop to fill a prescription. It's dark by the time we get back to the hotel.

Then there's the matter of getting me up to the room. The cab driver waits while Faiqa goes to get my chair. I'm feeling a little stronger, but the driver has to help me out of the cab. Faiqa gives him a nice tip.

I spend the last day of our honeymoon sick in bed. She brings me ice water, makes sure I take my pills, and hovers over me. I hold her close, but the mood is broken.

"I'm sorry I'm so much trouble."

"We're in this together, in sickness and in health, but don't you ever put me through this again."

~

On the flight back to Chicago, she says, "You have to let me know what to expect."

"I'll make an appointment with Dr. Brooks so he can tell you what it means to be married to me."

"Being married to you makes me happy. Dr. Brooks doesn't have to tell me that."

Other than that little trip to the emergency room, our honeymoon was great. She's everything I hoped for. And, even though I've proved to be a lot of trouble, she's staying with me. Incredible.

Before we land, she says, "You should have an Arabic name."

"Do you think so? What do you have in mind?"

"I want to call you Khalil."

"What does it mean?"

"Literally, friend. But, for me, it means my loved one."

Life isn't perfect, but she's my beautiful wife, and I'm her Khalil.

Ripples

Jennifer

In the morning, I reach for Nuruddin, finding Ahmed instead. I struggle through my morning fog, remembering what happened to my husband. He should be in Saudi Arabia now. I hope he's with Mama. I can imagine how much she needs him.

In the next few weeks, I must sell our furniture, pack for Pakistan, and get ready for a new life. I don't have a passport. Do I need a visa? Dad will know.

I don't know the first thing about living in Pakistan. Which clothes should I take? Should I bring Ahmed's toys, or should I buy new toys over there? How will I finish my degree?

And, how will I tell Mom? She's always worried that I would leave her and go to Pakistan. I told her I wouldn't be going anywhere for a long time. She won't be back from Mexico for another two weeks, and there's no way to reach her. I need her.

I'm washing my breakfast dishes when Dad calls. "Jamal and Muhammad want to do some lifting. Are you ready?"

I haven't packed anything. I'm not even dressed yet. "Yeah, sure, come on over."

I pull on jeans and a t-shirt, brush back my hair into a ponytail, and scan the apartment. Ahmed's toys scattered throughout the living room. Newspapers piled up in the corner. An unfolded basket of laundry.

I carry the basket to the couch and start sorting socks. Two for Ahmed. Two for Nuruddin. He'll need these, won't he? I hold up the black socks and stare at them. I miss his narrow brown feet keeping mine warm on a winter night. I miss the feel of his arms around me. I miss his lips kissing away my problems. I drop the socks and stare into space while Ahmed plays.

I jump at the knock. "Jennifer, it's us."

I slowly get up and open the door. Dad, Jamal, and Muhammad walk in. Jeremy and Raheema are right behind them. Raheema opens her arms and hugs me tightly.

"How are you?"

I hold on to Raheema. "What am I going to do?"

"Let's sit down." She walks with me to the couch. "Go ahead, Jennifer. Let it all out."

The tears flow freely while Raheema comforts me.

"Where should we start?" says Jeremy.

I have no idea. I cry harder.

Dad directs the traffic. When the tears are gone, I sit on the couch and watch my life being dismantled. No, this can't be my life. It must be a movie. They move in and out of the apartment, carrying furniture, toys, appliances, and clothes, and I know it can't possibly have anything to do with me.

∼

In five hours, it's finished. The apartment is empty. Jeremy rented a truck. He'll put our furniture and appliances in storage. My personal things and Ahmed's things are in Aisha's van. I hold tightly to Nuruddin's socks.

"You can talk to the landlord tomorrow. How much time is left on your lease?" Dad asks.

I don't remember. Okay, this is July. "Two or three weeks, I think." It's a good thing we haven't bought a house yet. Nuruddin was still doing the paperwork for an Islamic loan.

"That works well. You also need to call the utility companies tomorrow and have everything turned off. Give us another hour to put the furniture in storage. Go with Raheema, and we'll meet you for lunch. Are you okay?" He strokes my face

I nod, but I am definitely not okay. This is our home. Why is it empty now? Where is Nuruddin? Everything is happening too fast.

Raheema carries Ahmed out to her car. "We'll come back later for your car. You'll need to sell it. I can ask around."

She puts Ahmed in Nadia's car seat. "Where is Nadia?"

"My mother's watching her. We thought one toddler would be enough today. The packing went smoothly. When Jeremy and I moved last year, it took us weeks to pack."

"What's happening to me, Raheema? Why has everything changed? I want to go back to normal."

Ripples

She touches my arm. "A few weeks ago, my mother was talking about the day my father was shot. A policeman came to the door to tell her he would never come home. She was alone in a strange city, just her and her baby. A few days later, my uncle brought us to live with him in Chicago. Her entire life changed in a flash. When I dropped Nadia off this morning, Mom asked me to tell you that nothing will be normal for a long time, but you will get through it."

∽

During lunch, they all try to cheer me up. "I wish I could go to Pakistan," says Muhammad. "Will you email me as soon as you get there? Will you send pictures? I was so little when I went there, and I don't remember it very well. When can we go to Pakistan, Dad? Can I go with you and Jennifer?"

Dad is so patient. "I don't know, Muhammad. We'll have to see." Which is parent talk for, *I have no idea. Just shut up, and leave me alone.* But Dad would never say that.

"Raheema and I were talking about going to Bangladesh next summer," says Jeremy. "We'll stop by Pakistan, too, as long as we're in the neighborhood."

"Aren't Pakistan and Bangladesh a couple thousand miles apart?"

"I don't think it's quite that far. Anyway, I'll have to come see my favorite blonde sister."

He always calls me that. And I always say, "I'm your only blonde sister, silly."

"Made you smile!"

∽

After lunch, Jeremy and Raheema take me to Dad's house. Home again. I'm a married woman, with a child, but I walk through the door and step back in time.

"Jenny," calls Jeremy, "Come help bring in your stuff."

"Coming." I take a step outside, but, all of a sudden, I don't feel so well. I've been queasy since breakfast. I shouldn't have eaten those onion rings for lunch. I run to the bathroom.

Great. The last thing I need right now is to get sick. I hope it's just one of those twenty-four hour bugs.

∼

They unloaded my things while I rested. I've been lying here for the last two hours, too tense to sleep and too tired to get up. Aisha knocks.

"How are you feeling?"

"Come on in. I'll be okay. It must be something I ate."

"Do you feel up to attending a wedding?"

That's right. Kyle is getting married today. I would rather stay in bed, but it's Kyle. "Sure. Give me thirty minutes."

∼

It was a nice wedding. They looked happy.

I hope they have a good marriage, like Nuruddin and me. I stare out the window of the van, missing my husband.

I'm so tired I can barely keep my eyes open. And I can't eat without throwing up. It must be stress.

The second I walk in the house, Ahmed runs to me. "Mommy!"

I pick him up. "Why are you still awake? It's way past your bedtime."

"I tried to get him to sleep," says Jamal, "But he kept playing. So I yelled at him, and he started crying. I gave him ice cream so he would stop crying. Now he won't sit still."

"He'll be up all night."

"Sorry. I told you I'm not a good babysitter."

"No, it's not you. He's a two-year old. Thanks for trying. I don't know how I'll get him to sleep. I'm so tired I can barely walk."

"I'll take him," says Dad. "You go ahead and rest."

"Thanks." I head upstairs. Aisha walks with me.

"I know you're tired, Jennifer, but can we talk for a minute?"

"Sure. What's wrong?"

"You're tired all the time. You keep throwing up. Are you pregnant?"

Ripples

"I don't know. No, I can't be. It's not possible."

"Isn't it?"

"I'm moving to Pakistan next month. Ahmed isn't potty-trained. I can't handle another baby." She holds me while I cry.

"You'll be okay. Allah won't give you more than you can handle. I'll run by the store tomorrow and pick up a test." She stays with me until I settle down.

She's right. I've suspected it all week, but I didn't want to think about it. What in the world will I do with another baby?

What Happened to Isaiah

The tragedy of life is what dies inside a man while he lives.

—Albert Schweitzer

Isaiah

I close my eyes, but I can't settle down. I try sleeping on my right side. Then my left. For a while, I lie on my back and stare. Sometime during the night, Becky moves to the upper bunk.

It's getting light outside. I struggle out of bed and stagger to the bathroom. Uncle Ken passes me in the hall. He's still frowning.

After praying, I sit on the bed. I need to get ready to go to the airport, but I'm beat. And beaten.

Becky comes down and stretches out on the lower bunk. "I know you didn't sleep well," she says, rubbing my back. "Come back to bed."

"Ruth is leaving this morning."

"We don't have to leave for another hour or so. You can get a little rest first. Come lie down."

She helps me relax.

∽

I wake up and glance at the clock.

"Get up. We're late. Hurry."

I take a quick shower and throw on some clothes. We'll never make it in time.

Aunt Debbie is downstairs. "Don't you want breakfast?"

"We overslept. We'll come back later for our stuff." I slam the front door and speed toward the highway.

"Slow down," says Becky. "You know how these small town cops are."

"I won't see my sister for another year."

When I enter the highway, I get her up to eighty. These hicks down here are too slow. I weave in and out of traffic.

"Isaiah, I don't want to have to tell you again. You need to control yourself."

"If I stay in the right lane, will that make you happy?" I shout. "I'll get behind some old geezer and miss seeing my sister. Okay, whatever it takes to shut you up."

I've been in the right lane for two minutes. We're behind some old man going fifty. "I can't take this anymore."

I check the left lane. Two semis roar toward us. I can't wait. I speed onto the shoulder.

Becky screams.

The car slides. I grip the steering wheel and pray. One sharp move and I'm back on the highway, a few feet ahead of the old man. I floor the accelerator.

"Isaiah!" Becky shrieks. "You're going to get us both killed."

Ripples

Kyle: Part One

I just called my family to let them know we're back. Matt told me what happened. Mom and Dad flew down to Arkansas three days ago. They didn't want to disturb our honeymoon. I pray for them all.

This whole thing with Isaiah and Uncle Chris has got me thinking. Life is serious. Even after my accident, I treated everything like a joke. Laughing helped me forget the pain. I need to stop fooling around. I have someone who depends on me.

∼

I wake up suddenly. I don't know if it was a dream, a nightmare, or what. It's still dark outside. Time for the morning prayer.

I wash up and go back to Faiqa, gently shaking her. "Wake up, honey. We need to pray."

She rolls over. "Leave me alone."

I keep badgering her until she sits up and blinks at the clock. "It's 5:00 AM, Khalil. I don't have to get up for another two hours."

"We haven't prayed since the wedding. Don't you think we should go back to it? Remember what happened." I pull her closer. I don't want to think about losing her.

She yawns. "You're right. Give me a minute."

Her hair is a mess, her face has creases from her pillow, and her eyes are puffy. She's still beautiful.

When she's ready, we go into the living room where I lead my wife in prayer.

∼

Marriage is great. Coming home to her at night. Waking up to her in the morning. Sharing our moments. We don't have a television. I have better ways to spend my time.

I called Dr. Brooks' office today and made an appointment. Faiqa wants to know everything. Including what we'll have to do to have a child. Not yet. Someday.

339

I remember the day I knew Amy was dead. I cried for her. Later, I cried for myself. My life was over. At least once, I thought seriously about ending it.

Allah has given me a second chance, a better chance, at happiness.

Ripples

Jennifer

Aunt Melinda called here yesterday, crying. Dad left this morning. I don't know what to think. First Abdul-Qadir. Now this. Sometimes, I think I can't make it through another day. Then I try to imagine what Aunt Melinda must be going through, and I hold Ahmed closer.
I'm almost ready to leave. I sold most of our furniture. Someone is coming later this afternoon to look at our cars. On Saturday, I'll have a garage sale. I never imagined I would have to fit my entire life into three suitcases.
I'm constantly battling morning sickness. Aisha helps me find foods I can keep down and always encourages me to eat. I can't imagine having another child. Ahmed keeps me running day and night.
Everything is happening too fast. I'm moving to a strange country. Kyle is married. And then there's Isaiah. Poor Uncle Chris.

Jamilah Kolocotronis

Kyle: Part Two

We've prayed regularly for the last week. It makes me feel stronger somehow.

Faiqa's getting ready for her summer classes. Before leaving, she throws a pale pink scarf over her head. I glance up from my corn flakes. "You look nice."

"I keep thinking about Isaiah and his family. You never can tell what will happen. You knew that already, didn't you?"

"In a way. When it happened to me, though, I was too busy dealing with my disability and the deaths of my friends." I don't talk about Amy anymore. "It's different this time." Isaiah is as much a brother to me as Matt is. All those stunts we pulled when we were young. He got beaten for his mischief. I got away with a short lecture. I wish I had helped him then.

"I know you want me to cover, and, after this, well, I thought I'd experiment a little. What do you think? Does it look good?"

"You always look good, honey."

She gives me a long kiss before she goes.

I can't believe how great life can be. Isaiah had it, too. I don't care what everyone else thinks. Isaiah blew it.

Ripples

Jennifer: Part Two

Dad calls from Arkansas every night. I pray for them all, in my own way.

∼

Mom and Peter were due back late last night. She calls after breakfast.

"Jennifer, why is your phone disconnected? And why are you at your father's house?"

"A lot has happened since you left. Could you come over here so we can talk about it?"

"Can't you tell me over the phone?"

"It's complicated, Mom. I'll tell you everything as soon as you get here."

"I'm on my way."

I end the call and turn to Aisha. "What should I tell her?"

"Tell her the truth."

"She won't like it."

"She might surprise you."

∼

When Mom knocks, I'm sitting on the couch, watching Maryam play house with Ahmed. I feel awful. I can't keep anything down. I just want to crawl back into bed.

I quickly review my points: Abdul-Qadir died; Nuruddin went to rescue his mother; he has to stay in Pakistan to take care of her; I'm leaving in three weeks; I don't know when I'll be back. And, by the way, I'm pregnant.

Aisha lets her in. "Heather, how are you? Did you have a nice visit with Michael?"

"It was wonderful, but what's going on with my daughter? Jenny, where are you?"

"I'm in here, Mom."

"What is all this about?"

I have to say it all at once so she won't have a chance to ask questions. "The phone rang early one morning, about two weeks ago." I tell the story all the way to this morning when she called. Including the moment I knew for sure I was pregnant.

"Well," she says. That's all. I have never seen my mother speechless.

"I didn't think we'd have to live in Pakistan this soon, but his mother needs him, and I have to go with my husband."

"Didn't I tell you this would happen—" She stops herself. "No, I won't blame you. Your husband is gone, you have another baby coming, and you're leaving soon to live in a strange land. I wish I had been here for you." She puts her arms around me and rocks me.

~

While Mom comforted me, Aisha made lunch. She calls us in to the kitchen to eat.

Mom tells us about Michael and Gabriela over soup and sandwiches. "She's very nice, the kind of girl I always imagined Michael would marry. I never imagined, though, that he would find her in Mexico.

"They have a cute house, but it's very small. Only two rooms. Her parents asked us to stay with them. Her father owns a shop, and her mother teaches at the village school. They're good people. Her grandmother makes pottery. Peter and I learned quite a bit about the local art.

"I asked Michael why he did it. He said I had taught him not to harm any living creature, and he couldn't imagine going to a place where he would have to carry a gun. He knew what he was giving up, but he said it was his only choice. If he ever comes back, they will arrest him. Do you remember last year when that deserter was executed? I worry about him, and I miss him, but I have to admit he did the right thing."

"Do you have pictures?"

"Oh, yes, hundreds of them. I was going to email them to you, but I'd better make copies so you can take them with you to Pakistan."

I hadn't thought about that. I have to sell my computer, too. "I'm scared, Mom. It's so far away. I don't know anyone except his mother. I don't know anything."

Ripples

"I'm scared, too. I have one child in Mexico and another going to Pakistan. But Peter's artwork is receiving quite a bit of attention, and my reputation is growing. We've talked about having a show soon. We'd better get moving so we can pay for all these trips."

I walk with her to her car. "I wish I could stay longer," she says, "But I need to unpack. I'll tell Peter to plan our trip to Pakistan. I'll be back tomorrow. Make sure you eat something. Saltine crackers always worked well for my morning sickness." She hugs me. "Oh, I am going to miss you."

"I'll miss you, too, Mom."

Watching her car disappear into traffic, I wonder when Mom became so mellow.

Kyle: Part Three

On Wednesday, I pick up Mom and Uncle Joshua from the airport. Dad decided to stay in Arkansas for another week or two.

"How is he?"

Uncle Joshua looks down. "He's badly injured. They say he'll pull through, but he has a long road ahead."

"I stayed with your Aunt Melinda most of the time," says Mom. "She's not taking it very well. I can only imagine what she's going through. I'm glad I could be there with her."

"What about Isaiah?" How could he be so stupid?

"No one has seen him since it happened."

"Where do you think he is, Uncle Joshua?"

"I don't know. I was too worried about my brother. He's in bad shape." He shakes his head. "I don't want to think about Isaiah right now."

They squeeze into my little red car. "You'll need something bigger now that you have a family," my uncle says.

A family. I like the sound of that.

Separate Paths:
Isaiah's Redemption

*Narrated Abû Hurairah: Allah's Messenger said,
"The strong man is not one who is good at wrestling,
but the strong man is one who controls himself in a fit of rage."*

Prophet Muhammad (Al-Bukhâri and Muslim)

Part One

I darted from the shoulder into the right lane, barely missing the old man's car. He swerved into the median, seconds behind the semi.

"What did you do? We need to go back!" Becky screamed.

I checked my rearview mirror and spotted his car, watching as he got out to inspect the damage. "He's okay. Someone will come along to help him."

"*We* need to help him."

She was right, but I couldn't. "I have to get to the airport."

She badgered me for the next ten miles. I kept my mouth shut, gripping the steering wheel and trying to tune her out.

∼

Becky parked the car while I ran into the terminal. Ruth was still there. Her flight had been delayed. We hugged. I cradled David in my arms, barely noticing my father's anger. After a few seconds, he walked up and snatched David from me. "Stay away from my grandson," he snarled quietly.

Ruth looked at us both and started to speak, but she just shook her head. "Thank you for coming, Isaiah," she whispered, kissing my cheek.

My father glared at me. I backed away. I couldn't fight with him then, not with Ruth about to leave. I didn't want her to remember me that way.

Becky joined me on the sidelines. We watched while everyone said their last goodbyes. On her way through security, Ruth looked back at me and waved. And she was gone.

As soon as she was out of sight, I went after my father. "Why did you do that? I wanted to say goodbye to my sister."

He walked away. "You shouldn't have come. You're not wanted."

I followed. "I didn't ask to be your son!" I shouted.

He glanced around and lowered his head. "Don't make a scene," he said very quietly. "We must keep up appearances."

"To Hell with you and your appearances. I think it's time people knew the real Reverend Adams."

He clutched his head and grimaced. Mom came quickly to his side.

"Breathe deeply, Chris. Your tablets are in the car. Let's go." She took his arm. "Leave him alone, Isaiah. Can't you see he's suffering?"

Becky grabbed my arm. "Let's go, Baby."

"No." I jerked away from her. "You've seen the way he treats me. And I've tried, haven't I? I came down here and lost my job for it. That should count for something."

"You need to go," said Mom. "This isn't the right time."

"Is there ever a right time?"

They kept walking away from me. Dad was huddled over, clutching his head. Mom and the kids encircled him, forming a protective barrier.

I tried to break through their defenses. "Hasn't this gone on long enough? It's been over a year. Will I always be dead to you?"

We had reached the parking garage. He stopped and turned. "You don't know what you're asking of me."

"What am I asking? I only want to be part of this family again."

"You're the one who left. You abandoned your faith. You betrayed us." He continued walking.

"I'm here, aren't I? I wanted to see Ruth and the baby. You didn't have to snatch him from me."

He glared at me. "I don't want you anywhere near that baby. David will become the man you should have been."

I don't know what made me do it. Years of beatings or one lousy weekend. I pushed through his protectors. We were standing nose to nose.

"I have dreams," I said in the threatening tone he taught me.

He closed his eyes.

I pounced on him, knocking him to the ground. I waited for him to get up. I was looking for a rematch.

But he didn't move. I stared at his body, immobile on the concrete. Blood seeped from his nose and mouth.

"Isaiah! What have you done?" Mom shrieked.

"He's okay. He'll be okay." I stared a second longer before grabbing Becky's hand. "Let's go." I ran away from them, dragging my wife behind me.

Ripples

I jumped in my car, forcing Becky in, too. And I drove.

I headed for the highway. I thought about going straight to Chicago, but I needed to know. Had my nightmare come true?

Becky called 9-1-1 and reported an accident in the parking garage before starting her tirade. She screamed about how wrong, evil, and idiotic I was. "And how could you leave him like that?"

"What was I supposed to do?" What if I had killed him? I couldn't bear it.

"He is your father."

I had nothing more to say. She ranted until I pulled up in front of Aunt Debbie's house. We needed to retrieve our suitcases.

Before we climbed out of the car, I warned her. "Act normal. They don't need to know."

"What are you talking about? You can't hide something like this."

"Do this for me, Becky." I recognized my father's low, threatening voice in my words.

We walked up the porch steps and rang the bell. Uncle Ken opened the door. "Why are you here?" he growled. I was wondering the same thing about him. He should have been at the store.

"We need to get our things," I said tersely.

Aunt Debbie ran out from the kitchen. "I wish you didn't have to leave. At least you can stay for lunch."

Uncle Ken glowered. "You're weak, Debbie. I closed up the store and came home because I knew you couldn't handle the situation."

"But they're family."

"Let them go!" He shouted. My aunt shrank back.

We ran up the stairs, grabbed our stuff, and hurried out.

Once we were in the car, Becky started up again. "What kind of man are you?" She went on and on. I felt like pushing her, too. I gripped the steering wheel.

I wanted to escape to Chicago, but I couldn't leave. As I drove back toward Little Rock, I kept looking in the rearview mirror. The police would be coming for me. Where were they?

351

Part Two

For the last five days, we've stayed at this rundown motel near the hospital, eating fast food and watching TV. At night, I watch the cockroaches scurry across the floor.

The police never showed up. They must be looking for me in Chicago.

We're nearly broke. Tomorrow, I'll have to go out and get a job. I have eighteen hours to come up with a good story.

Every day, I buy a copy of the Pine Creek Tribune. It's only ten pages, cover to cover, but it tells me what I need to know. On Wednesday, they reported Reverend Adams' injury. He was taken by ambulance to a major hospital in Little Rock and admitted to the ICU. Today's paper said he's becoming responsive. He could be released in a few weeks.

I need to see him. I'm the oldest son. My family needs me. But will they ever want to see me again?

My wife ignores me, except when she's nagging or complaining. Which is all the time. "I want to go home." "I hate this place." "Why did you do that to him?" We're back to where we started. I don't know if we can get past it this time. I don't have the energy to try.

I didn't mean to do it. Something came over me. I wanted him to take me back. Instead, he replaced me.

I haven't had any nightmares since it happened. It's done now. But I never really wanted to hurt him.

~

Eight days ago, I assaulted my father. He's still in the hospital. Every day, I think about going. But I can't.

I found a job at a burger place two blocks away. It pays for the motel room, and they let me take home the unsold burgers and fries at the end of the day. We're not starving.

Becky won't even look at me. At night, she sleeps in the other bed. She won't let me near her.

I walk into our room at the end of my shift and toss her a dried out burger and some cold fries. "Dinner."

Ripples

Two days ago, she stopped nagging and starting giving me the silent treatment. At first, it was a welcome change, but I never knew anyone could be silent as loudly as Becky.

∽

I'm working the register. He walks up and orders two cheeseburgers and a salad. "My doctor keeps telling me to lay off the fries."

I adjust my orange cap—part of the costume I wear for the privilege of working here—and look up at him. "You need to take care of yourself, Uncle Brad."

"Isaiah. Where have you been?"

"We're staying at a motel down the street."

"They're looking for you. No one has seen you for over a week. Do you know what happened to your father?"

I'm sure they are looking for me. "Yes, I know."

"Your mother needs you. You can't imagine what she's going through. I hope they catch the man who did this. He needs to pay."

"What man?"

"The man who mugged your father in the airport garage. The police didn't get a good description. Everyone was too traumatized."

"How is Dad?"

"He's struggling. They give him morphine to help with the headaches. Much of the time, he's confused and disoriented. He's becoming depressed. He wants to get out of the hospital and go back to his church, but the doctor says he'll need another month or more to recuperate. Alhamdulillah, the seizures are under control now."

Confusion. Depression. Seizures. I turn away. "I don't have time to talk. The boss is watching."

He rubs the back of his neck. "Come see your father, Isaiah. Whatever problems you've had with him don't matter now."

"I'll try. Maybe tomorrow." I look at the woman standing behind my uncle. "May I take your order, please?"

Uncle Brad sighs and goes to a table to wait for his burgers.

Part Three

I've thought about it for three days. Uncle Brad is right. I should be there. And, if they want to punish me, I'll have to accept the consequences.

Or will I escape punishment? What's all that business about a mugging? Dad may be confused, but the rest of my family knows what happened. Why didn't they say it was me? Is it a matter of "keeping up appearances," or is it something more?

～

On Saturday, I get dressed early. "Where do you think you're going?" Becky asks. "Did they change your hours? Why didn't you tell me?"

"I'm going to visit my father."

"It's about time. Hold on. I'll go with you."

～

We ask for his room number at the front desk. Walking down the antiseptic halls, I remember how much I dislike hospitals. They smell like death and disease, made acceptable with chemical cleaners.

My father has been in many hospitals, visiting the sick as Jesus commanded. Often he made me come, too. I hated those trips. What was the point? The sick would go home, and we could visit them there. And the dying—well, what did it really matter anymore?

We walk into his room. Uncle Brad is here.

"Isaiah. Becky." He whispers. "I'm glad you're here."

"Where's Mom?"

"She'll come later. She uses the morning hours to take care of things at home."

My father is sleeping. He looks normal. I wonder why they're keeping him here.

"Chris is receiving therapy. When he hit the pavement, his brain was slammed against his skull. He had some bleeding inside his brain, and he was in a coma for four days. At first, we weren't sure he would make it."

Ripples

"How is he now?"

"He's better, but he has a long way to go. You'll see."

Becky puts the flowers we brought on a table, and we wait. I study him. He looks like he's taking a Sunday afternoon nap. I remember now. Sometimes, when I was little, I crawled next to him on the couch and fell asleep in his warmth.

∼

For two hours, I've waited. A few times, I glanced at his heart monitor. He's very still.

I'm halfway out the door, going for coffee, when Uncle Brad says, "How are you today, Chris?"

I spin around. My father's eyes are open. I walk quickly toward him, but my uncle holds up his hand. "Wait," he mouths.

"Chris, someone wants to see you. Isaiah is here."

Dad holds out his arms. "Isaiah." His voice is soft.

I rush to him. He puts his arms weakly around me. I lean down and put my head on his chest. Just like on those Sunday afternoons.

I'm still holding on when I feel a light touch on my back. "Isaiah."

I turn to look at Mom. I don't know when she came in. It's great to see her, but I don't want to let go of my father. I'm happy he's alive. He seems happy to see me, too.

Uncle Brad said he's still recovering. I wonder what he remembers.

∼

I had to go to work soon after Mom came. Becky stayed. She called me a few minutes ago, during my break.

"Hi, Baby. Your mom wants me to go back to Pine Creek with her. She needs my help. What do you think?"

"How long will you be gone?"

"I don't know. She wants me to teach Jacob, Benjamin, and Martha their lessons, and she needs someone to take care of the housework. People in the church have been cooking for her, but she really wants me there. She says it's lonely in that house at night."

"I'll miss you."
"I'll miss you, too."
"I'll drive up there on my day off."
"I love you, Baby."
I look around. I'm alone in the break room. "I love you, too."

Ripples

Part Four

I miss Becky. Mom tells me she's a big help. I'll drive up to Pine Creek tomorrow to see her and the kids.

I visit Dad every day. He's in rehab now. He doesn't talk much, and sometimes he seems confused. He asks for his glasses when he's wearing them. He tries to recite Bible verses, but he's forgotten much of what he knew. I wonder if it will come back to him.

∼

Uncle Brad left this morning. I drove him to the airport. When his flight was called, he hugged me.

"I'm glad to see you and your father together again. He asked for you every day, as soon as he came out of the coma. I hope you realize how much you mean to him."

I felt like a ten-year-old again as I looked into my uncle's eyes. "Did he say that?"

"Yes, he did." He gave me another quick hug and headed toward security.

∼

When I walk into his room, he's sitting up in bed. "How are you, Dad?"

He nods. "I would like you to read the Bible to me."

I agonize over his request for a full thirty seconds before turning to the Book of Psalms. I'm sure he would rather hear the Gospels, but I can't. I'm a Muslim.

"Blessed is the man that walketh not in the counsel of the ungodly," I start, "Nor standeth in the way of sinners, nor sitteth in the seat of the scornful. But his delight is in the law of the Lord; and in his law doth he meditate day and night. And he shall be like a tree planted by the rivers of water, that bringeth forth his fruit in his season; his leaf also shall not wither; and whatsoever he doeth shall prosper."

"Stop," Dad says.

"What?"

"I have tried to be that man."

I silently read the passage. Yes, that sounds like Dad.

"Go on," he says.

I continue reading. "The ungodly are not so: but are like the chaff which the wind driveth away. Therefore the ungodly shall not stand in the judgment, nor sinners in the congregation of the righteous. For the Lord knoweth the way of the righteous: but the way of the ungodly shall perish."

"Stop."

"What is it, Dad?"

"Which are you?"

"I'm a Muslim," I blurt without thinking. I need to be careful. I don't want to upset him.

"I know. But are you godly or ungodly?"

"What do you mean?"

"My brothers are Muslims. Though I disagree with them, they are godly men. Are you?"

"I don't know," I say softly.

He nods. "Think about it."

I pause.

"Keep reading," he says. "I want to hear more."

Part Five

I knock. Jacob comes to the door.
"Hey, Isaiah, it's good to see you. Come on in."
Becky is sitting on the couch, reading to Martha. She pauses and looks up. "Hold on, Baby. I need to finish this story."
Benjamin runs out of his room. "Isaiah. You're here." He hugs me. He's getting tall.
Mom walks in behind me. "Benjamin, did you finish your assignment?"
"Not only did he finish, he did extra work, too," says Becky. Benjamin smiles. Like me, he's never received much praise.
The house looks good. Everything is neat and orderly. Something is cooking on the stove.
Mom smiles. "That smells good, Becky. Did you make it?"
"I like Becky's cooking," says Martha.
I settle in, and we sit down to eat Becky's beef stew. This is what I wanted. I wish Dad was here.
At night, Becky and I snuggle in Ruth's old bed. It's good to be close to my wife again.
"Thanks for taking care of them."
"Your mom is one of the sweetest women I have ever met. And the kids are great. Especially little Martha. She's so cute, and smart, too." She shakes her head and clucks her tongue. "I don't know why you always said they were weird."
"Not weird, maybe. But different."
"Whatever it is, I like it."
I kiss her again. "Thank you."
"For what?"
"For staying with me, even when I act like an idiot."
She kisses me. "We're in this together, Baby."

Part Six

Dad is leaving the hospital today. Yesterday, I quit my job at the burger place. Becky and I will stay in Pine Creek for a week or two before heading back to Chicago for another year of school.

He's dressed and sitting on the bed, waiting for me.

"Hi, Dad. I'm sure you're ready to get out of this place."

He nods. "Yes."

The doctor said he has no major permanent brain injury—though he may have trouble with short-term memory, and he's still at risk for seizures—but he's different.

~

On the way to Pine Creek, I pass the spot where I ran that old man off the road. All the terrible memories of that day come rushing back. I can't stay quiet.

"Dad, do you know how you were hurt?"

"Yes, I remember."

"The police think you were mugged."

"Yes."

"But that's not how it happened. I did it, Dad. I was angry, and I knocked you down. You wouldn't get up. There was no mugger. It was my fault."

"Stop the car."

"We're on the highway."

"Stop this car, Isaiah. Now." Firmness creeps back into his voice.

I pull over onto the shoulder. What's he doing?

"Look at me, Isaiah. Turn around, and look at me."

I turn to meet his gaze.

"I know you hurt me. I remember."

"Why didn't you tell the police?"

He gently grips my arm. "I forgive you. We all do."

"But you were always so mad at me before. And what I did to you. It was worse than anything."

"I forgive you." He moves his hand to my shoulder and pulls me forward. I submit. We hug for long minutes next to the highway.

Ripples

Before going back on the road, I ask. "You never lie. Why didn't you tell the police the truth?"

"I love you, Isaiah, and, may God forgive me, I want to protect you any way I can."

"Why do you ask God to forgive you?"

"My love for you is of the flesh. I strive to be a man of the spirit, yet I still give in to my desires. And I can't do otherwise." He strokes my face. "God is perfect, and He sacrificed His son, but I am a man. May God forgive me for my weaknesses, and may He forgive me for trying to be like Him."

I don't agree with his theology, but I can't argue with the feelings behind it. I lean over to kiss him on the cheek. We sit by the highway, becoming father and son again.

∽

As we drive into Pine Creek, he says, "That day at the church, I said it would be better if you had died a physical death. That's not true."

"And I never wanted to kill you."

It sounds strange. But it needed to be said.

Separate Paths:
Kyle's Recognition

Richness does not mean having a great amount of property, but richness is self-contentment.

Prophet Muhammad (Al-Bukhâri)

Part One

My father-in-law stopped by my office today. "How is your uncle?"
"He'll live, but I don't know how long it will take him to recover."
"Alhamdulillah. May Allah help him." He briefly raised his hands in prayer before continuing. "I want Faiqa and you to come for dinner tomorrow night. There's something important we need to discuss."
Important? "You won't tell me what it is, will you?"
"Not until tomorrow night."
I ask Faiqa when I get home. "Is something wrong?"
"Not that I know."
"Does your father like me?"
"Of course, he does."
"He's said that?"
"Not in so many words, but I can tell when he's happy."
"So, I'm not in trouble."
"Stop worrying, Khalil." She kisses me. "You act like you're afraid of him."
"Aren't you?"
"Baba? He's just a big, cuddly teddy bear."
I've always pictured him more like a grizzly.

∽

We arrive promptly at seven. First, we sit in the family room and chat. Hannah asks about Uncle Chris. Faisal talks about applying to law school. I wait for the important discussion.
Hannah made lamb. It's delicious. I eat more than I should. Faiqa thinks I should lose a few pounds, but she doesn't say anything when I fill my plate for the third time.
While Faisal and Faiqa help their mother clean up, Mr. Hammadi asks me to come back into the family room. "Kyle," he says, "You're wasting your time."
"How, sir?" I don't watch TV or play video games these days.
"You're my son-in-law now. I told you to call me Gameel." He smiles and pats my arm. "You're too bright to be working at a non-profit agency in a dead-end job."

"I wouldn't call it dead-end. Kids Who Care has taken off, and I have several speaking engagements every month. I've received a few requests to present my ideas in other cities and help them develop similar programs, but I keep putting them off because Faiqa doesn't want me to travel."

"You've done a great job—no one would dispute that—but wouldn't you like to be earning real money? Maybe buy a nice house for your wife? I know you wouldn't mind being well-off."

"Of course not. Who would?"

He leans back and stares at me. "I want you to work in my company. I'll start you out at Naturally! as an executive. A good salary. Your own office, with all the amenities. And, when I retire in another fifteen or twenty years, you will be ready to take my place."

Faiqa peeks in. "That's a great idea, Baba."

I don't like it. I love what I'm doing—working with people and making a difference. Gameel's company does help people, in a way. Naturally! provides healthy alternatives to the junk they call food these days.

"I don't hire 'yes' men," he says. "I'll expect you to put your creativity to work. Develop new products and new ways of reaching people. Hope Center is in the business of helping others, and so am I. The difference is that, in my company, you will be paid what you are worth."

"Can I think about it and let you know?"

"I don't know what there is to think about. I'm asking you to carry on the family business. Consider the opportunity."

"You're right. But my father says that, before we make a major decision, we should pray about it. I think I need to do that first."

"*Salatul Istikhara*. Go ahead and pray. Come for dinner tomorrow night, and we'll make the arrangements."

He's handing me the world on a silver platter. I must be an idiot not to jump at it.

Faiqa sure thinks so. "What's wrong with you?" she says on the way home. "We would have more money. My father would have someone to pass the business to. What do you need to think about?"

"What about Faisal? Shouldn't he have a say in this?"

"My brother wants to be a lawyer, not a businessman. Not a corporate lawyer even, but a public defender. If Baba passed the business to him, he would probably sell it and give half the proceeds to charity. My father sees you as his successor. Do you know what an honor that is?"

"Let me pray about it first."

"When did you get to be so religious? I thought you became a Muslim so you could marry me."

"You knew?"

"It was very obvious."

"Anyway, I have a beautiful wife to take care of, and I need to take everything more seriously."

"If Baba hadn't let you marry me, would you still be a Muslim?"

"Yeah. I think I would be."

Jamilah Kolocotronis

Part Two

There was no way I could decline Gameel's offer. When we went back to their house for dinner last night, he laid out the specifics. I sure didn't expect to be making that kind of money, especially not without a college degree.

I asked Gameel to give me two weeks to wrap up my work at Hope Center. I've been there for nearly two years now, and I'm sorry to leave.

This morning, I called Bob Warren. "Can I come by your office? I need to tell you something."

"I'm in a meeting." He paused, probably consulting his schedule. "I can see you at four. Will that work?"

"Yes. I'll see you then."

I'll miss Warren. He treats me like a human being. That's harder to find than you would think.

I organize a file for my programs. Kids Who Care is running smoothly. I type up a short report and add it to the file.

My work with fatherless boys hasn't progressed as far. I have put together a small mentoring program with the help of community business leaders. Part vocational training, part moral guidance. I know what needs to be done to make the program stronger. I type it all up.

The work I started doing, recruiting and coordinating volunteers, has its strong and weak points. In some areas, we have more than enough qualified people. Other areas are still suffering. I write a few pages detailing what I've done so far and my recommendations for the future.

I'm ready for Warren. I pick up the phone and order a late lunch.

∼

At four, I show up at Warren's office, CDs in hand.

He's on the phone. He motions for me to come in. I wait while he wraps up the conversation.

"Kyle, how are you today? What can I do for you?"

I'll get to the point. "When I first came here, I was just a few weeks out of rehab, and I didn't know how I would get my life together. You

Ripples

gave me the chance to prove myself. I can't tell you how much I appreciate your support."

"You're a hard worker, Kyle, and you've brought some great ideas to Hope Center. Is there a problem?"

"My father-in-law has asked me to work in his company. I start in two weeks."

"I shouldn't be surprised. I'm sure Gil will be pleased to have you on his staff."

"I'll miss the work I do here at Hope."

"I'm certain you'll find a way to fulfill your dreams through Gil's company. Health is an important field. You realize that, of course."

"Sure. There's one more thing. I know you took me on as a charity case, but I think you need to hire someone to take my place. Kids Who Care is up and running, and the mentoring program is making progress. I have all the documents and reports you'll need on these CDs." I place them on his desk. "I hope you can have someone in place by the time I leave."

Warren walks around his desk and sits in a chair he keeps for visitors. "I admit that when your uncle first brought you here, I felt sorry for you, but soon I saw how capable you were. That's why I asked the board to give you a paid position. You have not disappointed me. I don't see you as someone who is disabled. You have a lot going for you, Kyle, and Gil will be lucky to have you on his team.

"I agree with you about the position. I'll run it by the board, and we'll begin advertising." He offers his hand. "It has been very nice working with you."

~

"That really is the way it happened," I tell Faiqa over dinner.

"What did you think he would say?"

"I don't know. Good riddance?"

She laughs. "You think you have everyone fooled with that false humility, but I happen to know you're full of yourself."

You can't fool all of the people all of the time, I guess.

Part Three

My last day at the center. My work is done. Everything is ready for the next person who sits behind this desk. They're still conducting interviews.

I brought a small box. I open each drawer and pack my belongings. When I open the top drawer, I find Amy.

"I'm married now, Babe. I don't think my wife will let me bring you home." I hold the picture frame over the trash can, but I can't let go. I put her picture in the box, next to my picture of Faiqa. My wife's picture will go on top of my new desk. I'll give Amy's picture to her parents.

I pack up my Qur'an and a few other books. That's it. I'm done.

"Are you busy?" It's Warren.

"No, I think I'm all wrapped up here."

"Good. I'd like you to come to my office. Let's go." He walks out, and I follow. I don't have anything better to do.

I'm glad they don't yell, "Surprise!" They clap instead. I look around. I think they're all here. I wonder who's running the center.

Faiqa is here, too. And Gameel. My wife hugs me. "Are you surprised?"

"Yeah, I am." I mean, they didn't have to do all this.

"Your new office is waiting for you," says Gameel.

We have cake and punch, and they say they'll miss me. Someone gives me a card. "We all signed it."

The party doesn't last long. They need to get back to work. As I finish my second slice of cake, Warren says, "I hope you don't forget us."

"I won't." I don't see how I could.

"You don't have to stay here all day. Unless you want to, of course."

I look at Faiqa. She smiles. "Let's go home."

On my way out, Warren hands me a present. "Something for your new office."

I tear open the wrapping. It's a plaque.

For Kyle Adams,
Founder of Kids Who Care

Ripples

You have made a difference.
You will be greatly missed.

From All Your Friends at Hope Center

I keep staring at the plaque as we head for the car. I will definitely miss this place.

Part Four

I've worked at Naturally! for a week. It's okay. Hope Center was better.

People here are nice, except for a couple of jerks. One guy, Lee, always talks to me in a raised voice. I keep telling him, "I'm paraplegic, not deaf."

Another guy, Russell, makes snide remarks about how I married the boss's daughter. Yesterday, he said, "I don't know how you managed to get this job. Oh, I forgot. You married into it." The word on the grapevine says he thought he would get this position.

Then there's Patsy, a nice old lady who means well but makes me crazy. If I'm going down the hall with some papers, she says, "Let me carry those for you." She opens doors for me and even tries to push my wheelchair. I want to tell her to back off, but she's old, and she doesn't mean anything by it. Hopefully she'll retire soon.

My title is creative consultant. In spite of what Russell says, I suspect Gameel created this job for me. Part of what I do is marketing—finding innovative ways to introduce our products. I also work on customer relations. Yesterday, I received an email from a woman who wants to buy chocolate chip cookies without nuts, eggs, milk, or wheat products, and made in a factory that doesn't deal with those ingredients. I told her I'll look into it. It's at the top of my to-do list.

We have a whole line of health foods, from wheatless breads to fishless tuna. All of our fruit and vegetable products are organically grown. We also provide hypoallergenic mattresses, soaps, lotions, medicines, you name it. There's a big demand these days for foods and products without chemicals. I like to think I'm helping to make the world a little easier to live in.

But I would rather be working at the center. I'm totally bored. I have a nice office and a parking spot with my name on it, but, when you're in a wheelchair, reserved parking isn't a big deal.

I miss working with the kids. They looked up to me. I miss coming up with ideas that could make a difference in the life of a kid. Most of our customers are middle-aged and older. Here, I'm just another guy wearing a suit. There, I was somebody.

Ripples

I don't say anything to Gameel. He's thrilled to have me at the company. But I tell Faiqa.

"You should have seen those kids. I was reaching them. They needed someone, and I was there for them."

"Why don't you find a way to help kids on the weekends? You know how much these community organizations need volunteers."

"Good idea. I'll check that out."

"Not every weekend, though." She kisses me.

I know Hope Center has someone in place. I go online and ask around. After two weeks, I find a midtown community center looking for a football coach. I start next week.

∼

I just finished coaching my first football practice. It was awful.

These kids don't know anything about formations or strategies. They ran into each other, tripped around the field, and treated it all as one big joke. I had to break up a fight when a kid took offense to being tackled. Another kid, smaller than the others, sat on the sidelines and whined about wanting to go home.

I'm shouting at them to shape up when one of the fathers approaches. He listens for a moment before tearing into me.

"You have no right to yell at my son."

"Your son and his friends need to take the game seriously."

"They're kids. Let them play."

"Then why do they need a coach?"

"Maybe they don't. What would you know about coaching football anyway?"

I don't want a confrontation, but I won't let that one slide. "You don't know anything about me."

"I know you're sitting in that wheelchair yelling at my boy. Why don't you go out on the field and show him how it's done? I'd like to see you do that." He laughs.

"What is your problem?"

"My problem is having someone who is obviously unqualified and probably knows nothing about football yelling at my son."

"Like I said, you don't know anything about me. I lettered in high school. I could have made All-American, and probably pro, if I hadn't gotten side-tracked. What I want to know is why I have to defend myself to you in the first place."

"What I see is a guy in a wheelchair screaming at my son, and I don't like it."

"What you see is the wheelchair. That tells you all you need to know about me, doesn't it?"

"Hell, yes. You can't play. How are you going to teach my kid?"

I wish I could play against this jerk, but the field's a little muddy, and I wouldn't get far. I wouldn't mind tackling him.

"I'll show you. Which one is your kid? Call him over."

"Noah. Come here, son."

The one who started the fight. That figures.

I turn to Noah's father. "Watch this. Noah, give me that ball over there. Now run deep. Deeper!" I yell. I throw a perfect pass. Noah runs all over the field, stops, waits for the ball, and watches as it drops fifteen feet in front of him.

"Come back here."

He walks slowly. We wait. When he finally arrives, I say, "Tell me what you did wrong."

"I missed the ball."

"I know that. What can you do differently next time?"

"I don't know."

"How about using your eyes? You were zigzagging all over the place, but you weren't watching the ball. Football isn't about guessing. Remember that. Never take your eyes off the ball. Let's try that again. Go deep."

I throw another great pass. He watches the ball fall toward him and makes a decent grab for it. I wave him back. He runs.

"That was better. Practice is over for today, but we'll work on that next week. You might want to practice at home. Get your dad to throw a football with you in the evening."

"My dad's too busy."

"I think he'll make time for you. Now go get your stuff."

"You have a good arm there," Noah's father says. "You wanted to go pro?"

Ripples

"It crossed my mind. You saw Noah. These kids act like they've never seen a football before. I need to be tough with them in the beginning. This isn't just a way to kill an hour on a Saturday morning. Football can teach them coordination, speed, strategy, and teamwork." I toss the ball into the air, catching it easily. "Do you still think I'm unqualified?"

"I'll be back next Saturday. Show me what you can do."

"You're on."

∼

Before we go to sleep, I tell Faiqa about Noah's dad. "I still can't get over his ignorance. But I showed him a thing or two."

"You didn't hit him, did you?"

"I thought about it, but there were too many witnesses. Seriously, there are a lot of people out there who need to be educated."

"You can say that about almost anything."

"I never asked you this. How did you feel, the first time you saw me in my chair?"

She comes closer and puts her arms around me. "I looked into those deep, brown eyes of yours, and I didn't see the chair at all."

∼

Working with the kids has given me some ideas for the company. I want to develop a line of health food specifically made for kids. After practice, while we're waiting for their parents, I talk to the kids about their diets. They like macaroni and cheese, pizza, hamburgers, and just about anything with sugar. They don't like vegetables, and they don't eat much fruit, except for the occasional banana.

I ask them to try an experiment. "For one week, I want you to eat only healthy foods, like fruits and vegetables, and fresh foods. No preservatives." I talk to them about natural foods and show them how to read the labels. Ten of the kids agree to take the challenge.

At the next practice, I don't ask how it went. I watch. The kids who took the challenge are sharper and faster. Noah said he would do it, but he's as sluggish and aggressive as ever.

I confront him after practice. "You cheated on the challenge, didn't you?"

"No, I did it. Honest."

"What did you eat for breakfast this morning?"

"Cereal."

"The healthy kind?"

"The kind with marshmallows."

"Did you drink juice with your cereal?"

"No, but I had a cola on the way here."

"Sugary cereal and cola are poison for your body. Remember what I told you about eating healthy food?"

"I forgot about it."

"Try again next week. You'll be a better player."

All day Monday, I work on the products. How can I make macaroni and pizza healthier for these kids, and still keep it convenient and affordable for their parents? I do the research and submit my findings on Thursday.

Gameel comes to my office on Friday. "I read your latest proposal. We'll develop the recipes and conduct consumer research. If the results are positive, I'll have them develop a major ad campaign. This could increase our company profile dramatically. Good job."

I did it to help the kids, not the company. It's great that I can do both. Gameel's happy, and, once kids start begging for healthy foods and learn how to focus, their parents and teachers will be very happy.

I wish someone had done this for my generation. Half the boys in my class were on prescription drugs to help them focus. I was, too, for a couple of years, before my mom read articles about the dangers of drugging kids. She stopped the Ritalin and taught me strategies to help me learn. I'm using the same strategies at work and teaching them to the kids out on the football field.

Separate Paths: Jennifer's New Reality

Be in this world as though you were a stranger or wayfarer.

Prophet Muhammad (Al-Bukhâri)

Part One

We leave in six days. Ahmed and I just got our passports. Dad bought the tickets. I made a little money from selling all our things. Earlier today, I bought hand lotion for Nuruddin's sisters—I have no idea what they would like—and new clothes for Mama. I forgot to get something for the sister-in-law who lives with Mama. I'll do that later.

Mom has invited everyone for dinner at her place tonight. We all pile into Aisha's van. This is the first time my stepbrothers have gone to Mom's condo. She has fragile, expensive knick-knacks in every room. Aisha reminds them to behave.

I walk in. The room is dark. They jump out. "Surprise!"

I blink. So many people. Everyone I know must be here. I see Clarissa, Jenna, and Mrs. Porter. And Deidre and Morgan, my best friends from high school. Mrs. Coombs, our landlady, hugs me. "Are you surprised?" asks Mom. I hold on to her and cry.

It's great. I talk to all those people I didn't have time to call. They give me presents, too. A book with everyone's contact information. An album full of pictures—high school friends, college classmates, our apartment, family, Chicago. Home. Bags of toys and books to keep Ahmed busy on the plane trip. Some people give me money.

We're eating cake when Dad calls out, "Jennifer, come over here." Everyone looks. Mom and Dad stand together, a package between them. "This is from both of us," says Mom. "I'm sure you can use it," says Dad.

Both of them? Mom and Dad haven't done anything together since I was six months old, except argue.

I open it and stare for maybe a minute before crying for the fifteenth time tonight.

"You can keep in touch with everyone, and you can keep up with your writing. You should write a book about your experiences there," says Dad.

"And you can take university classes online," says Mom.

"I made sure it complies with the electrical system in Karachi, and you'll get up to ninety-six hours from that battery," says Dad.

"Now you have no excuse for not staying in touch," says Mom.

I hug them both. "Thank you so much. It's just what I need." And thank you for doing this together.

Kyle and Faiqa give me their present—computer software for writers.

"Thanks, guys." I hug Faiqa.

"So, we're finally getting rid of you," says Kyle. "It's about time."

"Are you kidding me? I can't wait to get away from your face."

We eat and talk. I say goodbye over and over again, crying each time, until everyone is gone.

"Thanks, Mom." I hug her. "You don't know how much this means to me."

"The laptop?"

"The laptop, the party, everything. I'll miss you so much."

"We'll come in a few months," says Peter. "We've entered an art competition in Lahore, and the art institute has granted me a sabbatical to conduct research on South Asian art. Be ready for us in January."

I hug him, too. "You are an awesome stepfather."

"I try," he grins.

Ripples

Part Two

Every day is special because of the time I spend with my family. In the mornings, I visit with Mom. We talk while she paints. Brianna entertains Ahmed. Every afternoon, I have tea with Raheema. When Jeremy comes home, he joins us while Nadia and Ahmed chase each other around their house. In the evenings, I'm with Dad, Aisha, and the kids.

On my last evening in Chicago, we all go out for pizza. "You can get pizza in Pakistan," says Dad, "But it's nothing like Chicago's."

After dinner, we go for a short walk along the lake. "You'll be near the ocean. Make sure Nuruddin takes you to the beach."

Aisha offers to put Ahmed to sleep for me. "I'm going to miss this little guy. You can go and rest."

I lie down, but I can't sleep. I run through my checklists. I must be forgetting something. How in the world will I get through this plane trip with Ahmed? He won't sit still for five minutes, much less fourteen hours. What will I do when I get to Pakistan? I don't speak Urdu. I don't know anyone except Nuruddin and Mama. I don't want to go, but I miss Nuruddin so much. I squeeze my pillow, pretending it's him.

He called last night. He said Mama is waiting for me. He's trying to find a good job. He's excited about the new baby. He loves me. He can't wait to see us again.

I hear Dad getting up for the morning prayer. I get up, too. There's no use trying to sleep. I hope I can rest on the plane.

I try to eat breakfast, but, between nerves and nausea, I can't force anything down. I've never flown before. I can't imagine being trapped in that tiny space for hours with a restless child. Dad says everything will be okay, but that's what he always says.

We all climb into Aisha's van. I run another mental inventory. Passports, tickets, luggage, laptop, Ahmed's in-flight bag. Anything else? I think we're ready. Oh, the gifts. Yes, I have them.

Mom, Peter, Brianna, Jeremy, Raheema, and Nadia meet us at the airport. I don't know what to say. I start crying.

I'm giving my goodbye hugs when Kyle races up. "Hey, Jen. You weren't going to leave before I came, were you?"

"I wouldn't think of it."

381

"Chicago won't be the same without you. But we'll miss you anyway."

I want to outdo him this one last time, but I don't have a comeback. I make a feeble attempt. "I, um, I wish I could say I'll miss you, too."

"Take care, Jen. Stay safe."

They call our flight number. "I'll try."

A final hug from Mom, and I head through the gate.

∼

We boarded nearly an hour ago. The plane is about to take off. Ahmed fusses. "It's okay, baby. We're going to see Baba."

The plane speeds as we leave the ground. I feel dizzy. Air presses against my chest. Dad squeezes my hand. "You'll be okay."

∼

We've been over the ocean for five hours. Looking out over the endless water gives me a feeling of desolation. I hope we see land soon.

Ahmed wakes up. I read him a story. He wants me to read it again. After the third time, he wants to get down on the floor and play. When I won't let go, he struggles and cries. I carry him down the aisle. He grabs a woman's glasses. "I'm sorry." He pats a bald man's head. "Excuse me." I walk quickly back to my seat, exhausted.

"Let me try," says Dad. He plays peek-a-boo, flying, everything he can think of. Ahmed squeals. An older man looks back at us and frowns. Dad shrugs. "Okay, big guy, let's go for a walk."

They're gone for twenty minutes. By the time they return, Ahmed has his head on Dad's shoulder.

"How did you get him to settle down?" I whisper.

"Practice. Why don't you get some rest, too?" Dad asks the stewardess for a pillow. I lean into it and close my eyes. I'm so tired.

I dream of Baba. He's sitting next to me on the plane. "Why are you not a Muslim, Jenny?"

"I don't know."

He pats my hand. "You will be a Muslim."

Ripples

When I wake up, I feel better. Ahmed is still asleep. Dad is reading.

"Aren't you tired?" I ask him.

"I can never sleep on a plane."

"I just had a dream about Abdul-Qadir."

"I can't imagine going to Karachi and not seeing him there. But he died next to the Ka'bah. There's no better place."

"The last time I talked to him, before he went on Hajj, I promised him I would become a Muslim."

Dad puts his book down. "You did?"

"It would be better for Ahmed, wouldn't it, to have two Muslim parents? And I know Nuruddin would like it."

"Those aren't the right reasons for converting. What do you feel, Jenny, in your heart?"

"I've watched you follow Islam practically my whole life. My brothers are both Muslims. My husband is a Muslim. I believe in God. Muhammad sounds like he was a very special person. I like Islam, but I don't know if I could be a Muslim."

"Why not?"

"I don't want to cover my head. It would be hard to pray five times every day. I don't see how in the world I could fast during Ramadan. After what happened to Abdul-Qadir, I would be afraid to go on Hajj. And I don't want to disappoint Mom."

"Let's take things one at a time. You believe in Allah and accept Muhammad as a prophet of Allah. Is that right?"

"I think I do."

"You're nearly there then. If you really believe in Allah, wouldn't you want to worship Him in the best way?"

"I guess so."

"Islam isn't always easy. I get hungry during Ramadan, but I know I'm doing it for Allah, so I just keep at it. I pray because I want to stay in touch with Allah. Once you do it, you'll know what I mean. As far as Hajj is concerned, I just told you that Abdul-Qadir died in the best way. He is a martyr, and he will go straight to Paradise. Each of us must die when our time comes, and, if I could choose, I would rather die in Makkah than anywhere else on earth. Anyway, over three million people come back from Hajj each year, so Hajj itself isn't deadly. I'm going to ask you again, Jenny. Do you believe in Allah?"

383

I gaze at my sleeping son. "Yes. But what about Mom?"

He sighs. "Your mother loves you and wants what's best for you. I know she isn't crazy about Islam, but, if you give her time, I think she could accept any decision you make."

She is getting mellow, isn't she? "So, what do you think I should do?"

"I think you're ready to be a Muslim."

"Just like that? Don't I need to study? I'm not ready yet."

"Do you think I was ready? Mahmoud sent me to Pakistan because I was this close to going back to the bottle. I didn't know what I was getting myself into when I made shahadah, but I did it anyway. And I have never looked back."

I remember what Dad told me about his wild days. "Do you still have trouble fasting?"

"Sometimes. I get hungry and thirsty, just like everyone else."

"Okay." Which means I'll think about it. I look out the window. The ocean is gone. I see mountains. We must be getting close.

An hour later, Dad says, "Let me know. I promised not to jump up and down, remember?"

I laugh. He made that promise when I was sixteen. I can't believe he still remembers.

Ripples

Part Three

We're almost there. We've been in Pakistani airspace for the last hour. The pilot says we'll start the descent soon.

Ahmed is awake and fussing. "Hold on, baby. We're going to see Baba."

Dad holds my hand. "Are you ready?" Ready for the descent? Ready to start a new life in Pakistan? Ready to become a Muslim?

I smile at him. "Don't jump up and down, Dad. I'm ready."

He hugs me. "Allahu akbar," he whispers. I know what that means. God is the Greatest.

The plane drops slowly, steadily. Dad gazes out the window. I grip his hand. Long minutes pass before we finally touch ground. I breathe a sigh of relief. I can't wait to get off this plane and into my husband's arms.

When I try to stand, my legs feel weak. Dad takes the baby while I regain my circulation and get my things from the overhead rack.

I wait anxiously behind other passengers. A Pakistani grandmother struggles with her bag. Dad takes it from her and says something in Urdu. She nods and gestures for him to follow her.

We walk down the ramp and out into the airport. He's here. I drop my things and run for him. "Nuruddin." I fall into his arms.

He pulls away from me and whispers, "Not here, Jenny. People are looking."

Dad touches my arm. "It's okay, honey. You're in a different country now."

I'm starting to see just how different it is.

Nuruddin and Dad go to get our luggage. Ahmed's quiet, fascinated by our new surroundings. I'm petrified. There are hundreds of people here, and I can't understand a word they're saying. Some of them seem to be pointing at me. Look at that silly American woman.

It's taking them a long time. Ahmed wants to get down. I don't dare let go of him. He might be swept away by the crowd. He fusses. "Hush, baby. You're okay."

But I'm not. I'm tired. I'm hungry. I'm scared. I want to go home.

Nuruddin comes up behind me. "I'm so happy to see you, Jenny." He kisses me lightly on the cheek. "Wait until we get home," he whispers.

∽

We ride through the streets in a taxi. While Dad and Nuruddin talk, I look around. So many tall buildings. So many shops. And cars. And people.

The cab pulls onto a bumpy dirt road. Ahmed laughs. We go another mile, past a long row of old brown brick buildings, before stopping.

"This is it," says Nuruddin. "Welcome home."

Home? "Where?"

He takes my hand. "Follow me."

We walk down a narrow alley, stopping at a flimsy wooden door. He opens the door and walks in. "Assalaamu alaikum."

Mama runs and hugs me, giving me big, sloppy kisses. She reaches for Ahmed and yanks him from my arms. He screams. She whispers to him in Urdu. He doesn't know Urdu.

Nuruddin says something and holds out his arms. Mama gives the baby to him. Ahmed laughs and pulls his father's beard. Nuruddin holds him close.

Dad looks around. "Just as I remember it."

This is Abdul-Qadir's house? I knew he was poor, but I never expected this.

"Sit," says Mama, gesturing to a wooden chair. I am tired. I sit.

Another woman walks in, sweeping the green linoleum with a short broom. She stops and hugs me until I can hardly breathe. "Assalaamu alaikum, Jenny." She speaks rapidly in Urdu. Who is this person?

A little boy runs into the room. She scolds him and calls him Hamza. She's the widow of Nuruddin's brother. My sister-in-law. I forgot to buy her a gift. I'll give her something of mine. Not now. I'll think about it tomorrow.

Nuruddin rescues me. "Would you like to see our room?"

I look at Mama. She nods. "Go."

The rest of the house is tiny and old, but our bedroom is wonderful. "It's the best room in the house. Mama insisted we get it ready for

Ripples

you. She and Asma have been busy all week sewing curtains and making it nice."

"Asma?"

"My brother's wife. It's my duty to take care of her and the children."

"But you don't have a job yet."

"Any day now. Don't worry." He pulls me very close. "Welcome home."

~

Mama cooks my favorite curry and treats me like a queen. Asma plays with Ahmed. He giggles while she plays her own version of peek-a-boo. Her daughter, Leila, brings me bottled water and stares at me. Hamza practices his English.

"Do you like it here?" he says.

"Um, I don't know. I just came."

"You are from America?"

"Yes."

"Did you bring me a gift?"

"Of course, I did." I bought toys for both him and his sister, but I'm too tired to look for them now. "I'll give it to you tomorrow. Okay?" He winks. "Okay."

After dinner, Dad picks up his suitcase. "I'll sleep at the masjid. There's not much room here, and it's more proper."

"But, Dad." I look at him, pleading. Don't leave me.

"You'll be fine, Jenny. You're with your husband."

Mama and Asma go into the room they share with Asma's children.

Nuruddin takes me into our bedroom. Ahmed is sleeping on a cushioned mat on the floor.

I fall into my husband's arms. Now I'm home.

Part Four

I wake up to the sound of roosters. There are roosters in the city? Nuruddin is already dressed. "I'm going to the mosque to pray. I'll bring your father back with me."

Ahmed is still asleep. He must be tired from our trip. I look around. I'm here now. I'm with my husband again, and, even though I don't know anything about living in Pakistan, I am going to make this work.

I get dressed and walk into the kitchen, where I hear voices. Mama is frying bread. Asma is chopping vegetables. I'd like to help, but I'm still tired. I watch.

"Assalaamu alaikum." Dad is back. I run to the door.

He's limping slightly. "Are you okay?"

"It's just my back. I'm not used to sleeping on the floor."

"That's not right. You need a bed. We'll pay for you to stay in a hotel."

"No, Jenny, keep your money. I love being in the masjid. And the Prophet, peace be upon him, slept on the floor. If it was good enough for him, I have no right to complain."

⁓

Asma made curry. Nuruddin says most Pakistanis don't eat eggs and waffles in the morning, but it feels strange to have a full meal this early in the day.

After breakfast, I ask Nuruddin and Dad to come into the main room with me. I don't know how much English Asma understands, and I'm not ready to share this with her yet.

We sit on green cushions placed neatly on the floor. "Last night, I had a dream about Baba. We were in this room and he asked me, 'Why are you not a Muslim?' I couldn't answer. He reminded me of the promise I made before they went to Makkah. Then he said, 'When will you be a Muslim?' I said, 'Don't worry, Baba. I'll do it tomorrow.' Then I guess the roosters woke me up."

"Do you mean it, Jenny?" says Nuruddin.

"I had a long talk with Dad on the way here. I believe in God. I respect Muhammad. There are some things I'm not comfortable with,

Ripples

like covering my hair and fasting, but I admire the way Muslims live. And I promised Baba. That dream must mean something."

"Allahu akbar! Allahu akbar!" my husband shouts.

Asma and Mama come running from the kitchen. Nuruddin says something in Urdu. Asma hugs me. Mama cries. "Abdul-Qadir." She says his name over and over.

Nuruddin rushes out of the house. "I'll be right back, insha Allah."

"Wait. Where are you going?"

"He's going to bring the imam," says Dad. "Are you sure, Jenny?"

"Were you completely sure when you became a Muslim?"

"No, but I was ready to give it a try."

"I'm ready, too."

Ahmed wakes up crying. I start to go for him. Asma motions for me to sit. She carries the baby into the kitchen, speaking to him softly in Urdu. I'm surprised he goes with her so easily. He must know she's planning to feed him.

"When you become a Muslim," says Dad, "You start fresh. You should take a special bath."

"Yes, I'm ready for a nice, hot shower."

Dad grins. "You're lucky. They have a shower now. But it's not hot."

"You're kidding."

"No hot running water. Haven't you noticed?"

I've been too tired. "Why am I lucky?"

"Because, when I first came, they didn't have a shower. I had to dip the water from a container."

"Why do you like it here? Life seems so hard."

"Life is about more than soft beds and hot showers. It will be hard at first, but, at some point, you'll realize that your life has become richer."

Sometimes Dad's optimism drives me crazy.

"Assalaamu alaikum." I hear a strange voice outside.

"Please come in," says my husband. He escorts an old man through the door. "Please sit down, Imam Ihsan."

Mama walks in a minute later with hot tea and biscuits. Nuruddin takes them from her and serves our guest.

389

"This is my wife, Jennifer. She has just come from America. She would like to be a Muslim."

"Masha Allah, that is good news," says the old man. He turns to me, his eyes lowered. "Do you know what Islam is?"

I look down, too, to make him more comfortable. "Yes. My father has been a Muslim for a long time. I knew I would be a Muslim someday."

He nods. "I remember when your father was young, like you. He was a very good student. Please repeat after me."

He says the words. I've heard them, but I've never tried to say them. My tongue trips. I blush. "I'm sorry. I'm a little nervous."

"You're fine. Let's try again." He speaks slowly, and I'm able to keep up.

"Good. The words you said are very heavy. Do you know what they mean?"

This is easier. I was there when Uncle Brad made his shahadah, and I thought I might be doing this one day. "I believe that there is no god but the One God, and Muhammad is the messenger of God."

"That's it. Congratulations. You are a Muslim."

Just like that? Mama and Asma hug and kiss me.

"I know you won't be sorry." Dad touches my face. "All of my children are Muslims. Forget fancy hotels. This is what I need."

He doesn't jump up and down, but I can see how happy he is. I never realized how much he wanted it.

Nuruddin sits to the side, smiling. He'll hug me when we're alone.

I have to find a way to tell Mom.

Ripples

Part Five

On the day I became a Muslim, Asma gave me some of her clothes. I felt strange taking someone's used clothing, but Dad whispered, "She's showing her respect. Accept them, and wear them."

I put on one of the dresses this morning. It's mostly white, with green trim. She gave me a green scarf to wear with it. I drape the scarf around my neck, as I've seen some women do.

Dad's flying back to Chicago today. I wish I could go with him.

Before we leave the house, Nuruddin gently places the scarf over my head and kisses me on the cheek. "You're beautiful." He's said that a lot lately.

Mama and Asma cover their faces when they go out, but that's too extreme for me. They're staying home today. Asma carries Ahmed. "No problem," she says, explaining the rest in Urdu.

"She wants us to leave him here," says Nuruddin. "That will be easier."

"I need to say goodbye to my grandson then." Dad reaches for Ahmed. "Be a good boy. I'll come back soon to see you, insha Allah." He gives Ahmed a big kiss and tickles him. My son giggles and squirms.

While riding in the taxi, I look out at the people and buildings. It's been a week, but this place is still so strange to me.

Dad grabs my hand. "You'll be fine, Jenny."

We hug for the umpteenth time at the airport. "I wish you didn't have to leave."

"I'll come back when I can. Maybe Aisha and the kids can come with me. I expect to hear from you often. And your mom and Peter will be here in a few months." He touches my cheek. "I am very proud of you, Jenny. You are a beautiful young woman."

I don't want to let him go. I squeeze tightly. "You always know the right thing to say." I try not to cry.

He needs to leave. We watch him walk through security. Nuruddin puts one arm around my shoulders and uses his other hand to wipe my tears.

We wait at the airport until Dad's plane takes off. Now it's time to start my new life in Pakistan.

Jamilah Kolocotronis

Part Six

I want to go home.

Nuruddin just started a job with an architectural firm downtown. I hope we can move out of this tiny house soon. I'm glad he's working, but I'm stuck at home all day with Mama and Asma.

I miss my privacy. Yesterday, while I was at the market with Nuruddin, Asma walked into our bedroom, gathered all our dirty clothes, and washed them. I should be grateful—that's what Nuruddin said—but I don't want anyone touching my underwear. And one of my favorite shirts shrunk. I'll never be able to wear it again.

Mama watches everything I do. Yesterday, she told me to put warmer clothes on the baby. And, maybe I'm just being paranoid, but I could swear she knows everything I say to my husband. It wouldn't be hard. The walls in this house are paper thin.

It's not just Asma and Mama. Nuruddin's sisters come over at least twice a week. Sometimes all five of them. With their children. It's chaos.

Most of them are nice, but the youngest one, Nasreen, criticizes everything I do. My cooking. "You need to move faster." My mothering. "Don't be so protective. He must learn how to be a man." Even my marriage. "When your husband walks into the room, you should stop what you're doing and take care of his needs." Nuruddin and Nasreen are only eighteen months apart, and he says she always mothered him. I can't complain about her to him, but she is driving me insane.

Then there are the neighbors. They stare at me. When I cover my head, they stare more. I know my blonde hair makes me stand out, but it's more than that. It's my skin, my features, my name, my nationality. I'm the only American in this part of town, and, even though I'm a Muslim now, I know I'll never fit in.

Once we get out of this neighborhood, maybe I can meet other American women. I hope we move soon.

It's not even his family, or this house, or this neighborhood. I miss Chicago. I miss going to school and meeting my friends. I miss my family. I've been here for a month now, and I still know almost no one. I can't go to school yet. I don't even know if there are any English language schools in Karachi. Nuruddin keeps promising to show me the

Ripples

city, but he's always busy. I could go to school online, but the Internet connection around here is iffy. I don't know what to do or where to turn. I want to scream.

Instead, I take Ahmed into the bedroom for his afternoon nap and rock him to sleep. I hold him close to me and cry.

Jamilah Kolocotronis

Part Seven

Something exciting happened yesterday. We were finishing supper when a man knocked and called out, "Assalaamu alaikum." Nuruddin went to talk with him while Mama, Asma, and I stayed in the kitchen.

They talked for a long time. Mama and Asma listened. Asma prepared tea and biscuits, covered her face, and went out to serve him.

When the man left, Nuruddin hurried to the kitchen. The three of them talked excitedly in Urdu. Asma softly clapped her hands. Nuruddin finally turned to me.

"That was Abdur-Rahman Idris, the one who owns the butcher shop. He wants to marry Asma."

"Why didn't he talk to her?"

"That's not how things are done here. Not in our family. He came to me as the head of the household, and I carried his message to Asma."

"What did she say?"

"Can't you tell?"

I hugged Asma. I'm happy for her. She was so young when Nuruddin's brother was killed, and she has the children to raise. Now she'll have a second chance.

~

The wedding was six days later. I thought Nuruddin and I held the record for short engagements.

Asma wore red, just as Raheema did when she married my brother. Mama applied Asma's henna. Then she did mine. I never did have a henna party before my wedding.

Some women came to our house. I think they were all relatives. The men gathered at Abdur-Rahman's house. Nuruddin took Ahmed with him. "It's time for my son to learn to be a man," he said.

The day before the wedding, Nuruddin slaughtered a lamb. Abdur-Rahman's family cooked the meal.

The wedding was simple, but, afterward, the women danced and laughed most of the night. I watched them, not understanding, but still feeling a part of the celebration. I have no idea what the men did.

Ripples

After breakfast, Abdur-Rahman came for Asma and took her to his house. It was so sweet.

Hamza and Leila stayed with us for a few days. When Asma came for them, Mama cried and hugged the children. At first, I thought she wouldn't let them go.

Ahmed tried to go with Hamza and Leila. When we stopped him, he screamed and kicked. It took an hour to get him settled down. He fell asleep in my arms.

He just woke up. He starts running through the house. "Hamza? Leila?"

I put my arms around him. "They live somewhere else now. We'll go visit sometimes. And, in a few months, you'll have your own little brother to play with."

"Okay." He walks away and plays with his blocks.

Just like that? Kids are so unpredictable.

Jamilah Kolocotronis

Part Eight

I received a letter from Michael today. It's been months since I last heard from him. I rip open the envelope.

Dear Jenny,
 Assalaamu alaikum. Dad told me about your conversion. That's great.
 Gabriela and I are very happy. We're expecting next March. The doctor says we're having a boy. What about you?
 This is my home now. I'm fluent in Spanish, and I feel that I belong. Another hurricane hit our village three months ago. I'm helping to rebuild. This is what I was meant to do.
 I miss you. I would like to come to Pakistan one day. Maybe we can have a family reunion in Karachi. I don't know if I'll ever be able to go home. They're easing up on the draft, but I've heard they're still pursuing deserters. A few have been executed.
 Write back, and let me know how you are. How is life there? Is it different than you expected? Can you speak Urdu yet?
 How's my little nephew? Could you send a picture?
 I hope you're working on your writing. I think you'll be famous one day. Make sure you stick with it.
 I need to go. Our Internet service has been down since the hurricane. I'll email you as soon as I can. Take care of yourself.

Love,
Michael

I read his letter ten times. I wonder when we'll see each other again.

∼

I've lived in Pakistan for three months now. I can speak some Urdu, and I'm getting used to the strangeness of it, but I miss home.

Nuruddin just found an apartment in a nice neighborhood. We'll move next week, insha Allah. I can't wait.

Ripples

My biggest problem is boredom. Ahmed is at Asma's house most of the time. Mama works in the kitchen. Nuruddin goes to the office. I sit in our bedroom and stare at the walls.

Until I remember my laptop. I haven't used it much yet. Internet service is so irregular in this neighborhood that I finally gave up. I've been too distracted to write.

I take out my laptop and turn it on. The familiar hum. What a nice sound. I open a new document and stare at the empty page.

They say you should write what you know. What do I know? Marriage and motherhood. Pakistan and Islam. What can I do with that?

I try to clear my mind. It won't work. Concentrate, Jennifer. You know how to write. Just do it.

So, I do. I write, brainstorming freely.

"Mama!" Ahmed runs into my lap.

Where did he come from?

"Assalaamu alaikum," says Asma, peeking into the room. "He missed you."

I give my son a distracted hug. "Thank you," I say to Asma, speaking Urdu with a distinct Chicago accent. I save what I've written and take Ahmed to the kitchen to see about lunch.

∽

For the last few days, Mama and I have been busy packing. Sometimes, she laughs. "A new house," she says. Sometimes, she touches everything in her house and cries.

We're moving to a different part of the city, to a twelfth-floor apartment. I can't wait. I've already met one American woman who lives in our building. And the apartment isn't very different than the one we had in Chicago, except that it's newer. I'm looking forward to an easier life.

It's hard for Mama, though. She's lived in this house since Abdul-Qadir brought her here as a new bride over forty years ago. All eight of her children grew up here, and the two oldest were born in this house. She must have many stories to tell.

Right now, Mama is at the market, and Ahmed is at Asma's house. It's time for lunch. I fix a plate of curry and rice and sit at the table with my laptop. I have been waiting for this moment.

First, I read what I wrote. I have three pages of material here. I go through it twice, making corrections along the way.

I can turn this into something. A story. Or maybe a novel. I scroll to the next page and begin. "She looked into his dark eyes."

∼

I've worked on my novel for a full month now. I'm about halfway done, writing every chance I get. Ahmed plays noisily at my feet while my mind is far away. I should be helping Mama. I hope she doesn't mind.

I write as I go along. My story vaguely resembles my life, but it's much more exciting.

When I'm not writing, I make excuses to leave the apartment—going to the market or visiting Asma. Or even Nasreen. My Urdu is good enough now that I can go alone. People still stare, but I'm getting used to it.

While I'm out, I look for new ideas to put into my story. I am seeing the world in a whole new way.

All Grown Up

*The day the child realizes that all adults are imperfect,
he becomes an adolescent;
the day he forgives them, he becomes an adult;
the day he forgives himself, he becomes wise.*

—Alden Nowlan

Isaiah

On our way back from the hospital, Dad asked me to help him with it. We've worked on it for the last five days. I practically know it by heart. I hope he's ready to deliver.

This morning, he's returning to the pulpit. I know he's anxious. I went with him to the church last night. He asked me to change a couple of light bulbs and make sure the correct numbers were up on the hymnal board. A few weeks ago, I would have refused. I felt a little uncomfortable, but he needed my help.

Mom serves the pancakes. I get his coffee. "Are you strong enough?"

He nods. "I feel good. I miss my church."

After breakfast, Mom knots his tie for him—he can't remember how to do it. I drive him to the church. Becky will come with the family.

First, he prays. Then he goes into his office and sits behind his desk. "I need to get back to work. There are repairs to be made. The Baker boy is getting married next month. There were some meetings I was supposed to attend, but I've forgotten why."

I look down. "I'm sure it will come back to you."

"It will. The Lord has never abandoned me."

I peer out into the sanctuary. The church slowly fills. Mom, Becky, and the family arrive and take their seats in front. I hug Dad before joining them. "You'll be fine."

"I know I will. The Lord is with me."

The piano player sits on her bench. Dad steps out of his office and takes his seat behind the pulpit. Members of the congregation stand, hymnals in hand, and belt out the notes. I stand silently.

After the readings and choir performances, and a few more hymns, it's time. Dad stands behind the pulpit. "Good morning, brothers and sisters."

Some in the congregation murmur, "Good morning." A few say it loudly. I look behind me. The church is full.

Dad starts slowly. He reads that verse from Psalms about the godly man. "And what does this mean?" he says. "What is God telling us in this passage?"

Soon, he's back to his old form. The force. The fervor. The faith. The church rings with his voice.

At the end, he delivers his invitation, as usual. "Come forward and repent," he calls. "Turn your lives over to the Lord. He will forgive you and welcome you back into the fold as a shepherd welcomes a lost lamb."

I stay seated. We talked about it earlier, and I think he understands. Someone else comes forward. Willy. He kneels while Dad puts his hands on his shoulders and prays for his redemption. Aunt Debbie cries softly in the pew behind us.

∼

Becky cooked Sunday dinner. Roast beef and mashed potatoes. "Why don't you ever cook this well for me?" I tease.

"What would we do with all this food? This is a family-sized meal."

"Maybe you should think about having a family," Jacob pipes up.

"Maybe. Here, Dad, have another roll," Becky says, passing the basket to my father.

∼

After dinner, Becky and Mom clean up. The kids read. Dad stretches out on the living room couch. I sit across from him in the easy chair and close my eyes.

"Becky and you are thinking about having children?" Dad asks.

I open my eyes. "We need to finish school first, but we both want a large family."

"Good. It's not easy. You're going to make mistakes."

"I think we can handle it."

"You look at your newborn child, and you swear you'll be the best father to him, but sometimes you make the wrong decisions."

I think our relationship is strong enough now. I ask him. "Why did you beat me? I know it's in the Bible, but how could you have done that?"

"I thought it would make you stronger. I was wrong."

Ripples

I persist. "Why did you hit me and not Jacob?"

Dad opens his eyes and looks around. "Come closer."

I walk over and sit on the edge of the couch. He grasps my hand. "You are gifted, Isaiah. Jacob is good, but God made you special." He looks away. "Or so I've always thought."

Suddenly, I understand. He expected more from me. Maybe he even loved me more. I have been a disappointment—not because I'm a Muslim, but because I'm so stubbornly self-centered.

"I wanted you to be good," he adds.

"I'll try, Dad. You'll be proud of me."

He nods and closes his eyes.

"Being a father isn't easy, is it? I'll probably make some mistakes with my kids."

"I'm sure you will."

And, after all the shouting, arguing, debating, and fighting, that's all we really needed to say.

~

The car is packed. I kiss Mom. "Come up and see us in Chicago."

"It would be nice to visit, but I don't want to move back there. Not unless you can give me a house near the woods."

"Sorry. We don't have those in Chicago anymore." I shake Dad's hand. "Remember what the doctor said. Take it easy. Don't push yourself."

He hugs me. "Don't worry. The Lord will take care of me."

I say goodbye to the kids. Becky reminds them to do their work. We climb into our car and head back to the highway.

It's been a great two weeks. I talked with my parents day and night, seeing them in a new way. I never thought of them as real people before, with needs and dreams of their own.

Dad and I were able to resolve our differences, sort of. He wouldn't let me pray in the house, but he didn't mind if I did it in the woods out back. It was better that way. Praising Allah with the birds singing above me and the sun on my back.

We stopped talking about religion. We both know where we stand, and you can argue for only so long. But, one day, while I was helping

403

him with the sermon, I did ask him how he felt about my conversion.

He spoke slowly and carefully. "I think it was a mistake, but I've learned to accept it. I don't understand why some of the people I love the most have chosen that path. I will never turn away from my Lord and Savior, and, if I can ever find the right words to convince you, I will use them. Otherwise, I will stay quiet."

I never told him how ashamed I feel. Islam teaches that, as a father, he has rights over me, but I have violated his rights in many ways. He has forgiven me. I need to make it up to him.

∼

We pull into Chicago late at night and stumble into our apartment. Uncle Brad and Aunt Beth took care of the rent and utilities while we were gone. It's great to be home.

∼

On Friday, after the prayer, Faruq asks, "Where were you?"

I tell him my story. All of it. Including the part where I almost killed my father again.

"You know, don't you, that Muslims must always respect their parents. Whether or not they are Muslims."

"Why didn't you say that earlier?" I might have listened.

"You only said that your father beat you. You didn't tell me he was a God-fearing man."

I didn't see his goodness until it was almost too late.

Ripples

Kyle: Part One

Faiqa greets me at the door. "The visas came today. We're ready to go."

"Great. I can't wait."

"I bought more books to help us. We can ask my parents, too. They've been there."

"There's a series of talks about it at the masjid. Why don't we go next Sunday?"

"I think we'd better. I'd hate to go into this unprepared. Have you talked with your parents?"

"Their visas came yesterday. We're all set."

"Our family made *umrah* when I was fourteen. You can't imagine how it feels to see the Ka'bah. It's incredible."

We'll leave in three weeks. Gameel was happy to give me the time off. Fortunately, the Hajj season coincided with spring break this year, so we won't have trouble getting away from our classes.

∼

Hajj was awesome. Millions of Muslims, all in white, praying together and performing the rituals. The Ka'bah stood in front of us, uniting Muslims worldwide.

Dad, Matt, and I stayed together throughout the Hajj. Matt and I had to help Dad during the *tawaf* around the Ka'bah. The crowd was huge, and there was a lot of pushing and shoving. We kept Dad between us and held his arms. I was afraid he would fall and get hurt.

During the *sa'i*, as we raced between Safa and Marwa, he became very tired. We stayed with him and helped him complete it. I wanted him to use a wheelchair, but he refused. Many others passed us, and there was some jostling, but we stuck together, and we made it.

The part I liked best was on Arafat. We had a hard time getting there, but it was worth the effort. At night, we sat in our tent and read the Qur'an. Doing anything else would have seemed sacrilegious.

When it came time to throw the pebbles, Dad was really looking pale and weak. Matt threw for him. I threw for Mom. Faiqa stood by my side, throwing pebbles of her own. I worried about her getting lost in the crowd, but I should never underestimate my wife.

I offered to slaughter the lamb, but Dad insisted on doing it himself. I stood close by, ready to help.

"I'm the head of this family," he said. "Now step aside."

I think it was hard for him. Not because he was weak. He had never killed anything before. But he said "*Bismillah*," and went to work.

I was sorry when we had to leave. We made our prayers at Masjid Al-Haram one last time. Matt, Faiqa, and I made a final tawaf. Then we left to go back to what is generally known as the "real world." I can't imagine anything more real than Hajj.

∼

We came back yesterday. Uncle Joshua and Aunt Aisha greeted us at the airport. I kind of wished Jen could have been there. Can you imagine what she would have said about my shaved head? But she's a Muslim now, too. Maybe our wise-cracking days are over.

∼

Dad has this cough which won't go away. He's supposed to go for a check-up next month. We all keep telling him to go sooner, but he won't.

I don't think he can admit that he's sick. He still has dreams of beating Uncle Joshua at soccer. Maybe it's better if we let him hold on to his dreams.

∼

We came back from Hajj two months ago. Dad never regained his strength. I shouldn't be surprised when Mom calls me at the office.

"Your father just came back from the doctor's. They want to run more tests. He'll check into the hospital tomorrow."

"What's wrong?"

"They suspect cancer."

"I'll come over right after work. Don't worry, Mom."

Ripples

I hang up and close my eyes. Cancer isn't a death sentence anymore. Still, I don't want my father to go through that.

~

He's upbeat. During dinner, he even makes jokes about losing his hair. "It's all gray, anyway. Maybe when it grows back, it will be black again. Wouldn't that be something?"

But I'm worried. I know he has a hard time following his diet, and all those years of drinking took a toll on him. Tonight, for the first time, he looked old to me.

~

On my way to his room, I talk with the doctor. They conducted the tests. He has chronic lymphocytic leukemia. It sounds bad, but the doctor says it could be worse. They'll start him on chemotherapy soon.

He's reciting the Qur'an. When he sees me standing at the door, he stops.

"How do you feel, Dad?"

"I'm in great shape. They want to keep me here so they can get more money. Cancer isn't a killer anymore. By next week, I'll be ready to beat Joshua on that soccer field."

"You never beat Uncle Joshua at soccer."

"There's always a first time." He smiles and looks into my eyes. "You remember when I left home. Do you know why?"

"You said it was because you didn't want to stop drinking."

"That was a big part of it. But it was also because I couldn't get over my mother's death. Do you know I never told her I loved her? Not once."

I grasp his hand. "I love you, Dad."

"I know you do. And I love you, too, Kyle. I'm very proud of you."

It feels like we're saying goodbye. I don't know how many months or years I have to spend with him, but I can't imagine my life without him.

Kyle: Part Two

Faiqa and I just came back from Egypt. She has so many relatives. I never learned all of their names.

I loved the food. I gained at least ten pounds. Faisal says he'll help me work it off.

Most of her relatives live in Cairo, but she had to take me to see the pyramids. We rode a boat on the Nile. We spent two weeks in Alexandria, playing in the Mediterranean. We even rode camels. I don't know how I managed to get on that beast and stay there without falling. It was great.

Faiqa watched me closely. With her nagging, I kept up with my routine. No fevers.

She still has a couple years of med school, but we both want a baby. We're meeting with Dr. Brooks next week.

I love waking up in the morning, my beautiful wife by my side. My life awaits.

Ripples

Jennifer

Nuruddin found an English-speaking doctor for me. She says everything is fine. I have three more months. I'd better hurry up and finish writing this book.

∼

Yunus arrived this morning at 7:42 AM. He's healthy—nearly four kilos. He has a round face and a full head of curly blonde hair.
I cradle him in my arms as we study him. He's perfect.
"Let me see my little grandson," says Mom, her heels clicking across the tiles. "Oh, he's beautiful. Come to Grandma, little one."
"He is beautiful," says Nuruddin. "Like his mother."
"Don't forget his grandmother. Where do you think he got that hair?"
"Of course." He laughs. He is in a very good mood.
Mom is cooing over little Yunus when Mama walks in. She speaks rapidly in Urdu and turns to Nuruddin to translate. I caught much of what she said.
"She brought you soup," Nuruddin explains. "You need to eat it so you will be stronger. She said it will help your milk come in."
Mom laughs. "The women in my family never had any trouble with that."
Nuruddin doesn't translate. Mama wouldn't understand.

∼

In the evening, I call Dad. "His face is round, like yours. He is so beautiful."
"As beautiful as Ahmed?"
"Yes, every bit as beautiful. How is it possible to love more than one child?"
"It's a mercy from Allah."
"Have you heard from Michael? How is Gabriela?"
"Didn't you get his email? She had the baby last night. His name is Ilyas."

Last night there was morning here. I was in labor. "That's great. Two more grandsons. How do you feel?"

"Old."

"No, Dad, you can't get old. I won't let you."

"I don't think there's anything you can do about it."

∼

I wait in the wheelchair, Yunus in my arms, as Nuruddin pulls up to the front of the hospital. I'm anxious to go home. I miss my Ahmed.

As Nuruddin drives through the city streets, I remember the first day I came here. Everything looked so strange. Now I know exactly where I am.

Nuruddin pulls up to the door of our apartment building. We're home.

∼

A special package came for me today—twenty copies of my book. It's wonderful. I flip through the pages and stare at the front cover. *Home*, by Jennifer Adams Ali.

Ahmed picks up a copy and reads. "She...looked...into...his..."

I take the book. "I'll read it to you later, sweetie." With a little editing.

Yunus stares at my picture on the back. "Mama," he says.

"Yes, that's me." Finally. I am on my way.

Epilogue

Mikhail Adams was in third grade when he realized that other people thought his father was an important man. On career day, when Dr. Isaiah Adams came to talk to the class about history and show the class some of the books he'd written, Mikhail's teacher was visibly impressed. Mikhail didn't understand why. He was just Dad.

Mikhail didn't care too much about history. He was fascinated by religion instead. He loved listening to stories about Prophet Muhammad, especially the way Uncle Faruq told them. And he was in awe as he watched his Grandpa Chris deliver his sermons. Sometimes, Mikhail imagined himself speaking before hundreds of people with the same deep, strong voice of his grandfather.

About the Author

In addition to *Ripples,* Jamilah Kolocotronis has written five other books. Her first was the non-fiction treatise, *Islamic Jihad,* based on her doctoral dissertation. Her first novel, *Innocent People,* addressed the lives of Muslims struggling in the wake of 9/11. *Ripples* is the fourth book in her five-part *Echoes Series.* The other published books in this series are *Echoes, Rebounding,* and *Turbulence.* Jamilah lives in Lexington, Kentucky.

Another quality Islamic Fiction book published by Muslim Writers Publishing

Sophia's Journal: Time Warp 1857

by Najiyah Helwani

During a bike ride with her family near Lawrence, Kansas, anxiety-ridden Sophia falls into a river and is washed downstream. She emerges in 1857 – smack in the middle of Bleeding Kansas. Sophia is aghast to find that slavery is going on in her adopted community, and she begins to fight for the freedom of the slaves she knows. A local boy captures Sophia's heart, but when he proposes marriage, Sophia is torn about marrying outside her faith. An old Gambian slave, who is still a closet Muslim, helps her work out her fears, and this causes an exciting, dangerous and unexpected turn of events.

The author researched historical types of food, clothing and the way of life in 1857 Kansas, USA. Readers will love learning about the way of life early frontier settlers lived. The book has a glossary and some unique recipes that are specific to the book's period in history. This book will be a welcome addition to any Language Arts reading and/or American History program.

About the Author

Najiyah Diana Helwani is a teacher and freelance writer whose published credits include poetry and magazine and newspaper articles. *Sophia's Journey: Time Warp 1857* is the first book in a planned historical fiction series and her first published Islamic fiction novel. Raised on the windswept prairies of Kansas, Najiyah's love of her American roots blends beautifully with her Islamic faith, and she strives to show people that the two are not mutually exclusive. Najiyah currently teaches English in Damascus, Syria, where she lives with her husband and six children. When she is in the USA she conducts workshops on Islam and the history of USA relations with the Middle East.

Islamic Fiction Books

Muslim Writers Publishing is proud to have published *Ripples*, a quality Islamic Fiction book for older teens and adults. You can learn more about the availability of Islamic Fiction books and Muslim authors by visiting: www.IslamicFictionBooks.com

Islamic Fiction books: This refers to creative, imaginative fiction books written by Muslims and marketed primarily to Muslims. Islamic Fiction may be marketed to secular markets, too. The content of these books incorporates some religious content and themes, and may include non-fictionalized historical or factual Islamic content with or without direct reference to the Qur'an or the Sunnah of the Prophet (pbuh). The stories may also include modern, real life situations and moral dilemmas. Islamic Fiction may be written in many languages. Islamic Fiction books do not include any of the following Harmful Content:

- vulgar language
- sexually explicit content
- un-Islamic practices that are not identified as un-Islamic
- content that portrays Islam in a negative way

Linda D. Delgado, Publisher
Muslim Writers Publishing